Chapter 1.

1983, Chelsea. Misty

I remember nothing of the ambulance arriving or the transfer to St. Stephen's Hospital. After that, I remember only disjointed snapshots until I finally came round properly several days later. Davey was able to fill in some of the blanks – the shocking news that Andy had been found dead in a hotel in Knightsbridge – that someone had told the police of the 'toxic' relationship between us – how they had found clothing and other items belonging to me in the hotel room (no surprise there – he was always 'borrowing' my stuff) – how I was the prime suspect for his murder...

I lay on the floor, feeling the fibres of the carpet stabbing into my skin. Although everything still seemed to be more or less joined together, there was little if anything that didn't hurt. I had no idea how long I had been there or whether it was day or night. The heavy bedroom curtains were still drawn, but that meant little as I often left them that way. I knew I would have to try to get up sooner or later, but at that point had little incentive to confront the inevitable pain and nausea. I tried to remember what had led up to this latest mess, but everything was just blank.

I was lying more or less face down, which at least spared me the agony of having to try to turn over. As I tried to get to my hands and knees there was a loud crash as the door to the flat burst inwards and suddenly the room was full of noise. I heard someone shout "In here!" and none-too-gentle hands reached down and tried to drag me to my feet. I cried out in pain, the noise sounding unreal, as though it had come from someone else. I heard the crackle of a radio as an ambulance was called…

Chapter 2.

The present. Misty

My name is Misty. At least, it has been for some years now. My proper name is Michael – Micky - but I am better known as the singer in a band called Misty Blue. I was in my late twenties when my world came crashing around my ears and my life changed dramatically. Until that time things had been a whirlpool of work and largely self-inflicted dysfunction which had its roots in the fact that I was gay and, in the late seventies, although my lifestyle was no longer illegal, it was far from accepted.

As a band we had been together since our schooldays in Manchester. Four ordinary lads – myself, my best mate Davey who played drums, another mate Paddy who played bass and our lead guitarist Andy, the source of most of my problems...

Davey and Paddy had both married young and were already parents when we hit the big time. Andy had known he was gay from an early age and had never tried to hide the fact. I was my parents' only child, but both came from large Irish-Catholic families and I had always understood that my mission in life was to marry young and provide a large number of grandchildren. To begin with I was more than happy to try to fulfil my destiny, but it soon became clear that, while girls fancied me and were happy in my company, I really wasn't going to set the world on fire as a potential stud.

I don't think it was that failure which made me look in another direction – to be honest I already knew I was happiest in the company of my bandmates. When we were working Davey and Paddy generally avoided going out on the pull after a gig and were happy to stick around the hotel having a drink or four. Andy usually went in search of someone to amuse himself with but, if he was unsuccessful in his search, would then try it on with me, although it became clear fairly quickly that we were both looking for the same thing and that, just as I had failed with the birds, I was no better able to supply what he wanted. Unfortunately, he wasn't willing to give up easily, and was capable of reducing me to a quivering wreck in a very short space of time if he did not get what he wanted. It took a lot of graft by the other two to keep the peace between us and hold the band together.

After several years of very hard work, recording and touring the length and breadth of the British Isles and most of western Europe, our career had suddenly taken off and we had achieved a number of good chart placings. Things settled down into a routine of touring for six months, during which time Davey and I wrote new material, and then, after a few weeks' rest, we would rehearse and record before setting off on tour again to promote the new album. The rest periods allowed Davey and Paddy to spend time with their families and Andy would usually fly off to the sun somewhere, but it left me with a huge void in my life. I couldn't spend the time at home in Manchester under the eyes and ears of my family, and eventually acquired a flat in Chelsea which gave me somewhere to keep my stuff, and also quickly enabled me to find new ways of passing the time.

It was never down to money. While Davey and Paddy had families to support and Andy spent his money freely, travelling and entertaining his 'friends', I spent little. We earned good money, both from the constant touring and our album sales (and of course, as Davey and I wrote most of the material, we earned proportionately more in royalties). I had bought the flat at a good price and, as it was empty most of the time, the outgoings were comparatively low. I liked clothes and they were probably my main extravagance, but in proportion to what I earned it barely scratched the surface.

Chapter 3.

1960, Manchester, Micky

The first time I set eyes on Davey was my first day at school. Mam had taken me as far as the main door to the Infants' School, where I'd been handed over to one of the lady welfare staff who had led me by the hand to a room containing more children than I'd ever seen in my life, all sitting round larger versions of our kitchen table in groups of eight to ten, both boys and girls (possibly significantly, we were not segregated until moving up to the Junior school at the age of eight).

The lady, Mrs. Parker, told me to sit down on the one vacant chair, next to a much bigger boy with mousey-brown hair and huge brown eyes.

"Now, Michael, this is David – he's been here a year now, so he knows where everything is, if you follow him, he'll look after you. David, I'm putting Michael into your care – you must look after him – he's quite a lot younger than you – in fact he will be the youngest in your year…"

Davey grinned amiably at me and I smiled nervously back, unused to mixing with kids of my own age, as Mam had been careful to keep me away from the local children – my only real contact having been through Sunday school at the church, from which I recognised a few faces around the room. Mrs. Parker left us.

"What happens now?" I asked timidly.

"When all the other kids arrive we'll be taken into the hall for assembly, then we come back in here for lessons. It's really boring! The only good bit is lunch!"

I didn't get much chance to get to know him until 'break' at 11 o'clock, when we lined up to be given a tiny bottle of very unappetising milk and half a digestive biscuit each, before being allowed outside into the tarmac-surfaced playground for a short time. I didn't have to worry much about what to say to him – he did most of the talking - and by lunchtime I had learned almost all there was to know.

I didn't find the lessons boring, although as I could already read and could write my letters fairly well (from the combined efforts of Sunday school and Mam), I did feel a little impatient with the kids who were obviously finding life far more challenging. Davey, having already been through the year once, was reasonably proficient.

I don't know if I would have survived that first term without my 'protector'. I was small for my age – skinny and, at that stage, not over tall – and my blond curls seemed to make me a target for the bullies, but Davey took his duties as my bodyguard seriously, and several lads learned very quickly not to pick on me. Luckily, I could also run pretty fast and, by the end of that first term, had learned to hold my own in most situations.

As long as we were covering new ground I was fine, soaking up new information like a sponge. I realised before the end of that year that there was a real danger that Davey could be held down for yet another year. His father had died in an industrial accident, leaving his mother with nine children to feed and clothe, although the eldest were already out at work and able to contribute towards the rent and food. Davey had taken his father's death particularly hard, and despite already being nearly two years' older than me and at least a year older than almost everyone else in the class, he was struggling to keep up, and I set myself to trying to ensure that, either through his own efforts or, as a last resort, through a certain amount of cheating, we would not be separated. A good part of my later reputation for naughtiness was a direct result of trying to distract the teachers from Davey's lack of progress, most of which was down to laziness and grief, rather than any lack of ability.

I can't say that I enjoyed the academic part of school life, nor was I all that bothered by sport, despite being able to run well enough to be selected to compete for the 'house' and later for the school. Davey, on the other hand, and despite his fondness for food and his innate laziness, was much happier playing sport, especially football, although he was generally assigned to the position of goalkeeper (on the grounds that he blocked the net pretty well, even if he didn't move much...)

The one place where I genuinely enjoyed what I was doing was, of course, music. Until I started school no-one had encouraged me to sing or even notice music. Neither of my parents ever listened to the radio for entertainment and we did not own a gramophone, so I had absolutely no knowledge of popular or classical music, the only music I ever heard being in church. Fortunately for my later career, the school had a strong musical tradition, and we were taught to read music and sing properly from the very first day. The school also had a complete set of orchestral instruments, as well as the usual descant recorders, tambourines, maracas etc. and we were all given the chance to play everything at least once to see if we had any aptitude.

In the very early days neither Davey or I were assigned a regular position in the orchestra or even one of the smaller bands, but my voice was soon noticed, as was my early grasp of how to read a score. As a reward I was given the opportunity to learn to play the piano. Dad tried to block this but, once he was assured it would not cost him anything, and that the music master considered that I had exceptional ability, he little choice but to agree.

Chapter 4.

1967, Manchester. Micky

By the time we moved up to the 'big school' I was a fixture in almost all the choirs connected with the St Michael's Schools. I was still a skinny kid, although by now I had put on a sudden growth-spurt and was of similar height to Davey, albeit considerably thinner! I had passed the 'Eleven Plus' exam and could have taken up a place at one of the local grammar schools or even, probably, obtained a musical scholarship to a fee-paying school, but there was a problem: Davey had, predictably, not passed the exam, and I was dreading the possibility of leaving him behind at St. Michael's. However, for once, my father's reluctance to do anything to help me worked in my favour. Faced with having to buy uniform for me, pay bus fares or, worse still, boarding fees, he decreed that I would stay on at St Mike's. Mam was visibly angry and upset at this but, as always, was unable to say or do anything to make him change his mind, and I tried hard to hide my happiness at being able to stay with Davey in case Dad changed his mind.

With the new school year there was an influx of lads from other schools, one of whom was Andy. Before joining the school he had attended a small private school, his fees paid by his grandparents who wanted to give him a good start, worried that he would find life at a state school difficult. I suspect that, from more than one perspective, he would have found any school difficult, and from another, it would be the school who found things tricky…

From his first day he was something of a force of nature. Whereas in the Infants' and Junior schools there had been no actual uniform, boys being required merely to wear grey shirts, grey pullovers and grey shorts with grey socks and black shoes, in the Seniors we were supposed to wear grey shirts and pullovers as before, but with long black trousers and a striped school tie with an optional school blazer, although most of us simply wore a plain black jacket or anorak. Andy turned up on the first day wearing a white shirt with grey trousers and no tie. He was sent home but returned wearing white plimsolls, was sent home again…and again…and again, each time returning with one or more permutations of the wrong clothing. Having exhausted the possibilities of that piece of rebellion, the following week he turned up with his hair dyed green, then red, then blue; the next week he wore make up (not the sort of make-up later worn by Bowie as Ziggy Stardust, but full, almost orange foundation cream, blue eyeshadow, black mascara and scarlet lipstick…) and so it went on. In the end the school decided to ignore this blatant rebellion and merely sent the Truant Officer round on an almost daily basis to haul the miscreant back to the classroom, regardless of what he looked like.

These antics sharply divided the class. Half of us were amused by such outrageous behaviour, the other half were petrified of this exotic being and steered well clear. I have to admit I was fascinated; apart from seeing female impersonators such as Danny la Rue on television I had never seen anything like it (the TV watching was a rarity, as Dad would never watch anything so trivial, and it was only if he was out for some reason that Mam and I covertly and guiltily took the chance to watch Sunday Night at the London Palladium, The Good Old Days or similar on the tiny black and white set).

Once Andy realised that his behaviour was being ignored, he seemed to delight in seeing just how far he could go, turning up in his mother's silk shirts, accessorised with colourful scarves or jewellery, even coming to school in a dress during the summer months, although on that occasion he was escorted home and made to change into trousers, the dress being considered a step too far.

I soon realised that, in some respects, Andy was a kindred spirit; the only subjects he took any interest in were Art and Music. His singing voice wasn't great; he had perfect pitch, but his voice was not strong enough to sing a solo; however he was already an accomplished guitarist and could play a variety of other instruments to a greater or lesser degree, and was quickly found a role in the orchestra and several of the smaller units.

To start with I had felt slightly upstaged, and was worried that he would try to oust me from my privileged position as Head Chorister/Soloist, but once I realised that was unlikely to be a problem, I made an effort to befriend him by trying to find out what kinds of music he was interested in outside school. His response was to grab me and stick his tongue down my throat, at which point Davey grabbed him and, turning him upside down, threatened to drop him head-first down the stairwell…

While it would be fair to say that we never became best friends, it was not long before we discovered a shared love of pop music and a respect for each other's musical abilities, enabling a truce and the beginnings of what would become Misty Blue.

Chapter 5.

1971, Manchester. Misty

We had ended the gig around ten o'clock. The venue was a large community hall and was probably the biggest place we had played at that time. Gratifyingly, it had also been packed out, despite being a dance rather than a seated, theatre-style affair.

I emerged from the dressing-room, still on a high from the enthusiastic response of the audience. I knew that the van was parked near the stage door, but I also knew that Davey and Paddy had probably sneaked off with their girlfriends to the nearest pub to grab a few beers before closing time.

Paddy and Jan had been dating for over a year and had already set a date for the wedding; Davey and Tina hadn't been together quite so long, but I could see that they were getting serious, although I tried to convince myself that Davey's feelings were not as committed as hers were. I had no idea where Andy had disappeared to, but knew that he would probably reappear before the van was due to leave. I didn't fancy going to the pub – with the others being wrapped up in their romances I would be left to play gooseberry, drinking Coke as I was still too young (and looked it!) to legally buy alcohol, and having to fend off the hangers-on which we already attracted, particularly when playing anywhere local to Manchester.

Normally on such an evening I would spend the time helping our (one and only) roadie to load the equipment into the van, and then curl up in the back to wait for the others.

On this particular evening I didn't get as far as the van. Two girls emerged from the shadowy darkness and approached me, smiling coyly, although I could see that at least one of them was probably at least a year or two older than me and was well and truly 'tarted up' in a very short skirt, tight top and far too much make-up. The other girl was probably a little younger and rather fresher in appearance, with long strawberry-blonde hair.

"Yer Misty, aren't ya?" The first girl spoke, her accent betraying the fact that she hailed from further down the Ship Canal towards Liverpool

I nodded, expecting that she'd ask for an autograph or maybe just wanted to chat, but she grabbed me and glued her mouth to mine, sending me stumbling back against the wall of the theatre, unprepared for this sudden assault. Desperately trying to keep my balance I tried to pull away, but her hands had gone down to the buttons of my jeans, which she undid with an expertise that made me realise that she had had plenty of previous experience...

Despite everything, I began to feel aroused – I was, after all, a healthy lad of sixteen – and began to think that maybe I was finally going to lose my virginity, but just as quickly I experienced what was going to become a familiar feeling of deflation.

"What's the matter with ya?! Are you queer or something?! I can have any guy I want – no one's ever...you're just a waste of time, a complete..."

The rant, littered with language I had rarely heard from a young girl at that time (I was to get more familiar with it as my tally of failures grew!), lasted for several minutes as she continued to try to get a response from me. Eventually she pushed me away and her place was taken by the younger girl who, to my complete amazement, dropped to her knees in front of me and used her lips to try to breathe life back into my limp member…

I had actually found the blonde girl quite attractive, but I was, by now, so totally humiliated, anxious and repulsed, that there was no way she was going to be able to rescue me. After a few minutes the other girl told her she was wasting her time and the pair took off, teetering their way across the carpark towards the nearest pub. My legs gave way and I sank to the ground in an awkward heap, wanting to cry but desperate not to.

I heard footsteps approaching and, with nerveless fingers, frantically tried to re-button my Levis.

"Oh, look what we've got here! It's Foggy Culshaw himself, and he's got his tackle out! Having a slash, Mick?"

Oddly I felt absurdly relieved at the sound of Andy's voice. He stretched out a hand and hauled me to my feet, pushing me back against the wall and sticking his tongue down my throat. I gagged, unready for yet another mauling, but he took my hand and thrust it down inside his own trousers, his arousal being unmistakeable, while his free hand unbuttoned my jeans again.

The feelings he produced had far more effect than either of the girls had done, and I found myself enjoying his ministrations, but he stopped short of taking me the full distance.

"Come on, Micky, give it to me!"

I didn't realise to start with what he was asking, but he turned his back and dropped his flares, making it only too obvious. The anxiety came flooding back and the deflation washed through me like a cold shower.

"I can't!" I sobbed. "I wish I could, but I *can't*!"

"You're fucking useless! By which I mean you're un-fucking useless! You can just about sing, you can just about play guitar, but you're totally useless for anything else!"

He had pushed me back against the wall, unwilling to give up, but just as he was starting again, we heard footsteps and Paddy and Jan came up. It must have been fairly obvious what we had been doing – Jan looked horrified, but Paddy just pulled Andy off me and sent him sprawling across the uneven surface of the carpark.

"Are you OK, Mick?"

I gave a sob which was supposed to mean Yes.

"Get yourself straight and get into the van. Davey and Tina will be here in a minute."

He went over to Andy and hauled him to his feet, pinning him against the van.

"If you *ever* try that with Micky again, you'll have me to reckon with! Do – you – understand?!"

"I got the impression he was rather enjoying it…" Andy spat back sarcastically. Paddy shook him like a terrier with a rat, banging his head against the side of the vehicle. "Or are you jealous? Which of us would you rather fuck? I suppose it depends what turns you on, but I'd probably be of more use to you…"

He broke off as Paddy slapped him, hard, leaving him clutching his face.

Chapter 6.

Later 1971 to 1973, Various. Misty

Within a matter of weeks our lives had changed forever; a talent scout from London approached us, inviting us south for an audition. We were immediately offered a recording contract – initially for three single releases, but with an option (on the part of the record company) for further recordings, including an album.

Our first single scraped into the Top Twenty. A cover of a song which had been a hit in the US in the early 'sixties, it was not exactly ground-breaking but, aided by the professional pluggers employed by the record company, it received a lot of air-play and led to a number of prestigious bookings further afield than our usual circuit.

There was a lot of discussion as to what we should put out as the follow up. Most of our repertoire at that time was similar to the single – covers of standards and updated versions of lesser-known songs from an earlier era, but we had also begun to write our own material and occasionally included a sprinkling of these in our set, including a number which I had written, *Rock 'n' Roll Gypsy*.

This had become the song which we usually ended the evening with, although our small band of loyal followers had taken to demanding that we play it from early on in the evening, and this had caught the attention of the A&R team who, sensing that we were likely to have a ready market for at least a few hundred copies, decided that it might be worth taking it into the studio to see what they could make of it.

We worked on it for two days – a very long time in those days when singles were sometimes recorded in one take, or certainly within a matter of hours. The lyrics and tune were left as they were, but the instrumentation and arrangement were taken to pieces and reworked, making it more commercial. Andy, hungry for success and the fame and financial rewards it would bring, produced what would come to be his trademark, a stunning guitar solo which he also echoed in the intro and turned inside out for the outro, fading out in a plaintive, haunting instrumental break which needed no words. This took the time up to nearly five minutes – unusual for those days – although the radio stations usually cut it off after the final chorus, much to our fans' disgust.

The record was released at the beginning of December. For the first week it did little but, after our initial *Top of the Pops* appearance, it suddenly took off like a rocket and by the end of the second week was at No. 1, remaining there well into the New Year. We went back into the studio and recorded the third single, another self-penned song which I co-wrote with Davey, not as rocky as *Gypsy* but still 'danceable', Davey's main contribution being a clever drumbeat sequence which the fans soon developed into a set-piece dance.

We stayed in the studio for several more weeks, producing the tracks for the album which was now a foregone conclusion. This was followed by meetings with professional advisers who set up bank accounts and other financial arrangements for us. Unusually for that time, we were well looked after, and this stood us in good stead for the years to come. While we appreciated the guidance, we had agreed amongst ourselves that we would NOT sign with a manager but would deal with such matters ourselves. This was risky, especially as none of us were yet out of our teens, but we already had an agent to take care of our bookings and the record company machinery provided us with much of the support we needed and treated us very fairly.

Once the album was in the bag we immediately embarked on a long tour, starting with twenty dates around the British Isles and then immediately crossing from Scotland to Scandinavia before working our way across Europe. After months of little sleep (in the days of playing community halls, colleges etc.), it was a very strange feeling to receive bank statements showing sizeable credit balances, to be put up in comfortable, clean hotels and eat decent food. Instead of travelling in a Transit van, perched on top of the equipment, we now travelled in a minibus or coach, occasionally even flying to a destination.

The best part of all this was, for me, not having to return home and live under the same roof as my father. He had made it very clear, from the outset, that what I was doing was not what he had intended for me. He had tried hard to stop me, on the grounds of my still being under the age of majority, but once 'Gipsy exploded into the charts, the record company fought off his attempts to have me made a Ward of Court, making a good case that all the arrangements were very much for my benefit and that, in any event, at that point I was only a matter of months away from eighteen. In the meantime, Paddy and Jan having now married, Paddy was formally appointed as my guardian.

Although we had all been at school together, there was nearly two years' difference in age between Paddy and Davey and me. The older two had originally been in the same class at school but Davey, typically, had from early on done little or nothing in the way of schoolwork and had been held back a year, finding himself in the next class down with me and, later, Andy. Conversely although strictly speaking, age-wise, I should have been in the next class down from them, because I was considered bright I had scraped into the class with them, in spite of being just days short of a full year younger than Andy and almost two years younger than Davey.

Music had quickly brought us together; the seeds of the band had germinated when the others were fourteen and I was twelve. I was already, of course, known as a singer from my singing in church and I had learned to play the piano, and later the guitar, in the school music classes. Andy was also an established guitar player and we had taken to illicitly playing pop music before and after the official lessons. Davey, as my constant shadow, would improvise a rhythm on whatever was handy – a table, a cupboard – anything that made a satisfying noise – and it became apparent that he had the potential to be a useful percussionist, so much so that he was eventually promoted to play the school drum kit (such as it was). Finally, having found something worth working for, he exerted himself sufficiently to get a

Saturday job AND a paper round to earn money to buy his own kit.

By the late sixties of course the Beatles, the Shadows etc. were already considered rather old hat, but were still sufficiently influential for us to realise that we were missing an essential component – a bass guitarist.

Davey had remained friends with Paddy (helped by the fact that he lived only a few doors down from the Pryors) and persuaded him to take on the role. The band (or group as they were generally known then) was complete!

For the first couple of years we were effectively just playing at being a band, spending hours rehearsing in any space we could find that was large enough to accommodate us and from where we would not be speedily evicted. There was nowhere we could count on; my parents' house was out of the question, Davey's house was an occasional venue but, with so many of them crammed into such a small space, it had to be timed to coincide with periods of low occupancy. Paddy's mother could usually be depended on to tolerate us for a limited time, at least until his father got home, and Andy's parents possessed a garage/workshop which we were also able to use from time to time although, as their home was some distance from the rest of us, this was a mixed blessing.

Our first gig was at school, at an end of term dance. The music master had caught us in one of our jam sessions, and as a punishment/reward ordered us to provide the entertainment. Whether it occurred to him that we might be truly dreadful and he might therefore be bringing about the demise of the fledgling group I don't know – it seems entirely possible – but, having obtained permission to rehearse at every opportunity in the school hall for a full two weeks before the event, we turned in what must have been an acceptable performance, despite my voice being on the turn, making decisions about what key to play in a bit of a lottery.

For the remainder of our school time we were the automatic choice to provide entertainment whenever needed. This led to bookings for birthday parties and similar which, in turn, helped us reach a wider audience. By the time Paddy had left the school we were earning enough for him not to have to go to work at the Mill, although he supplemented his share of our earnings by working in the local pub at lunchtimes.

The following year our escape was complete. Andy and Davey finished the school year, leaving me in a kind of limbo. Dad was adamant that I was going to stay on for the sixth form and, in any event, I was in a grey area, age-wise, my birthday inconveniently falling right on the cut-off date.

We had work lined up across the school summer holidays, providing the entertainment in a holiday camp on the coast, with a second booking each evening playing in an 'end of the pier show' a few miles away. I wasn't keen on playing the same gigs night after night, but the money was regular and sufficient to allow me to indulge my passion for fashion, and for us to invest in some decent guitars and our own PA system. By the end of the summer we had further bookings lined up, taking us further afield, and I was seriously contemplating how I could manage not to return home between gigs.

It was at that point that our career had taken off, and we had spread our wings beyond the British Isles. By the time we returned to the UK I had bought the Chelsea flat and never returned to live in Manchester.

Chapter 7:

1972-1973, Various. Misty

In the days of travelling in the van with the equipment there had been little problem with Andy, other than the occasional situation like the one previously described. We all knew that he was queer – he'd made no secret of that – and we knew that after a show he went off in search of someone who would satisfy him. He was (then) a good-looking lad, though rather effeminate, something I knew that he played up. Later, years of drink and drugs took their toll and he became a caricature of himself. He seemed to have little trouble finding 'friends', but rarely seemed to be satisfied with whatever he'd found and would return to the van still hungry for more.

Before our success came Paddy had acted as my protector, stepping in to warn Andy off if he thought things were getting beyond banter. Although Davey would likewise have thumped Andy if he had seen any direct physical threat, he was too preoccupied with Tina to look out for me, and was not sufficiently sensitive to the point at which I found the constant harassment too much. When we started staying in hotels the problem moved up a gear. The original arrangement was for Paddy and Davey to share a room as they were both married/engaged and also roughly the same age, leaving me to share with Andy as we were both single and also closer in age.

For a while this seemed to work. After a show Andy would go off on the prowl. The rest of us would have a few drinks and then turn in. Andy usually returned to our room about midnight or later, often stoned. I quickly learned to sense whether he had found what he was looking for, although it rarely seemed to be enough. If he was totally unlucky, he'd be even more brittle and waspish than usual but, at the same time, with an element of vulnerability that was never normally apparent.

We were in Scotland, shortly before we were due to cross to Sweden on our first foreign tour. I heard him come into the room and could smell the booze on him before he'd even shut the door. I pulled the blankets over my head and pretended to be asleep. I heard him go into the bathroom and shower. A few minutes later he came back in, pulled the bedclothes back and climbed in beside me. Slipping his arms round me he started nuzzling the back of my neck. I tried to move away from him, but he tightened his grip.

"Don't be like that, Micky! You know that we're a pair of old poofs – be nice to me! You'll like it, I promise you. Remember that evening in the carpark? You enjoyed that, didn't you? Come on, let's have a nice time together…"

His hands were now exploring me - touching, rubbing, stroking…and I found I was enjoying what was happening – the first time (other than the carpark incident) that anyone had ever touched me like that. I rolled over to face him, and we kissed. Time seemed to become elastic – we probably continued like that for an hour or more – but then we arrived at the same point as before – he wanted me to screw him and I couldn't.

This time he didn't lose his temper but tried again – and again.

"Why?!" He wailed. "I don't understand you!"

"I'm sorry! Andy, I'm really sorry! I just can't! I don't know why – it's really great, what you were doing – I really liked it…Maybe – maybe if you do it to me it'll – it'll do something and I'll be able to…"

I suddenly realised he was crying – whether it was frustration, self-pity or something else I've no idea, but he was very definitely shedding tears.

"I can't!" he sobbed. "Why do you think I want *you* to fuck *me*?!"

He took my hand and shoved it down between his legs. He was completely limp, in spite of our recent activities.

"We're a right pair!" I said, laughing nervously. "All those birds out there thinking that we're 'sex symbols' and neither of us…"

I felt him shudder and thought maybe I should shut up. I hugged him and he clung to me, still sobbing quietly. We spent the rest of the night together and I thought that perhaps he'd leave me alone, now that he was aware of how things were.

We had to get up early the next morning to get the ferry; Jan and Tina had been with the others overnight and tearful goodbyes were being said over breakfast. I hoped that Paddy was too preoccupied to notice us but, as soon as we were on the ferry, he grabbed my arm and towed me outside.

"Are you OK? You look like you didn't sleep last night? Andy looks even worse…has he been bothering you again?"

"We're fine." I said firmly. "Andy's OK – he had a bad night, that's all."

"If he's been trying it on with you again, I'll break his bloody neck!"

"It's fine" I said firmly, genuinely at that moment feeling sorry for the very different, vulnerable Andy that I'd seen the previous night. I think that I honestly felt that we could maybe find a way to keep each other happy…

I should have known better. The next few days were worse than anything that had gone before. Andy, like the rest of us, was unable to speak any language other than English and a very small amount of schoolboy German and French, and found it impossible to communicate his desires. At that time our crew was supplied by the record company and were all totally straight, so there were no possibilities there, or with the local population. Strangely, in the years to come, Andy seemed to find a way to communicate with almost anyone, anywhere, but in those early days it just didn't happen and, after trawling any local bars and clubs, he would come back to the hotel and try it on with me – sometimes with more finesse than others. When he was being gentle and vulnerable, I was happy to go along with him as far as I was able, but often he would come back, drunk, stoned or both, and would try, none too gently, to force me to do what he wanted. The more brutal the attempts, the more impossible I found it to do anything that he found acceptable and it usually ended with me in tears, begging him to leave me alone.

By the time we reached Hamburg I was hollow-eyed from lack of sleep. Paddy kept interrogating me but, stubbornly, I could not bring myself to tell him the reason. Finally, when I broke down completely at the sound-check, it all came out. Paddy handed me to Davey to look after, dragged Andy outside and, when they returned, it was obvious that he had not stopped at giving him a tongue-lashing but had backed that up with a good kicking.

"In future you can share with Davey – I'll take care of Andy."

I looked at Andy but he wouldn't meet my eyes, staring sullenly at the floor.

"Go and get your head down – we've got a couple of hours before we go on."

Davey took me back to the room he had shared with Paddy, collecting my stuff on the way.

"What was that all about?"

Reluctantly I told him briefly what had been going on. He looked horrified but said little, other than promising to stay close to me, at the very least making sure that he was between Andy and me as far as humanly possible. I think that made me feel more miserable than ever.

"But I didn't *mind* what he was doing – I just couldn't do what he wanted! I was happy to…"

Davey looked shocked when I poured out my heart about how I had actually enjoyed Andy's attentions.

"Micky! How CAN you! You're not…?"

"I – I don't know – I think I might be. All the birds think I'm a waste of time. When Andy first started trying it on, I got far more turned on than I've ever been with a lass – I mean REALLY turned on – until he wanted me to…well, you know. He wants someone to…"

I found I didn't have the words to say it and ended up making a clumsy gesture.

"I think we're probably both…"

I heaved a heavy sigh, reluctant to admit in words what I suspected. Davey had been sitting on the edge of the bed but at this he got up and moved away.

"Please don't hate me! I can't help how I am, how I feel!"

"I don't hate you! How could I hate you?! We've been best mates ever since I can remember…I just don't understand how you can *want* to do that! You're gorgeous – all the lasses fancy you – it's not as though you're a raving old queen like Andy…"

I looked at him in abject misery, devastated that he seemed unable or unwilling to understand how I felt. It had been difficult enough to admit to myself that I was not normal (in the view of most people in those days) – admitting it to my best mate had been a major act of courage and his reaction confirmed my worst fears.

Just then Paddy let himself into the room to collect his things.

"You're supposed to be getting some kip."

He could see that something was obviously wrong.

"What's up? Micky?"

"Nothing…"

He came and sat down beside me.

"It doesn't look like nothing to me…Davey?"

"Micky's just…just told me that he thinks he's…"

"OK." Paddy seemed unfazed. "So what? Are you saying you'd rather share with Andy?"

"No, of course not! But…"

"We can talk about this some other time. Right now Micky needs to get some sleep."

"Paddy, please don't…don't do anything to hurt Andy…it's not his fault…"

"Micky, right now I'm supposed to be your guardian. You're still under the age of consent, and from the look of you Andy's been trying to bully you into doing things that you're not happy about, whatever you're now saying in his defence. I'm not going to stand by and see you getting ill…"

"I wanted him to do what he did! I *really* wanted it!" I shook my head helplessly. "But he wanted me to – to shag him and I *can't*…"

"Has he done that to you? Or tried to?"

"No…he can't either. That's the whole problem! We both want the same thing…"

Paddy squeezed my shoulder gently.

"How can you possibly know for sure? You'll find some nice girl and things will look totally different, you'll see…Just because you've had a few problems…hardly surprising the way some of those birds throw themselves at you – enough to frighten anyone…"

"No…!"

"Get some rest! Please Micky, just try and get some sleep, even if it's only for an hour…"

After he'd left Davey came and sat on the other bed.

"I'm sorry, Micky. I didn't mean to upset you – it's just such a shock! I never thought that you…"

I bit my lip, trying not to cry. I thought of the feelings that Andy had stirred in me, of the feel of his lips on mine, his hands.

"Are you really going to marry Tina?"

"Yeah."

I waited, expecting him to say something further, but he didn't.

"Do you love her?"

"I *think* so. We've – well, you know – it was OK. I don't want to find that she's up the duff and we're not wed. Her old man would kill me!"

I looked at him. Since leaving school he'd not had his hair cut and it was now well past his shoulders, a glorious curtain of rich mahogany where it had naturally darkened from the mouse of his childhood, his beautiful, dark-brown eyes with the black lashes framed between the remains of his fringe. His lips were full and well-shaped, currently pouting slightly as he contemplated things. I ached with the thought of him doing the things that Andy had done, longing for his touch. I thought of his strong hands…

"Davey…"

He looked up. I knew what I wanted to say, but was afraid to say it clumsily and spoil things between us, fearful of his reaction after the awkwardness earlier.

"Please don't – don't…"

"Don't what? Micky, you're my best mate – what you said just now really…I just can't believe…it won't affect our friendship, I promise you. But you need to give me time to get used to the idea…"

"I wish you felt the same way…" I ventured.

He shook his head. "No! No way! You're my best mate, but that's it! I'm not…well, you know…not that way…"

I got up and went through to the bathroom. I felt sick, a numb feeling which spread from my navel up to my throat. I rested my burning forehead against the cold tiles above the toilet. I think at that moment, if I could magically have been transported home I'd have gone, even back to my parents' house if I'd had to, though how I would have explained myself to Dad, God only knows.

Davey tapped at the door, which I'd closed behind me.

"Micky? Are you OK?"

"No!"

He tried the handle and, finding it unlocked, came in. He put his hands on my shoulders, gently pulling me away from the wall and turning me to face him.

"I'm sorry!" He said abjectly. "I didn't mean to upset you…I just don't know what to say to you…Teen and me are getting married…even if we weren't I don't think it would make any difference…"

I looked at him reproachfully, the big brown eyes were wet with tears and I knew that he was genuinely finding both the situation and the conversation painful. I opened my mouth to try to say something, anything, but the feeling of nausea chose that moment to manifest itself and instead I stuck my head down the loo just in time.

"I'll tell Paddy that we'll have to cancel tonight…"

"No, no, don't do that! It's too important…I'll be OK…"

Needless to say, I didn't get the prescribed sleep, but somehow managed to pull myself together and we played the gig – a large concert hall which was virtually sold out. It wasn't the best performance I'd ever given but, all things considered, could have been very much worse

. The audience seemed to think it was OK, although a few of the critics commented that maybe such a long tour was a little too much for such young performers, but generally they were kind.

We continued on our way further into mainland Europe, playing dates behind what was then still the Iron Curtain, before crossing back into West Germany, Austria, Italy and France. Paddy made quite sure there was little or no opportunity for Andy to try it on with me again. In some ways I found this unwelcome, although as the weeks wore on and Andy got more and more unable to find the amusement he craved, he was relying more heavily on pills to keep going and his behaviour grew correspondingly more reckless and erratic.

I was also feeling isolated; I was kept apart from Andy but, even though Davey and I were now sharing a room, he was finding it difficult to know how to deal with the situation, sometimes able to behave as though nothing had changed, but at other times a word or a situation would trigger a reaction which I found uncomfortable.

Paddy realised how unhappy I was and went out of his way to try to help, but there was little he could do; Davey refused point blank to share with Andy and I think Paddy was unwilling to leave either Andy or me on our own in case either of us did anything stupid.

In many ways it was a relief to get back to the UK. The third single had charted while we were away, and further dates had been added to the tour, sending the record to the No.1 spot.

Now we were back, Andy was able to resume his old ways and that solved most of our problems. Paddy and Davey were reunited with their ladies and I was left at a loose end again, but, freed from the stress of fighting Andy off, things didn't seem so bad and, now that I had turned eighteen and was able to at least have a drink with the others, I began to come to terms with my new circumstances.

The purchase of the Chelsea flat had been completed while we were away, so I was now freed from the obligation to return home to my parents. Once the tour ended, I was able to spend some time getting things how I wanted them. It felt very strange being completely on my own after month after month of being constantly with the band and crew, but I found that I actually quite enjoyed being able to choose the music I listened to or played, what time I got up or went to bed, and what I did during the day. All that was missing was someone to share it with.

*
■■■

Davey and Paddy had gone back to Manchester. I had no idea where Andy was and, in all honesty, wasn't that bothered. While I had enjoyed the contact we had had, I was also frightened by how easily he could lose his temper or inhibitions when he was stoned. At the same time, I ached to find someone, anyone, to explore those new sensations with. Although London had moved on from the Carnaby Street/King's Road era and 'Swinging London' of the sixties, it was still a magnet for a cosmopolitan mix of different cultures from all over the globe, but especially, at that time, from the English-speaking world. As a newly-fledged 'star' ('celebs' had yet to be invented) I found it easy to gain access to the many night-clubs, in spite of being well under the almost universal minimum age for entry which was still twenty-one or even twenty-four, despite the legal age of majority having recently been reduced to eighteen.

At first I enjoyed rubbing shoulders with other musicians, actors, TV stars et al, but realised fairly quickly that most of them were either very ordinary or very boring! The same problems I had encountered all too often before were still there, but at least now I could hint that there was a reason.

That in itself brought new problems; once the genie was out of the bottle, gossip spread rapidly, and I found myself the object of some very unwanted attentions from a number of ageing, would-be seducers, none of whom I found the least bit appealing. I made friends with a handful of other guys who pointed me to various gay-friendly haunts, but these all turned out to be full of similarly ageing and unattractive types behaving outrageously.

Thoroughly intimidated, I retreated to the safety of the flat, living a sort of half-life, only really existing when I was together with the rest of the band. Even then, the only person I was truly happy with was Davey although, generally speaking, Andy now left me alone, unless he was either desperate or out of his skull (or both!). Fond as I was of Paddy, for most purposes we were not on the same wavelength, our senses of humour being poles apart and, although he was fairly relaxed about me being gay (or, to be more precise, the fact that I had said that I was, given that I was still effectively celibate) he was very far from understanding how I felt.

Once he had got used to the idea, Davey seemed to have accepted the fact, although at that time there seemed little hope that he would ever change his mind about sharing my feelings. We never talked about it, but I suspected that he thought that, as I had yet to find a relationship of any kind, it might just be a passing phase and that, sooner or later I would meet a lass and would find myself 'cured'. By now he was the father of two and I knew that he adored the children and missed them like crazy when we were away, although I wasn't so sure that all was well between him and Tina…

Chapter 8:

1980, Chelsea. Misty

My extra-curricular career really began by mistake. We had arrived back from a tour of France and Germany just a couple of days beforehand. I had been dropped off by our tour-bus on its way from Dover back to Manchester and had fallen into bed at the flat, totally exhausted and hung-over from our end-of-tour party where, as well as splitting a bottle of Jack Daniels with Davey, we had also smoked several joints – the nearest any of us (other than Andy) got to doing drugs on tour.

There was little or no food in the flat and I had ventured out to get milk, bread and other essentials. The early spring sun was shining, and I wandered along the King's Road before turning down to the river and along towards Putney. There was a paved area with some young trees and seats, and I sat for a while enjoying the unexpected warmth. I felt disorientated and had little idea of what time or even what day it was, although I guessed it was probably around mid-morning.

I realised that someone had sat down at the other end of the bench and was looking at me. He was probably fifteen to twenty years my senior but still good-looking in a conventional way - well cut greying hair, chinos and a cornflower blue shirt and grey loafers.

I had left the flat in a haze and realised that I had just thrown back on the clothes I had been wearing when the bus dropped me off – skinny blue jeans and a garish, red-printed silk shirt, both of which almost certainly reeked of cigarettes and booze. I thought it time for me to leave!

"Are you looking for business?"

His voice was deep and warm, and his blue eyes crinkled as he smiled at me. I was startled and looked round to see who he might be talking to but there was no-one else near. My head reeled at the thought of the possibility of him touching me, of being taken in his arms…

There had been a few encounters since the debacles with Andy, but these had always been sordid, clumsy, drunken embraces close to a stage door with a variety of (usually young) stage-hands, roadies or others hoping for money or other favours, not anyone who I actually found remotely fanciable.

I knew I was playing with fire. It was unlikely that this man recognised me – wrong age group, wrong background altogether. He obviously thought I was on the game and looking for a punter. I felt an inward thrill and the daredevil inside made me answer in the affirmative. He raised an eyebrow.

"We can go back to my place." I said, trying to appear cool and not too eager.

"Is it far?"

I shook my head and led the way. He didn't attempt to make physical contact but followed a few steps behind so that it was not obvious that we were walking together. When we reached the outer door to the block he looked a little surprised, but made no comment. I led the way into the flat, apologising for the pile of luggage in the entrance hall.

"Is this your place?" I nodded. He spotted the guitar cases. "Do you play?"

"Yeah, I'm a musician"

We went through into the living room which, fortunately, had not yet been totally trashed.

"Can I get you anything? I don't have any milk for coffee – that's what I went out for, but I didn't quite get there. There's plenty of alcohol…"

He came to me then and placed his hands on my shoulders. I was trembling.

"I get the feeling you don't usually do this?" he said gently, "But you are gay?"

I nodded. He dropped a kiss onto my forehead before moving down to my lips. I went (literally!) weak at the knees.

"You can change your mind – it's OK. I won't force you to do anything you're not comfortable with."

"Please don't stop!" I whispered huskily. "I really want you!" My hands were shaking as I unzipped the chinos and went down on him.

Minutes later we were in the bedroom and I finally got to experience the definitive, earth-shaking ecstasy that had so far passed me by. Afterwards we lay there for a long while in silence. I was desperate for a cigarette, but knew instinctively that would probably drive him away. Eventually he said "I'd really like to see you again…"

"Me too – it may be difficult though. I'm here for a few weeks now, but after that we'll be recording – not sure where yet – if it's here in London then that could be a few more weeks, but then we'll be off on tour again…"

"Big time eh?"

I read the scepticism in his face.

"Well, you know…"

I tried to stay non-committal, not wanting to say or do anything to frighten him off.

"If money's a problem, I'm happy to pay your rent and living expenses."

I nearly choked. "No! No really, that's not a problem!"

Before I could stop myself, I blurted out that I actually owned the flat.

"I don't even know your name!"

"Alex. I don't know yours either?"

"M- Micky" I stammered, realising that 'Misty' was probably likely to trip me up sooner or later.

"How can I get in touch with you?"

I thought about this for a minute. I didn't want to leave too much to chance, but there were no mobile phones in those days. I gave him the phone number of the flat and promised to get an answerphone.

"I can't give you contact details." he said quietly, "No one must know about this."

"Maybe you shouldn't have told me that?"

He looked at me with a half-smile and shook his head.

"I trust you. You obviously are NOT a rent-boy, or if you are, you've a lot to lcarn!"

I watched regretfully as he dressed, longing for him to touch me again. I had waited so long to feel this way that I wanted the day to last forever. He realised that I was watching him and smiled reassuringly. I held out my hand to him and he came back and sat on the edge of the bed, gently running his fingers down my spine, making me shiver with desire.

"I promise I'll come back…" he said softly "You are too beautiful for me not to."

"Can't you stay a bit longer?"

He shook his head. "Not today. I have to be somewhere. I came out to – to get away from someone for a while. Now I must go home, change my clothes and go out again."

I realised that he had a very slight foreign accent, but we had done little talking so far, and it had not previously been apparent. He smiled at me again.

"It will be alright, Micky. I promise…"

He leaned over and kissed me on the lips, letting the contact linger, making me moan with desire again. I watched, feeling distraught and desperate for him to stay, as he left the room and heard the lock snap into place as he closed the door to the flat. I rushed to the window but couldn't see which direction he had gone in.

After he'd gone, I found a wad of £20 notes under the pillow. I lay down again, drinking in the vestiges of his cologne and his unique smell. I felt drunk with the emotional aftershock of the last couple of hours.

I'm not sure even now whether I had already fallen in love with him, or was simply grateful for the awakening of my whole being. My body smouldered with new life, aching for more, and I wondered how long I would have to wait, or even IF he would come back…

Chapter 9:

1980, Chelsea. Misty

Alex did not wait long before contacting me again after our first meeting. He told me little about his circumstances, other than that he was married but the marriage was childless. He had known from an early age that he was gay, but had married to advance his career.

His wife was (he thought) unaware of his 'other side', but he believed that she looked elsewhere for a physical relationship as they had not shared a bed for many years. She had not sought a divorce, and he assumed that she valued their lifestyle and the kudos of being married to him more than the freedom to marry again.

This went some way to explaining his need for absolute discretion, but I wondered why, if he suspected that his wife was also 'looking elsewhere', we could never be seen together in public. On rare occasions we went to the theatre, something I had never experienced until then, but he insisted on us arriving independently and taking our seats as strangers, leaving separately at the end.

As time went on, I was able to give him advance warning of when I would be home and when I would be away on tour or recording. Occasionally he would be unavailable for some weeks and, when that happened, I would find myself gravitating back to the place where I had first met him near the river, desperate for the physical comfort that he had brought me after so many years of loneliness. On these visits I would disguise myself by wearing something outrageous and painting on make-up so that I looked very different, not only from my stage persona, but also the far-less flamboyant Micky that Alex knew.

I rarely went home alone but always tried to play it safe, both in the partner I selected and in what I would or would not agree to do. If someone made me feel uneasy then, if possible, I would not agree to anything other than a quick grope in some dark corner, well away from the flat. This didn't always work – occasionally I would find myself with a black eye or worse, and at least once I was followed home and forced into decidedly risky sex by a punter who reeked of booze but was far from incapable. Each time I swore to myself that I would not do it again, but the temptation was always too much, and my resolve would fade with the bruises.

Alex couldn't fail to notice the black eyes and bruising, although I used to try to keep him away when they were at their worst. He'd scold me and try to make me promise to stop risking my life and health – the AIDS crisis was just breaking at this time – but when he was not around I was too lonely to stay at home waiting for him to call and would find myself drawn irresistibly back along the river path.

Chapter 10:

1980-1983, London. Misty

My relationship with Alex continued to blossom and grow right up to the time of my arrest. Although I was never financially dependent on him, emotionally I suppose I was mesmerised by him. This was the man who had, after so many years of longing, dreaming, searching, brought me fulfilment, satiation.

He rarely visited empty-handed, always bringing some small or not-so-small gift – jewellery if it was a special occasion, a bottle of good champagne, a silk scarf, a cashmere sweater - something to recognise that I had finally convinced him that I did not need his money. Occasionally he would arrive with a Fortnum & Mason hamper and we would picnic after making love, totally at ease in each other's company.

As a lover he was always completely assured, knowing how to give as well as take pleasure, always careful to ensure that he was not hurting me. Due to my peripatetic existence, and his uncertain work schedule, we rarely made plans – the theatre outings were always spur-of-the-moment, but a welcome diversion as he always chose shows which he knew I would enjoy, not things he thought I 'ought to' see.

A little before my world imploded he had begun talking about the possibility of us going on holiday – a friend would lend him a villa in Spain, we would travel separately before meeting up at the property. His wife, whose name I now knew to be Veronique, was going home to France to stay with her sister for an extended visit. He suspected that this was probably not entirely true, but it suited his own agenda not to enquire too closely.

Chapter 11:

1983, London. Misty

Once we reached the hospital I was officially under arrest and would be formally charged once I was well enough to be taken into custody. Davey was only allowed to stay with me after the doctors had intervened, alarmed at my failure to respond to the emergency treatment for my serious injuries. He had rushed to London immediately he'd heard the news and had camped out at the hospital until the police finally relented and agreed that he could sit with me (with an officer in the room in case I came round). The only other person allowed access to the room was the priest who had given me the Last Rites.

To start with the police had believed that I had killed Andy after a lovers' tiff and had then gone home and tried to kill myself. Fortunately, the medical evidence proved conclusively that it would have been impossible for me to have caused my own injuries; less conveniently it did nothing to disprove that I could have killed Andy, as the murder and the attack on me could have occurred several hours apart, although there was nothing to show which attack had actually happened first.

Once I regained consciousness Davey had to leave and the questioning began. The record company engaged a very expensive criminal lawyer, Angelo Daranda. He was the archetypal tall, dark and handsome – maybe a few years older than me and far more English than his name suggested. Despite everything, we hit it off immediately and I had no doubts that he would be more than able to extricate me from this nightmare, if anyone could.

Chapter 12:

1983, Chelsea. Misty

After I had recovered sufficiently to be questioned things had moved inexorably on. I was charged with Andy's murder, with an alternate charge of manslaughter.

Angelo was confident that the murder charge would be dropped at an early stage as there was plenty of evidence available that would show provocation. He managed to secure bail for me as there was little likelihood of me being a danger to anyone else, and the record company and my bandmates scraped together the enormous surety demanded. I was however effectively under house arrest, as I was required to report daily to the local police station and to be available at any time should the police wish to check up on me. Paddy moved down from Manchester to keep me company, followed shortly afterwards by Davey.

I heard nothing from Alex across this period; I was desolate, but realised that he had almost certainly seen the headlines and now knew exactly who I was, as well as what had happened.

The boys were good company – I can't think of anyone else who could have kept me from killing myself at that miserable time. Andy was seldom mentioned – even when we sat with our guitars and sang together, he was not really missed; if anything, it was a relief not to have the constant sniping and bitchy remarks.

Chapter 13:

1983, Chelsea. Misty

Angelo arrived one evening accompanied by another tall, dark, handsome stranger. Davey said later that he could read my mind with no difficulty whatsoever!

"Micky, this is Nathan Ainsworth – he will be representing you in court".

Nat held out his hand. His touch was like an electric shock and I gazed up into his deep-set, black eyes. His hair was equally black, and he was olive-skinned with strong features – very masculine but without any sense of machismo. His voice, when he spoke, was not as deep as I had expected, but quite similar in depth and tone to Alex', and it was no surprise to discover later that they had attended the same public school.

"Hello Micky. Angelo has told me your story. I've also received the papers from the DPP. Their case seems to be largely circumstantial, to say the least. That said, and although it is for them to prove their case, we do need to gather as much evidence as we can to challenge it, so we need to spend some time together – probably over several sessions, although I think once you and I have been through what we have so far, Angelo can probably follow up with you and brief me as we go along. I realise that you've not been out of hospital very long and I don't want to over-burden you."

I smiled uncertainly.

"I don't know what I can tell you." I said timidly. "I don't remember anything that happened that day or for several days either side of it."

"Nothing at all?"

"I remember waking up on the floor. I remember the door being smashed in – someone trying to pull me up – being put into the ambulance – then nothing until several days later…"

"What about beforehand?"

I shook my head. I'd been through this with Angelo so many times that now my head spun every time I tried to remember. Who had I been with that evening? Who had beaten me up so badly, possibly raped me? The only thing I was positive about was that Alex could not, would not have hurt me under any circumstances, even under provocation. Something nagged at the back of my mind but however hard I tried I just couldn't pin it down.

I had not mentioned Alex to Angelo – in fact no one knew of our relationship, not even Davey at that time. It was easier to keep quiet than to try to remember who knew and who didn't. Davey knew there was someone – he knew me better than anyone, and it had been impossible to hide from him the happiness that Alex had brought me and the subtle changes that came from that, in the way I looked, the difference in what I brought to our songwriting, but even when he questioned me, I kept quiet as to how Alex and I had met, his name or any of the very few details that I knew for sure.

Chapter 14:

1983, Middle Temple.

"Nat – is it correct that you are representing Michael Culshaw?"

Nat turned abruptly as he rushed across Middle Temple Lane towards the Inner Temple. He recognised Alex' voice immediately, but it seemed an unlikely time of day to find him there.

"Yes, that's right. What is your interest in the case?"

"Is he OK? Who's picking up your fee?"

Nat frowned and asked again what his interest was.

Alex hesitated, surreptitiously looking round to see who was nearby.

"Can we meet? Somewhere discreet?"

Nat sighed. Time was precious just then, but he'd known Alex since his schooldays and counted him as a close friend. He wondered what might have rattled the usually urbane façade. Not entirely reluctantly, he agreed to meet for dinner at a small bistro in Chancery Lane, not far from the Inns of Court.

Alex was already seated when Nat arrived, a large Armagnac in front of him.

"Now, what's this about?" Nat demanded, his eyes scanning Alex' face. "I doubt that poor Micky is of interest to HMG, however popular the band has been in the past".

He realised that Alex was pale and that his hands were shaking.

"Alex! I'm listening – what is this about?!"

"I know him – rather too well if you understand me."

Nat was about to make a 'smart' answer, but he rushed on. "Please, Nat! This is almost certainly not what you are expecting to hear.! I have known Micky for several years now and he means…" He struggled for the right words. "He means a hell of a lot to me!"

"You must tell me the whole story." Nat said cautiously. "I'm not promising anything until I know what I'm dealing with".

Alex sat in silence for some minutes. The food order was taken and, while they waited, Alex briefly told him the story.

"I met him down by the river. It was after I broke up with Nico, but I wasn't cruising. I'd had a row with Vero – the usual problems - and had gone out just to get away from her. Micky was sitting on one of those benches beyond the end of the park, near the river. The way he looked…I assumed he was for hire."

He smiled slightly at the memory

"You could have knocked me flat when he took me back to his place, but I assumed he already had someone funding him. And then…nothing was how I expected it to be! He was shy in so many ways, and totally – totally inexperienced, but at the same time so desperate - it was a whole new level for me!"

He stopped briefly, lost in thought.

"Please tell me he's OK? I hate the thought of him being frightened or unhappy!"

He stumbled on for some minutes more, telling Nat what he already knew – how Micky looked – the long, curly, pale blond hair, the colour of champagne; the grey-blue eyes that looked mauve in some lights; the slender figure; the facial features that were both masculine and feminine at the same time.

Nat realised that he was close to tears and nudged him gently under the table. The bistro was small and intimate, and he knew it well as a place to meet discreetly, but if Alex was seen to be in tears in such a public place, someone would be bound to notice and recognise him. If they did it would be plastered across the front page of every tabloid the next morning!

Alex pulled himself together with an effort and Nat could see how much he was already suffering.

"You have to help him!" he demanded.

Nat shot him a look.

"I have every intention of so doing!" he said indignantly.

Alex apologised. "Sorry, that was hardly tactful on my part. Who is footing the bill?"

"It probably depends on the outcome." Nat sighed. "The record company, the management and the boys themselves have funded the bail bond and I assume they will ultimately pay my bill. He's hardly likely to get legal aid!"

Alex said quietly "Don't worry about that. Just bill me – it's the least I can do."

He meant it. He was silent again for some more minutes, during which time the food arrived. He pushed it around the plate before apparently making a decision.

"If necessary, I'm prepared to come forward and say he was with me when the other boy was killed".

Nat stared at him.

"You're crazy! You're prepared to throw away everything you have worked for AND commit perjury…"

Alex cut in quickly. "How do you know it would be perjury? Whenever he's home I often see him several times a week."

Nat tried to read his face, but he was well skilled in inscrutability, both as an advocate and a politician.

"Will he say you were with him?"

Alex shrugged helplessly.

"I don't know. When we first met, I told him that our relationship had to be a secret. He's always been very good about that. I doubt he's even told the other boys."

Chapter 15:

1983, Chelsea. Misty

"How come you know Alex Hansen?"

Nat fixed me with his dark eyes, seeming to look into the darkest recesses of my heart. I pitied anyone being cross-examined by him in court…

I shook my head.

"I don't."

I was genuinely at a loss as, until that moment, I had no knowledge as to Alex' surname.

Nat gave an exasperated hiss through clenched teeth.

"Micky, if I am to represent you, you have to be absolutely straight with me. Alex is a personal friend of mine, as well as a colleague. He is in pieces over what is happening with you!"

My stomach knotted, and I burst into tears.

"I didn't know his surname!" I sobbed. "I didn't know anything about him except his first name – I still don't!"

Angelo moved across the room and put his arm round me.

"I believe him…" He said quietly. "Please Nat, he's been through a lot already; he's not on trial here!"

Nat's expression softened a little.

"Alex Hansen is a Queen's Counsel – a barrister - like me. He is also a Member of Parliament and a Privy Counsellor. He's desperate to help you and is likely to throw everything away in order to do so, unless we can persuade the judge to allow him to give evidence anonymously. He's one of the very few genuine good guys – it would be a tragedy if he is ruined by this."

I shook my head again.

"I had no idea – I was so intent on him not knowing who I was that it never occurred to me that he had anything to hide, except from Veronique. He said right from the start that no one must know, and we were always very careful, but I never thought that he was so…such…I loved him so much!"

"How did you meet him?"

I told him the story.

He nodded "That's pretty much what he told me. When did you last see him?"

I thought back desperately. Having been in hospital didn't help – I couldn't remember anything of the day of the attack at all, or for several days afterwards.

"I can't remember!" I said miserably.

"This could be really important!" Nat was staring into my eyes so hard it almost hurt. "Not just for you, but for Alex as well."

I shivered. Angelo still had his arm round my shoulders, sensing how difficult I was finding this. It seemed unreal that my sweet, kind Alex could be so important, but it all fell into place in a way that nothing had previously made sense, and I realised the huge risks he had been taking in maintaining our relationship. I shook my head again.

"I'm sorry, I just can't remember anything from that time…we were planning to go on holiday – Alex was going to travel out to Spain and I was going to meet him there – a friend was lending him a house…We went to the theatre…"

"What did you see?"

"*Cats.*"

"Who bought the tickets?"

"Alex – he always did."

"Was that the last time you saw him?"

I thought frantically, my mind scrabbling through shreds of memory from that time.

"What did you do after the show?"

"He had to go somewhere after the show – he didn't say where. I went home – but I think that was the Wednesday…"

Andy had died on the Saturday night. I had a yawning blank of three days. I tried to concentrate – when had I last seen Alex? – when had we last slept together? It would have been unusual not to have seen him for so long, but by no means impossible.

"Would your bank records give you any clue? If you go anywhere do you use cash or pay by card?"

"AmEx usually. I rarely have much cash. I'm sorry, I know I'm not being much help, but I really can't remember."

"What is the last thing you do remember?"

"Just snapshots – lying on the floor – the door being kicked in – being put into the ambulance – not much after that until I woke up and Davey was there – that was a few days later..."

"OK, before that?"

"Going to *Cats* I suppose – Alex going off to wherever he was going…"

I paused, unsure what came next.

"How did you get home?"

"By river probably…"

"What would you have done the next day?"

I sighed, shaking my head.

"Probably not much. A couple of hours of music, just hoping Alex would call…"

I broke off. Something was nagging at the back of my mind, just out of reach.

"Alex is devastated by what's happened – he – he really did love you… he still does for that matter – he'll be taking a huge risk if he gives evidence, even anonymously. He won't be able to contact you until all this is over in case anyone puts two and two together…"

I nodded miserably, longing for just one more kiss, one more chance to feel his hands on my body, bringing me alive, to hear his voice, smell his scent…

Chapter 16:

1983, Chelsea. Misty

The first time it had happened between Davey and me had been, certainly on his part, an accident.

Paddy had gone back to Manchester overnight to see his family, leaving the two of us together. The flat only had one bedroom but the living room had two enormous sofas and the boys had been sleeping there.

I had gone to bed late and had taken a long time to go to sleep. When I finally did, I dreamt badly – nightmarish images of Andy, soaked in blood, juxtaposed with a faceless, shapeless being holding me down, violating me - and I woke myself up, screaming.

Davey had stumbled in to find me, yet again, in floods of tears. He'd tried to calm me down, but I didn't want to be left on my own and he'd climbed into bed with me. Eventually we'd both managed to get back to sleep.

I came to with a jolt, dreaming that Alex was there with me. Davey had his arms round me and was nibbling the back of my neck, his body hard against my backside. I tensed slightly – my body ached for him, but I realised that he was still effectively asleep, dreaming that he was at home with Tina. By the time he realised his mistake he was already inside me. He swore and pulled away abruptly.

I rolled over so that we were lying face to face.

"That was nice!" I teased.

He shook his head.

"It was a mistake…" he muttered furiously.

"It was still nice!" I insisted.

I had nothing to lose – we had been friends too long for anything to damage our friendship now. I wriggled closer to him so that he was aware of my own arousal.

He didn't move away as I gently touched his face, gazing deep into his beautiful brown eyes. As he still hadn't actually pushed me away, I moved in closer still, kissing him gently on the lips, letting my hands wander from his face to his shoulders, his chest, down to his hips, touching, stroking…

"Micky –"

He breathed my name and I sensed he was about to try to stop me. I prevented him from saying anything more by kissing him more firmly. His breathing deepened. I knew he was struggling to stop himself from doing something he thought he would regret, and I slid my hand down between us, making sure that he was in no doubt about how I felt about things!

"I want you!" I insisted, sliding across so that I was straddling him.

"No –!"

He tried to pull away from me, but his body was betraying him and he came, gasping for breath.

We lay there for a long time without speaking. Eventually I started to gently caress him again, sliding my hands across his belly and sides, gently dropping kisses on his face, his throat, his chest, holding him against me until he couldn't resist any more and began to respond to me.

Aside from Andy's constant attempts to force me to have sex with him, sometimes rousing feelings in me which, in other circumstances, would have been more than pleasurable, Alex had been my only real lover. He had taught me how to give pleasure and, in turn, had given me my first taste of physical love – something far more wonderful than mere sex and which made me understand the difference between 'having sex' and 'making love'. Now. with Davey, I put everything I had learned into practice to try to convince him that what we had was more than special.

We were still making love several hours later when Paddy returned and walked in on us. He did a quick about turn and fled to the kitchen. Davey leapt out of bed and, pulling on his jeans, rapidly followed him.

I lay there for a minute or two more, luxuriating in the sensation of having made love with the person who had been the object of my desire, the love of my life, since adolescence, my body still alive with the feel of his skin against mine, the brush of his hair against my face, his own special smell, the mix of shower gel and shampoo...

I could hear raised voices, so reluctantly pulled on some clothes and also headed for the kitchen. The row stopped abruptly as I walked in and Paddy crossed to me, putting his hands on my shoulders.

"Are you OK?" he demanded.

I smiled.

"Never better!"

"Paddy's going back to Manchester…" Davey said quietly.

"You don't have to…" I said, meaning it.

I had felt so safe with them both there. Even with the developments of the last few hours, part of me wanted the reassurance of them both being there with me.

"I'm sorry, I just don't feel comfortable – I feel like a spare part. You'll be fine – I'll come back for the trial - or if you need me for anything in particular."

He collected his stuff together and was gone within half an hour, despite having just driven all the way down.

I looked at Davey. "D'you think he'll be OK?"

He nodded. "He'll be fine. But you can bet your bottom dollar the first thing he'll do is to tell Janice and then she'll tell Tina."

"I'm sorry!" I said abjectly.

I'd seen Tina's temper in action many times in the past and I knew that it would be more than rough.

"Don't be."

I blinked at him in total surprise. He shook his head.

"It's been over for a long time. I only stayed because of the kids."

He was close to tears and I walked into his arms and hugged him tightly. The silence seemed to last a long time, but it was probably only a couple of minutes.

"She made my life hell – and I let her! I'll have to find some sort of compromise so that we keep things normal for the kids. Perhaps we can buy somewhere not too far away from them and I can 'go home' like I've been doing. The kids'll think we've been on tour or whatever – they needn't know we've split until they're old enough to understand properly."

At this point Sally was just ten and Danny only eight years old.

My own childhood had been difficult. My father had been strict with me and Mam was enough in awe of him to go along with whatever he dictated. Always the performer, I had often been in trouble at school for playing the fool. In the days when corporal punishment was still allowed this earned me frequent beatings and, if he got to hear of them, further, similar punishment from Dad. So far as he was concerned my only redeeming quality was my voice, especially when I was given a solo to perform at Mass. I understood only too well what it was like to live in a home where the parents were at loggerheads or, worse, indifferent to each other and I wondered how Sal and Danny would cope.

"Are you sure?"

I looked into his eyes, trying to fathom what he really felt. My conscience was hurting badly – I knew full well that I had effectively seduced him and that we were now about to reap the whirlwind.

He nodded, forcing a wobbly smile.

"It's not your fault." He said firmly. "Don't think I haven't been tempted before – it's nearly broken my heart seeing you miserable and lonely. I've fought against the way I feel so many times, telling myself that I was straight – 'after all, I have kids' - and all that, but I can honestly say that I've never felt the way I feel about you with anyone else – certainly not with Tina."

I burst into tears. He smiled at me, returning my hug before kissing the tears away gently.

Chapter 17:

1963, Manchester. Micky

"Michael Culshaw! Come out here at once!"

I bit my lip rebelliously and shuffled to the front of the class.

"You never learn, do you? Go straight to Father Flanagan, tell him I sent you and tell him why!"

I was tempted to argue but I knew it was pointless. The incident for which I was to be punished had not been started by me but, as so often happened, I was the one who had been caught, red-handed.

I made my way to the Headmaster's office and tapped at the door timidly. The voice from inside called for me to enter and I turned the handle and went in.

Father Flanagan was a large man, probably at that time no more than mid-forties in age, but to a little lad of eight, he seemed ancient. His office had probably changed little since the school was first built in the late Victorian era; a large space for a large man, and the atmosphere was intimidating – probably intentionally so.

The décor was sombre – a dark oak-panelled dado beneath nicotine-stained, shiny cream paint, the floor covered with brown lino which had seen better days.

The room was high-ceilinged and there was one tall window, opposite the door, uncurtained, a range of old-fashioned Globe-Wernica bookcases with their glazed up-and-over doors and another bank of more modern, open-fronted bookshelves piled high with exercise books. A large Year Planner hung on one wall, below the inevitable crucifix.

The desk was large, also of dark oak and possibly only a little younger than the room, and was placed facing the door, albeit with a distance across the floor of at least eight feet. A number of mis-matched wooden chairs were arranged haphazardly to hand for the use of visitors or staff. An angle-poise reading lamp stood to one side of the surface of the desk, a large blotter filled with ink-spattered white paper placed centrally in front of Father Flanagan's padded leather chair. Opposite the blotter there was an elaborate ink stand. The only other items on the desk were a large glass ashtray, a black bakelite telephone with a braided cord and a filing tray with a number of thin files in it.

He peered across the desk.

"Oh dear, Micky Culshaw – again! What did you do this time?"

I could smell the Guinness and pie-and-mash he had consumed at lunchtime, over and above the reek of pipe-tobacco which always pervaded the room – a combination of smells which would haunt me for the rest of my life, particularly the pipe-tobacco.

"Please Father, I didn't do anything…"

I was trembling, already anticipating the bite of the tawse.

"If you didn't do anything Mr. Marshall would not have sent you to me! That will be two extra strokes for lying to me!"

He took the tawse from the top drawer of the desk, rose and came round to where I stood, my legs shaking in anticipation of what was to come. He *gestured that I should assume the customary position, hands on the edge of the desk, feet apart and leaning forward.*

He raised his arm and brought the thick leather strap down across my buttocks with a loud 'thwap', then again and again until I had received the prescribed six strokes plus the extra two.

Despite the protection afforded by thick cotton drawers and grey woollen shorts, the heavy leather strap stung and felt more as though it were made of wood or some other rigid material than anything more flexible. I could barely stand now, tears running down my face, my legs shaking. He was breathing heavily with the exertion – or maybe on this occasion it was something else?

Normally at that point I would have been summarily dismissed, but this time he said "You seem to have felt that today. I'd better have a look. Undo your shorts!"

Nervously I obeyed and he lifted my shirt to inspect his handiwork. His breathing grew faster and heavier and I caught another waft of Guinness, gravy and tobacco and then one arm came over my shoulder and clamped across my chest and throat, the other hand across my stomach, pulling me back against him and I felt something unbearably hard being forced between my buttocks and right into my most private region.

I tried to cry out – as much to relieve the pain as to attract attention but, like in a nightmare when you can't make a sound, nothing came out, the breath trapped inside me by the huge hand across my throat.

I was absolutely terrified, as well as torn with pain. I could hear strange noises – grunting and an almost animal-like whining and then a gasping noise and suddenly it was all over. His grip on me relaxed and I was able to tear myself away from him, frantically wrenching the door open and hurtling out into the corridor and down the stairs.

I ran, dragging my shorts back up as I went. There was blood running down my leg and I felt as though I had wet myself. My arms were bruised from his grasp and I was sobbing with fear and pain. My legs felt heavy and I could hardly see where I was going, blinded by tears and a blackness that threatened to swallow me.

I heard someone coming and took cover behind the bins where they were stored beneath the staircase. The footsteps passed but I stayed there, unable to make myself leave the safety of my refuge.

The bell rang for lunchtime. Many sets of feet passed and then someone stopped, level with my hiding place.

"Micky? Mick, are you there?"

Davey's hoarse whisper was the best sound I had ever heard, but I couldn't bring myself to speak, just sob. He pushed a bin to one side and slid in beside me.

"What are you doing in there, you dope?! You'll be in more trouble if you're found there! Why are you crying?"

I couldn't bring myself to tell him what had happened, but he could see for himself that I was badly upset.

"C'mon, I'll take you home."

"No! No, Dad'll kill me!" I begged.

"OK, I'll take you to ours – Mam'll clean you up."

We sneaked out of school through the hole in the railings which led directly onto the street where Davey's family lived, just around the corner from ours. His mother had nine children of her own so one more never made any difference. 'And they're not even Catholic!' my mother had once exclaimed in disgust, as though large families were only allowable for followers of Rome like us, but perhaps it was jealousy because it made her own inability to produce more than the one child seem the more obvious.

Our houses were identical in layout but, whereas our house provided my parents and me with a room each and one to spare, in Davey's home he and his four brothers shared one room and his four sisters another, in cramped but cheerful chaos. His mother welcomed me into the kitchen.

"Hello Micky love, in the wars are we?"

I nodded.

"C'mon, let me look..."

I shook my head.

"It's all right love, don't worry, you don't have anything I haven't seen before!"

"No, No it's OK, I'm fine!"

She fetched a flannel and gently wiped the blood from my legs. Just then there was a rapid knock at the front door. Davey went to answer it and came back in with my mother.

"What have you been up to now? Oh Micky, your father will have your hide!"

Mam scowled at Davey's mother.

"Thank you Margaret, I can look after my own if you don't mind!"

Davey's mother started to say that she thought that something was wrong, but Mam cut her off abruptly and, taking me by the hand, dragged me off home.

I tried to tell her what had happened and, for a brief moment, I thought that she believed me. I was bathed and put to bed with a mug of hot milk.

A couple of hours later I heard Dad come in from work and the hum of their voices below and I could tell from the rise and fall of the conversation that Mam was telling him what I had said. I could also sense, with a sinking feeling, that Dad refused to believe my story…

I heard his heavy tread coming up the stairs and burrowed down under the blankets, feigning sleep. The bedroom door opened and he came in. Grabbing the bedclothes, he tore them off me and, seizing me by the arm, pulled me out of bed

"You're a lying little beggar!" he shouted, shaking me by the arm, his face so close to mine I could smell the ale on his breath. "How dare you accuse that good man Father Flanagan of such an abhorrent thing?!! How do you even know such things at your age?!"

I started to sob, wanting to say that I only knew such things because they had happened to me, but I knew it was pointless.

He undid his belt, doubled it and, bending me over the edge of the bed, gave me another eight strokes, my thin pyjamas doing nothing to protect me.

When he had finished he left me as I was, kneeling on the floor, sobbing my heart out. I heard the key turn in the lock and knew there was no hope of Mam coming to comfort me. I was shivering with cold as well as the pain and fear, but it took all my strength to drag myself back into bed and pull the covers over me again.

The following day I was so bruised and sore I couldn't walk. Mam kept me off school and the Truant Officer came to the door, but she gave him the tale that I was sick and he went away without speaking to me.

If nothing else, I had learned to avoid getting sent to Father Flanagan again. I never told Davey what had happened – I felt too ashamed – but by some instinct he seemed to be extra protective of me after that day and, if it looked as though I was likely to get into trouble, he went out of his way to take the blame.

Chapter 18:

1983, Chelsea. Micky

We didn't have to wait long to find out whether Tina had learned what had happened.

The phone rang early the following morning. Davey answered it and turned as white as a sheet in the face of the torrent of vile abuse. I hoped the kids weren't within earshot! Once she had drawn breath, I heard Davey say quietly that they needed to talk things through. That unleashed a further volley of bad language which he ended by putting the receiver down, cutting off the call.

He phoned Paddy, asking him to come down to stay with me so that he could drive north. Paddy had the grace to apologise for precipitating events – Janice had wanted to know why he had returned so quickly, and he had told her the truth, not expecting her to pass it on – certainly not as quickly as she had done. Janice had however seen it as her duty to tell Tina, alarmed by the massive publicity currently being given to the AIDS epidemic, the 'gay plague'.

Chapter 19:

1983, Chelsea.

Davey woke from a deep sleep; for a moment he had no idea what had woken him but then he heard a terrified scream from the bedroom. Grabbing his jeans, he rushed in and found Micky sitting upright, arms wrapped round his knees, shaking and sobbing hysterically.

"What's up? What happened?"

Micky shook his head, unable to speak. Davey sat down beside him on the bed and put his arm round his shoulders. Micky was shivering violently, his teeth chattering.

Davey pulled the quilt round his shoulders, holding him tightly as he would have done with one of the kids. He'd lost so much weight he might have been the same Micky that he'd comforted nearly twenty years before, after yet another beating at school. Eventually Micky sobbed out that he'd been dreaming, a confused, terrifying dream full of impossible juxtapositions of their schooldays, his father, Andy's gory corpse...

There was no way he could leave Micky on his own, even with the light on, so he climbed into the bed with him and switched the light off, holding him, still swaddled in the quilt.

It was now ten years since Micky had come out as gay, although he'd kept it quiet until comparatively recently, the age of consent still being twenty-one for gays.[1]

Davey knew that for the last few years there had been someone special in Micky's life, but he'd never been told anything about him and had certainly never met him.

Although he'd been shocked when Micky had first confessed his feelings, Davey had quickly realised that, so far as they were concerned, nothing had changed – they were still best mates and, after he had made it clear that he could not share Micky's feelings, he had never raised the subject again and they had continued to share hotel rooms without any awkwardness.

Eventually they both fell asleep. Davey dreamed that he was at home with Tina – a warm, comfortable dream that bore little resemblance to reality. In the dream they were making out and he woke just as he was about to climax, to find that he was wrapped around Micky…

He quickly pulled away, muttering an apology, but Micky rolled over and snuggled up to him, obviously more than happy with what had happened. Before he could do anything to prevent it, Micky had taken control and had started to caress him, kissing, stroking, touching…in spite of himself, he couldn't stop him, finding his touch, his obvious passion, his complete love for him, totally irresistible and he came, emptying himself into him in a tsunami of ecstasy that he had never known before.

He found himself crying; hot, joyful tears of healing. Micky had turned back to him again and was

---

[1] Micky didn't reach twenty-one until 1976. The law didn't change until 1994 when it was reduced to eighteen, and then again to sixteen in 2001

laying in his arms, asleep almost immediately, with a look of utter contentment and peace that totally belied the torture of the last few weeks. Davey held him gently, promising himself that, whatever happened, he could not now pretend that he didn't share his love.

Time seemed to stand still. For the next few hours they slept, interspersed with more love-making, taking pleasure from touching, from the feel of each other's bodies, not needing words. Davey spent long spaces, while Micky slept, just watching him, loving the curve of his face, the way his hair curled more tightly where it clung damply to his forehead, the long eyelashes, the texture of his lips, the slight dent in his chin.

They didn't hear the key open the door to the flat. They were well into the throes of another bout of passion when the bedroom door burst open. Both had their backs to the door, so couldn't see Paddy's reaction, just heard the exclamation of shock. Tearing himself away from Micky, Davey pulled on his jeans, his legs like jelly, and stumbled through to the kitchen.

Paddy was leaning on the work surface, head down. As Davey entered the room he looked up, his face as white as a sheet, his unruly, black hair framing the strong nose and emphasising his Irish ancestry and the resemblance to Jimmy Nail.

"I'm sorry, mate – I panicked when you were missing from the other room – I never dreamed…"

Davey shook his head.

"Neither did I. It just happened…"

"Well it shouldn't have done! What the hell do you think you're doing? Don't you think he's got enough to cope with right now? How are you going to get yourself out of this one?"

"I'm not. It was over with Tina long ago. This has just finished it off. I'll do whatever is necessary to protect the kids, but Micky will be my life now."

"Tina will have your balls! I'm sorry, Davey, I can't stay here and watch this – I'm going back home…"

Micky came in at that moment and Paddy went to him…

Chapter 20:

1983, Manchester/Chelsea.

Davey had gone home with so much hope that Tina would accept his 'way forward'. Maybe he shouldn't have told her he was coming - when he got there, he found that the kids had been packed off to her mother's and the happy welcome he had been expecting was simply not there.

He let himself in - Tina was in the kitchen. There was a pile of stuff in the hall which he recognised as being all his gear – cases, drums, boxes of books etc. He peered round the kitchen door.

"Teen?"

"Just piss off! I don't want you here when the kids get home."

This was not a great start and all his carefully thought-out speech evaporated to nothing.

"Teen, please, we need to talk about this, for the kids' sake…"

"What do you want to talk about? How you prefer screwing Micky to living here with us? How you prefer sticking it up his arse…"

Davey stared at her, white with shock - he'd never heard her talk like that before.

"Is that what you've been doing all these years when you're away on tour? I knew Andy was a faggot, I suspected that Micky was, but I never thought that YOU…"

She burst into tears. He plucked up courage and crossed the room, trying to put his arms round her, but she swung at him with the milk bottle she'd been washing. It connected, but fortunately was still slippery and slid off without doing much damage. He grabbed her wrists before she could re-arm and pulled her into the living room where there was less weaponry to hand.

The moment he let go she grabbed a heavy glass ashtray and swung it at him, but he was too quick, and it sailed past him and smashed against the wall. He grabbed her again and forced her down onto the sofa, ending up kneeling awkwardly in front of her, still holding her by the wrists.

"Teen, please, just listen..."

"Nothing you can say will make any difference! We're finished – we were finished the minute I knew what you were doing. Haven't you heard about AIDS?!! He's probably riddled with it!! Is that what you want?! To bring it home to me and the kids!!!Just go!!"

"At least let me see the kids..." he begged "Please, Teen!"

"In your dreams! I'll make sure you never get anywhere near them ever again! If you even try to get access, I'll make sure what you've been doing is all over the papers! Now get out of the house!! Your stuff's in the hall, just take it and go!"

He went, feeling sick inside. He knew, from past experience, that once she'd made her mind up about something there was no point in arguing, and the threat to go to the press was the last thing Micky needed right now.

He packed his gear into the car. It was a tight fit and there was no way he was going to be able to drive back to London with it all, so he took it round to his mother's house and left the drums and books there.

She had obviously already been told the situation as she didn't seem surprised to see him. She tried to make conversation, but he was way beyond that, and she stood forlornly watching him carry the things to the spare room.

"Don't go back to London tonight! Please Davey, you're in no fit state to drive all that way…"

He shook his head without speaking, pecked her on the cheek and fled.

He remembered nothing of the journey, just of arriving back at the flat totally wrung out. Paddy looked at him, read the situation and handed him a large glass of Martell which he downed in one. He refilled it.

"I'll get you something to eat – you can't take all that on an empty stomach."

"Don't bother, I couldn't swallow it…"

"Bad?"

"She went for me with a milk bottle and one of those big glass ashtrays. She won't let me see the kids…"

Paddy put his arms round him and hugged him – he knew, as a parent himself, how much the kids meant to him and how much he missed them when they were away. He'd also known Tina as long as Davey had and understood that the situation was probably beyond recall.

"Where's Micky?"

"Asleep. He's been pretty miserable all day. The doc's given him a prescription for some tranqs so he's had a couple of those. I'll get going…"

Davey gave him an anguished look.

"Paddy, please don't go! Micky needs both of us here…"

Paddy shook his head.

"No, he's only ever needed you."

Davey looked at him, dumbfounded.

"Davey, maybe you were too close to see it, but all he's ever wanted is you. You broke his heart when you married Tina! I didn't want to believe it, I was stupid enough to think that if you were unavailable he might find a girlfriend…I could have saved us all that shit with Andy…"

"Don't say that!" he begged. "If you follow that thought logically, then it's my fault that Andy's dead and Micky's in all this trouble…"

Paddy hugged him reassuringly.

"That's probably taking it too far…"

"You always tried to protect Micky from Andy…why aren't you trying to protect him from me?"

"Oh… where do I start?! Micky's always wanted you – long before either of you knew what sex was! You and Micky are two halves of the same whole. Andy only wanted someone for sex – it didn't have to be Micky, but he was young enough to be …malleable, and wasn't liable to turn round and thump him like you or me! As it is, Andy was the one who turned Micky on to sex, despite my best endeavours. Don't forget, I was Micky's legal guardian for a while…and they were both way under the age of consent… Micky's nearly thirty now – it's a completely different scene. I care enough for both of you to want you to be happy – I don't have any problem with you being gay…"

"Unlike everyone else! Please stay, Pad!" Davey pleaded.

Although Paddy and he were the same age, Paddy had always seemed far more mature than him and Davey had always thought of him as an older brother – probably from he himself being the youngest in his family and used to be bossed around.

Paddy sighed heavily.

"OK, I need to go home for a couple of days to keep the peace with Jan, then I'll come back. It'll give you both a bit of privacy – you'll have stuff to talk about…"

Davey nodded. He didn't want Paddy to go, but realised that he probably felt a bit awkward after crashing in on them and triggering the current crisis, and also that he had a wife and kids of his own to think about.

He knocked back the rest of the brandy, poured some more and drank it and then dropped the door latch behind Paddy as he left.

He went back into the bedroom. Micky was lying face down across the bed – in the darkness he could just make out his shape beneath the quilt. He reached across and switched the light on, but Davey leaned over and switched it off again. Without bothering to undress he climbed in beside him. Before he knew what to say Micky had his arms round him, gently stroking his bruised face…

Chapter 21:

1983, Chelsea. Misty

Davey came into the bedroom – I could smell the brandy even before he got into bed. I reached over and switched on the light. Groggy though I was from the pills I could see he had a black eye. I wrapped myself around him, feeling him start to sob as the shock and exhaustion hit. I stroked his hair. Neither of us spoke – we didn't need words, just the comfort of contact. The physical closeness was too much for him and, without speaking or any attempt at foreplay, he rolled me over and took me roughly. When it was over we were both in tears.

"I'm sorry!" he sobbed. "I'm so sorry!!"

I hugged him tightly, shaking from the pain of the sudden assault.

"It's OK, it's OK, I understand…"

"Did I hurt you?"

"It's OK…"

I tried to reassure him. Eventually we slept, clinging to each other for reassurance.

Chapter 22:

Late 1983, London. Misty

Inevitably things eventually moved on and a date was set for the trial.

The murder charge had, as predicted, been dropped, but the DPP had insisted that there was sufficient evidence to justify proceeding with the manslaughter charge. Although Nat and Angelo were both entirely satisfied that I was completely innocent, both were worried that a jury might still convict, even if they managed to weed out any potentially homophobic jurors.

Alex had suggested that we should have some private psychiatric reports prepared as an insurance policy. This would entail me spending several days in a private clinic – a thought which terrified me. Eventually, after much persuasion from my team and from Davey, I reluctantly agreed.

Angelo drove me to the clinic which Alex had selected, and which was some way out of London in the Surrey countryside. Davey had wanted to come with me but, as he would not have been allowed to stay there with me, we decided that it would be too traumatic for both of us.

The entrance to the grounds was anonymous – just two high brick pillars marking the way into the long driveway, the grounds stretching away either side of the road like a country park. After some distance however, the drive was barred by two sets of high iron gates with an intercom on the outer one and a sentry box inside the inner. We were admitted into the space between the gates and the outer gates swung shut behind us before the inner set opened to allow us into the compound. Ahead we could see a rambling Victorian country house.

Angelo parked to one side of the gravelled turning-circle and I climbed out of the car, my legs like jelly. We approached the imposing double doors which stood open but had substantial, armoured glass doors inside. These slid open as we neared, and we entered a marble-floored lobby. A man in his fifties came toward us and nodded pleasantly to me.

"You must be Michael – and you are Mr. Daranda?" Angelo nodded. "I am Dr. Petersen – I will be responsible for Michael's care and assessment while he is with us."

Dr. Petersen was of similar height to me with greying, light-brown hair and wire-framed spectacles. He had a slight Scandinavian accent, his manner reassuring and friendly. He led the way into his office, and I sat quietly while Angelo completed the formalities.

"I will contact you once I have completed my assessment – it usually takes three to five days, but these things do vary, so please don't be concerned if you don't hear within that time. If you wish to have an update on progress, please feel free to telephone me."

Angelo shook hands with him, then turned to me, smiling reassuringly.

"You'll be fine," he said gently. "And we'll look after Davey for you, don't worry."

I nodded mutely, fighting the urge to fling myself into his arms or throw myself at his feet and beg him to take me back with him. I managed to do neither.

Dr. Petersen waited until Angelo had gone and then asked "What do you prefer to be called?"

"Micky…" I mumbled. "No one's called me Michael since I left school."

He smiled again. "OK. Let's get you to your room."

He led the way out into the lobby and through a pair of heavy double doors operated by a coded lock.

The corridor the other side was thickly carpeted, and our feet made no noise. We reached a plain white, panelled door which he pushed open and led me through.

The room was large – maybe sixteen feet by twenty or more, painted in a warm bluey-grey colour, a large window covered with a steel grille at the far end with a view across the gardens.

A male nurse brought me pyjamas of soft stretch cotton. The room was warm enough to be comfortable and go barefoot.

Dr. Petersen worked in one-hour sessions which could be extended if he felt that continuity was necessary. It felt strange to start with, but I trusted Alex' judgement and quickly grew to trust Dr. Petersen, who rarely pushed me beyond my comfort zone unless he felt it necessary to test my reaction to a situation or thought. After a few days my sense of safety had shifted so far that the thought of going back to the flat or, worse still, to the unknown, filled me with terror.

Davey and Angelo collected me. I was quiet on the drive back to London and said little until the next day when we were on our own. It had seemed strange to be sharing a bed again, but it was comforting to feel the warmth of someone next to me. We had spent the night just lying in silence, holding each other close.

Even though we had been intimate for a comparatively short time, our long and close friendship meant we could communicate as well without words as with them. I knew that he had missed me and had worried about me while I was away, just as he knew that I would have been anxious at being in the strange environment, and also because so much rested on Dr. Petersen's perception of me and his subsequent report.

Chapter 23:

Early 1984, London. Misty

Once it started, the trial moved slowly but steadily forward. I remained on bail as before, Angelo collecting us each morning and driving us to court.

The cumbersome procedure of selecting the jury and the other formalities seemed to go on forever and, despite my fears of the overall process, I just wanted to get on with it and for it to be over, whatever the outcome.

I had been brought up to accept that our justice system was good, and that if someone was innocent, they had little to worry about but, as the days passed, I began to feel less sure. While I could remember little or nothing of the day Andy died or, for that matter, the days either side, I *knew* that I would not, could not, have done anything that could harm him, let alone kill him, whatever the provocation. I had never been involved in a fight of any kind, even at school – it simply wasn't in my nature – and if someone had hit me or hurt me in any way I would either have run or just stood there and let them do it, too shocked to retaliate.

There had been a lot of debate among my legal team as to whether to put me in the witness box. There was no problem about Nat questioning me, but they were all worried that, if cross-examined by the prosecution, I wouldn't cope and would simply fall to pieces, probably doing more harm than good.

By the second week I was so wrung out that I just wanted it over. I had been sleeping badly, despite being given sleeping pills, and if left to myself, would have just thrown in the towel and changed my plea to guilty to get it over with. Anything (so I thought) would be better than this slowly grinding torture.

By the Friday of the second week it *was* over; Nat had made an impressive closing speech on the Wednesday afternoon and the judge's mercifully brief summing-up on the Thursday morning had seemed not only fair but favourable. The jury retired to consider their verdict.

The next twenty-four hours passed agonisingly slowly. I had no option but to sit it out downstairs in the cells although, when the jury were packed off to a hotel for the night, we were allowed to return home until the following morning.

After another sleepless night we returned to the Old Bailey and the cells. Angelo and Nat both stayed there with me until, finally, an usher came with the news that the jury were returning.

I was taken back up the steps into the courtroom. There was a deathly hush which I had not noticed previously. I glanced up to the gallery – Davey and Paddy were sitting in their usual seats, Davey clutching Paddy's wrist so hard I could see the pain in his face.

The judge turned to the foreman of the jury and asked him to confirm that they had reached a verdict.

"Yes, my lord. We find the defendant guilty of manslaughter."

The judge looked more than a little surprised.

"And is that the verdict of you all?"

The foreman hesitated.

"It was a majority verdict, my lord. A majority of ten to two. But we all feel that there was a high degree of provocation…"

The judge thanked them and stated that they were discharged. He turned back and looked directly at me.

"Michael Sean Culshaw, you have been found guilty of the manslaughter of Andrew James Freeman. Do you wish to say anything before I pass sentence?"

I shook my head helplessly.

"I didn't do it!" I sobbed. "I didn't do it!"

The judge called for silence as the courtroom had erupted by now – a slow rumble of voices reaching a comparative crescendo of noise. Paddy was having to literally hold Davey down in his seat.

"You will be held in custody over the weekend while I take advice and consider what sentence is appropriate in this case."

He rose and left the courtroom.

My legs wouldn't work, and the security guards had to virtually carry me back down to the cells. Angelo appeared within seconds.

"Nat's gone to see the judge." he said quietly.

"Why?! Why did they find me guilty?! I didn't do it, Angelo! How can they…?"

"I don't know." he said quietly. "I thought Alex' evidence was so strong it would cancel out everything else…"

"Did the judge really say that I'll be held in custody…why?!"

"I don't think he had any option – that's what always happens between a guilty verdict and sentencing, but Nat's going to try to see if maybe you can go to the clinic…"

I was beyond listening – suddenly all the weeks and months of anxiety and stress overwhelmed me. In my head I could still see Davey's stricken face. Angelo helped me to the bench that ran along one side of the cell. I sat down heavily, the room seeming to churn and swim around me.

A few minutes later we heard footsteps. The cell door opened, and Nat came in, still in his gown but minus his barrister's wig. He shook his head in answer to Angelo's anxious look.

"Micky, I'm so sorry, the judge has no discretion in this – the only thing I could do would be to try to get another judge to hear an appeal, but as it's the weekend it's unlikely to be heard before Monday at the earliest. I'm afraid you'll just have to sit it out. As you haven't been sentenced yet you will probably have a cell to yourself – they may even put you in the hospital wing…"

I don't think I took any of that in. I was nearly hysterical by now, as well as feeling faint and dizzy. Nat was about to go in search of a doctor when the security guards arrived to escort me out to the prison van. They produced handcuffs and, as I felt them close round my wrists, I completely freaked out. Nat and Angelo both protested that I required medical attention, but their words were ignored, and I was half dragged, half carried out to the waiting van.

As it pulled away I started to feel sick as well as faint. Because I was unable to see out, the movements of the vehicle as it braked and turned threw me around and I ended up in a heap on the floor of the compartment. Long before we reached the jail I had passed out and that was how they found me when the door was finally unlocked.

I was unceremoniously carried inside – presumably they were used to this happening – and laid out on the floor.

"Culshaw, Michael Sean, manslaughter, awaiting sentence."

"Don't know where you expect me to put him."

"In a cell!"

I was again half dragged, half carried and dumped on the lower bunk of an otherwise empty cell after the warders had removed the belt of my trousers and my tie, crucifix and watch.

I came to sometime later. All over the wing I could hear the sounds of people talking, shouting, even screaming, a constant hum of noise. There was a strong smell of bleach and disinfectant which didn't quite mask the smell of human life which seemed to leech out of the walls, the floor and, worse still, the mattress and blankets.

I could feel the tears running down my face and into my hair. Every part of me ached, both literally from being dragged around and the uncomfortable ride in the prison van, and figuratively, needing a friendly face, a friendly word, my adored Davey...

'Don't go there!' I thought wildly, fighting the sob which seemed to fill my chest...

Suddenly there was a mechanical 'clunk' and the lights went off. The hum of noise rose briefly and then gradually subsided. Lying there in the dark seemed both better and worse – better as I could not see where I was, other than a narrow strip of light under the door, worse for the same reason, as I felt even more alone in an alien environment.

I lost track of time completely. It was dark outside, but then at that time of year it would have been so by at least 6 p.m., and I didn't know how long I had been drifting in and out of sleep. I heard footsteps coming along the corridor, several sets of heavy boots and what sounded like bare feet. They stopped outside the cell door and I heard the rattle of keys and bolts as the door was opened. There were several different voices – a lot of swearing – someone was shoved through the door and then it was slammed shut again, more keys and bolts and the boots retreated back down the corridor.

I heard heavy breathing and lay as still and small as I could manage. The newcomer sat on the edge of the bunk and rolled in. The bunk was very narrow, and he immediately realised that it was already occupied.

"Bugger me, what have we got here?"

Hands began to explore – my face and hair, my body. A short laugh.

"Well, this is a nice surprise! Well, hell-o *sweet-heart!*"

The hands tugged at my shirt before pulling open my trousers. I knew what would follow and tried to get away from him, but he was much bigger than me – taller and a lot heavier – and he used his weight to hold me down, pushing me over onto my stomach and thrusting my face into the meagre pillow so hard I thought I would suffocate.

The pain, when it came, was excruciating, my scream cut off by the huge hand clamped over my nose and mouth.

But someone had heard me – footsteps hurried down the corridor, keys rattled, and the door was wrenched open. Several officers piled in and dragged him off me, pulling me onto the floor in doing so. The lights abruptly came back on and the noise, which had never entirely stopped, slammed back into life again – men shouting, a few cheering and catcalling.

It had taken several officers to remove my attacker. One remained in the cell with me, frantically checking for a pulse, calling my name, trying to get a response. More officers arrived.

"Get the M.O. – call an ambulance! Now!!"

The ambulance arrived before the M.O. and I was taken off to hospital – not St Stephen's this time. I was taken straight through to the emergency wing. My injuries were quickly assessed – I had lost a lot of blood

– and I was rushed through to theatre for emergency surgery to try to stem the bleeding and repair the damage.

The prison authorities had contacted Angelo – we had nominated him as my next of kin in the absence of any family, and as they would not accept Davey as any type of relative. He was understandably horrified that I had been attacked so quickly after being taken to the prison and, unwilling to break the news to Davey by phone, immediately went round to the flat.

It took a while for him to get anyone to answer the door. Davey had been absolutely distraught by the time they had got home, and Paddy had called out my doctor to prescribe tranquilisers, which he had proceeded to wash down with brandy, so that he was now almost comatose. Paddy had stopped answering the phone as almost all the calls were from the press demanding comments on the 'Guilty' verdict and, although in theory only approved visitors could get as far as the front door of the flat, not expecting anyone to call, he did not initially bother to go to the door.

Angelo persisted long enough for him to decide to at least go to see who was there and, on squinting through the spy hole and recognising him, he swiftly opened it.

"What's up?"

Seeing Angelo's grave expression Paddy grabbed his arm and dragged him inside.

"What is it?! What's happened?! Something's happened to Micky, hasn't it?! He's –?"

Angelo hurriedly said "He's in hospital. He was attacked…"

"Is he OK?! Which hospital?! Angelo…?!"

"I don't know how bad it is – the prison phoned me as his 'next of kin' – all I know is what I've told you. I've come to take Davey over there."

"I'm not sure if you'll be able to – he's drunk well over half a bottle of cognac and the doc's given him tranqs as well..."

"Paddy, we've got to get him there!! Whatever state he's in – if Micky is conscious he'll want Davey there…"

Chapter 24:

The same.

Davey had heard the doorbell, followed by the pounding on the door. He vaguely heard Paddy let someone in and then raised voices. Some instinct made him certain that it must be to do with Micky and that it meant trouble. He rolled out of bed and stumbled out into the living room.

Angelo was there, tieless but otherwise still wearing his formal suit. He was pale, his dark five o'clock shadow emphasising the pallor. Through the haze of alcohol and sedative Davey heard him say Micky's name just as Angelo saw him. He stopped mid-sentence.

"Davey – you must come with me, NOW!"

"What is it?! What's happened?!"

"Micky's in hospital – I don't know any more than that…"

The three of them hurried out to Angelo's car. They reached the hospital in around thirty minutes and were directed to the emergency department. There were several prison staff in the waiting area, including one in a grey suit. He obviously recognised them from the newspapers and went over to them.

"They've taken him into the operating theatre."

"What happened?" Angelo demanded.

"He was attacked by another prisoner."

"For God's sake, how did that happen?! I understood that he would be either kept in isolation or put in the hospital wing!"

"We're bursting at the seams. He WAS on his own, but then they transferred another prisoner in from Bedford after lights out– we had nowhere else to put him…I don't think anyone realised at the time that the guy was – disturbed... The officer had barely locked the door when he heard Culshaw scream – they got in there in a matter of seconds and secured the other guy, but it was too late. They called an ambulance immediately – it's probably less than an hour since it happened…"

"What are his injuries?"

The prison official looked uncomfortable.

"He has internal injuries – he's lost a lot of blood. They're operating to try to stop the bleeding. Depending on what they find he may need further surgery…"

"You mean he was raped?!"

Davey didn't hear any more – the room, which had been moving alarmingly, started to spin. Paddy grabbed him by one arm and then regretted it as he threw up. A nurse sighed impatiently but guided him to a chair and sat him down.

He started to cry, scalding tears of anguish at the thought of Micky, alone and probably terrified, and the ordeal he had been through. Paddy moved across and sat beside him, his arm round the heaving shoulders.

Angelo was still talking to the prison official, but there was little more information to be had and eventually all they could do was sit and wait.

The surgery took several hours but to those waiting it seemed an eternity. Having thrown up, Davey sobered up all too quickly, although the tranquilisers had stayed in his system and took the edge off the emotional agony he was feeling. Eventually a group of medics emerged from along the corridor and one, seeing the small huddle of figures, came over and spoke.

"You're waiting for news of Michael Culshaw?"

Angelo and Davey both leapt up, speaking at the same time.

"We've stopped the bleeding, but I think there's quite a lot of damage. I've repaired what I can see, but it will be necessary to do some proper scans, if and when he is well enough, and then we will almost certainly have to operate again. He's very weak and I would guess extremely traumatised. He was unconscious when he was brought in and hasn't regained consciousness at all yet – but with such injuries…" He shook his head. "Let's just say no-one would suffer that willingly."

Angelo hesitated, trying not to meet Davey's eyes.

"Are his injuries – life threatening?"

"I can't answer that. As I say, he's lost a lot of blood and is very weak. The trauma will make him vulnerable – he may not want to recover…"

"Please!!" Davey begged, "Please let me see him!!"

The surgeon shook his head.

"I'm sorry – that's out of the question at the moment. If he gets through the night, then maybe – *maybe* - you can see him in the morning."

Chapter 25:

The same

The phone rang. Nat rolled over and looked at his watch – it was only about 10.30.

"Nathan Ainsworth – who is this?"

"Nat, its Angelo…"

He felt a clutch of fear – he could think of no good reason for Angelo to be calling so late, especially as they had only parted a few hours earlier.

"What is it? What's happened?"

"It's Micky – he's in hospital. It's not good."

"I'm on my way – which hospital?"

He replaced the receiver and leapt out of bed, grabbing his clothes.

Alex rolled over and propped himself up on one elbow

"What is it?"

"It's Micky – he's in hospital. That was Angelo…" He saw the look on Alex's face. "You'd better stay here…"

"No."

Nat knew there was no point arguing. Alex was used to giving orders and the 'No' had been uncompromising.

They dressed quickly – Alex only had his court suit with him, but Nat pulled on casual clothes – the first that came to hand. They hurried out and hailed a cab.

The journey took what seemed like an eternity – the theatres were just turning out and the streets were busy.

When they reached the hospital Alex left Nat to pay the cabbie and ran inside. By the time Nat caught up with him he was deep in conversation with the doctor in charge of Micky's care. As he approached, he heard him ask to speak to the surgeon who had operated, but he was told that he had now gone off-duty. Alex dropped his voice, so Nat was unable to hear what was said next, but he and the doctor went off up the corridor away from the waiting area.

Angelo went over to Nat.

"What's Alex doing here – did you call him?"

"Erm – he was at my place when you phoned. Obviously, he wanted to know what was going on…"

Angelo gave him an odd look – whether he suspected the truth Nat couldn't tell.

"What happened?"

"We're beginning to piece it together. It seems that Micky was put into a cell on his own - as we had understood would happen - but the place is bursting at the seams. A prisoner was transferred in, late, from Bedford, and they put him in with Micky as there was nowhere else available. They'd barely shut the door when they heard Micky screaming…They got him out double-quick, but he's been badly hurt – there was blood everywhere. They've operated and stopped the bleeding, but the surgeon said he will almost certainly need further surgery – if – if he makes it. He's not regained consciousness at all yet, and his vital signs are not good."

Nat felt faint. He could see Davey, slumped in the corner, Paddy sitting next to him, stony-faced. Although he knew that there was nothing further that he could have done that would have prevented the current nightmare, he still felt a sense that this was all his fault – that if he'd been better at his job, he could have somehow prevented it.

Alex returned and, taking him by the elbow, led him away from the waiting area.

"I've offered to have Micky transferred to wherever he can be helped but – and I've spoken to the surgeon who operated on the phone – they think that he is too weak to stand being moved. They've done all they can for the moment. He's in an induced coma – all we can do is pray. The surgeon says that physically – and obviously apart from the current injuries – he was in good shape, but the damage done by the blood loss and shock are immeasurable."

He was fighting back tears and Nat marvelled again, as he had that evening in Chancery Lane, at the strength of the hold Micky still had on him, even now the relationship had, to all intents and purposes, ended.

"Alex, please, you must get a grip!"

He shook his head. "I can't stay here – I've got to do something…"

"There's nothing you CAN do!"

"There must be!" He said grimly. "I'll see you later."

He hurried off towards the main entrance leaving Nat to return to the others.

Chapter 26:

The same

Alex hailed a taxi outside the hospital. His head was spinning, trying to decide what he could do that was most likely to be effective. The cabbie asked him where he wanted to go. His first instinct had been to go to the Commons and use his office there, but well-established caution stopped him. He opted instead for his chambers in Gray's Inn.

At that hour there was only a handful of lights on, but the security staff did not seem surprised to see him. He went through to Chambers and let himself into his own room.

He hadn't been there for some time and the surface of the desk was empty apart from a filing basket containing a few memos and some strategically placed handwritten notes from the Clerk, mostly to the effect that, if he ever got to read them, could he please let him know his availability either to advise on a case or to appear. He found a piece of paper, wrote NO in large letters and dumped them back on the Clerk's desk.

He closed the office door, poured himself a large Armagnac from the bottle in the desk drawer, sat back in his chair and tried to think.

To begin with his head was filled with images of Micky – nightmarish images of his violation, his beautiful features contorted in pain, his body covered in blood. He took another large gulp of Armagnac and refilled the glass. Gradually he began to focus again.

He was in a delicate situation, to say the least. If he got it wrong it could have spectacular repercussions, not only for him but potentially for Micky, Nat, Angelo – all of them in fact - with the very real likelihood of embarrassing the PM and her government – not something she would take kindly to…

He looked at his watch – realising that if he was going to do anything, he had to do it now or wait until the morning. He picked up the phone and dialled. The call was answered almost immediately, the familiar mellow voice at the other end.

"Hargreave…"

"John, it's Alex…"

"I've been expecting you to call."

He hesitated – the words giving him a very real sense of panic.

"Alex, don't put the phone down – I assume you are at your chambers – get in a cab and come here – I'll expect you in fifteen minutes."

Alex obeyed automatically. The Right Hon. Lord Justice Sir John Hargreave had been his Pupil Master when he started his legal career, and it was very much thanks to him that he had achieved as much as he had. Hargreave had been a hard task-master – he had never been averse to insisting on one hundred per cent effort at all times. He himself had gone on to higher things – he was now the senior Lord Justice of Appeal and was likely to rise higher still.

He left Chambers and hurried out into Gray's Inn Road. There was little traffic and no taxi in sight, so he turned down towards Holborn where there seemed to be more activity. Within a minute or two he managed to flag down an empty cab and gave the driver the address in St. John's Wood.

The journey took rather longer than fifteen minutes. The cab dropped him at the kerb and he pressed the buzzer on the electric gates. As they closed behind him, he saw the front door open and Hargreave was standing there.

"What kept you?!"

"Traffic." Alex said wearily. "John, I'm so sorry…"

"Alex, I know you well enough to know that you would not be bothering me at this time of night if you did not have good reason. I also suspect that I have at least some idea of what that reason might be!"

Alex shook his head.

"I do hope not!"

Hargreave led the way through to his oak-panelled study and handed Alex a glass. Alex hesitated

"I'm not sure I should drink this…" he demurred. "I had at least two in Chambers and I need to keep a clear head."

Hargreave waved him to one of the leather 'club' chairs.

"Drink it! It's never caused you a problem before. Let me tell you what I think I know – that way you can correct me if I'm wrong, and you won't be spilling any secrets if I am."

Alex nodded assent.

"Very well. You are here because of the Michael Culshaw case. I am aware of the verdict and that the judge has remanded him for sentencing. I also strongly suspect that you are the 'Mr. X' who gave evidence on his behalf – I can only guess why, but I am pretty sure I would be correct."

Alex was silent for a few minutes and then simply nodded.

"Alex – you realise that your approaching me is highly improper…"

"John – I'm desperate…!"

"Is he blackmailing you?"

"NO!!" Alex was horrified. "It's nothing like that – Micky would never…"

John raised his hand.

"Then perhaps you'd better tell me everything."

Alex took a deep breath.

"I have known Micky for nearly three years. We were…in a relationship, up until the time of his arrest. I KNOW he could not have had any part in the death of the other boy…"

"How do you *know*?"

"Because I know Micky. He could no more hurt anyone than…"

He searched for the right words but, for once in his life, could not find a suitable analogy.

"And so you tried to give him an alibi?"

"No. I did not perjure myself – I appeared as a character witness only. How did you learn that it was me who gave evidence?"

"A little bird – in fact several little birds. What do you think I can do to help? I'm not going to tell the judge what sentence to impose."

"You haven't heard then?"

"Heard what?"

"Micky is in hospital. He is in a critical condition. He was attacked – RAPED – by another prisoner…"

Alex's voice shook with emotion. He took a gulp from the glass.

"I have spoken to the surgeon who operated on him, I've spoken to the doctor in charge of his case – I don't think they expect him to survive. I offered to have him transferred anywhere they could name for specialist treatment, but their opinion is that he is too weak to be moved. I just want to be able to offer him some hope, something that might make him fight for his life. If you had met him, you would understand…!"

He paused, lost in thought.

"Many years ago, William Rees-Mogg likened the treatment of Mick Jagger to 'breaking a butterfly on a wheel' – I can assure you that Micky's treatment has been far, far worse, for something of which he is entirely innocent. His legal team will fight to clear his name on appeal, but that will be futile if he is already – already…"

He could hardly bear to pronounce the word "…dead!"

Hargreave looked at him with great compassion.

"Alex – I have known you for a great many years, and I probably know you far better than any of my other pupils - and probably better than almost anyone else who knows you. I always suspected that you – looked elsewhere – for your pleasures, and until now you have obviously been more than discreet."

He paused, watching Alex intently.

"I will – speak to the judge – or rather I will speak to someone who will speak to him. I am not prepared to exert any pressure – the decision is his and his alone – however I suspect that, once he is aware of what has occurred, he will himself decide that Culshaw has suffered considerably already and if, as you say, there are grounds for an appeal against conviction, no doubt he will, in any event, be bailed pro tem."

Alex sighed, realising that this was probably as much as he could expect.

"Can I offer you a bed for the night? I don't think you are in any state to do anything further tonight, and from what I hear of Vero these days I doubt you are in a hurry to go back to Fulham."

Alex nodded. He wanted to go back to the hospital, but realised there was nothing useful he could do until the morning.

"Tell me about this boy – what is so special about him that you have been willing to risk everything…?"

Alex sighed again.

"I can't explain why I fell so deeply…we met almost by accident. I thought he was a – a rent boy… I couldn't have been more wrong! He'd never had full sex before – not with another man anyway, although he knew he was gay and was desperate to find…fulfilment. He was the most beautiful thing I'd ever seen – like Michelangelo's David, only more so. Not too tall, slender but well-formed. He has beautiful, golden-blond hair, the colour of good champagne, curling to his shoulders and violet eyes with long lashes, perfect teeth and lips…"

The alcohol was talking, allowing him the freedom of expression he had ruthlessly suppressed up to now.

"He is so gentle, so sensitive, but he is also intelligent and *interested* – you could take him anywhere and he would find something of interest and be able to talk about it. The thought of anyone hurting him – the thought of what has happened to him – the thought that he was frightened and in pain…"

A sob rose in his chest and he broke down, unable to stop the tears. As the alcohol had freed him to speak his mind, it now prevented him from exercising the rigid self-control that he had learned over so many decades, first at his public school and later as Hargreave's pupil.

Hargreave made no comment, nor did he make any move to comfort him, knowing that Alex would find that intolerable. Instead he took him up to the guest room, found him a couple of mild tranquilisers and left him to it.

The following morning he left him to sleep. When he eventually found his way downstairs there was fresh coffee, juice, cereal and fruit waiting and a short note giving him the number to call a taxi. Alex scrawled a note of thanks and made his way back to the hospital.

When he arrived there the prevailing mood seemed to have lightened a little. Nat had been sitting with Angelo but got up and went over.

"How is he – is there any news?"

"He's stable. The surgeon has been in to see him and he seems hopeful that the worst is over. Where have you been – I was getting worried…?"

"I – I went to see an old friend."

Alex thought it better not to say exactly who he had spoken to.

"The judge was here about an hour ago. Micky won't have to go back to prison when he leaves here. Did you have something to do with that?"

Alex heaved a sigh of relief but said nothing. Nat looked at him speculatively, trying to read his expression, and Alex suddenly realised that their 'arrangement' was beginning to mean rather more to him than he cared to admit.

Nat shrugged.

"He thinks we should appeal against the conviction – he can't see why the jury convicted on the available evidence."

Alex shook his head.

"I wonder if they resented the fact that I gave evidence anonymously – maybe that and underlying homophobia? Who knows! What did the judge actually say about the sentence?"

"He will record it as two years, suspended for two years. He's also said that he won't impose travel restrictions – he recognises that the band will need to tour. He went in to see Micky – he's very angry that the attack happened – he suggested that we should sue the Prison Service…"

Alex shook his head again.

"I'm not sure that would be a good idea - I suspect it could rebound, as the taxpayer would foot the bill if we won. There will be a lot of sympathy for Micky, but he could lose that…"

Despite a reasonable amount of sleep and the very civilised breakfast that Hargreave had provided he still felt washed out.

Nat said quietly "You look like shit – go and get your head down – you can use my place if you don't want to face Vero…"

"I have been advised to divorce her." Alex said flatly.

Nat looked at him, a little surprised.

"Will you?"

"I – I haven't had time to think about it yet. Apparently informed opinion is that it might be a good time to do so, otherwise she could be an embarrassment. I am not sure what the Whip's office will say! Certain people seem to know that I gave evidence for Micky…Nat…"

Their eyes met – neither of them spoke, but Alex thought the other understood what he wanted to say. Nat nodded.

"I'll see you later." He said quietly. "There's nothing much I can do here now."

Before leaving Alex went over to Davey. He looked as though he'd spent all night crying, dark circles under his eyes, the lids red and puffy. He felt a wave of compassion for him, glad that Micky had finally found real love. He had often talked about Davey and their special friendship, and Alex knew that he had longed for it to be more than just friendship. He wondered how and what had moved them on to become lovers…

He dragged a chair across and sat down close to Davey, who looked up and nodded in recognition.

"Davey, I'm so sorry about what's happened to Micky…" He nodded dumbly. "Have they said when you might be allowed to see him?"

"They're waiting for the surgeon to come on duty. Depending on what he says about operating again, and if he's still stable, they may let me sit with him. At least I can tell him that he won't have to go back to prison…"

"When he's well enough to leave here have you thought where you'll go?"

"No. Back to the flat I suppose."

"That would mean waiting until he no longer needs nursing. If I can arrange for him to go to Dr. Petersen's clinic – that way he would get both nursing care and treatment to help him deal with what has happened…would you agree to that?"

"That's up to Micky. He seemed to like Dr. Petersen…but I thought it was just a psychiatric clinic?"

"That's their main focus, but they have good medical facilities as well. They don't do surgery, but they can do most types of scan, so they'd be able to keep a close eye on his recovery. You could probably stay there with him if Dr. Petersen agrees…"

He broke off as the doors swung open and he recognised the doctor he had seen last night with another medic who he assumed to be the surgeon who had operated. They joined them.

"I'm pleased to say that Micky seems to be out of danger. Everything has settled down considerably since last night, and as far as I can see there hasn't been any further bleeding. I'll wait a few days and then we'll do an endoscopy before I decide whether he needs further surgery. There was so much blood last night it was difficult to see the extent of the damage, but the absence of bleeding now suggests that it was not as extensive as I originally thought."

"Is he conscious?"

"No. We'll keep him under for at least another 24-48 hours to let the shock wear off a bit."

"Can I see him – *please?!*" Davey begged, the brown eyes huge in his pale, unshaven face.

The surgeon smiled and nodded.

"You can sit with him – at least for a while. Keep talking to him – make sure he knows that he won't be going back to prison. Apart from that keep it light – talk about stuff that happened in the past – happy stuff."

He took Davey off along the corridor leaving Alex wishing it was him going instead.

Chapter 27:

The same.

The surgeon took Davey into the ICU room. Micky was lying on the narrow bed, covered in sensor pads, wires and tubes running from him to the bank of machinery which hummed and beeped. An ugly breathing tube disappeared into his mouth, held in place by micropore tape. There were still smears of blood on his chest and legs, a frame shrouded by a sheet across his hips doing little to preserve his modesty. His hair clung damply around his face, his skin deathly pale in the subdued light of the room. He looked scarcely more than a child and Davey had a momentary image of a small, frightened child hiding behind the bins at school…

He sat on the chair by the bed and took Micky's hand. The skin felt cold to the touch. The surgeon was watching one of the monitors.

"He knows you're here." he said quietly. "Now talk to him – keep talking. If you need anything - or you're worried about anything - press the call button."

He showed him where this was.

"I'll come back in a few hours. The nurses will check every 20 minutes or so and the Registrar every hour."

Davey was shaking – he had so wanted to be with Micky but now, faced with the reality of him lying there unconscious and looking so frail, he almost wished he had stayed in the waiting area. He tried to speak but all that came out was a croak. He tried again and managed to say

"You won't be going back to prison... I don't know who fixed that – the judge was here this morning and he's given you a suspended sentence. That means that if you keep out of trouble, you'll be fine. Think you can manage that?"

He couldn't think what else to say for a while, but then blurted out "I love you, man! Oh Micky – why did this have to happen? I love you! You have to get well again!"

Chapter 28:

A month later, London. Misty

Once the drugs which had kept me in the coma were reduced, the welcome reassurance of Davey's voice quickly brought me back to consciousness. His was the first face I saw when I opened my eyes. We both burst into tears. His grip on my hand tightened convulsively.

"I thought I'd lost you!" he sobbed, the tears dropping onto our hands.

"You don't get rid of me that easily!" I croaked, finding it difficult to speak after nearly ten days of silence, my throat sore from the breathing tube.

I could remember little of what had led up to me being in hospital again but, as I moved slightly, the residue of the pain hit me and it all came flooding back and I started to shake.

"Hey, hey – it's OK, nothing bad's going to happen now! You're free and you've got me to look after you now and I <u>promise</u> you I'm not going to let you out of my sight…"

He realised that I was not going to be able to stop without some help and pushed the call-button. A nurse hurried in, saw that I was conscious but in distress, and hurried out again, returning almost immediately with a doctor.

"Hello Micky. Welcome back! You gave everyone a real fright, but you'll be fine now – we just need to give you some space to recover. I'm going to give you something to calm you down a little – it won't knock you out again, just slow things down while your body recovers a bit more."

He filled a syringe and injected me. Gradually things did indeed 'slow down' and I began to feel more in control. He waited until he knew I was calm again and then said "I understand that you are going to be moved out now that you are back with us. That will probably take place either tomorrow or the day after, but if you would prefer to stay put a bit longer you must say so – I would understand if you want a bit of stability…"

Davey said quietly "We'll talk it over. Micky doesn't know what has been suggested yet."

"OK – I'll leave that with you."

He went out. Davey gently squeezed my hand.

"Alex has suggested that you should go to Dr. Petersen's clinic to recover."

"Alex? Has he been here?"

I felt a familiar frisson at the sound of his name.

"When you were brought in here the prison contacted Angelo and he contacted Nat – Alex was with him when Angelo phoned, and they arrived together. I don't know if he had anything to do with you being released, but he went off and came back the following morning after the judge had been here. He thinks that you will recover better at the clinic – they have the right facilities there to cope with your injuries and Dr. Petersen can help you…"

"I don't want to go anywhere without you!!"

I was close to panicking again. Davey grabbed my other hand so he was holding both tightly.

"I'll come with you…" he said gently. "That's the whole point – we can be together…"

"You won't mind?"

He smiled, a beautiful, wide, relaxed grin that made my heart leap.

"I don't ever want to be anywhere without you, so how could I mind? I want to be where you are – today, tomorrow, always…"

The door opened and Paddy came in.

"I heard you were awake." He grinned at me. "You gave us all a fright!"

"I seem to be making a habit of it…" I mumbled.

"We'd much rather you didn't!"

"How long have I been here?"

"About four weeks so far."

I tried to think back. I knew what had happened to me – my body was only too aware - but my mind was shutting out the actual events. I had flashes of the end of the trial, of being in the cell waiting for the van, of being in the van, of lying in the dark with the noises of the prison around me…each time I got to that point the shutters came down, protecting me from whatever it was that my memory did not want to process.

After that things moved very quickly. An endoscopy proved that the surgeon's guess was right – he had found the main area of damage and had repaired it in the emergency operation. Dr. Petersen arrived with a private ambulance and Davey and I were transferred to the clinic.

Chapter 29:

The same. Surrey.

They arrived at the clinic as it was getting dark. Davey had only seen the outside before, when he had gone with Angelo to collect Micky following his assessment. This time of course Micky was wheeled in on the trolley from the ambulance and they were taken straight through to their room, the same one, apparently, that Micky had occupied before. It seemed strange being away from the ICU and its bank of machines and monitors.

The next few days passed slowly but Micky seemed to recover far more quickly there than he had at the hospital and, by the end of the week, he was able to sit up and even, with support, to walk a few steps. The endoscopy was repeated and showed that the wounds had more or less closed, although the tissue was still very fragile.

Dr. Petersen had left them alone for that first week, dropping in only occasionally to see how Micky was doing, the day to day medical stuff being dealt with by the nursing staff, but once Micky was on his feet he dropped in one afternoon and suggested that Davey might like to walk in the garden. Davey wasn't that keen – it was still early in the year and he could see from the window that the wind was blowing strongly outside but, realising that Dr. Petersen wanted to talk to Micky alone, he took his jacket and went outside, despite Micky's protests.

He hung around outside within sight of the window. He could see that they were deep in conversation and, from quite early on, that Micky was finding the conversation difficult, both from his body language and later he could see that Micky was actually in tears. He longed to be with him so that he could comfort him, but he knew that Dr. Petersen would not push him further than he felt he could cope with.

By the time one of the nurses came to fetch him he was feeling very cold, having been outside for the best part of two hours. He returned to their room thankfully, to find Micky curled up on the sofa, hugging his knees. He looked pale and tearful and Davey hoped that the therapy was going to be worth the emotional cost. Dr. Petersen smiled as he came in.

"You look frozen – come and get warm! Micky has done very well – we've had a very productive session. I've given him a mild sedative just to help him relax. He probably won't feel much like talking for a while – just give him a little space."

Davey nodded. He went to sit in the armchair, but Micky held out a hand with an imploring look. He took his place beside him on the sofa and Micky curled up in the crook of his arm, his head on his chest, resting in the angle between his head and shoulder. Davey felt him tremble and hugged him gently. When he looked up again Dr. Petersen had gone. He wanted to ask Micky what had been said that had upset him so much but, heeding the doctor's advice, avoided saying anything that required an answer.

"It's bloody cold outside. Much better in here!"

A shiver.

"Do you want a cup of tea?"

Micky shook his head. A while later Davey realised that he was asleep. He wanted to move him to the bed, but knew he'd have to wait until Micky was at least almost awake again – there was no way he'd be able to carry him single-handed. Eventually one of the nurses came in with the evening meal and between them they managed to manoeuvre him to the bed without waking him up, although there was a small murmur of protest at being moved.

Chapter 30:

The same. Misty

The first therapy session was an ordeal. I'd never been in therapy before, and the assessment sessions I had previously had with Dr. Petersen were a totally different ball-game, as they didn't deal in any way with the past, only with how I looked at the world at that time.

The first session started with him asking me what my earliest memory was. I was silent for a long time, trying to think. Memories bubbled up in my mind, but none were much before the age of eight. I knew that I'd first met Davey when I started school, so that had to be earlier. More thoughts bubbled up, mostly memories of Dad belting me for something. Eventually I admitted that, although I knew that I'd met Davey when I was about five or maybe a little younger, I couldn't remember anything at all until later.

"Why do you think that is?"

It was an innocuous question, but I found myself trembling and the more I tried to find an answer, the more upset I began to feel. Again, I paused for a long time before answering. Dr. Petersen waited, watching my face through his rimless glasses. Memories that had been suppressed for twenty-five years surfaced – memories that I had tried so hard to forget. I opened my mouth to speak but all that came was a sound somewhere between a sob and a groan which ended in another sound, a sound which in itself brought the past flooding back all too clearly. I shook my head, trying to clear the thoughts. Still Dr. Petersen waited for me to speak.

"I – was –"

I stopped, not wanting to say the word, not wanting to repeat the story which had earned me a beating from Dad, not wanting to talk about something which I had not even told Davey. I gulped, forcing the words out.

"I – was – *raped…*"

The word came out almost as a hiccup, a squeak. Now I was sobbing as though I would never be able to stop. Dr. Petersen came and sat beside me, holding me tightly while I sobbed.

"Let it go, Micky. You've never told anyone about this before, have you?"

I sobbed out that I had told my parents, but that Dad hadn't believed me and had beaten me for lying.

"How old were you? You said you can't remember anything before you were eight – were you eight when this happened?"

I nodded.

"Who attacked you? Someone you knew? Someone you trusted?"

"F- F – Father Flanagan, - the headmaster of our school."

"A priest? Is that why your father didn't believe you?"

I nodded again.

"How did it happen?"

It was easier now that I had managed to say the word, and I sobbed out the story, including Davey finding me and Mam fetching me from his house.

"Have you ever told Davey what happened?"

I shook my head.

"What happened when you went back to school?"

"I made sure I never got sent to him again. The teachers commented on how much better I was behaving, how I never got into trouble any more. Ironic, isn't it?"

"You should go to the police."

"There's no point. He died while I was still at the school. I sang the solo at his Requiem Mass. Everyone said how beautifully I sang and how much I must have loved him as I cried all the way through it..." I said bitterly. "I wasn't crying for him!"

"How did what happened affect the way you felt – how you feel - about the Church?"

I shook my head.

"It wasn't the Church's fault. I don't go to Mass or anything anymore, but that's more to do with touring etc. than not believing or wanting to go, although I can't honestly say I often think about it. Obviously they're not great about gays, but until Alex came along that wouldn't have been much of a problem. Paddy still goes whenever he can. Davey's not Catholic so he's never had that problem."

"How come he was at a Catholic school?"

Dr. Petersen sounded surprised.

"The school always prided itself on offering something like a third of places to charity cases, regardless of whether the families were Catholic or not. Davey's parents had nine children – he's the youngest. As they lived virtually next door to the school they were obviously at the top of the queue."

"Has what happened affected you as an adult?"

"How would I know? I've never known any different. Davey was always the other half of me. I was heartbroken when he married Tina. He knew how I felt but he said he wasn't gay and couldn't share the way I felt. Andy wanted me to screw him but that wasn't what I wanted. When the band first started working, girls threw themselves at me – they still do – did – but I could never manage to do what they wanted, to get it up for them. I've only ever wanted someone who would look after me, make me feel safe. Until I met Alex all I'd ever managed was a quick grope up some alley, or occasionally a blow job from one of the stage crew if they wanted to earn some extra money. Then I found Alex and everything changed – suddenly I had someone who *did* look after me, who *made love* to me and I was so happy…"

I started to cry again.

Each day we made a little more progress, progressing through my teenage years, the band and our climb to success, the five manic years after we had our first major hit, when I had finally managed to break free from my family and Manchester; how I had dreaded the few weeks a year when I would be at home in Chelsea with nothing to do except sleep, deal with everyday stuff like replacing clothes or guitars, or sit and watch TV and listen to other people's music.

When I'd first moved down to London I'd visited a few clubs which I'd heard to be gay friendly, but I'd not been attracted to the scene – in my heart of hearts I wasn't looking for sex so much as someone to love and who would love me. I'd had plenty of offers of sex, but not from anyone I found remotely appealing, and had quickly reverted to staying in alone.

After that first session with Dr. Petersen I had finally told Davey about Father Flanagan. He was angry – not so much about what had happened, but that I had not told him at the time. He knew immediately which day it had happened, remembering clearly finding me hiding in the bin-store and what had followed. He had heard rumours from other lads at the school about the headmaster's penchant for young boys, but had been unsure whether this was just the tittle-tattle that circulated around most schools among pupils with over-active imaginations. He had never attracted that type of attention, possibly as he was not one of the flock, and might have been deemed more likely to kick up a fuss. In that theory he may have been exactly right, given my father's reaction at the time.

Eventually the sessions reached the day that Andy had died. This time Dr. Petersen took it very slowly and kept picking away at what had happened. Having made me lie down with my eyes closed, his voice was almost hypnotic as he re-created the interior of the flat as it had been that day, making me try to re-live what had led up to me being unconscious on the floor.

Like images from an early silent film, I kept getting pictures in my head of small time-bites, but could make little sense of them. Obviously someone had been there with me – who was it?

Images of a man AND a woman.

At the same time?

Not at the same time, I thought.

Were they known to me?

Maybe.

In my head, gradually, I could hear the woman's voice – a Manchester accent which seemed familiar, but not necessarily so. In my mind the man was Andy, but I dismissed that – the coincidence of it having been the day he died was too great, and, going on past form, Andy could not have been responsible for the rape.

Something nagged at the back of my mind but kept dancing tantalisingly, just out of reach.

The session ended without me remembering anything definite and I felt totally exhausted, physically, mentally and emotionally, but Dr. Petersen seemed pleased that we had made some progress.

Davey was called back in. He looked at my pale face and came and sat beside me, pulling me into his arms. Dr. Petersen asked me if I needed a sedative, but I shook my head – I was already beginning to feel a certain dependency, a sense of running away from reality and I had no wish to take anything if I could help it. Dope had never been my scene, other than the occasional joint, although I had been aware that Andy had frequently resorted to 'speed', and later cocaine, in order to keep up both his sex life and his energetic stage presence. Dr. Petersen exchanged glances with Davey who nodded imperceptibly.

"Are you sure you're OK?" he asked once we were on our own.

"No, I'm not sure. I'll let you know!" I said, a little grumpily. "The Doc. was on about the day Andy died – he was just stuck on that, over and over."

"Did you remember anything?"

"I don't know. Possibly. It was like frames of a film in my head – odd bits that didn't go together. There MAY have been two people in the flat – a guy and some woman – I think she came from Manchester – but we couldn't get beyond that. All I kept coming back to was Andy…"

Dr. Petersen tried again the following day, and the one after, but nothing further came to me and eventually he said quietly "OK. I'll leave it there. One day you WILL remember, hopefully under safe circumstances, and then you can come to me and we will deal with it. I'll talk to Davey about that. So, we are almost up to date, but there are still some important things we should talk about. How do you feel about Alex now?"

"Sad. Grateful…"

I bit my lip hard to stop myself from crying, but it almost had the opposite effect.

"Sad?"

"I was totally in love with him. When he didn't get in contact after my arrest I was devastated, but I suppose I knew he wouldn't be able to come to the hospital, and after that Davey and Paddy were at the flat with me. When Nat told me that Alex was prepared to give evidence – I didn't know what to feel… I was afraid for him, that his secret would be blown out of the water and I didn't want that – he'd been so kind, so wonderful, for so long…hearing his voice in court was…"

I gulped, shaking my head, fighting back tears again.

"Nat had told me who Alex was and why everything had to be so secret. I just couldn't believe that he was who he is – politicians always seem so remote, so straight… Alex was straight in some ways – the way he looked, the way he dressed - but he was also comfortable with how he is – he was never embarrassed about anything – everything always seemed so normal, so natural. I learned so much from him. I thought I knew who I was before I met him, but he found so much more…"

"This is an unfair question, but I need to ask it – if you had to choose between Alex and Davey…?"

"I don't even need to think about it – Davey! As I said before, he has always been the other part of me. I can't exist without him, especially since we became lovers. I will always have Alex in my heart, but we couldn't be together openly, and living like that isn't easy."

Dr. Petersen nodded.

"That's the answer I hoped you would give me." He smiled." Is there anything else you need to talk about, maybe about the time after you were released from hospital the first time, and while you were waiting to go to court?"

I thought back. I had been miserable to start with – the injustice of being charged with Andy's murder/manslaughter and the after-effects of the first attack, coupled with the yawning silence from Alex, but then things had suddenly changed radically when Davey and I had slept together that first time and he had made my wildest dreams come true by admitting his marriage was over and that he wanted to stay with me. Even the worries over the pending trial couldn't spoil that feeling.

The trial itself had seemed surreal and I had found it difficult to concentrate on some of the minutiae of evidence. Hearing Alex's voice when he gave evidence had been a great confidence-builder. He had spoken with no hesitation whatsoever and, although he was only stating his honest belief that I could not have been responsible for Andy's death, I couldn't see how anyone could disbelieve him.

The jury's verdict had come as an enormous shock after that. Because we had been so unprepared, Nat had not thought to warn me that, if found guilty, I would almost certainly be held in custody between the verdict and sentencing, so everything that followed the verdict was like falling off a cliff, the nightmare intensifying until that terrifying moment with its explosion of pain, followed by blackness.

I pulled my thoughts back to the present with an effort. Dr. Petersen was watching me carefully, measuring the time I took to respond, my expression, my body language.

"No." I said firmly. "I don't need to talk about anything from that time, and I can't talk about what happened in prison – not yet – it's too raw!"

"That is the very reason you need to talk about it." he said gently. "While it's there in your mind."

I considered the idea.

"How can someone *do* that? Just grab someone they have never seen before – not that he could see me – it was pitch dark in there – and do what he did? When I was – when I used to go down to the river looking for someone to sleep with – one or two people got a bit rough when I wouldn't do what they wanted – maybe you could argue that was because they felt they had a grievance – but that guy had never even seen me, never spoken to me, had no idea who I was – whether I was young, old, fat, thin, ugly…"

The words came tumbling out then.

Dr. Petersen held up his hand to stop me.

"You used opposing words – young/old, fat/thin – and then you said ugly. You didn't use its pair. Why?"

I thought about that. I managed a ghost of a grin.

"Maybe I don't want to think that I'm – Davey says I'm great – Alex used to say kind things – but I don't want to think of myself like that…"

"OK. Carry on."

I realised that he was not overly concerned with what I'd said – it had been a ruse to divert my attention – to break down the subject-matter into small pieces that I could process. I returned to my question.

"Why did he do it? For all he knew I could have been riddled with the clap, AIDS, any of that stuff. I don't get HOW anyone can just do it to order anyway – I can't even manage it for someone I love. He'd barely got through the cell door…"

"Tell me. Tell me what happened."

The voice was hypnotic again.

I closed my eyes and tried to concentrate on what had actually happened, without letting my mind dwell on the pain and fear.

"I don't remember much until it actually happened. When they took me out of the courtroom I was almost out of it. I remember Angelo being there with me in the cell and then Nat coming in, but I don't think I believed that I really was going to prison until they handcuffed me – then I just lost it! I was taken straight out to the van and put into one of those cupboard things. The first corner it went round, I was on the floor and I must have fainted. The next thing I knew I was in the cell at the prison. I remember the noise – it was like nothing else – and the smell…"

I heaved at the memory, my hand over my mouth.

"Then the lights went out and the noise quietened down a bit. I must have either been half asleep - or maybe I fainted again, but I remember hearing footsteps and the cell door was opened and they pushed this guy in. I couldn't see him in the dark – I dunno what age he was or even if he was white or black. All I remember was that he was big – taller than me and a lot heavier. I was in the lower bunk and he got in with me – he probably didn't realise there was anyone else there until then…"

I bit my lip hard to try to stop myself from crying again. I sucked in a breath.

"I'll never forget his voice - when he realised I was there, he started to grope me – he touched my face and hair and then said something like 'Hello sweetheart!' – like it was his birthday or something and then…then he was pulling at my clothes and shoving my face into the pillow…"

I gagged, remembering the smell of the bedding. I shook my head again, trying to clear it.

"…and then he just…just…"

I didn't continue. I couldn't continue - couldn't find the words to describe the sheer pain, terror, horror of those few minutes.

"What happened after that?"

"I've no idea. The next thing I knew I was in hospital and Davey was with me. I've absolutely nothing in between…"

"How do you feel about the guy who attacked you?"

I opened my eyes and looked at Dr. Petersen in amazement.

"How am I supposed to feel? I'd happily take a knife to him and make sure he can never do the same to anyone else!"

Dr. Petersen gave a small, mirthless smile.

"That's not really the right answer from someone who has a conviction for manslaughter!" He said gently.

I bit my lip again.

"However, I believed you before when you told me that you didn't kill Andy, and I have no reason to change my mind now, but I don't think you should share that thought with anyone else!"

"OK… I'll make a queue behind Davey."

"You understand that when someone rapes, it isn't usually about sex or desire, it's a violent crime, it's about *power*. The man who raped you was demonstrating that he was stronger than you, that he was the alpha male, and that even though you were in the cell, in the bunk, first, he was taking over the territory. Sometimes it's about humiliation – someone who has been humiliated themselves in the past wants to prove that they now have the upper hand."

"He was twice my size – he didn't need to …to do what he did to prove that! I've been…"

I struggled with the hated word

"…*raped* three times now, but I'm not about to go out and try to get my own back. I couldn't, even if I wanted to!"

"Does it bother you – that you can't 'get it up'?"

I shook my head.

"Why should it? That's not what turns me on. I do get a hard-on, just not enough to do anything with."

Ridiculously, I was beginning to feel slightly embarrassed by the conversation. Before Alex, apart from fighting off Andy's advances, there'd been little reason to use words. When girls had thrown themselves at me it had been literally that – I'd find myself being towed into a dark corner and snogged, usually followed by expressions of disappointment that there was nothing to follow, and I'd be left to slink away back to the dressing-room in abject humiliation. Later on, when I'd realised that I preferred guys, I'd been too shy to make the first move, especially once Davey had made it clear that he was not in the running. The crew had guessed my secret – they'd seen the humiliations too often to be in much doubt and, with Andy in the band, their gaydar was probably fairly high anyway. No-one ever really made a serious pass at me - I got the occasional half-hearted offer if someone was in need of beer-money, but it never went very far, and words were never necessary.

Likewise, Alex had always made all the running. After that first morning when I'd made it clear that I wanted him, he was always the one in control, although he would often ask if I found something pleasurable and I knew that if I wasn't enjoying it he would stop immediately, but words were never needed between us.

On the occasions when I walked the river path the discussions, such as they were, were usually monosyllabic, comprising an enquiry as to what I would agree to do and 'How much?' Discussing things in detail was a new experience – I'd waited so long to experience proper sex that I'd felt grateful for whatever was on offer – more aware of what I was unable to do than to discuss anything beforehand.

"Is talking about it making you uncomfortable?"

I nodded, my eyes fixed on the carpet.

"Why? You have as much right to decide what you like or don't like as anyone else. You say it doesn't worry you that you can't maintain an erection, but you could probably get help for that, and you might find that things a lot better, even if you don't actually want to penetrate anyone."

I shook my head.

"I'm sorry, I don't want to talk about it." I said firmly. "Things are OK as they are."

He realised that I wasn't going to continue the conversation.

"Micky, you've done very well, all things considered. You will almost certainly find that somewhere down the road there are other things you need to talk about, or maybe that you just need some space to think about things. I will always find room for you here, with or without Davey. I think my work with you is finished for the time being, and you can leave whenever you wish. There's no hurry – if you'd rather stay here a bit longer that's entirely up to you, there's no rush at all."

I felt a slight feeling of panic at his words, almost unwilling to deal with the idea of facing the outside world again, away from the safety of the clinic.

"Thanks. I'll talk to Davey – I don't know where we're going to go. It probably wouldn't be a great idea to go back to the flat right now."

"I think perhaps some of your friends have found an alternative for you." Dr. Petersen smiled at me.

I looked blankly back, exhausted by the session and the emotions it had roused.

"Are you too tired for a visitor?"

I pulled a face.

"Seriously? Who is it?"

Expecting him to say Paddy or maybe Angelo, I was stunned when he said gently "Alex should be waiting in my office. Shall I bring him through?"

I wanted to burst into tears again, my emotions so raw now that I hardly knew how to react. I nodded dumbly.

A few minutes later the door opened and Alex came in. He stood just inside the door and whispered my name. Hearing his voice tipped me over the edge, and now I did burst into tears. Lurching to my feet I ran to him. His arms closed round me and he held me tightly.

"You remember who I am then? Micky, I'm so sorry, I should have had the guts to face the world and stand up for you properly! I blame myself for what has happened – I should have been able to prevent it…"

"How could you have done?! Even *you* can't change the rules. You did everything you could – you gave evidence for me – even the judge said he couldn't understand how the jury could find me guilty on the evidence presented in court. You could have lost everything if you'd gone public with our relationship…"

"If I could have spared you what happened it would have been worth it! Micky, I know that you now have your Davey at long last, and I have no intention of trying to come between you – you have said so many times how much you love him – but what we had was very, very special and I will always treasure it. I know that things have moved on – and you will find out sooner or later, so I have to tell you that Nat and I are now…"

He didn't put it into words, but I knew what he was telling me.

"As you know, we are old friends... A very wise friend has advised me to divorce Vero – she is becoming indiscreet with her affairs and he thinks that times are changing, so that even politicians may be allowed a private life if they are *careful*. It is a great pity that it is too late for us, but then I think I would always have played second fiddle to your Davey…?"

He smiled the smile which always made me go weak at the knees.

"I want you to promise me that, if you ever need anything – and I mean *anything* – you will come to me. You may find things difficult for a while until people start to forget what has happened. I know you were 'comfortable' – I learned that the hard way – but you will find that money has a habit of going in only one direction when things are tough, and I suspect that Davey's wife will make things difficult for you both – at least until the children have finished their education. It goes without saying that Angelo, Nat and I will take care of all the legal formalities."

"You don't owe me anything…you are so kind! You did so much for me while we were together. If I hadn't met you, I'd still be paying the stage crew for a knee-trembler in some alley and drinking myself stupid whenever I was home alone – assuming I hadn't graduated to something worse from sheer boredom! Instead of all that you made a man of me, you showed me a different kind of life, you taught me *how* to love, and I will *always* love you, you will always have a special place in my heart! Yes, I love Davey and always will but that doesn't take anything away from what we had together…"

"Micky, if you say any more, all my good intentions about letting you go will desert me! I promised Dr. Petersen that I wouldn't say or do anything that would upset you or confuse you… I must go before I forget my promises - just promise me that you will remember what I have just said – if I can do anything to help you, you will ask me?"

I nodded.

"I promise. Alex – I really hope that you will be happy with Nat – he's gorgeous!"

Alex smiled, a little reluctantly.

"So are you! Look after yourself – and I'm sure Davey will look after you better than I did!"

I watched him go out of the door, fighting the urge to run after him. In my heart I knew that Nat was a much better match for him than I could ever be, as Davey was for me, but those three years had been so very special, as a first love affair always is, or should be…

Davey came in and grinned at me.

"We both had a visitor then?"

I frowned.

"Both? Who came to see you? Paddy?"

"No, Angelo! He's offered us the use of his family home in Portugal for as long as we like. None of the family live there any more, and he only goes out there a few times a year. He says it's beautiful at this time of year – not too hot but plenty of sunshine and really quiet. He's found a buyer for your flat and he's looking for somewhere for us to buy – well, for you to buy…"

He pulled a face.

"Tina's after all my money, as well as sole custody of the kids. I've told Angelo I don't care about the money, but I want joint custody."

I nodded. I wasn't hopeful that, given the circumstances, he would get it, but I knew how much it meant to him and I didn't want to upset him by saying anything that would take away the hope.

"I'm more than happy to buy somewhere for the two of us. I'd put it in joint names, but Tina could then claim your share if anything happened. I'll leave it to you in my Will – not that I'm planning on going anywhere just yet!"

Davey shivered.

"Don't even talk about that! I don't want to think about losing you – not now!"

He pulled me into his arms and hugged me, gently pulling my curls, twisting them round his fingers.

"I can smell Alex's cologne on you – did you snog him?"

I shook my head.

"No. We had a bit of a hug, that's all. It was all a bit weepy. We never got to say goodbye before. He and Nat are together now – I think they should be good together – I told him that… He made me promise that if I ever need anything, I'm to ask him. He's so kind…"

I was close to tears again.

Davey's arms tightened around me.

"I'm glad he made you happy, but I'm even more glad that I've got you now!"

We kissed. Davey manoeuvred me to the bed and gently pushed me down onto it, falling beside me.

Sometime later he asked "Well, how do you feel about going to Portugal?"

I smiled sleepily at him.

"Do they have beds in Portugal?"

He smacked my backside, none too gently.

"Does that mean you want to go?"

"We've got to go somewhere… If Angelo has sold the flat, then I suppose strictly speaking we're homeless…"

"I could always go home to mother. Not sure where that would leave you! Paddy might put you up…"

"Janice wouldn't let him – remember how quickly she split on you to Tina? She probably wouldn't let me in the house in case I passed something nasty on to the kids…"

Davey propped himself up on one elbow.

"They ran all the tests when you were in hospital – you're in the clear so far…"

"Probably more by luck than judgement! I always tried to be careful, but things did get a bit out of hand once or twice."

He kissed me gently.

"Now that we're together – you won't…?"

I hesitated just long enough for him to look worried.

"That's up to you!" I grinned at him. "If you keep me happy…With Alex I never knew for sure how soon I'd see him again – that's why I strayed…"

"In that case I'm not letting you out of my sight - ever!"

"Suits me!"

I wriggled on top of him, kissing his nose, nibbling his lips

"Why did we wait so long? I love you so much! Tina accused you of shagging me when we were on tour – we could have done that, and no-one would have been any the wiser…"

"If you want the truth, I was afraid that if I did, I'd not want to go home again… I've told you before that I was tempted – all those nights sitting behind you on stage with your bum wiggling in front of me, and then going back to some hotel and you parading round the room in the altogether – it nearly drove me mad sometimes, especially if we'd been away for weeks on end, or I'd had too much to drink or whatever. Or if you were upset about something – I'd want to put my arms round you and cuddle you, but I was terrified that if I did, I'd not be able to stop myself…"

"If I'd known how you felt I'd have made your mind up for you! Mind you, that's a small payback for asking me to be your best man when you married Tina –

I wanted to cry when you made your vows – or run away with you like Dustin Hoffman in *The Graduate*..."

"I only married Tina because she looked like you – I thought if I married her then I could pretend I was making out with you..."

I stared at him – it had never occurred to me that there was any resemblance between Tina and me, but now he'd said it I could see what he was getting at – when they married she had had long, curly, blonde hair like mine and her eyes were blue-grey, though not as violet as mine. She was also slightly shorter than me but, before the children came along, had had a boyish figure and, in those unisex days, had occasionally been mistaken for me in the half-light of the local dance halls.

"Seriously?! Did she realise that?"

"Not until I told her..."

"You're kidding! You ARE joking, right?"

He shook his head.

"No. I told you things were pretty much over between us when you and I...We'd been having a row – a real up and downer. She'd said something really nasty about you and Andy, and I snapped back something like 'I should have married Micky!', and that I'd only married her because she looked like you. I don't know whether she believed me or not – to start with she said she didn't believe me, but after that she kept throwing it back at me as though she did."

"No wonder she's being such a bitch about everything! Whatever possessed you?!"

He sighed.

"Twelve years of being married to her! You're right, I shouldn't have said it, but if you'd heard what she was saying..."

Chapter 31:

1984, Portugal. Misty

We landed at Oporto airport. Sure enough, a dark-suited driver was waiting, brandishing a card with 'David e Miguel' written across it. He seemed to recognise us even before we had worked out that the card was for us and, grabbing our bags, led the way out to a discreet grey Mercedes saloon. In passable English he introduced himself as Tomas.

The early afternoon sunshine sparkled on the Douro as he took us on a brief drive down into Gaia and across the bridge into Porto itself, before turning back along the river valley. The scenery was magnificent, the river waters the colour of an old wine bottle and as smooth as a mirror, in places far wider than the mighty Thames. As we progressed eastwards the scenery alternated between dark forest and vineyards precariously plastered on almost sheer slopes, tumbling down to the water. Eventually, after the road became an unmade track, he turned in between imposing gateposts, the high iron gates swinging open by remote-control.

The drive was smoother than the road had been, but only wide enough to take one vehicle. A few minutes later we caught sight of the house for the first time – a huddle of single-storey structures scattered across the high hillside, punctuated by huge rocks and beautifully landscaped gardens. The car pulled in under the shade of an open-sided porch.

The front door of what seemed to be the main building was standing open and a plump woman in her late thirties hurried forward.

"Bem vinda, senhors! Welcome to Portugal!" Her smile was infectious. "I am Mariana, I will be your housekeeper for your stay here. You have met Tomas –

he is my husband and he will take you wherever you want to go during your stay."

She snapped her fingers and Tomas picked up our luggage and led the way into the house. As we progressed from one part of the complex to the next Mariana pointed out where we would eat, our sitting areas and other landmarks. When we reached the furthest part of the buildings she led us into a huge bedroom suite with the most wonderful view across the valley.

Tomas placed our bags on the floor and Mariana indicated he should leave. Once he was out of earshot she said quietly "Senhor Angelo has explained to me how things are. You are quite safe here – there is only Tomas and me here and my daughters help if necessary, but I will be looking after you–" She searched for the right phrase "face to face – you understand? No one can see this part of the house, nor the garden around it, so you can – relax. But when you are away from here you must please to be discreet. This part of Portugal is not a tourist area and the people are – old fashioned – you understand? Senhor Angelo wish you to enjoy your stay so we not want any – misunderstandings – yes?"

"What about your husband?" Davey asked carefully.

"Tomas do what I tell him." Mariana said firmly. "He can be a bit – stupid - some time, but he will only see you when he drive you. We live close to door where you come in – he cannot see or hear you from there. I will not let him come through to this part of the house. Now – it is nearly time to eat – you come to dining room when you are ready – there will be food in maybe half hour."

She left us.

"What d'you make of that?"

Davey shrugged.

"Pretty much what she said, I think. 'Discreet' seems to be her favourite word, but I think she means that, as long as we avoid holding hands and kissing or worse when anyone can see us, we can relax and enjoy our holiday."

He came over to me and cuddled me gently.

"I can't believe that after all the shit you've been through, that we're here, together, in such a beautiful place!"

"How do you feel about eating? I'm not sure that I'm hungry."

"Come on, we've gotta eat! Got to keep your strength up!"

He winked at me, making me laugh.

"That's better! Go get showered and we'll go across."

We managed to find the dining room again without too many problems. The table was set for two, a carafe of greenish-white wine standing in a bowl of ice. The only other item on the table was a large bowl of fresh fruit, but almost as soon as we sat down Mariana appeared with a tureen of what turned out to be a cold stew containing chicken in a creamy sauce, new potatoes, green beans and a spicy seasoning. As soon as I started to eat, I realised how hungry I actually was. The wine turned out to be white port – something I'd never previously heard of, but which was also delicious and the perfect accompaniment to the food.

For a few days we simply stayed put, making full use of the small swimming pool and just soaking up the sun. Mariana suggested various things we could do but neither of us felt any inclination to go out and about. Eventually however curiosity got the better of me and I asked her about the possibility of taking a boat along the river.

"There is a boat which belongs to the quinta but it is quite small. You would be better taking one of the tourist boats from Porto. Is nice day out – they serve food and wine and you get a…" she searched for the right word "…history of what you see. Tomas will take you into town and show you where you take the boat from. Then you can either come back to Porto on the boat or Tomas can fetch you from wherever you decide to get off. Or there is a little train which follows the river."

Davey was a little uncertain about taking a tourist boat, but I couldn't see any problem. I wasn't so sure about the idea of the little train, and in the end we arranged that Tomas would be waiting at the boat station nearest the quinta, a mile or two upstream.

We boarded the boat around 9.30 the following morning. As it was early in the season there were only a few people aboard the large vessel, and we were able to move between decks and in and out of the saloon without worrying about losing our seats. Once we were clear of the city the scenery was similar to that which we'd seen on the day of our arrival, but far more magnificent viewed from the water, giving a vastly more profound perspective to the height of the mountains either side, the deep green of the water and its mirror-like surface.

I'd never been particularly interested in scenery before, despite (or maybe because of) the amount of travelling we'd done, but this was a whole new experience and I found myself wiping away tears at the sheer beauty of it all. I desperately wanted Davey to put his arms round me but, at the same time, after Mariana's warnings about the need to be discreet, felt it probably better that he didn't. To compensate, he grabbed a glass of port from a passing steward and handed it to me and I gratefully took a large swig.

The journey upstream took several hours before we reached the boat-station where we had arranged to meet Tomas. He was waiting on the quayside but was quite happy to wait for us while we went off to have a coffee in a quiet café.

Towards the end of the first week Angelo flew out to join us for a few days. Away from London he was far more laid-back, and we began to see a whole new side to him. The quinta belonged to his family and he explained that, generally, he was the only one who now visited it regularly, although he did so enough to justify keeping it running and staffed, albeit only by Mariana and Tomas, who were paid a small retainer plus their accommodation in return for keeping it maintained and attending to Angelo and his guests.

On the Saturday he took us out into the wilder parts of the estate, initially in a ramshackle Jeep and then on horseback – a first for both of us, but the horses were very docile and I thoroughly enjoyed the experience, despite being somewhat saddle-sore by the time we got back!

"I'll be going into Porto in the morning to go to Mass – would you like to come with me?" he offered.

I looked at Davey – I hadn't been inside a church of any kind since Danny was christened. I hadn't been to Mass for at least ten years – certainly not since I had left home for London in 1973. He shrugged – not being Catholic it was not his decision. Something made me accept, curious to see the interior of a continental church.

The following morning the three of us packed into Angelo's BMW convertible for the drive down into Porto. He had explained that the church we were going to, Sao Francisco, was probably the most beautiful in the whole country – certainly in Porto. It also had the added attraction of a parish priest who hailed from Ireland!

It was too early in the season for the church to be running an English-speaking Mass for the tourists but, even after my ten-year lapse, I found I was able (more or less) to follow what was happening. When the time came for the congregation to take communion Angelo stood up.

Davey nudged me.

"Aren't you going up?"

I shook my head.

"I can't – I haven't been to confession or Mass for over ten years!"

Angelo gently took my arm and whispered "It's OK – you can come up for a blessing if you don't feel able to take communion."

Slightly reluctantly, I allowed myself to be carried along with the throng and, reaching the front of the queue, crossed my arms across my chest and bowed my head to receive the priest's blessing. We returned to our seats.

When we were leaving the building, Angelo waited to speak to the priest, introducing us to Father Sean as guests of the quinta.

"Come to lunch" he urged.

The priest smiled.

"Angelo, you know how little time I get…"

"All the more reason to come and spend an hour or two in good company with a free meal thrown in!"

"Very well – it's probably quicker to accept than to argue!"

His accent was strange, the Irish brogue now intermingled with Portuguese overtones.

Over lunch we were to discover that he had left Ireland, and had eventually been assigned to Portugal by Rome, after becoming embroiled with Republican/ Nationalist politics after 'Bloody Sunday'. He had hoped to move on from what he considered to be a backwater, but he was popular with the local people and, so far, his pleas for a more challenging posting had fallen on deaf ears.

"My penance!" he grimaced.

He had obviously worked out fairly quickly the relationship between Davey and me, but seemed untroubled by it. He also guessed that I was a lapsed Catholic. Angelo steered the conversation round until I found myself agreeing to talk privately with him and we went through to Angelo's small office. We sat, rather awkwardly on my part, suddenly feeling slightly rebellious at the contrived situation.

He smiled encouragingly.

"Micky, you don't have to say or do anything you don't want – I realise that Angelo has manipulated you into this."

There was a long pause. I shook my head.

"No, it's OK. I just feel – I don't know what to say… You've obviously sussed that Davey and I are…"

"In love." he said firmly, a statement, not a question.

I looked at the floor.

"I don't have a problem with that. How long is it since you last went to Mass?"

"Probably about ten years."

"Well, I don't know what you were taught or told, but in most places now the Church preaches forgiveness and that we should love the sinner, while acknowledging the sin. My personal opinion is that, if you truly love someone…"

He didn't finish the sentence, but his eyes were looking deeply into mine, as though searching my soul for an answer.

I bit my lip and nodded.

"I've known Davey all my life." I said huskily. "I've loved him ever since I can remember. When I realised that he loved me…"

I shook my head.

"Do you want me to hear your confession?"

I thought for a while before replying.

"I don't know what you are expecting to hear?" I said eventually. "There's so much, and yet so little…"

"The truth will do. You don't need to spell it out."

I made a clumsy sign of the Cross.

"Bless me, Father, for I have sinned. It is ten years since my last confession."

I paused again, wondering where to start.

"I have been disobedient to the teachings of the Church. I was disobedient to my parents…"

I rambled on, unable to specifically refer to my 'sins of the flesh'. Father Sean eventually gave me the words I needed to deal with that without being false to my love for Davey. He gave me absolution.

"There – that wasn't so bad, was it?"

I gave a rather tearful smile and shook my head.

It was an odd feeling, making my peace with the church and yet knowing that my lifestyle was, for all Father Sean's gentle words, forbidden by it. And yet I DID feel at peace, as though something that had been unfinished business had now come full circle and I could now move on.

"How long will you be staying on here? Will you come to Mass again so that you can take communion?"

"I – I don't know. We haven't really thought ahead. At the moment we have nowhere else to go."

That question was about to sort itself out. After Father Sean had departed back to Porto, Angelo, looking conspiratorial, called us back to the dining table and, producing a bundle of papers from his briefcase, spread them out on the table.

"I have found you a new home!" he announced, looking at me, presumably because it was mainly being funded by the proceeds from the sale of my Chelsea flat, Davey's money, at least for now, being systematically drained by Tina. We had already decided that the purchase would be in my name only to avoid any complications.

"OK", I said cautiously, "Where, what and how much?"

"You won't be able to move in for another couple of months – there's a lot of work that still needs to be done, but I think it will be perfect for you."

I exchanged glances with Davey, worried that Angelo had not yet told us anything about the place. He pushed an expensive-looking estate agents' brochure towards me.

The photo on the front was not particularly promising, showing a run-down Georgian-style house. I picked it up and leafed through, looking for more photos, but there were very few – an overgrown walled garden, a large timber-clad barn that you could see right through in places and with several large holes in the roof, some unidentifiable, tumble-down outbuildings. There was a sketch plan showing how the buildings related to each other. No price was shown. I handed the brochure to Davey who looked slightly more interested.

"Hunt Kennel Farm – not sure that sounds quite our cup of tea." he commented after a few minutes.

"Where is it, Angelo?"

"Not too far from the motorway, a little north-east of Oxford."

"How much?"

He named a sizeable figure, but within our budget.

"It looks as though we'd need to spend twice that just fixing it up."

"No, that's the price AFTER the work is finished. And it comes with one hundred and sixty acres of land, so you won't have any problems with the neighbours."

"What are we going to do with a hundred and sixty acres?"

"You can let them out and earn some money from them, or you could buy some sheep…"

Davey snorted derisively.

"Farmer Culshaw – I don't think so!"

I tended to agree but wondered why Angelo was pushing us in this direction.

"Micky – I promise you that you will love it when you see it! It's the perfect size for you and the barn will make a terrific studio once it's been repaired. It's off the beaten track, so you won't have to worry about nosy neighbours or people dropping in, but it's close enough to the motorway so that Davey can get up to Manchester in a couple of hours. It's small enough to be manageable but big enough for you to have the children there and to provide accommodation for anyone using the studio. You will need a housekeeper or someone to cook for you, but apart from that you could probably manage with casual staff and someone to look after the gardens. The main outbuildings form a square behind the main house, so you have a private garden there, as well as the walled garden which can be used to grow fruit and vegetables – it's just perfect!"

"I get the feeling that I have already bought it?" I said nervously.

Angelo shrugged.

"Maybe. But I promise you, if you decide you really don't like it, I will make you a profit on it without you even moving in."

"I'll hold you to that!" I said, meaning it. "Angelo – we're really grateful to you for allowing us to stay here in this beautiful place, but we can't stay here for another couple of months…"

He held up his hand.

"That's taken care of too. Sir Peter Lawrence has offered you the use of his house near Bagshot – he never – or rarely – uses it during the summer."

Sir Peter was a music industry big-shot. He'd started out in a band in the very early 1960s and later, when their music had fallen out of fashion, had founded his own record label before moving into promotion and other related areas. A multi-millionaire, he was a well-known figure, not just for his business activities, but also for his colourful social life.

"Is there anyone you don't have contacts to?" Davey asked.

Angelo shrugged.

"Probably, but I haven't needed them yet! And in this case, he contacted me with the offer immediately after the trial ended."

Chapter 32:

1985, Surrey. Misty.

We were collected from the airport by limousine and swept off to our borrowed home as arranged. On arrival at the front door we were met by the housekeeper, a woman in late middle age with an elegant figure, dressed discreetly in a formal, navy wool dress with white collar and cuffs, her grey hair pulled back into an old-fashioned bun.

"Welcome to 'Sparrows Hill', Mr. Culshaw, Mr. Pryor. I am Grace Pritchard, Sir Peter's housekeeper. My instructions are that you should make this your home for as long as you wish."

She seemed genuinely pleased to see us and I wondered how often the house was actually used (in any meaningful sense of the word), although judging from the immaculate state of the gardens, the estate must have been fully-staffed.

Grace led the way into the house, leaving the chauffeur to bring our luggage. We were given a whistle-stop tour of the downstairs rooms before she took us upstairs to our guest suite, which comprised two large bedrooms, both with an enormous bed and en-suite bathroom, separated by a vast sitting room with large-screen TV, an expensive hi-fi system, cocktail bar and other comforts.

"Please feel free to use the 'phone as much as you wish, and if you want to be taken anywhere just dial 96 and the chauffeur will be at your disposal. What time would you like dinner?"

I looked at Davey who shrugged.

"What time would it normally be served?"

"There is no set time – Sir Peter is not here often, and when he comes it is usually late evening. You can order anything you would like – there is very little we cannot provide for you."

"Something fairly light please – maybe chicken or fish? Whatever the chef suggests."

Grace nodded.

"If you require anything just dial 91 to speak to me."

She exited.

We gazed round the suite, a little over-awed by the plush décor, heavy on the brocade and gilt. In the end we stayed there for just three days; somewhere along the way I had begun to get an odd feeling that it was not a happy house.

The food was faultless, and our suite was extremely comfortable. We had spent our time watching videos or listening to music from the seemingly endless supply. We both had guitars with us and used some of the time to try writing some new material but, to a great extent, were too much in limbo to really settle to anything very creative.

Several times Grace had seemed to want to say something to me but, for whatever reason, had thought better of it. However, on what turned out to be our last morning there, she had seemed particularly upset and close to tears. I managed to get Davey to leave us together and asked her straight out if there was anything wrong.

"Oh, Mr. Culshaw!" she said desperately, "I can't keep quiet any longer!"

"What is it? Have we done something wrong?"

She burst into tears and shook her head. Taking my arm, she led me out of the dining room and along the corridor into the servants' quarters. We went into a small room off the corridor. There was a bank of CCTV screens, a few showing the exterior of the house, but most plainly covering the main rooms of the house, including our suite.

To my horror, I realised that at least one camera was trained on the vast bed that Davey and I had been sharing, and that everything we had done would have been open for anyone to see.

Grace put her finger to her lips and took me outside the back door to where she obviously knew we could not be seen or heard.

"You're telling me that the staff – or anyone else – could have been watching Davey and me...?"

She nodded.

"It's worse than that – everything is on tape! Please, Mr. Culshaw, you must find somewhere else to stay - today! You're both nice lads, and you obviously love each other very much – you don't want all Sir Peter's nasty friends sniggering..."

"Don't worry, we'll be out of here this morning, even if we end up in a hotel somewhere! Oh Grace, you must come with us – you can't stay here and work for a slime-ball like that!"

Grace brushed her tears away.

"I have nowhere else to go." she said quietly. "I've worked here since before Sir Peter bought the estate."

"Come and work for us!" I said firmly, in no doubt that this was the perfect solution all round. "Is there somewhere you can go for a few weeks, until our new house is ready?"

She nodded.

"I can stay with my sister in Carmarthen for a little while. Do you really mean it?"

I smiled encouragingly.

"Of course – I wouldn't have said it if I didn't. Please Grace, we'll need someone to look after us, and we won't ask you to do more than you feel able to cope with. If you need help, we'll make sure you get it."

She hugged me, still emotional.

I went upstairs to the suite and, taking Davey to a corner I thought was out of range of the beastly cameras, told him quietly what Grace had revealed.

He looked absolutely horrified and, left to his own devices, would probably have stormed downstairs and created a scene, but I was anxious not to implicate Grace, and managed to persuade him simply to pack our bags and get someone to drive us to the farm, from where we could see if there was any possibility of moving into at least one room while the work was completed on the remainder of the house.

Chapter 33:

Same day, Oxfordshire. Micky

We managed to track down Paddy who, as luck would have it, was in London. He collected us within an hour and, curious to see our new project, was happy to drive us out there.

I had said an anxious goodbye to Grace, making her promise to leave Bagshot as quickly as she could. I gave her Angelo's contact details and told her that, if she found herself out of pocket from not giving whatever notice she ought to have done, that I personally would compensate her. I also asked her to make sure that we or Angelo could contact her to keep her in the picture as to when we would be able to provide her with a job and accommodation.

We arrived at the farm around midday. Not having been there before, we only had the address and vague directions and had initially turned into the wrong lane, ending up outside the Crossed Swords pub, a long, low, white-washed building, seemingly at the end of the lane. Davey went into the pub to ask directions.

"You're wasting your time – no-one lives there at the moment - it's been bought by some rock musician – bit of a rum do if you ask me! They're doing a lot of work there, putting it back together." The landlord told him.

Davey was tempted to say 'I AM that rock musician!' but thought better of it.

The landlord went on "Of course, if you're a builder or similar then maybe you DO need to find it?"

Davey nodded encouragingly.

"Go back down to the main road, turn left and then left again almost immediately. The entrance was quite overgrown but - all the lorries and stuff - it's a bit easier to find now. Go right down the track, under the railway bridge and you'll eventually find it. It's right at the end – you can't go any further."

Davey thanked him amiably and came back out. He waited until we were away from the building and then relayed the conversation.

We followed the directions – the access was indeed still fairly difficult to find, so it was hardly surprising that we had missed it the first time. The lane grew bumpier and bumpier before it dived under the railway, after which the concrete surface seemed newer. Eventually we could see the rooves of the house and barn peeping above the hedges and trees.

We pulled up outside the barn, the main part of the driveway being full of builders' vans. A burly Irishman came up to the driver's window.

"This is private property!"

Paddy grinned.

"And these are the owners!"

He waved his hand at the two of us. The Irishman ducked his head into the window and squinted at us.

"Bugger me! So it is!"

I was tempted to say that he wasn't my type, but thought he might not appreciate the lame humour. We climbed out.

"Are you the foreman?" I asked. He nodded. "We've just made ourselves homeless – are any of the rooms complete enough for us to use?"

He scratched his head.

"Even if you are used to roughing it, I don't think it's a great idea. The bathrooms aren't plumbed in yet, and there's no electricity apart from the generators we're using. You could possibly bring a caravan down and put it in the stable yard, but you'd be a lot better off at the pub – nice couple there, Gerry and Sylvia – they'll see you right."

"Davey's just met Gerry. We'd better go back there and see what they can do for us. Can we have a look round while we're here?"

"It's your gaff, I'll give you the tour."

He took us round the outside first, showing us the stable yard and walled garden and the barn. The external work on the barn was almost finished and the partitioning was in place dividing it into the actual studio, control room, rest area and facilities, although, as he had said, none of the plumbing or electrics had yet been installed, let alone flooring or other finishes.

Opposite the barn were the remains of the kennel runs. These were being converted into self-contained bedrooms with en-suite shower rooms and their own central kitchen and recreation area, providing accommodation for anyone using the studio. Again, the roof had been finished and the new walls and window-frames installed but, as yet, there were no doors or glazing, plumbing or electricity.

Beyond this area the drive opened up into a turning circle with what would be a central, raised fountain and fishpond in the middle. The Georgian house was set back at right angles to this, three wide steps leading up to the doorway. New windows had been installed but, again, no door. Inside, the square, double-height hallway awaited its floor surface. Doors led off to either side and a wide staircase rose from opposite the front door, branching off right and left from the mezzanine landing halfway up.

The door to the left led into what would be the dining room, again an empty shell. The room opposite was, at that point, designated as the drawing room, although it would eventually become the library/office with a secondary use as the best drawing room.

Mounting the stairs, the rooms above the dining room and drawing room were intended to be the principal bedrooms, but Grace would end up having what had been intended as the master bedroom and the other would become our best guest room. Both rooms had their own en-suite bathrooms and dressing rooms.

Double doors hidden behind the staircase led through into the oldest part of the main house. It had been the original farmhouse on the site, dating back well over a century before the Georgian house was added on, and both phases had their own roof structures. The ground floor of the farmhouse was being remodelled into a boot-room/cloakroom area with access through to the courtyard garden.

Walking through the boot-room to the left led through to the kitchen area – at this stage devoid of any fittings or equipment. The kitchen ran away from the main house along one arm of the kennel buildings, leading through into a utility room, a small lobby and then through to the rear corner of the kennels which would eventually become our bedroom, its en-suite bathroom leading off it into the furthest arm of the kennels, parallel to the boot room. A short, narrow corridor led past the en-suite into our music room/sitting room which formed the central portion of that arm, with a communicating door into the main bedroom range which backed onto the studio bedrooms. The bedroom range contained four double bedrooms and a large family bathroom. At the far end another door led back into the other end of the boot-room, completing the quadrangle.

I looked at Davey. He was grinning.

"Woww!"

The foreman, whose name was Seamus [Shay], looked anxiously at us.

"What d'you reckon?"

"It's fantastic!"

He looked relieved.

"A lot of thought has gone into the layout. It'll be easier to understand when we start putting in the fixtures and fittings. There are a few other rooms which can be used for storage."

"Where?"

I couldn't see that we'd missed anything.

"Above the boot-room range. The oldest part of the house is two storeys, but at the moment there is no staircase to get up there. If you're only using it for storage you could have one of those loft ladder things, or we can put in a simple staircase in one corner. There's also an upstairs in the barn, sorry – studio - above the rest area. Again, there's no stairs at the moment, but we can put in either a fixed ladder or a proper staircase – or maybe a spiral staircase might look good? You've also got cellars and attics in the main house – we'll get those cleaned out and damp-proofed before we finish up."

"How long will it all take?"

"We've a small army working on it – unless we find any major extra problems, I'd say maybe another three to four weeks."

"Even with the changes we've mentioned?"

He nodded

"What about the painting and stuff?"

"Mr. Daranda has brought in a designer to sort all that stuff. She comes up every few days to see how we're getting on. She has her own team of painters etc., and I understand they're ready to go as soon as we give the go-ahead. Obviously, as soon as we've finished anything, she and her lads can come in and make a start in that area."

"What about a garage – how about converting part of the stable yard?"

"We can do that if you want, although it's a pity to muck up the yard – it's all original to the time the new part of the house was built. We could convert the cart shed at the end of the barn – sorry – studio? That would give you room for three or four cars. Be easier to get in and out of too."

Eventually we'd had our fill of daydreaming and Paddy took us back to the pub. This time we both went in. Gerry wasn't around but his wife, Sylvia, was behind the bar. She gave an exclamation of recognition when she saw me.

"I thought it had to be you!" she said excitedly. "When my husband said something about this long-haired builder, I thought it must be you!!

"Well it wasn't me – it was Davey!" I grinned. "Do you have rooms?"

"For you, my love, of course we do! How long for?"

"For a few weeks, possibly. The builders think at least a month, probably longer"

"How many?" I looked at Davey – we hadn't thought about that – whether we would frighten the natives if we shared a double room…

"A double for us."

Davey winked outrageously at her. She rolled her eyes, only slightly embarrassed.

I heaved a sigh of relief.

"Paddy – are you staying for a day or two?"

"I wasn't – why?"

"In case we need to get around."

Paddy sighed with exasperation.

"I'm not your bloody chauffeur! Where's Davey's car?"

"Haven't a clue. Probably in the police pound in Chelsea, unless it's still at Micky's flat."

Neither of us had given it a thought since before the trial.

"Except that I don't own the flat anymore. You'd better call Angelo and see if he has any ideas."

Davey went off to phone Angelo and came back grinning.

"It's OK. Apparently the concierge rang him when he realised whose car it was. Angelo had it moved to his place – all I need to do is collect it."

Paddy sighed.

"OK, let's go."

"What, now?"

"I would like to get back to Manchester sometime this week, before Jan forgets who she's married to. I have to keep reminding the kids that I'm their father!"

Davey winced. This was a sore point – he hadn't been allowed to even speak to Sal and Danny since Tina had found out about us. Paddy realised he'd put his foot in it and apologised. They went off, leaving me to take our stuff up to the room Sylvia had shown us.

I unpacked our clothes into the vast oak wardrobe. The room was large and tastefully decorated, if a little chintzy. Judging from the twisted oak beams and unlevel floor, the building was even older than it appeared outside, but the bathroom had modern fittings and the bed felt comfortable.

I went back down to the bar. Sylvia made me a coffee and I perched on a bar stool and chatted, there being no other customers around at that time. I asked whether we were likely to get problems with the regulars.

"You may get a few humorous comments, but they will be just that. Once they get used to having you around, they'll be fine. They're a good lot around here – everyone mucks in together and if anyone has any sort of problem there'll be someone who can fix it." She grinned. "It's not as if you're raving queens in pink tutus! You're just two nice guys with long hair. They'll probably tease you more for being pop stars than for whose bed you share. Will you be eating with us or eating out?"

"Here I would think – at least tonight and probably for the first few days, until we get settled and know our way around."

"How's the building going? Some of the builders come in here at lunchtimes or on Friday nights and we hear bits and bobs. They say you're having the whole place taken apart and put back together again."

"So it seems! Our lawyer has put the whole plan together – we had nothing to do with it...In fact, I think we came up here today expecting to dislike it and put it straight back on the market, but that's not going to happen, unless we get run out of town."

"Have you thought how you're going to use the land?"

I shook my head.

"Not really. Angelo – our lawyer – suggested we could rent some of it out, or maybe get some sheep. Not sure I fancy that much."

"I'm sure you won't have any difficulty renting out the fields – there are plenty of girls with horses who want grazing round here, and Eddie at the farm always used to rent the big fields nearest his place. He grumbled like heck when your place was sold up and he lost the use of them. If you were happy to rent out some of the boxes, I could probably put you in touch with someone."

"Boxes?" I was puzzled.

"The stables – they call them loose boxes as you don't have to tie the horses up in 'em. I know someone who would like to offer livery that's when people pay someone else to look after their horses. You can't really do that with just a field, but if she could rent a few boxes from you, plus a field or maybe two, she'd have the makings of a good thing to offer people."

"I'd have to talk it over with Davey." I said cautiously. "I'm not sure we'd want people coming and going all the time, especially when the studio is up and running and we have other musicians around – some of them are quite neurotic about their privacy."

"You could open up the old gates at the far end of the yard – they open directly onto the bridleway. That way no-one would have any excuse to come anywhere near the house."

It was apparent she knew the layout of the property.

"I'll have a look and we'll talk it over. We may be glad of the money!"

It seemed no time before Davey came back, his elderly Volvo estate looking much cleaner than I remembered seeing it before.

"Angelo had it cleaned – his neighbours were complaining!" He grinned. "You're going to have to learn to drive, you know. We can't live round here if I'm the only driver."

I pulled a face.

"I hope Grace can drive!"

He shook his head.

"So do I, but she'll have more than enough to do without being your chauffeur as well. We'll start you off up and down the drive, at least you'll learn how to change gear before you go out on the road."

Gerry came back in at that moment.

"No need to do that." he said. "There's a disused airfield up the road – all the local kids learn to drive there. Much safer!"

Gradually the bar filled up. We soon found out that during the week there was little or no passing trade, but there were a good number of locals who came for a pint or three and a chat. The food Sylvia offered was limited – a daily Specials board with a handful of choices, but all home-cooked and appetising.

As predicted, we got a few pleasantries but, generally, people went out of their way to make us feel welcome. We were introduced to Eddie, who wasted no time in lobbying to rent the fields closest to his farm. We learned that there had originally been a 'big house', for which ours had been the Home Farm. We later discovered that the old part of our house had in fact pre-dated the mansion, and I felt a slight satisfaction that the Farm had outlived its more illustrious successor. When the mansion was demolished in the early 20th century the Farm had been taken over by the local hunt, who had been displaced by the loss of the bigger house, hence its designation as Hunt Kennel Farm. The kennel buildings had been converted from earlier farm buildings, so our current re-invention of the place was far from being its first.

"What was the mansion called?" I asked.

This triggered much argument and head-scratching and no conclusive answer, other than a suggestion that we should contact the local county archives.

"We thought of changing the name to Old Kennel Farm…" I ventured.

There was then some discussion, involving some friendly ribbing, about townies buying country properties and trying to re-invent rural life. I had to kick

Davey hard on the ankle to prevent him starting an argument on the merits or otherwise of hunting – I thought it was far too early in our new life to risk being branded as any sort of fox-cuddling animal-rights types. Sylvia told me later that the reason the Farm had been put up for sale was due to the local hunt being merged with another some distance away, mainly due to lack of local support, and that, so far as she knew, none of the regulars had ever been more than lukewarm supporters.

At breakfast the following morning we got a call from Shay to say that the designer had arrived on site. We scrambled into the car and went up there to find an elfin 'girl' in her mid-thirties holding forth to Shay because no part of the site was yet ready for her to work on.

The tirade continued regardless of our arrival until Davey, courageously I thought, tapped her on the shoulder. She swung round.

"Who the devil are you?!"

"I'm Davey Pryor and this is Micky Culshaw, the owner."

She took a gulp of air before continuing, only a couple of decibels more quietly, to hold forth about the state of the building work, accompanied by a fair amount of arm waving.

"Could you at least introduce yourself?" I asked quietly.

She stopped again and looked me in the eye.

"I am Natasha Forbes-Elliot. Mr. Daranda commissioned me to design and execute your interiors. My boys have been kicking their heels for weeks, waiting to come on site, and today there is STILL no power supply for us to use, nor is there even one room that we can start work on!"

I felt some sympathy for her – Davey, on the other hand, was laughing helplessly at the thought of her 'designing and executing' our interiors.

She swung round and glared at him.

"I don't see what is so funny!"

"I must apologise for my other half." I said gently. "His sense of humour is rather childish!"

I glared at him meaningfully.

"Why don't you and I have a look at your plans while Davey sees if he and Shay can find some way of organising things so that you and your team can make a start?"

I shot Shay another meaningful look as I guided Natasha into the house. We went through into the kitchen where, fortunately, there were some cabinets, albeit still in their cardboard shrouds, which we were able to use as a table. She unzipped her folio case and produced paint charts and fabric swatches.

"I tell you what" I said, a little intimidated by a creeping suspicion that she was about to *tell* me what we were to have, rather than this being any sort of discussion. "Why don't we walk through and you can tell me what you have in mind for each room while we are there?"

I have to say that her plans were not only totally in tune with the property, but also had a distinct contemporary feel. Our only slight disagreements were where we had adjusted the designation of some of the rooms – the master bedroom, the library/office and the room which Davey and I had decided was more suitable to be our bedroom. Obviously these would require a re-think from her but she, maybe slightly reluctantly, accepted that this was to be our *home* and that we knew what we wanted from it.

She had used more adventurous schemes for the studio/kennel rooms – each had its own theme and a humorous twist. The bedrooms which would be used for Sally and Danny – if we ever got the chance to have them with us – were to be left as blank canvasses so they could choose their own schemes.

We went across to the barn. She was less sure of herself here and had only, so far, proposed schemes for the rest area and facilities. We discussed the finishes for the floor, walls and ceiling of the studio itself – obviously these had certain critical requirements as they could affect the recorded sound. I proposed that the control room should be finished mostly in black so that it would disappear when viewed from the studio, so as not to distract anyone recording. She suggested that instead we should use an electronic two-way mirror window which could be switched off to allow see-through visibility when required. That would then allow the control room to be decorated in a less funereal fashion than I had suggested – something I didn't even realise was possible...

Davey and Shay joined us there, having decided the fairest option now was for his men to finish the barn/studio, followed by the studio bedrooms, as these were self-contained and Natasha's team could then work on them without getting in their way. Shay promised to chase up both the electrical team and the fitting of the sanitary-ware, as nothing could be started until these were in place.

I felt that we had actually managed to achieve something that day, although I wondered how long it would be before Davey unintentionally upset someone…

When we came down to breakfast the following morning Angelo was already there.

"You're a bit keen!"

Davey exclaimed, suddenly waking up. Angelo grinned sleepily.

"Well, various things made me realise that you two were getting around, so I thought I'd better come and find out what you are up to. You obviously retrieved your car?"

Davey nodded.

"What happened at Bagshot? I've had Sir Peter on the phone bending my ear…"

"I'll bend more than his ear if I ever come face-to-face with him!!"

Davey was about to launch into a tirade and I hurriedly shut him up. While I felt that we owed Angelo an explanation, I didn't think it desirable to do so where we might be overheard.

"We'll tell you about that later." I said firmly.

"He says you've stolen his housekeeper – or at least she left when you did?"

"She had her reasons – and Yes, she is going to come and work for us."

"So you've decided to keep the Farm?"

I grinned. "It'll do for the time being."

Angelo grinned back.

"You mean you love it!"

"I mean that I think we will love it if it ever gets finished!"

He frowned. "Problems?"

I shrugged.

"Dunno. Shay's a nice enough guy and seems to know what he's doing, but they're waiting for this and waiting for that, so there's nothing that is actually ready for Natasha to get going on. She's not a happy lady, although I think we managed to find a way forward yesterday."

Angelo grinned again.

"You're not just a pretty face, are you?"

I laughed. "We'd not have got very far if I had been! You either have to learn how to handle people, or pay a lot to someone else who can. We weren't planning to go over there again today, but if you want to come and have a look for yourself…"

He nodded. "Think I'd better, as it's my name on the contracts!"

"Yeah. There was a lot of Mr. Daranda this, Mr. Daranda that…"

We went in Davey's car as Angelo wasn't over happy to take his BMW down the rough lane.

Shay didn't seem too surprised to see us again so quickly and was happy to show us that the 'sparks' team had arrived and were putting in the general wiring to the barn/studio and would then move on to the kennel/bedrooms once the window glazing had been completed, hopefully that same day. Delivery of the sanitary-ware had been promised for the following day. He had also had confirmation from Natasha that the specialist materials for the floor and walls of the studio had been ordered and were likely to arrive early the following week.

We walked Angelo through the house – he had not previously visited it, despite having bought it on our behalf.

"You'll be getting a lot of house for your money!" he commented. "And a lot of scope to earn money from it with the studio, the stables and the farmland."

"We may need that!" I said. "We will have to really work our tails off to get back to where we were two years ago."

We were back at the car now.

"OK, can you *please* now tell me what went wrong in Bagshot?"

I checked the car windows were properly closed and took a breath. While I was wondering how to start Davey took over.

"That guy's a pervert! He had cameras in the bedroom and taped everything…"

There was a stunned silence while Angelo absorbed what he had heard.

"You – are – joking! Are you sure?"

"Yes." I said. "And this is absolutely not to go any further – Grace – the housekeeper – showed me the screens in the servants' quarters – anyone could have seen everything and somewhere there are tapes…"

Another stunned silence.

"I'm really sorry! – I had absolutely no idea... When he contacted me, he just seemed genuinely to want to help you after all the publicity and everything…"

"It wasn't your fault. That's why we offered Grace the job – she was really upset about what has been going on there. I was really worried about what might happen to her if they put two and two together about us leaving so quickly. She's a lovely lady – she deserves better than working for that creep."

"What about the tapes?"

"I think we'll just have to live with the fact that they're out there somewhere. I don't see that we can do anything about them without it all getting into the public domain – the publicity would probably do more harm than the tapes themselves – he's hardly likely to put them up for sale!"

"Would they be very – harmful?"

I blushed deeply.

"Um – well, they're not exactly likely to be family entertainment! OK, our fans are mostly now in their twenties or even thirties, but – well, y'know – we had no idea anyone could see us, and we weren't just playing Scrabble…"

It was Angelo's turn to blush.

"OK, I don't need diagrams. You are probably right – it's probably best to leave well alone, unless we find that copies are circulating. Guys, I'm really, really sorry! Where is Grace now?"

"She said she would stay with her sister in Wales. I gave her your contact details in case she had to leave there before the house is ready. I also said that if she is out of pocket from leaving without notice I would see her right."

Angelo nodded. "OK, no problem. If she gets in contact, I'll let you know. Was Natasha OK about the changes you made?"

"I think so," I said cautiously. "I think she got the fact that it will be our home. Her ideas for the bedroom in the house were great, but I think we'd prefer to be a bit further from the front door – the corner room works better for us as we can just walk out into the walled garden if we want to AND it's next door to the music room, so if one of us gets an idea in the middle of the night we can just go through and play with it."

Davey snorted and muttered something about 'ideas in the middle of the night' but I ignored him.

Angelo smiled, happy that we seemed to be settling down after the long months of misery.

"The corner room is also more private – there's a good buffer-zone between it and anyone else's accommodation."

Chapter 34:

Several months later, Old Kennel Farm. Misty

Now that we knew what was ahead, the work seemed to move agonisingly slowly, despite our best efforts not to upset either Natasha or Shay. To be fair, the delays were never their fault, but that is little consolation when you are living in one room at a pub, knowing that less than half a mile away across the fields you own a large property with (potentially) every facility you could possibly want.

We tried not to keep going up to the house to see what was going on, and generally limited ourselves to visiting once a week unless Shay or 'Tash actually asked us to give input on site. Frustratingly the studio was actually completed several weeks before any of the accommodation, the only upside to that being that at least it meant we could go up there and do something useful - and also see what was going on - without feeling that we were breathing down their necks.

Davey suggested that we could camp out in the rest area of the barn but, although there were shower and toilet facilities, there was nothing other than a microwave and a kettle in the way of a kitchen. We could of course have slept there and gone to the pub for our meals, but that seemed like the worst of both worlds.

While we were waiting to move in we made full use of the airfield and Gerry taught me to drive. Davey had tried, but did not have a lot of patience and often gave directions which confused me. Gerry had realised that the constant aggravation was likely to cause problems between us and stepped in, offering to teach me himself.

He proved to be a natural instructor and, when I finally got a test date through, I passed first time, despite still being, if not a nervous driver, then certainly on the cautious end of the scale. I celebrated by buying myself a small Peugeot as a runabout, as I found Davey's Volvo estate far too big for just going into Oxford or the nearby village, although later on I used the Volvo if I wanted to take the dogs anywhere so that I could pen them into the boot area.

Finally, though, the day came when the kennel rooms were completed, and we were able to move in to one of the rooms there. Grace had been in contact via Angelo a number of times, anxious that we should not forget her, and, the moment we said that we were able to move in, she arrived with all her worldly goods squashed into an elderly Renault 5.

"Grace! Lovely to see you – you're looking so well!"

"It's lovely to see you too! I've been bored stiff staying with my sister – it was lovely for a week or so, but after that I hardly knew what to do with myself! I'm so happy to be here – what a lovely part of the world too!"

I helped her carry her bags into the kennel room furthest from that occupied by us. Although the rooms were well built and had been made as soundproof as possible, I didn't want to inadvertently embarrass her.

I then took her on a tour of the rest of the property, showing her the room we had designated as hers which was still to be decorated and, far more important in her eyes, the farmhouse-style kitchen and utility room.

"It's lovely Micky! A lot of thought has gone into all this, and the gardens will be wonderful when they're established."

"It's a bit smaller than you're used to…"

"That's all to the good, lovey. At Sparrows Hill I had an army of staff!"

"Grace, I promise you that if you need more help, we'll get it for you. We've already been promised someone to do the gardens and a cleaner – you must say what other help you need. As far as we're concerned, the most important thing is our meals and someone to keep everything running smoothly. I've never had to manage a house before – my flat was just a dumping ground for the few weeks I was at home and Davey had a wife to look after everything. We won't be having endless dinner parties or anything like that, and if we do entertain, we can get caterers in – Sylvia at the pub does all that sort of stuff. If anyone comes to use the studio and stays in the kennel rooms they have the option of looking after themselves or paying for stuff to be brought in."

Grace patted my cheek gently.

"Don't you fret! I'm not going to turn tail and run. I'm just so glad you helped me get away from that place, and that you've given me a home and a job. You're nice boys, and I'm happy to be here and look after you both."

"You must talk to 'Tash about your room – she has a colour scheme etc. in mind but if you don't like it you must say so. The same goes for the furniture – it's your room! The kitchen's almost finished but again, if you think there's something that doesn't work for you or anything else you would like, just say so – better now than in a year's time."

She nodded gratefully.

"I can see that working here is going to be much easier than I'm used to!" she smiled, a little tearfully. "Now, where's your other half?"

With perfect timing (as you would expect from a drummer) the Volvo crunched onto the gravel in front of the house and Davey leapt out, running up and hugging Grace almost in one fluid movement.

"Thank God! Are we pleased to see you!!" I hid a grin behind my hand. "I can't tell you how tired we are of eating at the pub – and Micky can't cook…"

"Neither can you!" I retorted. "You've never had to live on your own…"

"How often did you cook when you did?"

I shrugged.

"Not that often, admittedly."

That was slightly economical with the truth. Alex was actually quite an accomplished cook and had taught me the basics of a number of things – enough to at least attempt most dishes – but it had become a habit to eat at the 'Swords and the very basic facilities in the kennel suite did not really provide for cooking more than a fry- up or microwaving something pre-prepared. The virtual completion of the main kitchen had enabled us to send for Grace, so for the time being the baton had passed me by.

Grace was smiling tearfully at the pair of us.

"I'm so happy to be here!" she said again.

She reached into her bag and handed me three videotapes.

"I think you should have these now…"

I stared at her.

"Are these what I think they are?"

She nodded.

"I didn't want to post them to you in case they went astray. I could have given them to Mr. Daranda, but I wasn't sure how far you trust him…"

We both went to hug her at the same time, colliding and crushing her between us, causing a protest.

"Oh Grace, I love you more than ever!!" Davey gasped. "These are definitely the originals?"

She nodded again.

"Oh yes, I managed to grab them without anyone knowing just as I was leaving."

Davey grinned. "We gather that Sir Peter wasn't too happy about us stealing you – wonder how much of that was to do with the tapes going missing too? Oh Grace, you have made me very happy! I was having nightmares about them turning up in the middle of my divorce hearing!"

"I was in two minds about whether to destroy them, but I thought you ought to do that yourselves so that you know they have definitely gone."

"If you had told us you had done it, that would have been good enough." I said gently. "After our stay at Sparrows Hill I don't trust anyone except Davey and you and possibly Angelo!"

Having helped Grace to unload her car we left her to talk to Shay and 'Tash about finishing the kitchen and her room in the main house and retreated to the studio which was fast becoming our refuge during the day. Fortunately, this week, we had it to ourselves.

"How are we going to obliterate those tapes? Put them through the shredder?"

"Put them in the incinerator would probably be the best plan, but we ought to check them over first." Davey grinned.

I pulled a face.

"Really? Fancy ourself as a porn star do we?"

He grinned again.

"Just to make sure it's the genuine article…"

"We can't very well run them in the kennel sitting room – Grace might wander in!"

"There's a video machine upstairs in the rest area here – we can go up there later when the builders etc. have gone home."

We took Grace to the 'Swords for dinner to introduce her to the locals and to prevent her from insisting on cooking for us after her long drive. Having seen her safely to her room, we headed for the studio and climbed the spiral staircase to the rest area. The tapes were carefully labelled with the dates. Davey fed the first one into the machine and switched on the screen.

The cameras had obviously been set up to record when they detected movement, and ran from us entering the room that first evening after having dined in the downstairs dining-room.

We'd both had a fair bit to drink and I watched through my fingers as Davey had gently pulled me into his arms before kissing me passionately and undressing me. He'd wasted no time in taking me from behind. We'd fallen onto the bed and I was glad that the film had no soundtrack as I could see that I'd almost certainly been making a fair amount of noise.

"OK" I said, not wanting to watch any further. "That one's obviously the right tape – switch it off!"

"You don't have to watch if you don't want to. Go to bed – I'll be over when I've checked the other two."

I realised that he was set on watching them through, but I'd seen more than I wanted to already and took myself off to bed.

By the time I'd showered and got into bed he'd arrived. He came and sat on the edge of the bed. He seemed more subdued than when I'd left the barn.

"What's up?"

He bit his lip and I realised that he was close to tears.

"Davey – what is it?"

"When we – when I – am I hurting you?"

"Of course not! Why?"

"You've only ever hurt me once," I said truthfully "- the night you came back from Manchester when Tina had whacked you with the bottle. I knew you couldn't help it, so I didn't say anything at the time. It wasn't that long after I'd been attacked – the day Andy died. That's probably the only reason it hurt as much as it did."

"You've been attacked again since then – not that long before Sparrows Hill – are you sure I didn't hurt you – you really do look as though it's hurting on the tape?"

"I promise you I was fine. I was probably coming – a different kind of agony altogether!"

I managed a grin to try to reassure him.

"For heaven's sake don't worry about it – there's nothing more guaranteed to ruin our love life! Tomorrow we'll burn the beastly things!

I slipped my free hand behind his head and pulled him down so that I could kiss him, and then pulled him all the way down so that he was lying across me. He tried to pull away from me, but I knew by now exactly what to do to make sure that he couldn't get away, and I rolled over onto him, pinning him down…

Chapter 35:

Late 1985, Old Kennel Farm. Misty

Eventually the house was completed and suddenly, after months of tripping over builders, decorators and sundry contractors, the place felt very empty with just the three of us there. We held a house-warming party – two in fact – one for the locals and one for our mates, both catered for by Sylvia and her seemingly endless extended family.

At the first party, attended by the usual suspects from the 'Swords plus Shay and his lads, we were presented with an array of house-warming presents, the highlight being a pair of Jack Russell puppies from Eddie-at-the-farm, which I promptly named Pipkin and Pipsqueak (who quickly became known as Pip and Sprout). Davey was less than thrilled about them, and I had to agree to them being housed in the boot room at night rather than in our bedroom. When they were tiny I thought this was extremely heartless but I suppose, realistically, it was a sensible move, especially later on when two expanded to four and subsequently a fluid population which, by the time Sal and Danny were able to visit, had peaked at six, plus the cats which had migrated from the stable yard, and the flock of bantams which lived in the courtyard garden (on the grounds that it was more fox-proof than the walled garden and also that there was less chance of them finding their way into the house via our bedroom). The bantams had also been a house-warming present, this time from Gerry and Sylvia.

The second party, attended by most of our muso-mates, plus 'Tash and her crew (who had blagged an invitation to it on the grounds that they were artists not builders), Angelo, Nat and Alex (who seemed somewhat bemused in the bohemian company but, by the end of the evening, had formed lasting friendships with several of our more cerebral friends) was a somewhat bigger affair and far less well-behaved, due to large quantities of wacky-baccy and possibly other dubious substances circulating. Fortunately, being so far off the beaten-track, we were unlikely to attract the attention of the Oxfordshire Constabulary and everyone seemed to have a good time in a very relaxed atmosphere.

The party had more or less dispersed by 4 a.m., those who had decided to stay over being housed in the kennel rooms or, for the overspill, in the rest area in the barn. Fortunately, the weather was relatively warm for the time of year and the barn was well-insulated to keep the acoustics stable, as well as for the well-being of the recording equipment and any instruments which might be in there.

Chapter 36:

1986, Old Kennel Farm/Manchester. Misty

Davey and I were in London overnight when the universe suddenly shifted again. We had gone up by train for a meeting with the record company. Paddy was also there but it was one of those frustrating chicken/egg arguments – we had new material, but the record company were not interested unless we could tour/promote it, and we were reluctant to go through the exercise of trying to replace Andy without some sort of new deal/plan to offer as a carrot. We already knew that we would have difficulties putting a tour together without a new package to promote – and so it went on round.

We met Alex and Nat for dinner at a small, fashionable restaurant in the West End. The food was good, and I think we both enjoyed being with two such articulate and congenial people, and we sat for a long time after finishing our food just chatting. Nat would have been happy to drive us home, as by then it was too late to get a train, but we decided to stay overnight in a hotel near to Paddington, so that it was mid-morning by the time we got back to the farm.

Grace greeted us at the door. I went through and released the dogs (who were nearly hysterical at hearing my voice), so I didn't immediately register what Grace was saying to Davey, who suddenly vanished into the office.

"Where's he gone in such a hurry?"

"He's gone to ring his mother – she phoned yesterday evening."

I shrugged. Davey was in fairly regular contact with her, but it was usually left for him to phone her.

"Have you had breakfast?"

I grinned. "Yes, of course – can you imagine him going anywhere without eating first?"

I headed for the music room, Grace promising to bring coffee shortly. About ten minutes later Davey joined me, looking serious.

"What's up? Is your mam OK?"

"She's fine." He hesitated. "Micky, your father died yesterday…"

"So? What has that got to do with me?"

"*Micky*…the funeral will be next week. Your mam has asked for you to be there…"

I shook my head.

"I'm not going. He made it quite clear that I was no son of his. After all he did, I don't feel that I owe him anything."

"OK, - you're not going for his sake. Your mam wants you to be there – you'll be doing it for her…"

Because my parents had come as a package, I had not been in contact with either of them since I'd left home nearly ten years before. I suppose I'd known that sooner or later something would happen but, with everything else that had been going on in my life, I'd buried that thought.

They'd not been in contact during my nightmare, nor in relation to Davey's split with Tina and the ultimate reason for it, even though they must have been made aware of it. They'd obviously known about all those things, but I'd heard nothing, not even third hand via Paddy or Davey's mam.

"I've told Mam that we'll go. You don't have to go to the house – you don't even need to speak to your family if you don't want to, but you must be there…We can stay with my mam…"

"No. IF we go, we'll find a hotel."

I found myself caving in. I didn't want to go. I knew that the funeral would be at St. Michaels, the church next door to the school which held such bitter memories for me – the very last place I wanted to revisit, particularly now that I was rebuilding my life and things had seemed to be improving – I had Davey, we had the farm, Grace, the dogs, our local friends…

The funeral was at the end of the following week. We drove up the night before, even though we could easily have got there in time for the Mass – I think Davey thought that I might manage to delay our journey somehow…

We stayed in the nearest decent hotel so that we could get to and from the church in the shortest possible time. The church was already quite full when we arrived the following morning, but the ushers obviously recognised me, and we were escorted to the second row, so that I was sitting almost directly behind my mother, who was sandwiched between various uncles and aunts on both sides of the family.

I was already a bundle of nerves – the very fact of having to wear a suit for the first time since appearing in court had been enough to nearly tip me over the edge. My dark suit had perished when I was attacked at the prison and I had refused to buy another simply for a funeral I had no wish to attend, so I was wearing a mid-grey suit, white shirt and black tie – another cause for discomfort. Davey had given me a reassuring grin when I had emerged suited and booted.

"You look gorgeous!"

"Well I don't feel it! I feel ready for the hangman!"

We took our seats and I knelt briefly to pray – since Portugal I had started going to Mass locally, either in Bicester or Kidlington or, less often, in Oxford itself – not regularly, but every so often when I remembered that it was Sunday. Occasionally Davey would come with me but, more often than not, he would use it as an excuse for a couple more hours in bed.

I sat back and cautiously looked round to see if I recognised anyone. The uncles and aunts were easy enough, although I wasn't entirely sure who was who – there were too many of them and, not having seen them for so long, the ageing process had made them less distinctive than I remembered.

A number of people were staring at us, and I wondered whether this was due to fame or infamy – were we 'His son, the pop star/musician' or were we 'His son and his gay lover' or, worse still perhaps, 'His son the convicted killer'?

Mam's brother, Uncle Sean, who was sitting on one side of her, had turned round to see who it was and had whispered urgently in her ear. She briefly turned her head and our eyes met. She was pale and had aged a lot since I had last seen her. I couldn't read her expression, but I thought there was perhaps the ghost of a smile. Uncharitably I wondered whether that was because she had won in getting me to be there…

The priest who took the Mass was probably around my age, so had obviously not been there when I was at school. He spoke well and had presumably known my father for quite some time. I wondered what he would have thought had he known of the brutality I had suffered…

We reached the Giving of the Peace. Mam turned round and briefly took my hand, but the uncles and aunts did not. The guy next to me clasped my hand and then hugged me warmly and I wondered whether this was for my benefit or whether he was making a point to someone else.

I went up for communion and could feel eyes boring into my back from all around, but I was in full communion with the Church, and my conscience was clear.

The Mass ended and the coffin was carried out. The Church no longer had its own burial ground, and the interment was to take place at the municipal cemetery a mile or so away. I had not intended to go, but the guy who had hugged me said quietly "I'm your cousin Joe – Sean's son. Would you like a lift to the cemetery?"

I hesitated and looked at Davey who said "Thanks – that's kind of you."

I shot him a look, but he pretended not to catch my eye. We climbed into Joe's XR3i and he pulled out to join the end of the cortege.

"Thanks for coming." he said. "When Dad said that Auntie Ann hoped you would come, I thought you would probably bottle out – it means a lot that you're here."

"I didn't want to come." I said quietly, feeling that honesty was the best policy. "Davey made me."

"It's brave of you, after all that's happened. I don't suppose your dad was much different to mine. He certainly made his feelings clear about you and Davey!"

"I bet he did!"

Somehow, I didn't feel uncomfortable with the conversation, and it was only a mild surprise when he confessed that he was also gay, although he didn't have a regular boyfriend. Uncle Sean had thrown him out when he first came out, but had since relented and allowed him back home. I wondered how far the spirit of liberalism had permeated the rest of the family…

We arrived at the cemetery and made our way across the grass to the area where some of the family were already at rest. The priest read the burial rite, and we took it in turns to scatter a few ounces of soil into the grave. No one else spoke to us and I intended that we should leave then and go back to the hotel to change and then drive home but, before we could escape, Mam took my arm.

"Micky…please come back to the wake…"

I shook my head.

"If you won't come to the wake, please come and see me tomorrow, before you go home?"

Her voice shook with emotion and I found myself nodding reluctantly. She pressed a piece of paper into my hand.

"That's the address – you may not know we've moved?" She turned to Davey. "You will make sure he comes, won't you?"

He nodded. She patted his arm and then turned back, to be engulfed by the crowd of her brothers and sisters and the various in-laws.

Joe offered to take us back to the hotel, but Davey assured him that it was comfortably within walking distance.

"You could still change your minds and come to the wake?" He said hopefully.

"I think Micky's probably had as much as he can cope with." Davey said gently. "Nothing personal – but I suspect you're probably one of the few who will be there who would give us the time of day! We'll go and see his mam tomorrow like she asked, but I think we both need to go home now."

"Manchester's still your home!"

Davey shook his head.

"Nah. Not anymore. You'll have to come and visit. It's out in the middle of nowhere – you won't find any wild parties or anything – but we have everything we need and *real* friends! That's where we belong now."

I'd never heard him say how he felt about things before, and I was surprised at just how much feeling he had expressed. I squeezed his hand, a wave of love flooding through me.

We said goodbye to Joe, having exchanged addresses, and went back to the hotel and up to our room. I shed the suit and pulled on my jeans and a clean shirt. Davey handed me a drink from the mini-bar.

"You looked very sexy in that suit!" he said, a twinkle in his eyes.

I pulled a face.

"It reminds me too much of going to court!" I said, my voice catching.

"You still looked good. It's a sort of dichotomy – is that the right word? The severity of the suit – and the type of people who wear suits – y'know, bankers, accountants, lawyers and stuff – against the innocence of your angelic looks…"

I snorted.

"Innocence? When was I last innocent? Quite apart from everything that's happened to me – I've spent the last twenty-odd years trying to get laid…"

"You still look like a choirboy, especially in a white shirt."

He took a step closer to me, took the glass from my hands and wrapped his arms round me.

"You did good!" He said gently. "That wasn't a good atmosphere in church, but you kept your head held high and you didn't let it get to you - AND you went up to communion! I was really proud of you! I expect they're all talking about us right now – wonder what they're saying?"

We overslept the following morning. The bedside phone rang – it was Mam making sure that we had not sneaked off without visiting her.

"Sorry – I think we were both really tired. We'll be with you shortly. We'll take you out to lunch – your choice."

Much to Davey's disgust we skipped breakfast and went straight out to the suburb where she now lived. The property was a 1920s bungalow, perched on a slight ridge above the road – a far cry from the red-brick terrace I'd grown up in. I was slightly taken aback when Davey's mam opened the door.

She smiled at me. "Annie was worried you weren't coming – I'm so glad you have!"

Davey pushed past me and hugged her.

"Ouch! Be careful you great ruffian – I'm getting old you know!"

"You're coming out to lunch with us!"

"Are you sure? I don't want to gate-crash…"

"Of course you must come!" I said, anxious to even things up a bit.

She smiled and patted my cheek.

"You were always a kind lad, Micky. Thank you for making my baby boy so happy…"

Davey spluttered.

"Baby boy! I'm thirty-three now, Mam!"

"You're still my youngest, so you'll always be my baby boy!"

Mam appeared behind her shoulder and gently but firmly moved both mother and son out of her way. She looked me in the eye, gauging perhaps whether I was feeling friendly. I forced a lukewarm smile.

"Thank you for coming!" She said quietly. "I wasn't sure you would. And thank you for coming yesterday - Mag said that Davey would make you come, but I wasn't sure…"

"I didn't want to. You know how Dad treated me…"

I heard her sob and then suddenly she was in my arms. For a moment I froze, but then instinctively tightened my arms round her.

Davey took his mother outside, leaving us together. I could see that the sitting room was through the doorway beside us, and I guided her through and sat her down on the sofa, sitting beside her. She clung to me, sobbing as though her heart would break and I began to worry that she would make herself ill.

"Mam…"

I didn't know what to say, and tried desperately to collect my thoughts.

"Mam, please, you'll make yourself ill!"

She took a gulp of air.

"Micky, I *hated* the way Joseph treated you! I tried everything I could to make him stop, but there was nothing…"

"You could have left him!" I said bitterly.

"And gone where? I had no money – he wouldn't let me work – he said it would make him look a failure if I went out to work when we only had the one child to support. I couldn't go to my family – they had all they could do to support themselves - and there was no social security for single parents in those days. I couldn't afford a solicitor and even if I had gone to court he would never have paid up! He used to hit me too, you know…"

I didn't. It had never occurred to me that he might hit her as well. I had always assumed it was me he hated…

"I didn't know. I'm sorry." I said, meaning it.

"When he started hitting you, I used to try to make him stop. I learned the hard way not to defy him. I thought if I kept him sweet he'd not be so hard on you – I don't know whether it made any difference. When – when Father Flanagan – did what he did - I tried to make him go to the police. He went crazy – knocked me across the room – told me if I ever said anything to anyone, he'd kill you and me too…"

I shivered, realising for the first time the reality of the situation and what kind of man he had been.

"I'm sorry." I said again. "OK, he's gone now. We'll have to start over. Get to know each other properly."

She hugged me tightly.

"I must have seemed a terrible mother to you! I loved you so much – you looked like a little angel with your blond, curly hair – and you sang like one too! Micky, I can never make up to you for what you suffered when you were little, but I hope that we can at least be friends now…"

Chapter 37:

1987, Old Kennel Farm. Misty

Davey's divorce from Tina took an agonisingly long time to go through. The sticking point was access to the children – Tina was adamant that she didn't want them to have any contact with either of us. I had (with a heavy heart) offered to be away from home whenever it was Davey's turn to have them to stay, but even that was seemingly unacceptable, and Davey had instructed Alex to go all-out to get full, joint custody.

By now the children were fourteen and twelve and the judge had had the wisdom to see them in chambers and find out what they themselves wanted. Both had said unequivocally that they missed Davey and wanted to spend time with him.

That seemed to nail it and the divorce was finalised – the children would continue to live with Tina during the week in school term-time, but would come to us at weekends and during the holidays, except when we were touring - assuming we ever managed to resume our career.

Alex brought Davey home after the final ruling. He stayed to eat with us, but the mood was subdued, and I quickly realised that Davey was drinking far too much.

I walked Alex out to his car. He said quietly "I suspect it's not over yet – Tina will probably not comply with the court order and Davey will need to go back to court to enforce it."

I nodded. Alex moved in closer, his lips hovering just above mine. I was trembling, worried by his closeness. Part of me was still a little in love with him – our relationship had ended so abruptly when I was arrested that he was unfinished business, but at the same time I was now so deeply involved with Davey that I couldn't bear the thought of hurting him in any way.

Alex cupped my face in his hands and kissed me gently, just as he had that very first morning. He slipped his tongue between my teeth, gently pushing me back against the car. I tried to duck under his arm but was trapped by his weight and my own weakness. He breathed my name.

"No! Please Alex…!" but things had gone too far, and it ended messily.

"I'm sorry!"

He sounded genuinely remorseful.

"I thought perhaps you still felt something for me?"

I bit my lip, blinking back tears.

"I do!" I whispered shakily, "But I love Davey so much…"

I shook my head.

"I *was* in love with you, but that was a million years ago now, before everything went wrong. You'll always be very special to me – you were my first proper lover and it was – it was more than wonderful, but we can't go back… you have Nat now…"

Alex bowed his head and nodded slightly, stirring the gravel with the toe of his shoe.

"Yes, I have Nat now. But that's a different matter entirely! We suit each other, it works, but I don't think either of us is in love, or necessarily even that we love each other, for that matter. You were something very precious to me and I wish things hadn't ended the way they did!"

I tried to make some reply but couldn't get the words out and ended up pulling away from him and stumbling back into the house.

Grace was waiting by the door. "Are you alright? Micky?"

I shook my head. She took me into the kitchen and sat me down in the corner, pulling up another chair.

"It was Sir Alex, wasn't it?" she demanded. "The 'Mr. X' who gave evidence for you?"

I nodded, trying to hold back the tears.

"Oh Micky!"

The compassion in her voice tipped me over the edge and I dissolved into floods of tears. She took my hands in hers and held them tightly and then, when the tears kept coming, put her arms round me and held me until I managed to stop.

"Now," she said firmly, "I've made up the bed in the guest room – you'd better sleep in there tonight. Davey's drunk far too much and I'm worried that he'll take it out on you…"

"No! No, I need to be with him!"

"But lovey, he might hurt you! I know he won't mean to, but…"

"I don't care! I said bitterly. "If he does, it's no more than I deserve! Oh Grace, I'm so confused – I've loved Davey ever since I can remember, but I never thought we'd be together. I loved Alex so much, and then it all went so horribly wrong and I lost him but got Davey instead…"

Grace put her finger to my lips.

"Sshh! I'm pretty sure Davey's out for the count, but don't even say it! You're much better off with him! You love each other – proper love - even when things aren't going well for you. You can't turn the clock back – things have moved on and you should count your blessings. Davey needs you now, just as you have needed him, and will do again."

She hugged me tightly.

"Now!" she said, "I'm going to make you a hot drink and then you must go and try to get some sleep. I still think you should go to the guest room but if you want to be with him maybe that's what's right for you."

When I reached the bedroom, Davey was sprawled untidily across the bed, still fully clothed. With difficulty I managed to undress him and move him enough to be able to squeeze in beside him. I snuggled up to him, but he didn't show any sign of waking, although he was breathing noisily so I knew he was reasonably OK.

When I woke it was daylight outside. Davey was in the bathroom, throwing up. I went in – he was kneeling over the toilet, holding his hair back with one hand while the other clutched at the cistern.

"Are you OK?"

He managed a hollow laugh.

"No!"

I draped a bath-sheet round his shoulders and padded out to pull on some clothes, before making my way back through to the kitchen. Grace was breakfasting, the dogs visible through the other door, scrapping over their own breakfasts.

"How is he?"

"Suffering!" I grinned.

I filled a jug with some strong coffee and loaded it onto a tray with orange juice and dry toast. Grace handed me a pack of paracetamol. I went back into the bedroom. Davey had emerged from the bathroom and was slumped on the edge of the bed, his face colourless, skin clammy. I put the tray down next to him and popped three tablets from their foils. I handed them to him with the glass of juice.

He groaned.

"I don't think I can swallow them!"

"Yes, you can. Come on – you'll feel better when you've had something. There can't be anything else to come up!"

"Yes, mother!"

He put the pills in his mouth, took a swig from the glass and swallowed noisily, gagging but managing to get them down. He drank the rest of the juice and I poured some coffee. He pulled a face – normally I drank coffee while he stuck to tea, but this time he was desperate enough to drink it black. Finally he ate some toast.

"How much did I drink last night?" He demanded.

I shrugged.

"No idea. I haven't checked the bottles. Grace was sufficiently worried to try to get me to sleep in the guest room, and you didn't wake up when I undressed you, so you must have had a fair bit…"

He groaned again.

"Why did you let me?!"

I shook my head.

"I didn't notice how much you had had. I went out to see Alex off and when I came back in you had already gone to bed." I said carefully, being economical with the truth.

I wasn't about to tell him about Alex's pass, nor the time I'd spent with Grace…

He turned to me and took my hand. The clamminess was wearing off, and he was beginning to return to his normal colour.

"I wish I could marry *you*…" he said quietly, "but we can still commit to each other…"

"I thought we already were?" I said.

I could tell that he was serious, and I found myself trembling.

"I mean something more – more visible. I want to take you into Oxford and we'll buy rings. Does that sound OK?"

He looked anxiously into my eyes.

"Yes!"

I felt a shiver of excitement.

"Yes please!"

It wasn't the thought of the ring itself – God knows Alex had bought me enough jewellery to satisfy anyone other than Elizabeth Taylor. It was the symbolism, the public acknowledgement of us as a couple. Civil Partnerships were still 18 years away, the concept of gay marriage just a pipedream.

Davey had, until then, been wary of making any overt display of our relationship, partly so as not to inflame the situation with Tina. Now, apparently, the Decree Absolute had drawn a line under that obstacle, and he felt secure enough to display our love to the world.

He still wasn't exactly functioning, so I found clothes for him and helped him dress. We went through to the kitchen. Grace looked up as we entered and smiled slightly when she realised that Davey was at least on his feet.

"We're going into Oxford. Is there anything you need?"

She shook her head.

"What about lunch?"

"We'll get something in town. Otherwise it'll be late by the time we get back."

"Right you are. Do you want anything special for dinner?"

Davey answered before I could.

"Yes please – something special!"

He exchanged glances with Grace, but I was in a world of my own and didn't pick up on the significance.

I drove – Davey would still have been well over the limit. Luckily it wasn't term-time and we managed to park fairly easily. He led the way to the Covered Market – he seemed to know exactly where he was going and took me into one of the smaller units, tucked away in a corner.

The girl behind the old-fashioned mahogany counter was petite, her long blonde hair elaborately braided and tied with multi-coloured ribbons. She looked up from the piece of jewellery she was working on and, obviously recognising Davey, greeted him warmly.

"Hi, I was beginning to think…"

Davey smiled.

"Things took a bit longer than I had hoped. Are they ready?"

She nodded and turned to unlock the heavy antique safe behind her. She took out a single leather box and handed it to him. His hands trembled as he opened it and I gasped as I craned my neck round his shoulder.

The box contained two rings, identical in design, but one slightly larger and wider than the other. The rings were made of yellow, white and rose gold, ornately chased and fashioned into a design of rose-gold hearts, entwined with white-gold ivy on a black-enamelled, wide yellow gold band. I had never seen anything similar and was amazed that human hands could produce anything so exquisite.

"They're beautiful!"

Davey smiled at me.

"No more than you!" he said softly.

I had tears pouring down my face as he took the smaller ring and slipped it onto my wedding finger. It fitted perfectly – he'd obviously used some subterfuge to get the size right.

I took the other ring from the box and slipped it onto his hand. He grasped my fingers and raised them to his lips, oblivious to the jeweller who was quite misty-eyed herself by now.

I turned to her.

"Did you design them?"

"Let's say it was a collaboration. I made some suggestions, but your…other half already had a pretty good idea of what he wanted. I just advised him what was possible. The design will eventually wear down, but generally it will just look better and better. They're quite heavy duty."

"They're amazing! I've never seen anything remotely similar. Where did you train?"

"I did an apprenticeship in London, but I've also travelled a lot, looking at different techniques around the world. Some of what has gone into your rings owes *homage* to some time I spent in Russia – the Faberge legacy."

"Do I owe you anything extra?"

She shook her head.

"No, you were more than generous in what you offered when you commissioned them."

"Thank you! I think you can see for yourself that we both love them…"

We both kissed her goodbye and she hugged us in return.

I suggested that we should have lunch nearby, but Davey neatly ducked that.

"No, I want to get my hair cut."

"Don't you dare!"

I loved his long, thick, glossy, brown hair. I loved the feel of it on my skin, I loved running my fingers through it...

"I want it a bit shorter and more styled. That was the old me – this is our new life and I want it to be different."

I could see that he wasn't going to change his mind and, as I didn't want to spoil this magical day with a row, allowed him to lead the way to the side street where our hairdresser had his salon.

As we went in, Carlo was blow-drying an expensive-looking lady of a certain age, but he quickly put the dryer down and hurried over.

"Darlings – how are you!! Micky you look fabuloso!!"

I waved my ring finger at him and he pounced.

"Oh my bambino! Wonderful, wonderful!!"

He turned to Davey.

"It's about time! At last, you make an honest man of him!"

"My divorce was only finalised yesterday!" Davey protested. "I couldn't do anything before that or Tina would have screwed me for every penny AND barred me from ever seeing my kids again!"

Carlo waved that aside.

"Micky, I refuse to touch your hair – not for another month!"

"I want you to cut my hair, Carlo!"

Davey made a scissors gesture with his fingers. Carlo's eyebrows went so high they disappeared under his bleached-blond fringe.

"Cut your hair! But you never let me cut your hair! You mean *trim*?"

"No, cut! About six inches off the back and layered at the sides, but not too much or Micky will kill me..."

Ignoring the still-damp, previous client, Carlo sat Davey down and swept a nylon cape around his shoulders. I could hardly bear to watch as he ruthlessly chopped squarely across the back of Davey's very long hair. He then carefully sectioned and layered the sides and fringe, combing and sweeping it round until it hung loosely around his face and shoulders in a glorious, glossy curtain. I had to admit it looked one hundred per cent better and made Davey look a lot younger.

"There! Is that what you wanted?"

"Absolutely what I wanted! You're a genius!"

"But of course!"

Davey handed over his AmEx card to cover the very immodest cost of the genius' work. As we left I could hear Carlo making soothing noises to the, by now, totally furious but bemused lady client.

We headed back to the car.

"I just want to pop in to the 'Swords on the way home."

"Why? We've not had lunch yet."

"Not very hungry – still a bit hungover."

I drove homewards and turned into the lane that ran parallel to our access. The pub carpark looked quite full, but I managed to squeeze into the one remaining space.

Considering the number of cars outside there didn't seem to be many people in the bar. Gerry looked up from his crossword and grinned.

"Look who's here! Bit quiet in here today, as you can see. I should go through to the other bar – think there are a few people you know in there."

Still unsuspecting, I led the way through.

The lounge bar was festooned with streamers and a banner which read 'Congratulations M&D'. The banquetting table was laden with food, and a quick glance round told me that this was far from being a spur of the moment thing and must have been planned well in advance. As well as our local friends, Grace, Paddy, Angelo, Nat and Alex were there along with a number of other close friends from the music industry.

Sylvia came towards us with glasses of champagne. She patted my cheek affectionately.

"Your face is a picture!"

I shook my head, seeing everything through a mist of tears.

"I had no idea!"

Davey had his arm round me, gently rubbing my shoulder. He twisted his head and kissed me gently on the lips which earned a big "Aahhh!" from the assembled company. I buried my face in his shoulder, suddenly feeling ridiculously shy, especially for someone used to showing off in front of hundreds, if not thousands or even tens of thousands of people.

The rest of the afternoon and evening passed in a haze. I drank rather too much champagne, the rings were inspected and much admired, as was Davey's new haircut.

Around six o'clock Gerry sidled up to us rather sheepishly.

"I don't suppose there's any chance of you giving us a few songs...?"

I exchanged glances with Davey. We hadn't performed in public since before my arrest, although obviously we had carried on singing and making music at home. We hadn't actually made a conscious decision to stop performing, but our agent had made it clear that, while our records were still selling steadily - even the new material we had been putting out - promoters and venue management had indicated that they were still unwilling to take the risk on booking us, both from the perspective of whether they could sell enough tickets but also whether, in those less-enlightened times, it might provoke trouble from anti-gay protestors. There was also the as-yet unaddressed problem that we were short of a lead guitarist, as we had never got round to replacing Andy.

This wasn't a problem when recording – I was perfectly capable of supplying lead, rhythm or any other type of guitar track - but obviously on stage this was not going to work. We had also put out material using guest musicians but, again, we could not expect our friends to trek along on tour with us.

Davey looked at me intensely.

"How d'you feel about it? These are all our friends here – I'm sure they'll help out. Paddy's here..."

"But we've not rehearsed anything…" I said doubtfully. "Besides which I'm pissed!"

He grinned.

"Well that won't be the first time!"

"Our gear is all at home…"

"No, it isn't, it's here – Paddy fetched it earlier."

I realised that I had been well and truly stitched up. I sighed and gestured submission. Gerry grinned and gave a thumbs up.

The pub had its own reception room with a small stage at one end. Everyone drifted through and Davey, Paddy and I took our places on the platform and had a quick, whispered consultation about what we would play.

My legs were shaking, and someone got me a bar stool to perch on.

I picked up my acoustic guitar and nervously picked out the opening notes to '*Misty Blue*' – the way we always opened a show. It sounded odd without the lead guitar part, and I quickly changed to finger-picking the chords to make a fuller sound. I realised that Davey and Paddy had not joined in but were leaving me to carry the haunting song by myself. You could have heard a pin drop, but when I ended it the room erupted and I suddenly felt totally at home again.

I then switched to my Les Paul and went straight into 'Rock'n'Roll Gipsy', one of the first numbers I had written, and which had become our first self-penned hit. With this much rockier number Davey and Paddy were right behind me, and gradually our mates unpacked their guitars and took it in turns to join us, contributing their own takes on Andy's solos as we alternated between our own material and well-known standards.

I lost all sense of time and was amazed to discover that we had been playing for well over two hours. Grace had slipped off home to let the dogs out. Alex had called me over about halfway through and had handed me a sealed envelope.

"By way of an apology." he said quietly. "It was very wrong of me, what happened yesterday."

I bit my lip, tempted to tell him what to do with it but, not knowing the contents and, slightly mollified by the genuine-sounding apology, slipped it into my pocket unopened.

"I have to get back to town – there may be an important vote tonight. I've already been paged once this evening. Micky – please believe me, I hope you will be very happy. I just wish it was me!"

He dropped a kiss on my forehead in his customary way and I caught the familiar waft of cologne.

"Maybe we can talk sometime? I promise to behave myself!"

I nodded, unable to make any sensible reply, and then he'd gone. Davey got up from his drum stool and came over to me.

"What was that about?"

I shrugged helplessly.

"I'd forgotten what a turn on it is sitting behind you and watching you wiggle your ass!"

I grinned. He kissed me gently and went back to his seat.

We closed the set with '*Angel of the Morning*', a song I'd been singing at home but had not previously done live. As with '*Misty Blue*' earlier, you could have heard a pin drop and, apart from a spellbinding solo played by one of our friends, I was unaccompanied by Davey or Paddy. To say that there wasn't a dry eye in the house would be an understatement as I wrung every last drop of emotion from the beautiful words.

I didn't think any more about the envelope until after we arrived home, and even then, didn't get round to looking at it until the next morning. We were both too drunk to drive, so Paddy took us back home. A few of the others also came back to sleep in the kennel rooms rather than making their way back to London or further afield. Nat had gone back to London with Alex, and Angelo gratefully accepted our offer of one of the spare rooms in the house.

I was still on the high I always had after singing live. I don't think either of us got much sleep that night, despite the remnants of Davey's hangover from the night before.

When we eventually crawled out of bed the next morning and made our way to the kitchen for breakfast, we discovered that our guests had found their way into the dining room where Grace was providing prodigious quantities of the full English. Angelo was enjoying rubbing shoulders with some of the cream of British rock music and Paddy was winding everyone up with some of his tall tales. The entrance hall had somehow become filled with an ever-growing number of baskets of flowers which were being delivered by florists' vans from the surrounding area.

Gradually the over-nighters dispersed. Paddy had indicated that he was also going but we managed to hang onto him until there were just the three of us.

"What are we going to do?"

Davey opened the conversation without any preamble. We both knew what he was talking about, but Paddy wouldn't meet my eye.

"The way I see it we have two choices – replace Andy and go back to how things used to be or just carry on recording without playing live."

"I think we should try to replace Andy – even if we just use session men until we find someone who fits." I said, still on a high from the night before.

Paddy still wouldn't meet my eye.

"Pad? What do you think?"

There was a heavy silence. We waited and eventually he spoke.

"I – I'm not sure. I – don't – know – if – I – want – to - tour – as things are now…"

He'd said it, but I didn't want to understand what he was saying. Obviously there had been the incident way back when he'd crashed into the Chelsea bedroom and found us *in flagrante*, but that was over four years ago now. I didn't want to believe that someone who had been like family for most of my life was now unwilling to live in close proximity to us. He was staring at the floor.

Davey broke the new silence.

"Why? What's so different?"

Another pause.

"You and I used to share. We stopped that when Andy started laying into Micky – I inherited Andy. Presumably I would now have to share with the new boy or the temp or however we work it. I'm not sure I want to do that! You and Micky would be like a married couple on tour. I can't bring Jan because of the kids and school and all that – not that I'd want to…"

Davey sighed.

"Is that all? There's no reason why you can't have a room to yourself. Micky and I have always been 'tight' – writing together and all that. I thought you were trying to say that you didn't want to tour with us because we're gay, or because of the AIDS thing…"

Paddy shook his head and I heaved an inward sigh of relief.

"Look Pad, Micky and I are not Misty Blue – you're a part of it too! You get just as much input as we do. You'll have just as much of a say on who comes in on guitar and if you aren't happy then we won't go with them, it's as simple as that."

He grinned.

"I promise we'll go with the butchest, most straight guy we can find – or maybe we should get a girl on guitar – someone like Suzi…"

"No way!! It was bad enough with Andy in the band! No girls!! Can you imagine the practicalities? More to the point, can you imagine how Jan would react?!!"

The tension evaporated. Davey had handled the crisis in his usual blunt, practical way.

Paddy stayed until after the motorway rush hour would have passed. During his remaining time with us he made me promise to explore whether we could record '*Angel of the Morning*', which he predicted would be a sensational way of launching us back onto the live circuit. I wasn't entirely happy with the idea but, after he'd gone, Davey picked up where he'd left off.

"But I was pissed!" I objected. "I don't think I could sing it like that again even if I wanted to…"

"OK, we'll make sure that, whenever you sing it, you're pissed again!"

I laughed, despite my doubts. When I'd sung it the previous evening I had been singing it right from the heart to Davey. I really wasn't sure that I could reproduce that level of passion night after night. There was also the problem of the guitar solo. The night before it had been played by one of the greatest guitarists in the UK, probably in the world. He was a mate, and would almost certainly agree to play on the record, but who would be able to emulate that live?

As I was undressing that night Alex's envelope fell out of the pocket of my jeans. Davey spotted it before I did and pounced.

"It's about time you opened this!"

Reluctantly I took it from him, a little worried about what Alex might have written, but obviously I couldn't now keep it from Davey, whatever the contents.

I opened the envelope to find airline tickets and a short note written on House of Commons notepaper:

'Dear Micky and Davey, please accept this small gift as a token of my regard for you both. The air tickets are undated – all you need do is contact the airline to confirm your dates of travel and return, although you may wish to leave the return date until later. I have made similar arrangements with the Hotel Europa in Pisa for your arrival there. The Hotel will arrange for rail travel to take you on to Florence where you will have the use of my apartment for as long as you wish. Your rail warrants will also be valid for onward travel

to Venice with accommodation in an apartment off Santa Maria Formosa. The return air tickets are valid from Marco Polo. All you need do is phone my secretary, Martin [he gave the phone number] *and he will confirm the bookings for you. I hope that you will enjoy your honeymoon – my love always, Alex'*

"Bloody Hell!" Davey looked at me. "Did you know he was going to do this?!"

I shook my head, close to tears. It was typical of Alex' generosity, and I guessed had partly been prompted by his bad behaviour earlier in the week, but was also, I think, a sign of his continuing feelings for me.

"We don't have to go..." I said, worried that Davey might feel undermined by the pre-arranged itinerary.

"Are you kidding? It sounds perfect! Think of all that wonderful Italian food and wine! We've only ever seen Italy from the back of a tour-bus on an autostrada or whatever they call them out there."

I hugged him, happy that he did not seem to resent the source of the gift.

"How long d'you think we can be away?"

"As long as you like – we're not doing anything else at the moment..."

However, word of our impromptu show had quickly spread, first in the local area but, very rapidly after that, the story was picked up by the media, and we had to field enquiries from the main TV channels as well as the music- and general press. We referred everything to Benny, our agent, who immediately turned up on the doorstep to talk tactics.

Our previous recording contract had expired – our recent releases had been through our own independent label – but our former label now wanted us to re-sign with them. After a lot of discussion, we decided to go with that as they had more clout to negotiate the necessary permissions to record and release '*Angel*', which we were now realising could be pivotal to our chances of a successful re-launch.

The publicity also had another bonus: a number of guitarists contacted us to offer their services, either permanently or on a tour-by-tour basis, and we had an enjoyable time auditioning them in the studio. In practice this became a series of jam sessions, playing through a few of our better-known numbers, along with some golden oldies, to assess whether they were able to reproduce our sound and whether they would bring anything of their own to it as well. Each session finished with a shot at '*Angel*' to see if we could re-capture the magic from that special evening. A few came close, but one was head and shoulders above the rest.

Bird's career had run parallel to ours – he was of similar age, had had a similar amount of success with his previous band, and was also from the north of England, though sadly not from Manchester but from Preston, a little further north-west and nearer the coast. Happily for future relations, Paddy was more than pleased with this outcome and had been the first to suggest that we offer him the chance to join us.

He grinned.

"I don't even need to think about it! Yeah, man, when do we start?!"

"We've not confirmed anything yet. The permissions for '*Angel*' will hopefully come through soon and we can get that down and released. The record company are being a little cautious – they want to see how that sells before we start on an album, although we could work on that in the studio here. Same goes for tour dates – we have a provisional itinerary for the UK but only a quarter of the dates have been contracted so far. Are you happy to spend some time here and work on the album and maybe start rehearsing for the tour? Maybe you can discuss it with Paddy – obviously he needs to be happy with how much time he spends away from home."

Bird seemed happy with that – in fact I don't remember ever seeing him anything less than happy. His old band had been huge in the early- to mid-seventies but had faded away to nothing with the demise of the hippy era. Unlike so many others, Bird did not seem to have had any sort of drug problem and had come through relatively unscathed. He still dressed the part, but in a low-key way which was as much cowboy as hippy, and would not be too far removed from our overall image, although he had indicated that he was happy to modify both clothes and hair if we wanted. The guitars he had brought along with him were both classics and, by now, virtually priceless, and I asked if he planned to use them on tour.

"Sure man, why not? They're there to be used, not put in a museum. I don't dig cheap guitars…"

I grinned, happy that someone shared my passion for good gear.

After we'd waved both Paddy and Bird off on their separate ways home, we went back to the house and settled down comfortably in the music room.

"He didn't give any indication as to whether there is a Mrs. Bird?" Davey mused.

"Or a Mister!" I laughed. "He doesn't seem at all phased by the idea of working with a pair of…"

Davey cut in "Don't you dare! But, as you say, he seemed quite OK about everything. I suppose he does know about us?"

"He must do! C'mon, with all the publicity about me after Andy died, your divorce and our engagement party – even an old hippy couldn't have missed all of that! Besides which, wasn't he one of the ones who offered his services as a result of the last lot of publicity?"

"Yeah, think so. But he might just have heard on the grapevine that we were looking…"

"Well, now that's sorted, maybe we can do something about our 'honeymoon'?" I ventured.

Davey grinned.

"That occurred to me too. I'll phone Martin in the morning."

Chapter 38:

1987, Italy. Misty

Martin managed to get us onto an early flight to Pisa the next day, flying First Class with a small airline. We landed around midday and took a taxi the short distance to the hotel.

Our room had a ringside view of the famous Tower and its adjacent historic buildings. Although we had, quite literally, travelled the world during the band's heyday, and stayed in many top-notch hotels (and just as many really crap ones!), this one somehow seemed to be extra special – maybe something to do with the circumstances of our stay - and in the years that followed we would return there regularly whenever we wanted a few days to ourselves without imposing on the generosity of either Angelo or Alex.

We took things easy for a few days, breakfasting late before doing all the tourist things – the Tower and Baptistry etc,, the lovely old churches and designer shops in the new town the other side of the river, and just enjoying the sun while eating lazy lunches in some pavement café.

Eventually we ran out of new things to do and, with the aid of the hotel receptionist, got ourselves onto the train for Florence.

The journey was quick, and we arrived early in the afternoon and followed Alex's instructions to find the apartment, situated in a narrow street which ran roughly north/south behind Santa Maria Novella, just a short distance from the station.

The building had a narrow frontage to the street, and the apartment was on the top floor, up an amazing number of stairs, which meant that one of us had to wait downstairs with our luggage while the other struggled up, carrying as much as he could (the amount of luggage having increased exponentially due to the temptations of the designer shops in Pisa). Davey cursed the lack of a lift but, once we had finally carried the last of the bags up, we found that we rarely noticed the stairs in our general comings and goings.

The view from the windows, both front and back, was incredible and, being the top floor, the apartment also had its own roof terrace where we could sit until late at night with a drink, watching the people far below and the lights of the city and even the traffic on the river, as well as regular son-et-lumiere displays around the Duomo.

There was a little market nearby where we added to our luggage, buying an eclectic selection of items for the house – tapestry cushion covers and wall-hangings, leatherwork and other things that would enhance the period features of the older parts of the house, without clashing with Natasha's modern schemes. We also bought things which would make gifts for the children, Grace and our mothers.

Again, we spent days exploring the city, visiting the Uffizi as well as some of the more spectacular churches and yet more 'antique' markets. Occasionally Davey was enthused by a particularly elaborate interior but, in general, he preferred digging around in the markets and sampling the local food and drink. When I offered to wander round while he sat and had a coffee or glass of wine, he would summon up enough enthusiasm to assure me that, as long as I was there, he was happy, and he didn't want me to go off on my own.

I wasn't too sure whether this was as much because he didn't fancy being on his own in a foreign city, where he spoke nothing of the local language, as it was concern for my safety or (maybe) that he thought I might get up to mischief without him to keep an eye on me. If the latter, that made little sense – I could just as easily do so in Oxford as anywhere else and I had, so far, not felt the slightest bit tempted to stray- except maybe with Alex - but that was a whole different thing. Mostly I was just overwhelmingly happy to be with him, sharing our days and nights.

It seemed oddly familiar staying in the apartment – in many ways it reminded me of my flat in Chelsea – and every time I opened the wardrobe, I could smell the familiar scent of Alex' cologne – so many memories but, for once, only good ones.

All good things have to end. This was probably the most restful part of our 'honeymoon' but, eventually, we decided that if we were to spend any worthwhile time in Venice, we should move on.

Chapter 39:

1987, Venice. Misty

We arrived in Venice late evening, only to find that all the public services were on strike and there was no way of getting ourselves and our luggage across the lagoon to St Mark's Square and on to our apartment.

As neither of us spoke any Italian beyond being able to order coffee or wine, this seemed to be something of a problem, but we eventually managed to ascertain that we could still get a water taxi at reasonable cost and, with the aid of the boatman, loaded our luggage into the tiny boat. I showed him the piece of paper with the address of the apartment and we set off at what seemed like a reckless speed towards the lights on the other side of the water.

Once we arrived on the far side the boat nosed its way along the waterfront before turning into a very narrow entrance and proceeding along what seemed to be little more than a ditch at a snail's pace. Davey seemed worried that we were being abducted but, with difficulty, I managed to gather that the lagoon was now at very low water and that we would be lucky to make it through to Santa Maria Formosa, our destination.

After several false starts we found ourselves in a small pool of water, barely bigger than a corporation swimming pool. The boatman cut the engine and leapt, cat-like, onto some steps leading up to the quayside. He fastened the boat and quickly unloaded our bags onto the cobbles at the top of the steps and then wrote some figures on a piece of paper. All things considered, the cost was reasonable, and we gave him a generous tip on top of it, having enjoyed the romantic arrival by moonlight.

"OK, Marco Polo, how do we find the apartment and, when we do, how do we get in?"

I looked around. It was now getting on for midnight and there were few lights showing around the square. I spotted a Cambio which looked as though it was still open and, leaving Davey to guard the bags, walked across and pushed the door open.

"Speak English?"

The large guy behind the grill nodded but gestured that this might be limited. I showed him the piece of paper with the address. He looked blank for a minute and then nodded. He pointed towards the corner of the square.

"First door." He said hesitantly. "Hotel – he has key."

I thanked him effusively. As I was not one hundred per cent certain that the directions were going to turn out to be correct, I went back to Davey and told him where I was going before making my way along the path to the corner of the square.

There was no sign for a hotel, but there was a large door in the wall, studded with medieval-looking nails, and a rather more modern entry-phone. I pressed the button and, after a pause, a voice drawled "Si?".

With great difficulty I managed to make myself understood and the door clicked open. I walked through into what looked like a scene from a nineteen-fifties historical film – a stone-walled chamber with a vaulted ceiling, lit by what at first glance looked like blazing torches, but which proved to be electric-powered, a wide flight of stone steps leading upwards. I looked up the steps, unsure whether to venture up them. As I did so a youth in his late teens looked over the parapet at the top of the flight.

"I help you?"

"Signor Hansen – apartment?"

I kept it brief, thinking rightly that the less I said, the easier it should be to understand.

"Ah! You are Signor Coolsure?"

I grinned, liking the new name.

"Si."

"You wait – I get key. Have luggage?"

"Outside. With my friend."

The boy disappeared briefly, reappearing seconds later and galloping down the stairs two at a time.

"You follow."

He led the way back into the square and then immediately across the cobbles and into the path that led back parallel to the one we had just left.

I heard a shout of protest from Davey, who could not carry everything on his own, and was obviously reluctant to leave anything unattended. I called back that I would come back for him as soon as I knew where we were going.

The boy stopped at a wide wooden door covered by a wrought-iron grille, and unlocked it, leading the way into a small lobby with two doors opening off it. He opened the first one and switched on the lights.

The apartment had obviously recently been refurbished and was sparsely but tastefully furnished in pale wood with cream linen blinds, the floors bare of rugs and surfaced with 'marble' tiles. There was one large room, a vast double-bed close to the window, and the rest of the room furnished with an enormous leather sofa and chairs, divided by a small dining table and low room-divider, a door beyond leading into a marble-lined bathroom. There was no kitchen, but the dining area also contained a microwave and kettle.

"Bene?" The boy asked anxiously.

"Molto bene, grazie!" I smiled.

"I help you friend with luggage."

He disappeared abruptly and returned what seemed impossibly quickly afterwards, laden with what looked like most of our bags, followed by Davey, also laden, breathless from trying to keep up with him.

I found some money and pressed it into his hand.

"Is there somewhere we can eat?" Davey asked anxiously.

The boy looked at his watch.

"Is late!" He frowned.

"Yes, but we are very hungry – it doesn't matter what it is. Or a shop where we can buy bread…?"

The boy scratched his head, his brow furrowed, but then inspiration obviously struck.

"Si. I know! I take you – is not far."

We followed him out into the alley again, across another side of the square, and over a footbridge into yet another alley. A short way along there was an open door with a few steps leading down into one large room containing a number of long refectory-style tables. The boy indicated that we should sit and vanished through a curtained arch at the far end of the room. He came back with a burly man wearing a none-too-clean apron.

"Alfredo give you food. There is not too much choice, but is good food. You like meat?"

We both nodded.

"What you drink? There is no vino here but you can have birra…"

We nodded enthusiastically again.

"Is good. I go now."

He vanished so quickly I almost wondered if we had imagined him. Alfredo did not seem to speak much, if any, English but nodded to us before returning to his lair. Only a few minutes later he returned with plates of steak and fried potatoes, with a small mound of pasta in a tomato sauce, which he placed in front of us before producing two bottles of continental beer, which he uncapped and plonked on the table. As an afterthought he disappeared again before returning with a basket of coarse bread.

We ate. The boy was right – the food was very good, made all the better by our extreme hunger. The beer also tasted good, although Davey pulled a face and said he'd rather have a pint of best bitter. Despite that he managed to down two more bottles before we made our way, slightly unsteadily, back to the apartment. The meal had cost less than £10 for the two of us.

We stayed in Venice for another ten days, drinking in the wonders of the city, travelling up and down the Grand Canal on the water-bus to visit the galleries and museums, exploring St. Mark's Square and the cathedral, crossing to Murano where we spent a lot of money on beautiful glassware (which we arranged to have shipped home rather than trying to carry it safely ourselves). We tried a number of far more expensive restaurants and cafes but often ended up revisiting Alfredo and his miraculous steaks.

Eventually, reluctantly, we both decided that it was time to return home. Every time I had seen someone walking a dog, I had a twinge of conscience about mine, although I knew that Grace would take the greatest care of them, and that there had been any number of willing helpers who had offered to walk them while we were away. I also knew that we had bookings for the studio which required one or both of us to act as session musicians – something that we were honour-bound to fulfil, especially as some of these were reciprocal arrangements where our mates had contributed to tracks we had recorded.

Chapter 40:

1987, Old Kennel Farm. Misty

We landed back at Luton having paid a small fortune in excess baggage charges. We had only told Grace that we were coming home, but Paddy met the flight, grumbling at how much stuff we were cramming into his car. Fortunately, like Davey, he drove a large estate and we managed to eventually stow everything in.

"How did you know we were going to be home today?"

"I tried to phone you and Grace mentioned that you should be flying in. She didn't know which flight, but it didn't take too much to find out."

"Where's the fire?"

"Work!" He said, conveying a sense of urgency that even Davey couldn't miss. "The permissions for *Angel* have come through and Benny is fighting off TV and radio stations both here and overseas and has already booked almost a full tour."

I stared at him in alarm.

"But we haven't even recorded it yet! No-one's heard it, apart from anyone who was at the 'Swords that night!"

"Maybe that's almost better than it being out there and being plugged night and day. It's become an urban legend. Bird and I have put down our parts but obviously it needs your vocals and the drums…"

I frowned.

"But when we did it at the pub we didn't use bass and drums…"

"What has been suggested is that we do two versions – the acoustic version you did at the party and a full version - and we issue it as a double-A, - then people can choose which they prefer. The acoustic version may not work too well on radio, especially a car radio. The record company have already taken a vast number of advance orders…"

"That's crazy!"

"No, it's not! Everyone at the party was blown away by the way you sang it. Word has got around and there are some very influential people out there who are talking it up. It's likely to go to No. 1 the moment it hits the shops."

I felt a moment of panic, similar to what I'd had at the party, only a hundred times worse. I wasn't at all sure that I was ready to perform in public again, let alone on TV…

"I've not sung a note for nearly two months…"

"You'll be fine! Bird's at the farm. All you need to do is a day or so's rehearsal and put down the track – we'll get it engineered and off to CBS…by the time it's out we'll be ready to rock."

Davey put his arms round me. He realised that I was far from relaxed about the speed with which things were happening.

"You WILL be fine!" he whispered into my ear "And if there's anything that turns out to be a problem, it will just whet people's appetite even more if there's a delay. We're all in this together and you've got me now…"

I didn't reply. Our 'honeymoon' had been an escape from reality, just as our Portuguese stay had been a convalescence after the shit that had gone before. I knew that I couldn't just run away from the future and that, sooner or later, I needed to engage with real life again, but I realised it wasn't going to be easy...

Before Andy's murder it had always been my role not only to front the band, but also to deal with the media, record company, promoters, technicians and almost every aspect of what we did - and that had never bothered me - but everything that had happened since had diminished me in so many ways. I had lost so much of my self-confidence, my sense of invulnerability. I'd been viciously attacked – not once but twice – and the experience of being arrested, charged, tried and jailed had destroyed any sense of self-worth, something which had, at best, always been a brittle, fragile part of me after my unhappy childhood. If I had not had Davey in my life I am absolutely sure that it would have destroyed me, but I now needed a much greater amount of reassurance than before, and I knew that any degree of negativity would bring me down quicker than you could say blink, and each setback would take a measurably longer time to recover from.

I opened my mouth to speak but all I managed was a pathetic whimper.

Davey hugged me again.

"You'll be fine" he repeated.

We arrived back at the farm. The dogs hurtled down the steps to meet us, pointedly ignoring Davey and Paddy and launching a concerted attack on me instead. I ended up on my back on the gravel with the four of them squirming on top of me. Grace appeared and called them off – amazingly they responded (almost) instantly, forming a comical line, as though waiting for a military inspection.

"I took them to obedience classes." She said, trying and failing to keep a straight face. "I decided it was time they learned to behave!"

"They always behave for me…" I said defensively.

"Like they just did?"

Davey hid a grin.

"Welcome home, boys. It's good to have you back!"

"I'm not sure you mean that!"

Davey grinned at her.

"Oh yes I do! It's been far too quiet without you here. If Paddy and Bird hadn't been here for the last week, I'd have ended up talking to the dogs and chickens…"

"You'd probably have had a more sensible conversation if you had!" I said, rather uncharitably. "I hope they didn't have you running round after them?"

"I just made sure they had enough to eat." She said primly.

I sighed – obviously they had made themselves at home in the house, rather than in the kennel rooms. I suppose really, as they were the other half of Misty Blue, that was probably a reasonable thing to do, but it still rankled slightly with Davey and me being out of the country and not there to OK it.

I was feeling quite washed out after the journey home and Paddy's bombshell, so I made my excuses and went to bed. Davey stayed to talk to Paddy and Bird for a while before following an hour or so later. I was half asleep, but he snuggled up, nuzzling me awake irresistibly.

"Bugger off!"

"That's one idea!" he whispered gently.

I groaned, not totally averse. Although we'd been together for several years now, I was still very much in love, and still craved the intimacy of sex with him as well as the physical turn-on. What he lacked in technique (in comparison to Alex), he more than made up for simply by the strength of the love between us, and I rarely said No.

I rolled over and kissed him. He grinned at me hopefully.

"Where do you find your energy?"

"Well, when you are super-fit like me and follow a proper nutrition plan..."

"You do talk bollocks at times! You never take any exercise and you eat for two – generally junk food..."

"Now who's talking bollocks? You try playing drums for hours at a time! I use every muscle in my body..."

"You haven't played for months!"

"And I haven't been eating junk food either! We ate some wonderful food in Italy and Grace certainly doesn't serve up junk food."

His hands were exploring and I gave up arguing, surrendering to him, secure in his love.

Later I lay in his arms, gazing at his profile, out of focus beside me. He realised I was watching him and opened his eyes.

"Go to sleep!" he ordered. "I'm knackered!"

"You didn't take any notice when I said that earlier!"

"I didn't hear too many complaints?"

"What d'you feel about what Paddy was saying?"

"Sounds good to me – a chance to earn some real money again after all this time."

"Always provided I can get somewhere close to the way I sang it at the party." I said, already feeling nervous about the whole project. "And what do we put on the B-side?"

"Bird's idea about that works for me – do it the way you played it at the party – totally acoustic apart from the guitar solo – then do a second version with all the bells and whistles and issue it as a double-A. We could also do an extended version and put it out on a 12-inch, maybe with one of the new album tracks as a B-side to that, as a teaser to get people listening to the album when it comes out. Paddy says that Benny has already booked us onto a whole load of things   radio and TV and stuff – to promote it."

I groaned. I didn't mind doing shows where we played the song we were promoting, preferably live, but I knew that after the events of the last few years, the media would almost certainly want interviews, some of which were likely to be inquisitions, and I was not at all sure that I was ready for that, even if I could drag Davey along with me. I knew there was no chance of anyone settling for Davey or Paddy going along in my place; I was the face of the band and that was that – not only that, *I was the one who had been at the centre of the storm…*

We went into the studio the next day. I hadn't touched a guitar since before our 'honeymoon', and it took me an hour or so even to manage to finger-pick my way all the way through the song without fumbling a note. At one point Bird gently suggested that I should try to put down the vocal track either *a capella* or with him playing the guitar, and then deal with the guitar track later, but I was never happy doing things that way – I needed to feel the guitar in my hands and shape the music and my voice to fit each other.

Finally, my hands seemed to find their stride again, and I started to work on the vocals. I sang the song through several times and Paddy played the tape back to me, but it sounded emotionally flat. I tried again, trying to re-capture the emotion of that special evening, but it still lacked something. Davey came into the studio with me and, switching off the microphone, gave me a talking to.

I tried again, and again, and again. A few attempts were getting close, but I was nowhere near happy. Eventually we called it a day and walked across the fields to the 'Swords where I proceeded to get well and truly hammered. Davey eventually decided that I had had more than enough, and we staggered home leaving Paddy and Bird to it.

As we were passing the barn Davey dragged me back inside.

"Give it one more shot."

"Don't be ridiculous – I'm far too pissed!"

"You said before that you only sang it the way you did BECAUSE you were pissed!"

He caught me to him and kissed me, pushing me against the studio wall, hands exploring roughly, taking me to the edge.

"Now!" he ordered, "I'll be just the other side of the glass in the control room – give it all you've got!"

Suddenly it all came together. With just the two of us there I was able to sing it from my heart, the arousal and intimacy taking it to the highest possible level.

He played the tape back to me; I shivered, ghostly fingers running up and down my spine.

I looked at him, tears in my eyes.

"Was that really me?" He nodded. "Wow!"

He hugged me.

"Let's go finish that cuddle properly – I think you deserve it!"

The following day, once the hangovers had been washed away, the four of us went back into the studio and finished off the tracks in their various permutations.

Paddy and Bird had been blown away by the vocal recorded the previous night, and Bird provided a guitar solo at least as good as the one played at our engagement party, playing it on his vintage Gibson ES335 semi-acoustic for the acoustic version and then, almost note for note, on his Gibson 'Goldie' for the electric version. Making sure we kept copies of everything securely in the studio safe, we sent off the tapes by courier to be properly mixed in London.

A few hours later the phone rang – a very over-excited record producer in London who had just listened to the raw tapes. We explained our ideas and, amazingly, he agreed with everything Bird had suggested. The bottom line was that the main single would go out with the acoustic version just as we had recorded it coupled with the full version, which he would very slightly polish to adjust the sound balances.

He would then re-mix the two versions together to make the extended cut – he would get back to us if he needed any further material to complete that version. In the meantime, we were to supply another five or six tracks for him to select the B-side to the extended version.

The next few days passed in a blur; we spent hours in the studio, working until late at night, writing and recording possible tracks. While Davey and I provided the songs, as we always had, the creative input had shifted, with Bird supplying a new and very welcome dimension to our music, bringing a different feel to the band while retaining its identity enough for people to recognise us.

I loved his playing style; Andy had been an exceptional guitarist and had provided some barnstorming solos on our hit records, but he had rarely stepped outside his own formula. Bird seemed capable of supplying an endless variety of unique interpretations of whatever Davey and I were looking for. We had already agreed that, when working live, he would, as far as possible, replicate Andy's recorded work so that no-one could complain that we were altering much-loved hits or trying to erase Andy in any way, but here in the studio we were creating new music and that gave him free rein to stamp his own contribution on things, which he did with his gentle humour, musicianship and absolutely no sense of intrusion.

Those two weeks allowed us to bond again as a band. Paddy was more than happy with our new direction, both musically and in terms of the internal dynamics of the band. When Bird eventually took himself off home, once we had reached a natural break in what we were doing, Paddy remained behind for a further 24 hours, allowing us to have a review of where we were and what we would be doing over the next couple of months.

"I dunno where Bird came from but I'm certainly glad we've got him! No disrespect to Andy but…"

"Don't say it!" I begged.

Although I had played no part in Andy's death, I still felt uneasy talking about him. He'd made my life a misery for so long – had to a great extent spoiled what could have been an unbelievably great period – that I had often wished that he was not part of the band, but I would never have wanted him to die in the way he had, and I felt uneasy even thinking about how much better things looked to be now.

Davey sensed what was on my mind and put his arm round me.

"It wasn't your fault!" he said, gently but firmly.

He'd said it before numerous times, but he knew that however many times he said it, the thought would continue to haunt me.

Paddy poured me a drink and handed it across.

"Micky, I didn't mean to remind you…"

"I know, but it just feels wrong, being glad that he's not around anymore…"

"After all he put you through, no-one who knew what went on would have blamed you if you had done something! We know you didn't have anything to do with what happened but,,,"

Davey shook his head, indicating that Paddy should leave it.

"Wonder how long we'll have to wait before we hear from Benny and CBS?"

The answer to that was 'Not long'.

Benny rang the next morning with a list of media bookings. Various journalists would be visiting over the next few days, all looking for 'exclusive, in depth' interviews. Advance copies of the single were being distributed immediately, with promotional TV and radio appearances the following week. He wanted to confirm that we were happy to kick off a low-key, mini tour within a couple of weeks, limited to the UK and lasting just a month, playing some of the middle-sized venues – small enough to sell out, but large enough to accommodate a sufficient number of people if the single sold quickly enough to attract more than a modest number of ticket sales.

I began to get butterflies about the whole thing. Davey took the phone away from me and just said "Yes, yes and yes" before replacing the receiver. I looked at him reproachfully, but he just said "You'll be fine. You wouldn't be any more prepared next month, so let's get it over with and get back to normal."

"I can't remember what normal is!" I said miserably. "We haven't been normal for four years!"

"We're more normal now than we've ever been. You and I are together now, and we've got Paddy and Bird and everyone's happy."

I noticed that he had avoided saying 'and no Andy to screw things up'. *The elephant in the room again...*

"Quite apart from anything else, has anyone thought about the fact that we no longer have a stage crew and all that non-essential stuff?" I said sarcastically.

There was a pregnant pause. Davey's face assumed an expression of mock panic, but then he grinned.

"That's all been taken care of. The record company have a flying squad company they use who provide a basic stage set and lighting and sound crews. They generally do small stuff like weddings and conferences and things like that, but they are used to picking up the pieces when people's lorries break down or stuff gets nicked or whatever. It won't win any awards, but it'll get us through the next month which is all that matters."

I gave up. I was shaking inside but realised that I had been out-manoeuvred.

"You'd better ring Paddy and Bird." I said, my teeth chattering. "I'll go and tell Grace."

"You'd better go and break it to the dogs as well."

I glanced at him sharply, but he was grinning at me.

"Micky, it'll be fine - *you'll* be fine. The hardest part was recording the vocal for the single – the rest of it will sort itself out, you'll see."

I shrugged. I went through to the kitchen, stopping on the way to talk to the dogs. I picked Pip up and kissed her silky head, trying to ignore the halitosis. She writhed with pleasure, wagging her tail ecstatically. I rested my head on hers, opening my eyes to see her bright little eyes peering into mine anxiously.

"It'll be fine!" I said, echoing Davey's words, trying to convince myself. I put Pip back into her basket and fussed the others before continuing to the kitchen.

Grace looked round as I entered. Seeing my face, she put down whatever she had been doing and came over to me.

"What's up lovey?"

"We're going to be touring for a month, the week after next."

"Well, that's good isn't it?"

"I don't know! I don't know if I can do it anymore!"

"Why ever not? That's what you *do*, isn't it?"

"Grace, it's four years since we last toured... I'm four years older, my personal life has been splashed all over the media, I've been...I've been attacked – twice – and I've been in – in a mental hospital..."

She put her hands on my shoulders, reaching up to do so, looking me in the eyes.

"Micky, you had a rough time – a *horrible* time – but you came through it and now you are stronger – you have Davey, and Paddy, and Bird – it's not just *you*. I've heard you sing, and I've seen you perform – you are at least as good as anyone else you'll see on TV or anywhere else – and a lot better than many! Most of all, you have Davey – he will look after you, whatever happens."

"There'll be journalists, coming here, over the next few days, to do interviews and stuff. Next week we'll be in London doing a load of TV and radio stuff..."

"How exciting!"

I shook my head, reluctant to accept that the comparative anonymity that we had enjoyed since moving to the farm might be coming to an end.

I went through to our bedroom and opened the wardrobe doors, looking for anything that might be suitable to wear on stage. There wasn't much. Most of the things I'd worn pre-Alex I had ditched when I realised how flash they looked.

Until my arrest, while we were still working, I had used a fairly limited range of clothes, but a lot of those had either long since fallen apart as I'd continued to wear them as everyday clothes, or they were so out of fashion as to be ridiculous, or were now too young for me or, worst of all, I realised there was no way I would be able to fit into them where I had filled out – partly from lack of exercise and partly through the natural maturing process – I was no longer the eternal youth I had been!

I went back to find Davey. I found him in the studio, sitting at his kit, doodling a staccato rhythm on the snare drum, interspersed with the deeper 'bom' from the floor tom (another drum).

"Did you speak to the others?"

"Paddy wasn't home yet but I spoke to Jan. She sounded more than happy – I think she was getting a bit fed up with little money coming in. I also spoke to the present Mrs. Bird – she also sounded OK."

We had finally established that Bird had no less than three ex-wives, as well as the 'present Mrs. Bird' who he always referred to as such, and a whole tribe of children, some from the four wives and a few from other relationships.

I'd been a bit shocked when we'd first learned this but, after working on the recordings with him, I grew to realise that he wasn't the archetypal philanderer – he was just so laid back that things tended to get a little out of hand! He remained on good terms with the three previous Mrs. Birds and was generous to all the offspring, who ranged in age from their late twenties, with kids of their own, down to several toddlers.

"I need to buy clothes."

He groaned.

"Need to?"

"Need to! Without sounding like a 1950s housewife, I don't have a thing to wear! I can't exactly go on stage dressed like this…"

He looked me up and down. I was wearing threadbare cord jeans, a shirt which had come off second best from a tug of war with Sprout and socks with holes in.

"Need to." He conceded. "Don't you have *anything*?"

I shook my head.

"No. I've just looked. Apart from stuff like this, the only thing left is the suit I wore to Joe's funeral. What do people wear these days?"

Davey gave a crack of laughter.

"You were always the fashion-plate! How the hell do I know? You watch Top of the Pops these days and they're all wearing completely different stuff – and definitely not the sort of thing that people our age wear! Unless you fancy an Armani suit – and I don't think that really fits our image, do you?"

"Can you imagine Bird in an Armani suit?" I grinned. "Do you reckon Sera would come shopping with me? I can't think of anyone else with the right sort of taste."

Seraphina was the lovely jeweller who had designed and made our bethrothal rings, and had since supplied other gifts for us, both to each other and to the children and various other members of our circle.

Davey nodded.

"Good idea – I'm sure she would. Or 'Tash?"

"Yeah… Not sure she'd really have the right vibe. She'd probably insist on the Armani suit!"

I drove into Oxford. Sera was very happy to see me and enthusiastic about the proposed shopping expedition.

"Always happy to help other people spend their money!" I grinned. "What sort of look are you after?"

"I've absolutely no idea! It's one thing choosing clothes when you are young and pretty, it's quite another when you are thirty-plus…"

"You're still pretty – you've still got all your hair and teeth AND your figure – you're a lucky boy!"

I felt myself going pink. It was a long time since anyone other than Alex or Davey had paid me a compliment, let alone a young[ish] lady…

"I don't really know your music, other than *Angel* of course. I keep meaning to get hold of some of your earlier stuff and listen to it, but it's not easy to come by at the moment. You'll have to do a Greatest Hits album…"

I pulled a face. I'd never been keen on retrospectives and at that time had a big problem listening to anything that dated from the time leading up to Andy's death. The thought of having to select tracks to go on a 'Hits' album or, worse still, re-record it, did not appeal. I suddenly realised that I was going to have to sing at least some of that material on the forthcoming tour…

"Urghhh…that's a horrible thought! I'll do you a tape of the stuff we've just recorded."

I knew Davey would hit the roof, but I trusted Sera to be discreet with it.

"And you'll have VIP tickets for whichever gig you want to come to!"

"That's not helping with the current problem is it? What sort of music do you mostly do? Is it all soul-type stuff like *Angel*?"

"No, not at all. We've done all sorts of stuff in the past, but I suppose you'd say we were AOR – adult-oriented rock. A bit like Dire Straits maybe, but not quite so instantly recognisable. I could put together a compilation of our stuff and you'd probably swear it was twenty different bands. It's very guitar-based, and on the records there's quite a lot of harmony stuff going on, but when we play live that can be a bit difficult to reproduce - on the records we multi-track my voice, but on stage it's really only Paddy and me singing, although we use stereo or echo a bit to fill out the sound."

"Doesn't Davey sing?"

"Not if I can help it! He sang on some of our earliest stuff and he's done one or two album tracks on his own, but he really doesn't harmonise well."

"Sing something for me – so that I can see how you would move on stage."

I suddenly felt very shy. It's one thing being up on stage with three other guys and you can't see the whites of the eyes of the audience – it's something quite different singing one-to-one in the middle of a small shop with people passing the door!

"I – I can't! For a start I don't have a guitar with me – I wouldn't know what to do with my hands…"

She grinned at me.

"I don't know many men who would use that as an excuse! Wait there, there's a guy the other end of the Market who is a luthier – he usually has a few guitars in his shop."

She dived out of the door before I could stop her and returned a few minutes later with a beautiful, old, twelve string – no recognisable maker's label, but I could see from the wood and the fittings that it had real quality.

"He said that it may not be quite in tune and to be careful with it."

I took it from her.

"I'll certainly take care of it – it's a beautiful instrument! He must trust you, to just hand it over like that!"

She smiled. "They're mostly a good crowd here. If they're not they don't last long… We keep an eye on each other."

The tuning was almost perfect, and I tweaked it only very slightly, enough to give me the feel of it and find its tone. Sera nudged the door shut and bolted it and pulled down the blinds so that I wouldn't be distracted by passers-by.

I strummed for a few minutes, getting used to the action and stalling slightly while I decided what to play. I started a little uncertainly with *Angel* and then rocked it up a bit with *Rock n' Roll Gypsy*.

"I remember that one!" she said. "I didn't realise that was you!"

"I wrote it. It was our first proper 'hit'."

I played a couple more. Someone tried the door and I was suddenly conscious that I could be heard outside the shop.

"Is that enough? We may be causing a traffic-jam out there!"

She nodded.

"Thank you! I can just about remember seeing you on the box a long time ago. It's a little weird – you're so different now, and yet the same – I can't really explain what I mean…"

I smiled. "No, you're right! You probably remember me from very early on. Things were a lot different – I was miserable – Davey and I weren't together. I over-compensated by being totally over the top with everything – I even wore make-up – a bit like Bowie or Boy George sometimes – because I had almost zero self-confidence…"

"I hope you won't be doing that now? I think you're probably just a tiny bit *old* for that sort of thing!"

"Don't worry, I won't! I had a very – close friend - before Davey and I got together – he taught me how to dress properly – how to present myself…"

"OK. Let's go! I have some ideas, but if you don't like my suggestions for heaven's sake say so! I don't want you to spend money on stuff you don't like and won't wear!"

We went out into the Market. She led the way back to the luthier's shop and I returned the guitar. I asked how much he wanted for it, but he wasn't sure whether he wanted to part with it, so I left my phone number with an open-ended offer to buy it if he changed his mind.

We then wandered round the rest of the Market. There was a tiny shop crammed full with Indian-style clothes in jewel-like colours, beautifully embroidered and embellished. I was a bit worried, but Sera carefully picked out pieces that stopped short of being garish or flamboyant, only choosing things in colours which were stunning against my hair or which enhanced the violet/blue of my eyes.

I squeezed into the minute changing cubicle at the back of the shop, trying things on reluctantly at first but, buoyed by my reflection and the reaction of both Sera and the shop-owner, began to enjoy myself.

"If you wear those things with skinny jeans it will keep the look just within tasteful. We'll buy some accessories – scarves, belts and stuff, so that you can change the look a bit when you want to, but you'll need a decent jacket and something respectable for your feet – ideally two of everything."

I followed her gaze to the scruffy trainers I was wearing…

Having paid for what seemed like half the shop, we deposited it back in Sera's unit and then we were off again in yet another direction, where she led me to a tiny cubicle tucked away in another corner of the maze. This contained a tiny, gnome-like figure surrounded by piles of supple leather skins which had been dyed every colour of the rainbow. Above them hung numerous pairs of the most amazing shoes, boots and slippers.

"Micky, this is Roo. Roo, we're looking for a couple of pairs of something wonderful for Micky to wear on stage."

The little gnome peered up at me from the rickety, antique chair he was perched on. He looked me up and down several times without comment, before stretching out a skinny arm and selecting a pair of mustard-yellow pixie boots which he offered to me.

"Will they fit me? They look tiny!"

He shrugged and gestured that I should try them on. I sat on the floor (there being little option) and pulled off my trainers. Amazingly the boots fitted perfectly and looked fine, even with the threadbare cords. Roo stretched out his arm again and handed me a pair of lace-up shoes in soft red leather with a slight heel. Again, they fitted beautifully.

"How can you tell someone's size and fit just by looking at them?! They could have been made for me…"

Sera grinned.

"I've never known him get it wrong. If you buy those, he'll have two more pairs in stock for you in a week's time – or any other time you like. I think he must have been a wizard in a previous life!"

Roo, who had not yet spoken, finally found his voice – surprisingly deep and strong, which took me a little by surprise.

"No more than yourself, Seraphina! I keep telling you that we should get together…"

"You're just after my shop, Roo! You think that if you get round me, I'll let you move into my unit where you'll have more room!"

They had obviously known each other for a long time and had a relaxed relationship.

"Are two pairs enough to be going on with? I hope those –" he nodded at the remains of my trainers "are not your only footwear?"

"No, I have a pair of Hunter wellies…" I teased. "Just about everything else has fallen apart…"

"Like the socks?!"

"Like the socks. It's crazy – I used to live for clothes and stuff, but I've got out of the habit…"

"So, if I make you a couple more pairs? Boots or shoes?"

"Boots for preference. Maybe a black pair and a white pair?"

He nodded assent and I had a sense of having passed some sort of test of approval.

The final stop inside the Market was an expensive-looking, bespoke tailor right in the centre where I found myself commissioning a made-to-measure velvet jacket in a deep blue/purple. This would not be ready for a couple of weeks, so we then went outside and walked round to one of the little streets near Carlo's salon where there was a small men's boutique. Having now got used to the idea of spending money again, I bought myself a black, three-quarter length coat that was more styled than a classic one would have been, but not so trendy as to be out of fashion before the season was over, and also a beautifully cut and styled blue denim jacket with embroidered collar and cuffs.

"OK, I think that's enough…"

"Oh no you don't! I'm taking you to Marks and Sparks and you are going to buy some new socks and underwear! You're almost embarrassing in those – thank God everyone round here knows you don't belong to me!"

I grinned at her, unused to being bossed around. Davey would never have thought of telling me when or what to buy anything - would never have noticed that it was necessary!

"OK, but after that I'm taking you out to dinner"

She threw up her hands in horror.

"You can't do that! I've had a whale of a time spending your money! What will Davey say?!"

"He'll probably say I've spent too much money – but it's *my* money! I'll phone him and tell him what we're doing – he can come and join us if he wants, but I suspect he'll either stay put or go to the pub."

As I suspected, he was too idle to drive into town. We went to the small Italian bistro in Little Clarendon Street where Davey and I usually ate if we had been to the cinema or theatre. The waiter seemed totally confused to see me with an attractive young lady, and his efforts to assure me that he would be very discreet made it difficult to keep a straight face.

Sera helped me to carry my bags to the car. The inevitable parking ticket was a pain – it was usually Davey who collected them, as he often forgot to buy one in the first place. On this occasion I *had* paid to park – just nowhere near enough to cover the length of my stay! I was beginning to feel like a rock star again – the massive shopping spree, dinner and a parking ticket! The high life…

I offered to take Sera home but her flat was only a few steps from the Market and there were still plenty of people around, and she assured me she would be perfectly safe. I thanked her again.

"Any time! Like I said, I'm always happy to spend other people's money!"

When I got home, Davey was still at the 'Swords. I debated whether to walk over to join him but, by now, I was beginning to feel totally knackered. I carried the shopping in and deposited most of it in the library, before letting the dogs out and taking them through to the music room.

Davey arrived home an hour or so later, relatively sober. I was more or less asleep on the sofa. He removed the dogs and flopped down beside me, tweaking a toe which was poking through a hole in my sock.

"You've been spending money!"

"Mmm. I had a wonderful time!"

"Did Sera help?"

"Oh yes! She knew just where to go and what to buy. It was really great!"

"Where did you eat?"

"*Rosetta's*. That was good too. Mind you, I got a parking ticket…"

"I thought that was my trick? Did you forget?"

"Nah. I just overstayed by a few hours…It's your turn next…"

"To get a parking ticket?"

"Don't be a chump! You'll need new clothes too – you're spilling out of everything – you need to get clothes that fit!"

"I'll soon lose weight when we get going again."

"Not that much! Ask Sera to help you…"

"You know I hate shopping! Can't you do it for me?"

I looked at him appraisingly. Although he was going through one of his chubby phases, he was in fact still reasonably in proportion and I reckoned that, provided I measured him accurately and chose clothes that would disguise the worst bulges, I could probably manage without him and would escape the associated bleating that inevitably went with taking him shopping.

"OK. I'll do my best - if Sera will help me again. I'll have to go through your wardrobe to see what you need…"

He groaned.

"Everything! I'm nearly as bad as you were - except that my stuff doesn't fit any more rather than being out of fashion. But don't get me any fancy stuff – I don't want to look like a total Muppet!"

"What about shoes?"

"Oh, *they're* OK. You know I only ever wear boots and they still fit."

I phoned Sera the following morning – happily she agreed to come with me again and we spent another pleasant afternoon buying clothes and accessories for Davey. This time however, she chose a limited range of stuff, mostly either black or denim, the intention being to keep the rest of the band low key. Paddy only ever wore black on stage anyway, and I had never seen Bird in anything other than his cowboy-style denim and rawhide gear, so keeping Davey in black and/or denim would keep the overall picture fairly coordinated as well as, hopefully, disguising the flab.

Shortly after this, and having rapidly cobbled together a reasonably coherent set which we rehearsed as thoroughly as time allowed us, we set off on our abbreviated tour. In between rehearsals we seemed to be fixtures on TV, either guesting on the usual random selection of popular shows, making the obligatory appearances on Top of the Pops after *Angel* went straight to the top of the charts, or appearing on all the major chat shows to talk, with varying levels of sobriety, about the nightmare of the last few years and recent events.

The latter were mostly me on my own, although I always tried to insist that Davey should also be there to field the inevitable questions about our personal life as, after all, it was his privacy which was being invaded as much as mine. Generally speaking, even if the show's producer dug their heels in, I managed to ensure that Davey was at least able to come with me as far as the pre-show green room.

On the whole people were kind, the one exception being a show host who I knew for certain was himself gay, but who covered this up by being particularly offensive in rehearsal. Luckily on that occasion Davey was with me and threatened to 'out' him if he upset me on screen. He took the point and modified some of his questioning, but was still sufficiently obnoxious to arouse the wrath of the popular press (and public opinion) and lost himself a lot of respect by his behaviour. I suppose that, if you believe that 'any publicity is good publicity', he achieved his aim, but it took a long time for people to forgive him and I made it plain that I would never appear on his show again.

After that, the tour itself was light relief. I felt good in the new clothes that Sera had helped me pick. Carlo had given me a new version of my hairstyle which went well with the new-look clothes, and once I had got beyond the first night, I was able to achieve something approaching the level of energy and extroversion that I had had when we had last performed in public, nearly five years before.

The first night had been a total nightmare; I had been literally sick with nerves and we eventually went on nearly half an hour late – something I had never done before. It had taken a couple of joints and a large amount of gin before Davey eventually managed to drag me onto the stage.

Bird had started playing the intro to *Misty Blue* a good ten minutes before I stumbled to the front of the stage, but this only served to heighten the atmosphere in the crowd, and they went wild when I eventually got to the microphone. I ended up singing it through twice, as I doubted the first-time attempt could be heard for the cheering. Someone told me later that a lone voice had yelled something very abusive and the guy had quickly been thrown out by a few people who had been close enough to hear what he'd said. By the time we closed the set with the extended version of *Angel,* I felt as at home on stage as I had before everything had gone wrong.

We had started the tour in London, so were able to get home after the first show – a great comfort and a quick reality-check. Most of the regulars from the 'Swords had been there, and Gerry had driven us home and had come in for a drink – a nice turn of the tables!

After that we headed for Manchester – an acknowledgement of our roots which also seemed to go down well. Cousin Joe was there with his new boyfriend and joined us for a meal afterwards, along with Mag and my mam who had also been there.

I was almost sorry when we reached the end of the tour. Bird had quickly made himself a favourite with the fans, his unique solos becoming a growing sensation each night. We took to duelling the extended version of *Angel* in the finale – a tradition that in the years that followed we were never allowed to drop from the repertoire, even long after the song had been superceded by other, self-penned material.

As the record company had hoped, the tour triggered massive album sales and, on the back of that, a clamour for further tours both at home and overseas. We talked this through carefully. Paddy didn't want to be away from home continuously, his children now being at a critical stage of their schooling and in need of a greater degree of stability with both parents at home. He would have preferred to tour only during the school holidays, but Davey was worried that, if and when he ever managed to get access to his children, the holidays were the very time when he was most likely to see them. Eventually a formula was worked out limiting overseas tours to no more than three weeks away at any time, even if it meant splitting a longer tour into two or more legs.

Chapter 41:

1987, London. Misty

As Alex had predicted, Tina continued to try to stop Davey from seeing the children but, eventually, faced with losing the more than generous financial arrangements and the children's own insistence that they wanted to see their father, she caved in. Her final act of malice was to insist that our living arrangements should be comprehensively inspected by Social Services before Sally and Danny could visit the farm, although Davey was allowed to meet them on neutral territory in London.

I travelled up with him. The meeting was to take place at Angelo's office, and Paddy and Janice had been appointed to accompany the children from Manchester and provide adult supervision and comfort if necessary. I waited in another room, ready to pick up the pieces if Davey found things too much. Angelo's secretary had shown me that there was a discreet peep from which I could see (but not hear) most of what was happening.

The children were already waiting. I was stunned to realise how grown up they now were – I hadn't seen them at all for over five years and, even before that, had only rarely seen them since I had moved to London. The children I remembered had morphed into a lively, though slightly plump, teenager and a slight but sporty-looking twelve year-old.

From my vantage point I saw Davey cautiously enter the room. Sally's hand flew to her mouth and I could hear her yelp "Daddy!!" as she threw herself into his arms.

That was too much for him and I saw him burst into tears. Danny hung back, a little shy, but Davey extracted one arm and held it out to him and he joined the hug.

I could only catch the odd word. Sally seemed agitated about something and I saw Davey shake his head a couple of times. I assumed that she was complaining about the long gap since she had been allowed to see him.

They moved to one of the vast leather sofas and sat, huddled together. The conversation seemed a little hesitant at first but quickly settled down to a rapid exchange of words. The hour passed only too quickly, and I could see Davey's distress when Paddy and Janice had the difficult job of removing the children.

As soon as the office door had closed, I emerged from my concealment. Davey turned to me, his face a pale mask of misery.

"C'mon," I said gently "– at least you've seen them now. Hopefully this is just the start…"

He was shaking with emotion, and I could think of nothing to distract him, so all I could do was lead him out to the car for the drive home.

"Sally wanted to know where you were." He said after a long silence. "She *really* wanted you to be there as well! I didn't know what to say – if I'd said that you couldn't be there because her mother insisted. she'd have gone home to have a row and that would have rocked the boat again."

"What did you say?"

"I just said that you weren't allowed to be there this time – maybe next time."

"What is the next step?"

"Hopefully another meeting like today – perhaps with you there at least part of the time. I don't know how soon the social workers will come to inspect us. I don't know what they expect to find – a bondage dungeon or cannabis plants in the kitchen!"

"Maybe we should have separate bedrooms – I could move into the guest bedroom for a while…"

"Not bloody likely!" He said grimly.

Out of the corner of my eye I could see a bitter grin. I relaxed a little, knowing that this was probably a sign that he was beginning to feel a little less uptight.

"I can't believe how much they've grown in the last four years. Sally's still Sal but there's so much MORE of her! She's nearly a woman already, and I just didn't know what to say to Danny – he seemed so lost – I'm going to have to find some way we can communicate."

"It'll be fine!" I said, almost certainly with more confidence than I felt at that point. I knew only too well how it felt to feel isolated and confused at Dan's age.

By the time we got home he had more or less recovered and had begun to share what the children had said. I wondered how Tina would react when faced with Sal's strongly-expressed wish to see me, although such a meeting was inevitable following the judge's ruling on shared custody.

Chapter 42:

1987, Old Kennel Farm. Misty

We didn't have to wait long to find out when the social workers would visit. The doorbell rang at 8 a.m. the following morning.

As always, Grace was already up and answered the door. I could hear the dogs making their usual raucous racket and sleepily wondered who would ring the bell that early.

The bedside phone rang.

"Micky, there are two people here from Social Services – they want to see you."

I frantically tried to think of some way of putting them off until later, but knew, with a sinking feeling, that it was probably not a good idea.

"OK." I managed to say. "I'll be right out."

I woke Davey none too gently, telling him the worst, while I frantically pulled on some clothes.

"For God's sake get up and dressed NOW!! And pull the bedclothes as straight as you can - I'll go and talk to them and I'll try to bring them round the other way to give you a bit more time."

"Please tell me this is a bad dream…"

"Just do it!" I hissed, heading for the door.

I went round via the kitchen and through the boot room to find a woman in her late thirties, accompanied by a younger man, talking to Grace. They were obviously closely questioning her about the house, the studio and ourselves. Being Grace, she was answering them amiably and fluently, but without giving much away, and I thanked God, not for the first time, that we had bagged such a complete treasure as our housekeeper.

I arrived just in time to hear her assure them that she would, of course, take great care of the children and ensure that they would not be allowed to attend any adult parties or similar.

The woman turned as I emerged from the stairwell. "Are you Mr. Pryor?"

"He's on his way. I'm Micky Culshaw – this is my house. Can I show you round?"

"Thank you. I am Shirley Jones, the senior case officer for the Pryor children. This is my colleague, Trevor Lake."

She waved her ID and I saw that she was from the Oxfordshire council rather than from Manchester.

I led the way back under the stairs and through to the bedroom wing, explaining the layout as we went. I emphasised that we had left the children's rooms as blank canvasses so that they could choose their own schemes.

She queried who else might use that wing, and I was able to say that it would only be close friends such as Paddy, and probably no-one at all if the children were there with us.

We went through the music/sitting room and into our bedroom. There was no sign of Davey and the room was relatively tidy, the French doors which led into the walled garden standing open, showing the garden in all its well-ordered splendour, rows of home produce to one side and the formal rose beds to the other, surrounded by espalier fruit trees.

"What a beautiful space!"

Ms. Jones seemed surprised. I grinned.

"We enjoy it, but I can't claim much personal input – we have a great gardener from the village who comes in regularly. He and Grace plan what produce is to be grown. Most of our fruit and veg is home grown now."

We went through the utility room and into the kitchen. Davey met us as we entered, apparently having come in from the front of the house, which seemed to me to be a good move. I introduced him to the visitors and then took them up into the recreation room – again emphasising that this would be the children's personal space.

After quickly showing off the posh part of the house we went across to the studio and I showed them the kennel rooms, stressing that all that area was entirely self-contained from our home, and that there was no reason for the children to come into contact with visiting musicians or technicians. More questions followed about the use of the stable yard, and I showed them how the communicating gates and Judas door were normally locked from our side.

We went back into the house – Grace had provided coffee and refreshments and we were asked a few more questions, but our visitors seemed to be more than satisfied with what they had seen. The only comment that was made was that we should ensure that the door between our room and the passage from the bedroom wing should be locked or bolted.

Davey looked a little shocked by this.

"But what happens if one of the kids wants us in a hurry?!"

Shirley Jones grinned a little wryly.

"Surely it's better for them to have to bang on the door, than to risk bursting in on you…?"

I put my hand over my mouth to hide a grin and suspected that her report would be favourable.

It obviously was. We heard nothing for a few days but then a suddenly flurry of letters, forms to sign, phone calls etc. told us that the access arrangements had now been agreed, and to expect the children to arrive on the Saturday morning.

As before, dear Paddy provided the transport, Tina having remained obdurate over allowing Davey to go anywhere near her home.

The car pulled up in front of the house shortly after 10 o'clock. Davey hurtled past me and almost went headlong down the steps, the dogs in a sea around him. I hung back in the shadow of the porch, watching carefully to see the children's reaction to the house, the dogs, the situation.

Sally had again thrown herself into Davey's arms, but this time Danny was only a little slower. Obviously, the fact of coming to our home had made the meeting seem less difficult than the formality of Angelo's office.

He spotted the dogs.

"Oh how cute!! Are they all yours?"

Davey grinned.

"Nothing to do with me – they're Micky's".

Sally must have heard my snort of derision as she looked up and saw me. Tearing herself out of Davey's embrace she hurtled up the steps and threw herself on me, sending me staggering back and nearly flattening me. The dogs followed, unsure whether to protect me or join in the game.

"Oh Misty!! I have really, really missed you! It's been so long since we last saw you!!"

I hugged her tightly, overwhelmed by her greeting, thankful that the acrimony of the last four years had not, apparently, soured her affection for me.

Paddy helped carry in the seemingly endless luggage and then departed, having agreed the pick-up time for the following evening. We took the kids through to the bedroom wing, laden with bags. Natasha had painted their names on the doors of their rooms and we showed them how to operate the curtains which covered the skylight windows.

"You must decide how you want the rooms decorated." I said "– I know they're really boring at the moment – we left them that way deliberately so that you could do them how you wanted."

"How long have you been here?" Sally asked curiously, and I realised that Tina had obviously not told them anything about what had been happening since she had thrown Davey out.

I wondered how much they knew of the events which had been all over the media for so long – probably most of what had been in the papers, I guessed, knowing how children talk and would have delighted in using it as ammunition for bullying at school.

"Two years or thereabouts. Come on, let's show you round."

We went the long way round, showing them the big bathroom with its whirlpool bath and vast shower, the music room, our bedroom. I pointed out how, in the summer, we were able to have the French doors open and walk straight out into the walled garden.

Danny seemed a bit nonplussed at the notion of 'our bedroom' but made no comment. Sally seemed to take it for granted. I wondered what Tina had told them (I was soon to find out!) and what they had gleaned from the media/other children at school.

We went through to the kitchen. Grace had set the table in there for lunch and greeted them warmly, emphasising to Sally, in particular, that, if she needed anything, she was to ask her. We carried on back into the boot room, taking them up into the recreation room, now accessible, like the one in the studio, by a reclaimed spiral staircase.

We had equipped the room with a large TV and music centre, an old synthesiser from the studio, a couple of old guitars, loads of books and magazines, games – whatever we could think of that we thought might keep them amused on a rainy day or dark evening.

I don't think either of us got much sleep that night; Davey sat up in the music room for a long time after I had gone to bed, just in case one or other of the children didn't settle and came looking for reassurance, but eventually he assumed that, as all was quiet, it was safe to turn in.

I had fallen asleep with the reading light on and he gently removed the book I had been trying to read, switched my light off and slipped in beside me.

The following morning we arrived in the kitchen to find the children up and dressed, bright eyed and raring to go. Before their arrival we had discussed various possible excursions that we thought might appeal to them, but they seemed happy to stay put, playing with the dogs and just hanging out.

Sometime in the afternoon Davey had taken Sal off to the stables to see the horses and I assumed that Danny had gone with them but, as I lounged on one of the sofas in the music room, picking out the beginnings of a new tune on my acoustic guitar, he wandered in and perched on the piano stool, watching for a while in silence.

I was never that great at being creative in company – I even found Davey's presence off-putting, as he would often start to make helpful suggestions long before I was ready for any outside input – so I switched to just doodling, finger-picking some related chords and improvising existing tunes beyond their normal format. I began to get the feeling that he wanted to say something, so I stopped and watched him patiently.

Eventually I said "Something on your mind? Do you want me to show you how to finger-pick?"

"Misty – does Dad really stick his willy up your bum?"

A long silence ensued as I wondered how to reply to this totally unanticipated landmine of a question. I wondered how far away Davey was…Finally I decided that, at twelve, Danny was neither too young for an honest reply nor too old to need one.

I took a deep breath.

"Errmmm – yes."

"Does it hurt? Why do you let him do that?"

"No, it doesn't hurt. He does it because we love each other very much, and it's a way of showing love – like kissing someone, only more so. When a man and a woman love each and want to make babies…"

"Yes, I know all that – we did that in biology at school. But they didn't say anything about…"

"No." I said, trying to keep a straight face. "I don't suppose they did!"

"And *you* can't have a baby!"

I bit my lip, not knowing whether to howl with laughter or cry, because I was beginning to feel way out of my depth. I was absolutely sure that Danny genuinely wasn't winding me up, and suspected that either Tina had voiced the accusation as to what we got up to or maybe some - rather more worldly - lad at school had said something, possibly based on what had been in the papers two years previously.

"Do you do it to him?"

I shook my head.

"Why? Don't you love him?"

"Yes, of course I love him, very, very much, but – but I can't do that, and I'm not sure he would want me to, even if I could. Danny, I'm not sure that you should be talking to me about this – you should be asking your dad…"

He swung his legs, studying the floor, and I was suddenly conscious of how much he looked as I must have done at around the same age. I really hoped that he hadn't had to experience some of the stuff that I had by that stage…

Just as Sal had inherited Davey's lustrous brown hair, huge brown eyes and tendency to put on weight, Danny had inherited Tina's blonde, curly hair, blue eyes and slender physique. Having not quite reached adolescence he was still childlike in appearance. At that age my hair would have been a fair bit shorter, as was the fashion then, although I had been allowed a certain latitude as a chorister, in order to milk the angelic look when in my robes. Danny's hair was closer in length to how I wore mine at the time of the conversation, and it struck me that, if Davey and I could indeed have had a child, it would probably have looked like Danny.

He looked up as I watched him and gave me an odd, slightly wistful smile.

"Thanks," he said. I shrugged, not entirely sure why he was thanking me, but he added "I don't think Dad would have talked to me properly – he'd either have made a joke or just changed the subject."

I smiled back, feeling a certain conspiratorial closeness to him.

"I'll always try to be honest with you." I said gently. "But your dad's your dad, and you should always be able to talk to him about things, you know – especially things like that. He's not as dumb as he looks!"

At that moment Davey and Sal came in, preceded by the dogs. Davey usually grumbled if I allowed them through to this part of the house, but clearly the rules were being relaxed, at least for the time being.

Pip leapt onto my lap, colliding with the guitar which produced a protest noise, causing her to leap off again. I carefully put the guitar onto its stand and picked her up, cradling her upside down like a baby. She kicked her hind legs in ecstasy, laughing up at me and making me fan away the dog breath. I rubbed her chest, causing more leg-kicking. Sal tried to pick up Sprout, but he took refuge behind the sofa.

"He's not used to you yet." I said consolingly. "He needs to get to know you a bit more."

I handed Pip over to her and showed her the best way to cradle her, without making her feel trapped.

All too soon Paddy arrived to take the kids back to Manchester. Both seemed reluctant to leave, but Davey assured them that it would only be five days before they'd be back again.

After they'd gone he was subdued for a while, but admitted he'd found it quite tiring having them there.

"That's only because you were trying too hard." I said gently. "You wanted everything to be perfect, and I'm sure they thought it was. It'll be the holidays soon and they'll be here almost all the time, which will probably be much easier, daft as that sounds."

"Were you teaching Dan to play?"

Davey pointed at the guitar.

"Not really. I was working on something and he just wandered in, so I stopped and we were talking."

He wandered over to the tape machine, rewound the tape and pressed play. The fragments of what I'd been working on played back, followed by the improvisations I had switched to and then, to my horror, I realised that I had left the tape running right through my conversation with Danny.

I frantically tried to distract him so that I could switch it off but, before I could do so, he heard Danny ask the fatal question. He looked at me, stunned.

I hid my burning face in my hands.

"Switch it off, for God's sake!" I begged.

He shook his head.

"No way, step-mummy!"

I dived out of the room and took refuge in our bathroom, bolting the door behind me.

Five minutes later he came into the bedroom.

"Micky! Micky come out of there!"

He knew I was in there – I could hardly have locked the door and not been, so I was well and truly trapped.

"Micky please!"

I forced myself to unbolt the door. He was grinning, his eyes moist with tears of laughter.

"You did brilliantly! I'm so glad he asked you and not me! I don't think I could have been so honest, and yet you didn't say anything wrong – there was nothing there to frighten him or anything – but I'm not sure I'll ever be able to look him in the eye again!"

He gurgled with laughter.

"I'm glad you think it's funny!" I retorted, mortified "For God's sake PLEASE erase that tape – I'm reaching the stage where I wish magnetic tape had never been invented! Every time I step into the studio now, I'll be remembering Sparrows Hill and now today and I won't be able to sing…"

He chuckled again.

"Seriously, you'll make a brilliant step-parent for the kids – if you can handle *that* the way you did, you can handle anything! Didn't you think he might have been winding you up?"

"I did, for a minute or two, but he's so young for his age, that I realised that he was obviously reacting to something someone had said. If he had been putting it on then he ought to be at RADA, not the local secondary…"

"Probably bloody Tina, although I'm not sure that even she would stoop so low as to deliberately say that in front of him. He probably overheard her talking to someone else."

"You don't think it was the kids at school?"

"I doubt it. I think if it had been, he probably wouldn't have believed them. If that had been the case, he'd probably have asked Sal – they're pretty close, considering she's the older one and a girl. I think she's been mothering him. God knows what Tina's been saying about us, but I don't think she'd have said anything too specific in front of the kids – they're her kids too, after all, she wouldn't want to hurt them – ME, yes, but not them."

I shrugged, not having the experience to know whether he was right or not. My own childhood had been such a travesty of how things should be, that I really had no idea of how parents ought to interact, either with their children or each other.

He came over and hugged me. I buried my burning face in his shoulder.

"I love you so much!" I said, my voice muffled. "And I love your kids too. Have you noticed how much Sal looks like you now…?"

"And Dan looks like you did around the same age! If I didn't know better, I'd be wondering if you were his father!"

"That's really not funny!" I said crossly. "I've never done anything that could have got anyone pregnant – not for want of trying when I still trying to please my parents – but…"

He realised how upset I was and wrapped his arms tighter around me.

"I'm sorry! You know me – it was a cheap and feeble attempt at a joke – I wasn't thinking. Mick – I'm *really* sorry! The last thing I'd ever want to do is upset you, you ought to know that by now. But it goes back to what I told you – about how Tina looked so like you before we got married. And you were around so much when they were tiny – Sal thinks of you as a godparent or an uncle – so it's almost as though they had three parents anyway."

"I hope you never said THAT to Tina – that's almost worse than telling her you only married her because she looked like me! You have an amazing knack for saying the wrong thing…"

"I've said I'm sorry…"

I looked up – the expression of remorse on his face was almost comical. I bit my lip and sighed.

"OK. You're forgiven – this time!"

I hugged him tightly, trying to reassure him that I was, at least to some extent, only pulling his leg. He returned the hug.

"If ever I say or do anything that upsets you for God's sake TELL me! I know that I can be clumsy sometimes, but I do try not to be…"

"Only sometimes?" I teased gently.

We overslept the next morning, waking only when Grace, obviously reluctant to make any direct intervention, let the dogs into the walled garden and they started scratching at the French doors leading into our room. I opened my eyes to see four little faces peering in eagerly, tails wagging. Davey slept on, so I quietly opened one of the doors, allowing them to bound in and leap up onto the bed.

"What the…?!"

Muffet immediately stuck her tongue into his mouth, leaving him spluttering in revulsion and me splitting my sides with laughter. He gave a roar of rage and threw a cushion at me which missed, and the dogs promptly threw themselves onto him, loving the game.

"Micky! Get these bloody animals out of here!!"

I whistled and they came to order and I shoo-ed them out of the doors and back into the garden. He looked at me reproachfully.

"That was a rotten trick!"

"Grace must have let them into the garden. She probably thinks it's time we were up, and she's right – it's gone eleven o'clock!"

He groaned.

"Urgh… I was going to go into Oxford this morning."

"There's not much morning left. Go after lunch."

"Can't. Nick's coming to use the studio and he wants me on drums."

Nick was an old friend – someone neither of us would want to mess around.

"I could go into town – what did you want?"

He shook his head.

"Nothing you can do for me…"

I gave him a quizzical look, but he obviously wasn't going to let me in on whatever it was.

"S'no good, I'll have to go in,.. I can't just leave it. If I'm not quite back when Nick arrives tell him I'll not be long."

Fortunately Nick was pretty late turning up so I only had to stall for a short time before Davey arrived back. The late start meant that their session went on well after the usual time and I had eaten and gone to bed long before Davey came in. I waited until he had slipped in beside me before pouncing.

"OK, Pryor, are you going to tell me where you went earlier on?"

He didn't reply but tried to distract me by rolling over and pinning me down, kissing me until I had other things on my mind.

Some time later, when I remembered what I had been trying to ask, he was, or pretended to be, fast asleep, and it was some months after that before I eventually got to the bottom of the matter.

Chapter 43:

1997, Old Kennel Farm. Misty

The sun was beating down. Davey and I were sitting on the retaining wall around the fountain in front of the house. We had been working in the studio, overseeing a session by a hot young singer. I had been providing guitar tracks, her own band guitarist not being quite proficient enough to work on the recordings, and Davey had been acting as engineer for the session. The youngsters had just departed back to their posh hotel in Oxford and we were enjoying being out in the sun, the dogs arrayed around us on the gravel, panting in the heat. Pip was an old lady now, Sprout just a happy memory, but we still had two of their puppies and several from more recent generations, keeping the line going.

We were sitting face to face, astride the wall, bare feet dangling in the water, playing footsie. I had just leaned in for a kiss when we heard a car approaching at a little speed up the drive towards us.

"Are we expecting anyone?"

Davey shook his head.

"Maybe one of the youngsters left something behind?"

The car came into sight and we realised it was Sal.

"Wonder what's up? She didn't say anything about coming down when I spoke to her on Monday".

The car slid to a halt and she climbed out. The tubby teenager had morphed into a shapely young woman. Today she was wearing a cotton dress which emphasised her slim waist and brought out the golden glints in her brown eyes. She came up and hugged us both silently.

"What's up, Sal? You didn't say anything about coming down..."

She shook her head but still didn't speak.

"Sal – is something wrong? Danny?"

Another shake of the head.

"Do you want to speak to one of us alone?" I asked gently.

She shook her head again. I began to feel uneasy.

"Is something wrong? Your gran? My mam?"

Yet another shake of her head.

"I just wanted to see you both…"

She managed to say that much, but I could see she was close to tears.

"I can't stop, I just wanted to see you both."

Davey had untangled himself and moved to put his arms round her, but she pulled away from him and without saying anything further ran back to her car, got in and drove back down the drive, leaving us staring after her.

"What the fuck was that all about!?"

I shook my head blankly.

"That was my daughter, wasn't it? The one who always says what's on her mind, however embarrassing…"

"Should we go after her?"

"Don't be daft – she could be halfway to anywhere by now. I'm going to phone Mam…"

"No, no don't – you'll only worry her – it's not fair at her age. Try Danny…"

Davey went back into the barn but came back minutes later shrugging his shoulders.

"I tried his flat, his office and his mobile. I got the answerphone at home, he's not at work and his mobile's switched off. Something's going on! I'm going to ring Paddy."

He went back into the barn, returning after sufficient time for me to feel I ought to go after him.

"He knows something but he's not telling. He just said that Sal will tell me all about it when she's ready…Micky…"

I put my arms round him and hugged him tightly, feeling his agony.

"We'll just have to wait. Sal's obviously OK – she looked the picture of health – and if it had been something to do with Dan, either she or Paddy would have told you…"

We didn't have to wait much longer. As we were having dinner that evening the front doorbell rang and Grace came back with Nat. I jumped up.

"Nat?! What's up – it's not Alex is it..?"

He shook his head, smiling slightly.

"Alex is fine – he sends his love and he'll see you soon. I have some news for you both…"

"Good or bad?"

Davey had also got to his feet.

"Probably both, I'm afraid."

He hesitated.

"Maybe you'd better sit down…"

"Let's go through to the library." I suggested.

We crossed the hall and took our seats on the leather chairs.

"Drink?"

Nat shook his head. He took a deep breath.

"First the not so great news. Tina died this afternoon. She had cancer which was inoperable by the time it was diagnosed. She was in the Royal Marsden for quite a long time, but she actually died in a private hospice."

I got up and poured a large glass of brandy which I handed silently to Davey. His hand shook as he took it, and the glass rattled against his teeth as he swallowed most of it in one gulp.

Despite the bitter power-struggle which had surrounded their divorce, she was the mother of his children, and for that reason alone the news had come as an enormous shock to both of us. We waited. Nat was obviously summoning up the right words for the next part of his news.

"I'm not sure whether I should tell you this now or let you deal with what I've already told you…"

He looked at me as though seeking permission to continue. I had no idea of what might be coming next, but he had started by saying that the news was good and bad. I couldn't see that, after all these years, we were likely to see Tina's death as good news, so I assumed that whatever remained had to be better than that.

"Maybe I should tell you –?"

He looked at me enquiringly.

"No – if it concerns us both, tell both of us, and if it concerns Micky then he'd probably prefer you to tell him with me here anyway…" Davey found his voice.

Nat nodded.

"OK. It's still to do with Tina".

He hesitated.

"Before she died – once she knew that it was inevitable - she asked to see me. She has made a sworn statement – about the day that Andy died…"

My hand flew to my mouth. The jumbled thoughts that had haunted me for nearly fifteen years suddenly began to assemble themselves into some kind of order and, as Nat spoke, I was half a sentence ahead of him. Davey looked at me, sensing my distress.

"On the day that Andy died, Tina had come down from Manchester to see you. She was worried about Davey, she was worried about their marriage, and she wanted to talk to *you*, as Davey's best friend, to see if you could help her to try to make things work again. She had Davey's key to your flat, so she was able to get into the building and let herself into the flat without the concierge knowing. She'd rung the bell but there was no answer, so she let herself in to wait for you. She found you on the floor, like the police did later on. She thought you were dead to start with, but apparently you came round for a few seconds – long enough to tell her that Andy had attacked you. You then lost consciousness again and she thought you really had died. She didn't call anyone because she thought she might be suspected of attacking you, and she wanted to confront Andy first. She says that she intended to call the police after she'd seen him…"

Davey shook his head disbelievingly.

"Maybe she did, maybe she didn't. She knew that Andy was at the hotel as he'd dropped the key in the flat, so she knew where to find him and even had the room number…When she got there Andy was stoned out of his head. She accused him of attacking you and he laughed at her. He was rambling, rubbishing you, rubbishing Davey, saying a lot of stuff about you…" He looked at me "- in particular. He told her that he had come to see you and had tried to get you into bed, but that you had given him the brush off. You'd had a couple of joints together and he'd tried again, but you told him to bugger off, so he'd tried to force you to have sex and things had got out of hand. He didn't deny that he knew he'd hurt you badly, but said that Tina could never prove it. She couldn't say whether he tried to hit her or maybe strangle her first, or whether she lost it and attacked him, but she says that she grabbed the knife in self-defence and he ran onto it. He was so stoned that the first wound didn't stop him and she had to stab him several times to get away from him. She then bolted back to Manchester without calling the police or ambulance because of the children…"

Davey was shaking his head again, obviously close to tears.

"When she heard on the news that you were still alive, but that Andy had died, she took fright even more, and then when Janice told her that you and Davey were sleeping together, she was so angry that there was no way she was going to try to save your neck…"

"Oh my God!" Davey burst out "I can't believe she put us through all that…"

"No, it's true." I said flatly. "All those bits I remembered before now make sense, and what she says is absolutely right, so far as what happened at the flat is concerned. Andy was there, stoned out of his head. He kept trying it on, and in the end I lost my temper and tried to throw him out. I got him halfway to the door, but he was so stoned he was too strong for me, and he got me down on the floor…"

I started to cry as it all flooded back into my mind – the pain, the ugly words he was saying and the things he was doing to me.

Davey got up and got me a drink, kneeling beside me with his arm round my waist. I was shaking so much I couldn't hold the glass and he gently held it to my lips and helped me drink.

"Do you want to call the doctor?" Nat asked anxiously.

"No, I'll be OK. It's just such a shock! Oh Nat! After all these years, to finally know what happened!!"

"What happens now?" Davey asked quietly. "Will this clear Micky's name once and for all?"

"I hope so. She signed a full statement in the presence of several witnesses, including doctors and the hospice chaplain. They didn't know what was in it, of course, but I made sure that she acknowledged that she knew what she was signing."

"Did Sally know what Tina was doing?"

"Yes. Tina told both the children before she asked to see me."

"Does anyone else know?"

"I've told Alex."

I looked at the floor. My stomach was churning, and I felt sick. Part of me wanted to say *'Let's just forget it – it's a long time ago'*, not wanting to pursue something that might bring hurt on the children. Davey sensed what was going through my mind – the telepathy that had always passed between us acutely developed over four decades.

"Please Nat – do whatever you have to do. We must clear Micky's name – we've lived for over twelve years in the shadow of this…"

"Sweetheart – we should talk about this…do you really want it all in the media again? Now, when things are back to normal?"

His arm tightened around me.

"I don't care what it costs! You are far more important than anything else!"

"More important than Sal and Dan? It's their mother we're talking about and she's just died!"

"They would say exactly the same – they love you – you saw Sal this afternoon – she came here to reassure us…"

"Did she? Or was she trying to tell us that Tina was dying and that she needed us to comfort her?"

"I've talked to Sally at length about this. It was partly at her insistence that Tina asked me to take care of things. Tina told her what had happened, and Sally immediately said that she had to do something to clear your name."

"What about Danny?"

"He hasn't said much, but he agrees with Sally. He loves you both very much and he's very angry with his mother for letting you take the blame. If you don't take the opportunity to clear things up, I don't think he'd ever forgive her. In that way you'll be helping them to make sense of things."

"What happens now?"

"Alex has applied for the case to be re-opened."

I felt sick. Abruptly I got up and left the room, half-running through the boot-room, across the courtyard garden and into our room, locking myself in the bathroom. I leant over the basin, resting my head against the cold tiles.

A few minutes later someone tried the door.

"Micky! Open the door!"

I didn't answer.

"Mick, open the bloody door or I'll break it down!"

Reluctantly I unlocked the door. Davey came in and enveloped me in a bear hug. I started to shake again, totally overwhelmed. Neither of us spoke for a long time. Eventually he manoeuvred me back into the bedroom and sat me down on the edge of the bed.

"We've got to get this sorted out." He said firmly. "You've had years of people wondering whether you killed Andy. OK, no-one who knows you thinks you did it, but there are plenty of people out there who think that the Court found you guilty so there must be some doubt."

"But Sal and Dan – she was their *mother* – "

"Micky – they're nearly as much your kids as they are mine! They know you didn't do it…"

"That's not the same thing as knowing that their mother did it! I don't want to do anything that might hurt them..."

He put his hands on my shoulders and gently shook me.

"Sweetheart, they're grown up now – I *know* that they'll want to put things right..."

"Is Nat still here?"

"No, he's gone. There's more going on, but he wouldn't tell me yet – he wants to wait for 'the right time' – whatever that means."

We weren't going to find out for another month or more.

We went to the funeral – Sal had asked us both to go, which made me feel very uncomfortable, but rather than cause her more distress, I agreed. Tina's parents – both still living but, by this time, in their late sixties – ignored us (hardly surprisingly), but there was no overt hostility. Davey's Mam was also there but, slightly to my surprise, mine was not. Worried that she might be ill I asked Mag why she wasn't there.

"She's fine, sweetheart. It's just that she never got on all that well with Tina's mam, and she didn't think she'd be welcome."

That seemed reasonable: Mam had always been (or thought herself) a 'cut above', and had occasionally commented on Tina's brassiness, so I didn't think any more of it at the time. Later her absence made a lot more sense.

As we were leaving the Crematorium (we didn't go to the wake), I caught Tina's father looking at me with an indefinable expression but, again, assumed that it was just a reasonable representation for someone looking at his ex-son in law's gay lover, and mentally shrugged it off.

Sal and Dan were staying in Manchester overnight, and would not be returning south until they had seen Tina's solicitor the following day and put arrangements in hand for the sale of her house. Sal was by now living with her fiancé and Dan had his own flat near where he worked, both in London.

We drove home, both rather quiet. Despite the circumstances, it had come as a shock to lose someone we had grown up with. Whilst we had lost friends to the curse of drugs and, more recently, to AIDS, Tina was the first contemporary we had lost to natural causes, and it had given each of us a sense of our own mortality.

We heard nothing more about the application to reopen the manslaughter case for several weeks, apart from a copy of a letter sent to Alex acknowledging the application and giving an approximate date when it might be considered. If anything, I was grateful for the delay – it made it seem less distasteful.

About six weeks after Tina died, Nat phoned to say that he would be coming the following morning with someone from Scotland Yard.

By now Davey and I had talked through both the situation and what I remembered of the day Andy died – much more now, having been prompted by Nat's account of Tina's statement, which I had not yet seen. The ability to talk about it had helped me to come to terms with the situation and to deal with the prospect of having to re-live the nightmare of twelve years earlier with more composure than would once have been possible.

They arrived in two cars – Nat and Alex together and, shortly afterwards, a Detective Chief Inspector and a Detective Sergeant.

I hadn't seen Alex for a while. He was beginning to look his age, but still had the ability to make my stomach contract with desire at the memory of what we had once shared, and his smile was enough to make my head spin. He greeted me with a hug, broken off hurriedly as the policemen approached.

"Are you OK?" He whispered.

I nodded.

"Just listen to what the DCI has to say. I have something to tell you afterwards."

We settled in the library – Davey and me on the Chesterfield, Alex and Nat in the armchairs, and the detectives remaining standing. The DCI took some papers from his briefcase.

"I understand that you have been made aware that Christina Pryor made a formal, sworn statement in front of witnesses shortly before her recent death?"

I nodded.

"You are aware that in that statement she stated that she believed that she had caused the death of Andrew Freeman, whose manslaughter you were charged with, tried and found guilty?"

I nodded again.

"A copy of that statement is already in the hands of your legal representatives. Mrs. Pryor also stated that she came to your flat and found you, badly injured, on the day of Mr. Freeman's death. She said that you briefly regained consciousness and that you told her that Mr. Freeman had attacked you. She then confronted Mr. Freeman at the hotel where he was staying. There was a scuffle, during the course of which she stabbed Mr. Freeman several times."

I nodded silently. He continued.

"A formal application has been made for the case against you to be re-opened. I have been instructed to re-examine the evidence and, if I find that there is sufficient cause, to submit my findings with a view to having your conviction set aside. To this end the forensic evidence gathered at the time will be re-submitted to examination. Do you understand what is meant by DNA analysis?"

I looked at Davey but neither of us had any idea of what he was talking about, the discovery of DNA being comparatively new at that time, and its application to forensic science only just being understood.

"DNA is genetic material which is unique to each of us. It can be obtained from such things as hair, skin, blood, bodily fluids – you get the picture. We have samples of material which was gathered on the day that you were attacked and Mr. Freeman died. This has already been re-analysed. Samples were also taken from Mrs. Pryor before she died – with her permission – and these have also been analysed. The presence of matched samples in various locations indicate that her version of events is possible or even probable, and therefore I will be sending the necessary papers forward. You must understand that this does not mean that your conviction will automatically be set aside – it is possible that the judge could order a re-trial ..."

Alex cut in.

"But that would be unusual – yes? Given that Mrs. Pryor effectively made a death-bed statement admitting her guilt."

The DCI nodded.

"Yes, sir. We would however ask that Mr. Culshaw should submit a DNA sample for analysis.

There are some – anomalies – which the forensic people would like to try to clarify. As I have indicated – this is a very new science and is not fully understood yet. There is also the factor that the samples originally taken may have deteriorated over the last fifteen years – a new sample could make the difference between a clean result and something less clear."

"Where do we have to go?"

Davey spoke for the first time.

"Nowhere. One of our forensic people will come out tomorrow or at some time to suit you."

The detectives left. Alex and Nat stayed on. Nat opened his own briefcase and took out several envelopes. He hesitated – looking at Alex for guidance, who nodded.

"I waited to give these to you until the police had the results of the original DNA tests. The DCI mentioned anomalies – these letters may explain what he was talking about. They are from Tina – there is one for each of you – and before you ask, the children are already aware of what they contain."

Alex said gently. "I think maybe you should come with me before you read yours, Micky – you probably both need to digest what she has said on your own."

Davey indignantly tried to protest but Alex had already swept me out, through the house and into the walled garden.

"What are you playing at?!" I protested. "Davey and I have no secrets…"

"I think you will find what Tina says will come as a shock to both of you. Nat will take care of Davey, and I am claiming seignorial rights to take care of you again, just this once."

He sat me down on one of the rustic benches in the rose garden. My hands were trembling as I opened the envelope, wondering frantically what could be so earth-shattering. Was Tina going to tell us that, ironically, she had AIDS and that we were at risk? What else was likely to cause us so much heartache?

I started to read the letter. To my surprise she had opened it to '*My darling Micky*'. I blinked and read on in disbelief; the further I read, the more blurred the words became by the tears that sprang to my eyes. Snatches leapt off the pages:

'*You are my brother – Joseph Culshaw was not your father. Annie is your mother, mine is Jean, but we share the same father. I have known this since I was seventeen and started dating Davey. Mam was worried that I might start dating you and thought I should know the truth... I was always jealous of you – you had so much and were so close to Davey - when you stole him from me I thought my heart would break, but I realise now that I had stolen him from you – please forgive me...please look after him and my darling Sal and Dan – I know how much they love you and you them....Please also forgive me for letting you take the blame for Andy's death, but I had to think of the children... I know how much grief he put you through over the years, and I saw what he had done to you that awful day. I didn't mean to kill him, but the things he was saying about you and about Davey were unbearable...*'

The pages fluttered from my hand and the ground came up to meet me. Alex dropped down beside me, gently trying to help, but I was out cold, pale as a ghost.

Grace must have been watching from the kitchen window as she was there within seconds. Between them they managed to get me up onto the bench again, pushing my head between my knees. Once I was semi-conscious they quickly got me the short distance into our bedroom and onto the bed.

Grace looked at Alex.

"What have you done to him?!"

Alex shook his head.

"I am innocent, Grace! I know you don't like me much, and you probably have some justification, although in my defence I must protest that I have only ever wanted Micky's happiness…"

He handed her the letter.

"I know that Micky trusts you, so I am sure he won't mind you reading this."

Grace put on her reading glasses and quickly scanned the pages, catching her breath as she read the secrets so long buried. She handed the letter back to Alex who carefully folded it and replaced it in the envelope, which he placed on the bedside cabinet. He sat on the edge of the bed, stroking my hair.

Voices approached from the courtyard garden and Davey and Nat came in. Davey looked at my inert shape on the bed and, shoving Alex out of the way unceremoniously, sat down heavily beside me, taking my hand.

"Oh Micky!"

Tears ran down his face unnoticed. He looked up at Grace imploringly and she gave him a reassuring smile.

"Don't fret!" she said quietly. "If you're worried, I'll call the doctor, but he's only fainted – he'll be fine in a while, you'll see…"

Nat gave Alex a significant look and they slipped out, leaving us alone. Davey sat beside me, cradling my head against him, stroking my hair and, after a few minutes, was rewarded when I opened my eyes and looked up at him, albeit totally disorientated.

"Are you OK?" he asked anxiously.

I blinked.

"I've no idea." I croaked. "Was I dreaming? Or are you now my brother in law, as well as my significant other, and are my step-children now my nephew and niece?"

He smiled gently at me.

"That's what we are supposed to believe, yes. Although I suppose you are strictly my ex-brother in law..."

"Don't you believe her?"

"About her being your half-sister? Yes. That explains how Danny looks like your son, not mine, and Tina's – *your* father – was notorious for screwing anyone who came within range and, more often than not, getting them pregnant, There are probably a dozen more of you out there –."

I glared at him reproachfully and he bit his lip contritely.

"I'm sorry, Micky. I should have engaged brain – that was extremely tactless…"

"At least I now understand why Dad – Joseph Culshaw – hated me so much. Poor Mam! When she said what she did about single parents and her family, there was more to it than I realised! I suppose Joseph offered to marry her, and she felt she had no option. He would have been a good catch for her, with his job and everything, although he was a lot older than her. All her airs and graces were because everyone knew the situation and she was just making sure they understood that she had had the last laugh."

I felt the tears starting again. Davey lay down beside me and hugged me to him, kissing the tears away.

"Which is worse?" He asked gently. "Having Joe Culshaw as your father, or Sam Whittaker?"

I groaned.

"What a choice! At least Sam would have been absent! I've only met him a couple of times – at your wedding and the kids' baptisms, and now Tina's funeral. He gave me a very odd look the other day – now I know why! – He obviously knew all along that I was his son, but this was the first time he's seen me since you and I – got together."

I managed a wobbly grin.

"That must be really weird for him – you being married to his daughter, and screwing his son!"

Davey's arms tightened round me.

"I'm sorry!" I said. "Now it's me being tactless! Do you think these DNA things are going to sort it all out once and for all? It sounds like witchcraft to me!"

"Sweetheart, even if the DNA stuff doesn't prove it one way or the other, I am sure that what Tina said is right. It was so obvious, and we just didn't see it! Especially the way Joe treated you and the way your mam just let is happen – as he'd taken you both on, she must have felt so indebted to him she just *couldn't* stand up to him. And however much Tina put us through, I think I knew her well enough to know that, under the circumstances, she would be telling us the truth. I don't know exactly what she said in her letter to you but hers to me is heart-breaking…"

I nodded.

"She started by calling me 'Darling Micky' – she'd known that we were brother and sister right from when you first started dating – Jean told her in case she moved on from you to me…"

Davey grinned.

"Not exactly a likely scenario!"

I stuck my tongue out at him.

"That's not true! In those days I was still trying to do my duty and provide grandchildren – I was only fifteen when you started dating Tina, remember."

"I remember! Do you really believe what she says about the rest of it though? About coming to see you because she was worried about me…"

"What other reason could she have had? Especially as she had managed to get hold of your key to the flat..."

"You don't think she was planning to have a go at you, but Andy got there first?"

I shivered.

"I think that what she says in her letter sounds more believable…or maybe that's what I want to believe…why? Don't you believe it? Or do you?"

"I dunno… Maybe I want to believe it too, but after all the shit with the divorce…"

"Yes, but that was *after* she'd killed Andy and effectively framed me for it – or at least left me to take the rap. She was probably desperately trying to hang onto the kids – it would have been devastating for her if she'd done all that and then lost you, the kids, everything that mattered to her. I just *wish* I'd known the truth while she was still alive – I wish I'd been able to talk to her as my sister…"

I felt the tears start again, an aching void in my stomach at the loss of someone who had been part of my youth, the mother of my step-children, and was, I now knew, my only sibling – or at least the only one I was aware of - although as Davey had pointed out, there were likely to be others.

"What are you going to do? Will you confront him?"

I shook my head.

"No – what's the point? I can hardly ask him to maintain me - it's more likely that he'd try to get me to maintain him! I'll have to talk to Mam, but I don't want to upset her – just ask her to tell me the truth after all these years."

I forced a smile.

"In a way it's a big relief to know that my father was the local stud and not that – that –."

I lost it then and burst into tears. Davey pulled me into his arms and held me tightly, stroking my hair, soothing me as he had done so many times before.

Eventually I hiccupped to a stop.

"Come on," he said gently, "Let's go out somewhere – have lunch somewhere nice…"

"We can't!"

I suddenly remembered the studio – we were still supposedly working on the young star's recordings.

"What about Sapphire?"

"Don't panic – I phoned the hotel and said that you weren't well, and I've phoned Bird and Paddy and they're coming down to take over tomorrow."

"I'll be fine by tomorrow…"

"No, you won't. I don't think you should even try to work until we've at least got the final results from these tests or, better still, until we hear that your conviction has been overturned. This will be all over the media tomorrow and probably for the next few weeks – longer maybe. What we need to decide is whether to lie low here or go away somewhere."

I groaned.

"I think I'd rather be working…"

"Your mind won't be on what you're doing – it's not as though you'd be working on our own stuff, and it's not fair to screw up someone else's sessions..."

"That's right! Be tactful, why don't you?!"

I felt rather narked that he was suggesting that I would be unprofessional enough to let my emotions interfere with my work, but I suppose, deep down, I knew he was right.

I sighed.

"OK. But we'll stay here and work in the music room on our own stuff."

Paddy and Bird arrived early evening. We ate together in the dining room before crossing to the studio to play them the tapes of what we had done so far with Sapphire. Bird made a few suggestions which made perfect sense and I was happy that the recording and the guitar contributions would be in safe hands.

Leaving him in the control room immersing himself in her work, I took Paddy off to the library to update him on the situation. To my amazement he seemed unsurprised to hear our news, both as to Tina's confession and to the change in my parentage.

"Well I always knew that you hadn't killed Andy – it was just a question of who HAD done it – and I always thought that you and Tina could be twins, but I didn't dare say so…"

"We weren't twins – we had different mothers, but, as you say, there was less than a year between us."

Paddy hugged me.

"I'm really glad that this seems to have put you in the clear – it's about bloody time!"

I buried my head against his shoulder.

"I know it sounds ridiculous after everything that happened, but I really wish I'd had the opportunity to get to know her as my sister. OK, we knew each other as kids and when she and Davey got married, but it's not the same as having a sister…I can't believe that she knew I was her brother and then gave us all the shit when Davey left her…"

"I'm only guessing, but from her point of view it was probably the last straw that not only had Davey left her - and that he'd left her for another guy - but that you were her brother…"

I realised that he was trying not to laugh, and it suddenly sank in how absurd it sounded.

"Yeah – yeah OK, you're right as always! I'm sorry, we live in our own little bubble here. I guess that we're too close to it – that and trying to make it easier for Sal and Dan... We're so conscious that they've lost their mam, and that's been made so much worse by finding out that she was responsible for what happened all those years ago. If I had known her better, it would be easier for me to know what to say to them."

"Yeah. I get that. I'm not laughing about the situation – I know it's not funny and I get what you're saying. It's just that when you break it down bit by bit…What happens now?"

"Alex has lodged the papers to try to get my conviction set aside. It may not be straightforward as Tina's not here to confirm her statement, but at least it was done properly and witnessed."

We didn't have to wait too long for the outcome of the application. The original trial judge had been so unhappy about my conviction that, as soon as he became aware of Tina's confession and the application to set aside, he added his weight to it and we were quickly informed that the application was unopposed, and the conviction would be stricken from the record.

Chapter 44:

The same. Misty

Once the conviction was overturned and things began to get back to normal, I went up to Manchester to try to talk to Mam about the difficult subject of my parentage.

I didn't tell her I was coming – I didn't want her to start fretting, or give her time to perhaps invent an alternative version of the truth. I doubted whether she had heard of DNA testing or, if she had, that she would realise that it is more or less foolproof.

Davey had tipped Mag off as to what was coming so that she was there with Mam when I arrived, but she had agreed not to give her any hint that I was on my way or why.

Mam had seen the car pull up and had opened the door with a smile.

"Micky! Why didn't you let me know you were coming? There's nothing wrong is there?"

"No Mam, everything's fine. I just need to talk to you, that's all."

"But Davey's not with you! Are you sure there's nothing wrong?"

By now we were inside. Mag went out to put the kettle on while we went through into the sitting room.

"I want to ask you something, and I want you to tell me the truth." I said gently, holding her hand.

It felt fragile in my grasp and I wondered whether I should go ahead with the conversation, but I needed, after all the years of deception, as well as the abuse I'd suffered at the hands of her husband, to hear the truth from her, together with her version of what had happened.

She looked at me, a little anxiously, but met my gaze steadily with her blue-grey eyes.

"I'll do my best!" she said quietly.

"Mam – who was my father?"

I let that sink in for a few seconds before adding "I know that Joe Culshaw was NOT!"

She looked at her lap for several minutes before she raised her head again and looked straight back at me.

"No. You're right – and you deserve the truth, now it no longer really matters! Your father was Sam Whittaker – Tina's father –."

I heaved a sigh of relief that she had now given me the real truth and not another prevarication. I was about to ask her for more, but she continued unprompted.

"I'm sorry, Micky. Times were different then. Sam was two-timing me – he hadn't actually married Jean when I found I was pregnant, but she was too – much further along than me – and Sam was far more scared of her old man than of my mam, so he married her, and I was left to pick up the pieces. There was no abortion in those days – not that I would *ever* have done that, even if there had been – or anything much in the way of contraception for that matter - and I was nearly out of my mind! Mam and I were living with your uncle Sean and his family, and they insisted I had to leave – they didn't want my sin associated with their home. I was working at the Mill and I knew that Joe Culshaw liked me. I don't know whether someone told him I was pregnant, or whether he just guessed it, but he offered marriage. He was the overlooker, so he was on a good wage and already had a house of his own – he was a good catch for a girl in trouble! And he was quite presentable – always well turned out, and he had lovely manners. He didn't drink himself stupid like most of the lads, and he was a churchgoer…"

Her voice tailed off and I realised she was crying.

"What I didn't realise was that he was a pig of a man, a vicious bully who wouldn't get into a fight with anyone who could hit back, but would happily beat a woman or a defenceless child! And then go to Mass as though nothing had happened! I wonder what he told the priest at confession? Mind you, if it was Father Flanagan then he'd not have been in a position to …"

I put my arms round her and held her. Again, I realised how frail she seemed, my arms used to the far more robust form of Davey.

"It's OK Mam! It's OK! You don't need to say any more…"

I explained then about the DNA testing and Tina's letter (which I showed her).

"I'd much rather have Sam as my dad than old man Culshaw. I didn't realise from what Tina said that Sam had been dating you both. Davey said that Sam had fathered half Chadderton…"

She forced a slight grin.

"He was a very attractive lad! You and Tina were the first as far as I know, but, yes, Davey's right – there are quite a few others as well as Jean's brood."

"Tell me about him…"

"There's not too much to tell. Like the rest of us, he worked at the Mill. He was taller than most of the lads, blond hair like yours – well, you've seen him! He had a way with him – much more confident than most of them – didn't need to get blind drunk to ask for a dance – and – and he'd get your knickers off before you'd notice the draught!"

She giggled, and I suddenly felt that I'd learned more about her in those few words than in the sixteen years I'd lived under the same roof, catching sight of the pretty young girl she had once been.

She'd said that Culshaw had been a catch, but I reckon that, even pregnant, he'd had the better bargain. I remembered how elegant she'd looked in the beautiful clothes she'd worn when I was a child. She'd been a good seamstress and had made a lot of them herself. but she'd also been able to treat herself with good accessories to set them off.

I took both of them out to lunch at the pub we'd been to before. I was tempted to go on to confront Sam, but decided to leave it for a while – after all, it was only a matter of weeks since Tina had died - and I had no reason to suppose that he had been anything other than a good father to her, despite the various unofficial progeny. After all, he'd stuck with Jean (and she with him) for forty-two years, which had to count for something.

It was dark by the time I got home. Davey had, as usual, taken himself off to the 'Swords to save Grace from cooking. As I'd already eaten I didn't bother to follow, and spent a little while sitting in the kitchen chatting to Grace.

Alex had of course shown her Tina's letter, so she knew why I had gone up north, and she nodded approvingly when I said that Mam had confirmed the story without any prompting. Since our original reconciliation Mam had come down to stay with us a number of times and she and Grace had got on extremely well together, so much so that Mam had occasionally come down to cook for us to give Grace a break. Under normal circumstances no-one was allowed to use 'her' kitchen - not even us!

"I always thought your mother was a decent woman – I'm glad it's now all out in the open. Are you going to contact your father?"

I sighed.

"I dunno. Part of me wants to, but it seems ridiculous after all these years! What do I say to him? What do I expect him to say to me? 'Hello son, sorry I missed your birthday – all forty-two of them!'?"

"I know it's a long time, but if you leave it too much longer it could be too late, and then you wouldn't be able to do or say anything and you'd always wonder…"

I sighed again. I knew she was right – I knew myself well enough to know that if I missed the opportunity, I would beat myself up ever after, but it still seemed too soon after Tina's death to confront him.

I went to bed early, tired out after the long drive. Davey rolled in around ten, waking me up.

"Did they run out of beer?" I asked sarcastically as he flopped onto the bed, nearly bouncing me onto the floor.

"Ha ha! Very funny! I just wanted to make sure you were safely home. How did it go?"

"She confirmed what Tina said without any prompting. It's not quite how I thought – she and Jean were both dating Sam – Jean got pregnant first, so Sam married her. Uncle Sean threw Mam out. Old man Culshaw offered to marry her – she didn't have much choice…"

"What are you going to do about Sam?"

"Oh, I dunno! Grace thinks I should go to see him before it's too late... I suppose I feel the same way really, but I can't say I'm looking forward to it much."

"You might be surprised…"

I switched the light on and looked at him. Something in his voice made me suspect that he knew more than he'd let on.

"Come on, Pryor! You know something, don't you?"

He gave me a sheepish look.

"You knew that he was my dad before Tina's letters, didn't you?!"

He nodded.

"How long?!"

"More or less since the divorce…"

I stared at him, incredulous.

"D'you remember that day when we overslept? I was supposed to go into Oxford in the morning and then Nick was recording here in the afternoon – the day after you told Danny the facts of life…"

"That's ten years ago!! You've known all this time?!"

He looked uncomfortable.

"Sam came down to see me. I was supposed to meet him in Oxford that day – well I did – Nick was able to manage without me for a couple of hours, so I sneaked off in the afternoon. I suppose the divorce and the situation between Tina and me made Sam feel that he was losing any real contact with you. Maybe he was just curious – I think it was difficult for him to get his head round me being gay – y'know – the father of his grandchildren and all that…I'm sorry Micky – I didn't really feel comfortable about keeping you in the dark, but everything was so raw for all of us, what with one thing and another. You'd been through so much, I didn't want to give you another problem to cope with."

"But what did he want? What did he say?"

"He just more or less came out with it. He started off by beating around the bush a bit – 'Sorry about the divorce' etc. 'Didn't have you down as a shirt-lifter' – that sort of thing."

"You're kidding!"

"Yup!" he grinned. "But I think he genuinely finds the whole idea of two guys together a bit of an uphill struggle. Maybe being such a ladies' man himself? I dunno. He talked about how angry Teen was about the whole thing and then he came out with it. '*Of course, Micky being her brother was the last straw*' – as though I already knew, which I didn't! Teen had never said anything about that, but of course it all made sense then – her reaction when I said that I only married her because she looked like you and all the rest of it. I *know* I should have told you, but there never seemed to be a right time – there was always something going on, and the longer I left it the harder it would have been."

I was silent for quite a long time, wondering if he was going to add anything, but he didn't.

"Did he say anything at all about me?"

"Yeah – he's always taken an interest. I think he'd have been around when you were a kid if it hadn't been for Joe. I don't imagine that he would have taken it too well if Sam had tried to contact you! I think your mam probably warned him off too – there was a lot to lose, one way and another. He knows you've been through it, but I haven't told him much beyond what's been in the press – he doesn't know about what happened when you were a kid – he'd have killed Father Flan if he'd known about that! He's always been quite proud of you – I don't think that helped with Teen much, either. Please Micky – go see him – soon! I've always got on well with him, and he IS the kids' grandfather. He's not such a bad guy – just a little careless about fathering children…"

My emotions were doing cartwheels – Davey had known…Sam could have been there for me…he had wanted to stay in contact… my head was spinning. Davey's arms tightened around me, feeling me tremble, sensing that I was close to tears.

"OK..." I said quietly. "I'll go – if you'll come with me..."

"It's probably better if he comes down here. I don't think Jean knows that we kept in touch and it might not be a good time to ..."

"Here? Has he been here, to the farm?"

He shook his head.

"No. No, he's not been here – we've always met in Oxford, apart from a couple of times at Mam's. It had to be somewhere we weren't likely to bump into Teen - or you – or Jean."

"Will you contact him? Or shall I write to him? I don't know what to say..."

"I'll do it – but you must promise to go through with it – not back out at the last minute..."

"I promise!" I said, making the cross-my-heart gesture.

I suddenly felt a strong urge to meet the man who had given me life. I knew little about him really. I knew he was Catholic – most of the neighbourhood had been, Davey's family excepted – but, as far as I knew, the Whittakers had not been particularly observant, beyond some of the kids going to St. Michael's. Sam had obviously shared his blond curly hair with Tina and myself, as well as passing it on a generation to Danny. We had also inherited his above-average height and slender build but, those superficial resemblances aside, I had no idea of his character or interests. I didn't remember ever exchanging more than half a dozen words with him, or him ever showing any sign of even acknowledging my existence, so it was more than a bit of a surprise to hear that he had wanted to retain even the slightest contact.

Chapter 45:

1997, Oxford. Micky

I didn't have to wait long to meet him. Davey phoned him the next morning and he came down the following day.

Davey drove me into town and we met him in the King's Head, near the New Bodleian Library. The pub was a warren of small rooms, jumbled haphazardly together, but Davey had obviously met Sam there before and led me to a small nook in one corner.

Sam was already there. He looked up as we entered the room and stood up quickly, nearly knocking his pint over as he did so. He gave a half-smile, followed by an anxious look. I had stopped suddenly in the doorway and Davey gave me a shove, sending me stumbling towards him. We stopped, several feet apart, and stared at each other.

"Micky?"

I bit my lip, desperate not to show how traumatic I was finding things. I opened my mouth to try to say something polite, or even conventional, but all that came out was a croak which sounded superficially like "Dad…"

He obviously thought that was what I had said, as he seemed to sigh and held his arms out. Davey gave me another shove, straight into Sam's embrace. His arms closed round me in an awkward man-hug. He was shaking.

"Oh my God! I've been awake all night trying to work out what to say to you, but it's all gone…"

I closed my eyes. There was something primeval in the strange familiarity of his smell. Maybe that is something to do with DNA – I have no idea – but, just as the day when Mam and I made our peace, suddenly I experienced the strangest sensation of belonging, of completeness. We sat down on the settle, side by side. Davey went off to get drinks, leaving us alone together.

"Micky, I know you were upset that Davey didn't tell you the truth - about me - but that was partly my fault. I thought things were complicated enough at the time. I know you've been through some – some bad stuff – and I just wish I could have been there for you...You probably know that there are a few more little Sams around, as well as my kids with Jean... I'm not making any excuses – I was a randy little so-and-so when I was younger! Tina was the eldest, but if I could have chosen, I would have married your mam – Annie was always my special girl – but Jeannie's dad was not one you could ignore...I used to look at old Culshaw and think of him with Annie and it used to eat me up...The others –"

He shrugged

"I can't make any excuses. If it was on offer I took it! I collected affiliation orders like other people collect parking tickets, and there are probably others where it never went to court..."

I looked at him for a few minutes without saying anything. Part of me understood, part of me felt as bemused by what he had said as he probably felt about Davey and me.

Close to, the resemblance was even more striking. If you had photographs of Sam, me and Dan, you would probably have thought we were the same guy at different ages. Sam's eyes were a truer blue than mine and Dan's hair possibly yellower, but our features, and even some of our mannerisms, were identical. I caught a glimpse of how he must have looked alongside Mam – they would have been a stunning couple - and I could understand his comment about the thought of Mam and Joe…such a tragic waste!

Davey came back with the drinks to find us deep in conversation. He put the glasses down and tiptoed out again.

Sam looked up to see him retreating and said quietly "I'm glad you're happy with Davey. I must admit it was a huge shock when it all happened, but he's a top bloke and I knew he wasn't happy with Tina. He's been a good father to the kids, and I know they adore you, too. They're a great pair!"

"If I hadn't had Davey, I wouldn't be here!" I said simply.

"But you had another – boyfriend – before Andy…?"

"Yes. His name is Alex, and it was…" I shook my head. "… it was just wonderful, but Davey has always been the love of my life. It broke my heart when he married Tina. After that I had no one until Alex came along, and I was in a very bad place. Then, after Andy…died…Alex vanished from my life – or at least, he had to keep his distance – and I was – suicidal. Davey and Paddy were great – they stayed with me through it all and stopped me from killing myself, but it was horrible. And then –" I smiled at the memory "and then suddenly Davey and I were together! I never set out to take him away from Tina and the kids…"

Sam gently put his hand under my chin and turned my head towards him.

"Hey – I realise that! I could see that marriage unravelling a long time before it finally did. Tina trampled all over him and he obviously didn't want to be there. I understand how difficult it is – I stuck with Jeannie and we made things work somehow, but it's never easy. We stuck together for the kids, but Sal and

Dan were better off when Tina and Davey were apart – even with Tina bad-mouthing their father at every opportunity! Like I said, Sal and Dan both adore you especially Dan – he says he can talk to you about anything…"

I nodded ruefully.

"Yeah. I'm not sure that's always been a good thing…"

"It's better that he can talk to you, than not having anyone to talk to! He told me what you said to him a long time ago, about how much you love Davey. And Davey has told me that too…You are a son to be proud of, Micky! When Davey and Tina first split up I didn't get it at all, but I do now. I've seen the change in Davey, and I've heard it from him and the kids, and it's changed my thinking. Once upon a time I'd have disowned you – now I'm proud of you! You're a survivor, you're a MAN! And a great musician, and a great parent…"

There were tears in his eyes, his voice husky with emotion.

Davey had obviously been lurking within earshot as, the conversation having fallen away, he came back in, looking anxiously from one to the other of us. He seemed satisfied with what he found and moved a chair close to me and sat down.

Eventually, reluctantly, Sam indicated that he had to leave. We ran him back to the station and I hugged him, promising that we would now keep in touch as best we could, although it would have to be done in such a way as not to risk upsetting Jean.

I was quiet on the journey home; much to my surprise I had bonded with Sam immediately, and now felt desperate to see him again and to keep in touch, the sense of having missed out in my childhood making an ache inside which nagged so much it became a physical pain.

We stopped off at the 'Swords, but I wasn't feeling all that sociable and after a couple of drinks I made my excuses and would have walked home across the fields, had Davey not insisted on driving me, a little worried that I might not be in the calmest frame of mind.

I went and sat at the piano in the music room, doodling the beginnings of a melody. After a while Davey, obviously bored, took himself off to bed, but I stayed there. A chorus began to form in my mind '*You gave me life…*' over and over. It fitted the melody and then some verses followed. As always, I had set the recorder running...

Several hours later Davey came to find me, worried that I hadn't come to bed. He found me almost asleep over the keyboard and gently woke me.

"What are you up to? Do you know what time it is?"

"Eh? No idea…"

"It's almost three o'clock! Come to bed…What have you been doing?"

He switched the recorder off, ran it back and listened to the last ten minutes or so, his eyes widening as he heard the raw emotion in my voice.

"Bloody hell, Mick! That's sensational! Did you just write that? I've not heard it before…"

"I wrote it for Sam." I said simply.

Davey looked at me in amazement.

"For Sam?! It sounds like you're singing to a lover!"

"I suppose it could mean a lot of things, depending on how you hear it, but it's for Sam."

"Are you going to record it? We MUST record it!!"

I shook my head.

"No – it's too personal…I was going to put it on a tape and send it to him…"

"If you do that, Jean'll kill him! It would be far more to the point if we record it, and then you can tell him that you wrote it for him. That way he can listen to it without Jean suspecting anything. I promise you, it'll go to No. 1 with no trouble! I reckon it will outsell *Angel* and everything else we've ever done!"

I looked at him doubtfully, too tired and too emotionally close to it to know whether he was right or wrong. He switched the machine off and gently but firmly took me off to bed, pulling my clothes off and tucking me under the duvet before slipping in next to me. I was asleep even before he'd turned the light out.

In the morning he phoned Paddy and Bird before I was awake and then came and woke me with a tray of coffee, juice and fruit. This was a rare event, and I knew he was trying to get me in a good humour in preparation for a possible power-struggle over whether to record the song, but by now I had had time to think it over and accepted that he was probably right – not so much about the likely success of the record, but about it being an acceptable way to present it to Sam.

We were in the studio when the others arrived. I had recorded the vocal properly, with a few minor changes suggested by Davey to make the song slightly less Sam-centric and more credible as a love song, while retaining its personal message from me to Sam.

I had accompanied myself on the electric piano in the studio, adjusting the tone to get it as close to an acoustic piano as possible. I had never done this before, the guitar always being my first choice, but this suited the song better and Davey had added some gentle percussion to give a framework.

Paddy and Bird arrived together and, while we drank coffee, they listened to the raw track. Paddy nearly spilt his coffee when my voice first hit the chorus, cracking with emotion on the first '*You gave me life…*'

"Christ! Micky – how did you do that?! Did you really write this for Sam? It sounds more like something you'd sing to Davey…"

"Or Alex…." Davey teased.

I glared at him reproachfully, my sense of humour totally absent that morning. Bird was still listening intently, and I knew he was thinking of possible arrangements and how best to treat the song.

We put the nascent track to one side, having made a working copy, and Bird and Paddy went into the studio. Paddy laid down a simple bass line, reinforcing Davey's percussion with a light touch. Bird tried a number of ideas for a guitar accompaniment, but eventually decided that the most striking treatment was to supply a vibrant middle-eight solo, leaving the rest of the track without any guitars. He put his Gibson down, having completed the solo to his satisfaction, and went over to the synth.

He called me in.

"Now, what I think would work would be some strings, just dotted here and there to highlight the rest of it. A string intro – and maybe between the verses - and then a short outro with strings reaching a crescendo and then just leaving it hanging."

I nodded, happy that he was on message. I hoped that he would take over, but he shook his head and gestured that I should sit down at the keyboard. Together we selected the voices required, and then he hummed what he could hear in his head and we put it together, piece by piece.

"Now", he said gently but firmly, "I'll mix it!"

We went into the control room and he wove the various tracks together until he arrived at the result he wanted. Davey and Paddy had long since got bored and had vanished over to the house, but I phoned across and they came back to listen. By this point I was sitting with my fingers in my ears, unable to listen to any more.

The completed track was just short of five minutes – longer than average, but by no means over-long. I saw Paddy exchange glances with Davey and then with Bird and then saw them all grinning hugely. I shook my head crossly, thinking that they were laughing at me and the emotion.

Paddy leapt up and came over and hugged me.

"You are a total fucking genius!! That is the best thing we've ever done and if it doesn't go platinum I'll give up music and go work in the Co-op…"

He played it through again, making me listen this time. As with *Angel* I could hardly believe that it was my voice. This time though, I had written it – a cry of anguish and love to Sam.

Davey came to sit beside me.

"If you'd written that for anyone other than Sam I'd kill them!"

He put his arm round my shoulders and kissed me gently. I squirmed slightly, experiencing one of those moments of intense shyness, but also wishing that it was just the two of us there.

As before, we sent a copy of the recording down to London by courier. Predictably, a few hours later CBS were on the phone demanding a B-side within 24 hours.

I shook my head hopelessly.

"I can't" I said simply. "I'm totally knackered – I couldn't write a nursery rhyme let alone a song!"

"Haven't you anything you've been working on?" Paddy asked quietly.

"Nothing suitable for this. Can't we do what we did before – two different versions?"

"You can get away with that once, but I think it would be taking the piss to do it again."

I looked at Bird who looked a bit embarrassed.

"I've got something – if that's not treading on your toes…?"

"You can tread all you like as far as I'm concerned" I said, looking round at Davey, who nodded.

Bird proceeded to play us a simple, acoustic-backed song with a slightly Mexican feel. I'd not really heard him sing before, other than his harmonies to my lead vocals. He had a good voice and I liked the song – it was lightweight, but a good contrast to the power of *Gave Me Life.* We all agreed to use it and went back into the studio, eventually using Bird to sing the lead with his own acoustic accompaniment. I added a few discreet harmonies and a few strategically placed, counterpoint acoustic guitar riffs. As with the A-side, Paddy and Davey supplied some very gentle bass notes and percussion, adding to the Mexican feel.

As had happened with *Angel,* CBS pushed it out within a matter of days and again the media went mad. Davey phoned Sam and told him to listen to the radio. The record went to the top of the charts in its first week and the whole circus started all over again…

This time round it was me who was the least enthusiastic about touring, I still loved performing, I loved the buzz of provoking a reaction from a crowd – the bigger the better – and the sheer scale of the sound in a big venue. At the same time, I also liked playing the really small, intimate places. What I had begun to hate, or even dread, was the endless travelling and being away from home. Now that I had a real father who I loved, as well as a mother, and as they were not getting any younger, I wanted to see as much of them as I could, as often as I could, and I dreaded being away in case anything happened while I was too far away to get home quickly.

I shared these thoughts with Davey who, his own mother in mind, understood only too well how I felt, Mag being a fair bit older than either Sam or my mam. For those reasons we drew up a set of stipulations for Benny, limiting our live appearances to a maximum of ten per year, spread over two months, with various geographical formulae intended to ensure that we would never be out of reach for more than 48 hours if an emergency arose. In the same way we also limited the number of media appearances we would do when promoting the issue of a new record, although that could be more flexible should we be in line for an award. Media appearances overseas could be managed by taking advantage of a satellite link or pre-recording interviews in the UK for broadcast elsewhere.

Chapter 46:

1997, Old Kennel Farm. Misty

Danny had arrived on the Friday evening, ostensibly to spend the weekend with us as in the old days.

He spent Saturday morning hanging out with Davey, and after lunch I went through to the music room, intending to do my daily practice – essential these days to stop my hands from stiffening up. I realised that Dan had followed me through.

"What's up? If you're bored get your guitar and we'll jam…"

He shook his head.

"I need to talk to someone," he said quietly. "I thought I might talk to Dad but…well, you know what he's like – he doesn't listen properly…"

"Only too well! OK, will I do?"

"Yeah – but not here – can we go for a walk?"

"OK. It's muddy across the fields, we'll need wellies…"

We wandered off, through the stable yard and out onto the bridleway, heading north as that would give us a longer walk without the likelihood of bumping into anyone. The path was reasonably wide in that direction, giving us a good margin from the riverbank. We walked in silence for a while and I thought it might be easier for him to open up if we found somewhere to sit.

There was a rusting and long-abandoned harrow, tucked just inside a field gate, under some trees, and I went through and perched on the end, inviting Dan to sit beside me. I waited for him to speak. He began to try to start the conversation a couple of times, but without giving me any clue as to what he was trying to say.

Eventually he sighed heavily, took a gulp of air and, without any other preamble said "Misty – how did you know you were gay?"

I studied the toes of my boots and thought for a while. Carefully avoiding any mention of Andy, I eventually said "I don't know. I'm not sure that I did. I only ever wanted to be with Davey – he was the only person I ever felt really safe with. I tried dating girls but – um – well, kissing was OK, but I could never – er – never…so I thought I might be - was possibly - gay. I – er – I tried it on with your dad, but he said that he wasn't -wasn't interested. He was already dating your mam, and they got married not long after that – I was heartbroken! After that I didn't know what to do. I went to a few gay clubs – or at least, clubs that I had heard that were gay-friendly, but it really wasn't my scene – all the leather and studs and moustaches and stuff – it scared me to death! When we were on the road, I used to bung someone in the road crew a few quid for a quick snog and a cuddle or whatever, but until I met Alex that was as far as it went…"

"How did you meet him?"

"I went out to buy milk and came back with him instead!"

I smiled at the memory of that sunny morning.

"Seriously! It can't be as simple as that…?"

"You must remember that this was before the AIDS thing started… It was a lovely morning and I'd walked from my flat in Chelsea along the King's Road towards Putney, before turning down towards the river. I was very hung over from an after-tour party. There was a bench in the sun and I sat for a while. This guy – Alex – sat down at the other end. He thought I was on the game and propositioned me – I thought all my Christmases had come at once! I took him back to the flat and – and that was that. We were lovers for three years or more until – well, you know the rest…"

"So you've only ever actually slept with Alex and Dad?"

I crossed my fingers behind my back before answering.

"Mmm."

It wasn't a total lie – as far as sleeping was concerned it was true, but there had of course been the punters I had picked up on my other rambles along the river, and my horrific experiences…

I suddenly realised what he was asking me.

"Danny – are you trying to tell me you think you might be gay?"

He sighed deeply again.

"I'm beginning to wonder… I just don't seem to get it right with anyone! I've tried dating girls, but they either turn me down flat or we go out and they either end up going off with someone else or spend all evening talking about someone else."

"Have you tried dating guys?"

"No! I've had a couple of black eyes though…"

I bit my lip to stop myself from laughing.

"Poor Danny! Have you not managed to get anyone into bed?"

He shook his head ruefully.

"Is there anyone who you've really felt attracted to? Someone who you really felt you wanted to take to bed?"

"Not really. There were one or two girls at school that I fancied, but I'm not sure how much of that was that I actually fancied them, or that everyone else did – you know how it is…"

"What about boys?"

He shook his head again.

"Not at school! There was a huge amount of homophobia around – you'd never have dared to even look at anyone that way, let alone try anything!"

"College? Work?"

"Nope. Micky – isn't there anyone that you know who'd take me to bed and…"

I shook my head.

"It doesn't work that way, Dan. At least, not among the people I know... Maybe in some circles, but your dad and I aren't exactly 'on the scene'. I'm the only guy he's ever…at least, as far as I know… OK, we know quite a lot of other gays, but they're people like Alex and Nat – people who've been together a long time. You need to be very careful these days…Wouldn't it be better, and easier, and safer, to find yourself someone female to sleep with first?"

He sighed again.

"How?! I've tried, but they just pat me on the head, or use me as a meal ticket…OK, I could probably find a hooker, but I don't think I could…"

"You ought to meet Sapphire…" I suggested. "She's your sort of age…"

Danny stared at me before letting out a crack of laughter, sounding uncannily like his father.

"What's so funny? She's working here in the studio…"

"Misty!! You of all people!! Don't you get why she calls herself Sapphire?"

"No idea – she always wears blue and silver – I thought it was just part of the image…"

Dan shook his head despairingly.

"For Sapphire read Sappho – she's gay you idiot! Her girlfriend is the band's guitarist – the one whose guitar parts you were supposed to be providing…"

"Don't be idiotic! The band are all guys…"

"When did you last get your eyes tested?! All five of them are girls…"

I stared at him, suddenly feeling very old, as well as very stupid.

"Their original name was Sappho and Sliver, but the BBC wouldn't give them airtime, so they changed it to Sapphire and Silver. In a lot of ways, the Beeb did them a favour, because it gave Sapphy the idea to dye her hair that colour and the whole shiny image – I don't think they'd have caught anyone's attention without all the publicity – or at least, not that quickly."

I was tempted to say that it was a pity they hadn't had time to literally get their act together a bit better but, given their huge success, decided that was probably way too bitchy, and that I was just feeling miffed at having been caught out…

We walked back into the stable yard, only to find that someone had bolted the Judas door from the other side. I groaned, Short of growing wings, we had the choice of walking three sides of the farm to the main road and back up the drive, or back in the opposite direction along the river, round past the 'Swords and across the fields via the footpath – liable to be a muddy walk, even if neither of us actually managed to fall into the water.

Danny grinned and pulled out his mobile – something I did not yet have, and had been unconvinced of the necessity for, although Davey had had one since they had first been available and had been the size and weight of several bricks.

"Dad – you've locked us out – we're in the 'yard."

I could hear the crack of laughter from where we stood, and then the sound of the bolts being drawn back.

"Serve you right for sneaking off without me!" he grinned. "Where've you been, anyway?"

"Boy talk!" I said shortly.

Danny went off with his father and I let them go, feeling that after our chat he might appreciate the time to talk to him.

I started to walk towards the studio but spotted Sapphy perched on the wall of the fountain. She looked a little pensive but, hearing me approach, looked up and smiled. Apart from her trademark, electric-blue hair, she was comparatively soberly dressed today – black skinny jeans and an electric-blue T-shirt, eyes ringed with kohl. If it hadn't been for the black lipstick she'd have looked pretty.

"Hi!"

She seemed genuinely pleased to see me.

"How are you? Are you feeling better?"

I frowned, forgetting that Davey had told her that I was 'indisposed'.

"Sorry about letting you down – things suddenly…happened…"

"No worries! Bird's been brilliant – he's got some great ideas, and he's been teaching Jo how to play the guitar parts, for when we're doing them live."

"I hope he hasn't been teaching her anything else!" I said warily, thinking of the four wives etc.

Sapphy grinned.

"I get the impression Jo is happy anyway!"

"I thought she was your girlfriend?"

Sapphy grinned again.

"Oh that! That's all a publicity stunt! And it certainly worked – we'd still be playing around the colleges if the Beeb hadn't banned us…"

"You're not gay?"

She shook her head, still grinning.

"Not in the least! I'm not entirely sure about the 'guys' – I'm not saying that they're completely straight – a lot of giggling goes on – especially on the tour-bus in the dark, but Jo and our tour manager definitely have a thing going…"

"What about you?"

She pulled a face.

"No-one special at the moment. Are you offering?"

I felt myself blush.

"I'm twice your age! And you must be aware that Davey and I are …"

"Pity!"

She smiled flirtatiously.

"The age thing doesn't bother me. I think you're really cool!"

She touched my cheek gently, letting her fingers slide down to trace the line of my lower lip. I felt an odd stirring that normally only Davey or Alex could provoke.

I tried to concentrate on the things about her that I didn't like, but the black lipstick really was the only thing… That aside, she was gorgeous! I tried to analyse this – she didn't have a particularly boyish figure – her breasts, although small, were only too obvious through the tight T-shirt, and her waist was tiny in proportion to her hips. I tried to think of her as a cross-dresser, but she was far too pretty – very definitely female!

She was watching my face.

"Misty?"

I pulled myself together with an effort.

"No!"

I said, as gently as I could.

"I really am very flattered, and you've given me feelings that I can barely remember, but – No! I'm sorry, Sapphy, but I couldn't do anything that might hurt

Davey. We've been together a very long time now – most of our lives, one way and another…"

"I know. I read the papers!" she smiled. "You've had some real bad stuff. Is this latest story going to set things straight once and for all?"

"Oh God I hope so!" I said with feeling.

"That guy you were with just now – the one who looks like you? Is he your son?"

"He's Davey's son and my nephew. His mother was my sister – half-sister…"

"You sure like to keep things in the family, don't you?"

I winced a little at the implications, but realised that it was probably fair comment, and also that I now had the perfect opportunity to introduce her to Dan. I wondered how to broach the subject without risking embarrassing him.

"Danny would really like to meet you. Why don't you come to supper with us?"

"Do I get to sit next to you?"

I sighed.

"If you promise to behave yourself! Remember what I said about Davey…I'm asking you to come to meet Danny, not flirt with me!"

She pouted prettily, fluttering her eyelashes sexily, but I suddenly twigged that she was just playing with me. She realised I had rumbled her and burst out laughing.

"Oh Misty! I'm so sorry! I really DO fancy you, but you've made it quite clear that you are out of bounds and I respect that. Too many people would be happy just to grab and go. I promise I'll behave myself – at least with you and Davey – I'm not making any promises about Danny – if he's as gorgeous as you, I may not be able to help myself!"

"Be gentle with him." I warned "He's more than a little confused at the moment, especially having just lost his mother. You may need to be patient with him…"

"Message received and understood! It must have been tough for him – how old was he when his parents split?"

"About eight, though I'm not sure how much he was told at that point. Both kids were used to us touring, so Davey not being at home wasn't anything new."

"Both? Who's the other one?"

"Sally. She's two years old than Dan. She lives in London with her boyfriend – I get the feeling they'll probably marry soon."

"So, she'd have been ten? That's rough. I was about that age when my parents split. You're dealing with a lot of stuff, without suddenly losing a parent."

"You seem to have survived!" I said drily.

"I found music. Until then I was a basket case – anorexia, dope, totally unsuitable guys…"

"Like me?"

She grinned.

"Other than the fact that you're gay, and a *little* older than me, you would be extremely suitable, compared to most of my early boyfriends! Seriously, what you see now is straight, in every sense of the word, and a model citizen. Music did that – and a fair amount of therapy…"

"Are you happy to try to help Danny? I don't want to do anything that might tip him over the edge…"

She made a cross-my-heart sign.

I went back inside and told Grace that we'd be one extra for dinner. I found Davey in the music room watching children's TV.

"Where's Dan?"

He blipped the remote and switched the set off.

"Went to get cleaned up. What was it all about?"

I hesitated, unsure whether to share what had been said, although Danny hadn't actually told me not to tell his father, the problem having been the wish to talk to someone with some sensitivity, rather than it being a secret.

"Micky, I'm his father..."

"Yeah, I know... He just felt I'd be easier to talk to, that's all. It's – it's nothing too earth-shattering..."

"Well then, what? Don't tell me he's got some bird up the..."

I shook my head quickly.

"No, definitely not that! That's part of the problem."

I let that sink in before saying "It's probably our fault, but he's not sure whether...whether he's..."

"Arthur or Martha?"

I didn't reply, not entirely happy with the expression, which had been common currency, along with a lot far worse, in our childhood.

"Is that what you are trying not to tell me? Oh Micky! Please tell me you're winding me up!"

I shook my head.

"I think the main problem is that he's no experience either way. He seems to be too shy to make the first move, and he's obviously not giving out the right signals to anyone, one way or the other."

I watched Davey's face as his expression went through the whole spectrum.

"Davey – he's not saying he's gay, he's just saying that he doesn't know who he is! I can understand that, although I think I always knew that *you* were what I wanted, but it was so difficult in those days – especially living with Joe Culshaw – it was a far bigger deal. I really tried to be 'normal', but even when I knew for sure I couldn't be, there were still so few options, especially living up north where everyone knew me. Even in London the clubs were horrible if you were a bit shy – and then when we became successful I didn't dare do anything that would have outed me. I was desperate to find someone - if I hadn't met Alex when I did, I don't think I'd be here now…"

He got up and came to me, pulling me into his arms.

"Don't talk like that! I can't bear the thought of you being so unhappy – or the thought of you doing anything so stupid…"

His lips found mine and we kissed with an intensity that took my breath away. Before I knew what was happening we were on the floor and he was tugging at my jeans. I was worried that Danny might walk in on us, but suddenly my mind flipped back in time and images of being on the carpet in the flat, Andy on top of me, the images interspersed with others, even darker, of the floor of the cell and the agony…

I screamed hysterically, tearing myself away from him and rolling up protectively, incapable of getting up, paralysed with fear and nausea.

"Micky! Micky what's the matter??"

Davey's voice broke through the nightmare in my head. I was sobbing helplessly.

The door from the bedroom wing crashed open and Danny rushed in. He took in the fact that we were both in a state of disarray.

"What the fuck are you doing to him?!! Micky, Micky are you OK?"

He knelt beside me, accusation in his eyes as he glared at Davey who was by now also in tears.

"I didn't DO anything. We were – something obviously upset him, but I have no idea what –."

Danny gently pulled me up and onto the sofa, wrapping his arms round me protectively.

"It's OK!" He said gently. "It's OK. I'm here, you're safe. Dad you'd better go…"

"Don't be ridiculous! Micky, I'm going to ring Dr. Petersen…"

"No!" I sobbed. "No, please! I'll be OK…"

"What was it? What upset you?"

My thoughts were still whirling, but I managed to piece together what had happened.

"It – it must have been because we were on the floor – you must have touched me somehow and I thought I was back in the flat with Andy – and then I was in the cell and that guy was – was –"

I still had difficulty in saying the words. I knew now, after so many sessions with Dr Petersen, exactly what had happened to me on both occasions. Davey had obviously, inadvertently, touched me in a way that my body recognised as being a preliminary to that practice – something I would never have willingly endured. I was shaking helplessly, but at least I had managed to stop crying.

"Do you want a drink?"

I shook my head. Davey rolled a joint and we shared it between the three of us. Gradually I began to feel calmer.

Grace tapped at the other door. Davey went and opened it enough to speak to her, but without her being able to see in. There was a mutter of conversation before he closed the door again.

"Dinner's ready. Sapphy's already here, in the library. Dan, you go and talk to her – we'll be out in a few minutes – if Micky feels OK…"

Dan looked panic-stricken, but recognised that he had little choice under the circumstances.

We showered quickly and put on fresh clothes before joining the youngsters in the library. The hot water had restored my equilibrium and there was little trace of the hysteria of twenty minutes earlier, but I still felt shaky inside and was happy to let the others do the talking.

Danny shot me an anxious glance, but said nothing, presumably not wishing to say anything in front of Sapphy. Davey poured me a large gin and we went through to the dining room, he and I sitting on one side of the table and Dan and Sapphy on the other. She was good company, with a very dry sense of humour and a quick intellect. I could see that Danny was very taken with her, and mentally crossed my fingers that things would go well.

After the meal had ended, Danny invited Sapphy up to the games room upon some pretext or other. I was feeling very tired by now and went off to bed, Davey turning in some time later.

"Is she still here?"

"I haven't seen any sign of her leaving, so I suppose so. She's good fun, isn't she? Did you put her up to this?"

"Not exactly. I suggested she should come to eat with us and meet Dan. I may have said that he'd like to meet her, and I did tell her to be gentle with him. I didn't exactly suggest she should seduce him! I don't think she would deliberately hurt him... Her own parents split when she was about the same age, so she understands what he's been through. Her whole persona is an act – underneath all the brashness I think she's a nice girl, although it sounds like she's had a few battles of her own in the past."

When we entered the kitchen the next morning, Sapphy was there with Dan, tucking into a vast cooked breakfast.

She was still wearing the clothes she had been in the previous evening but was make-up less, so I assumed she had stayed the night. Danny looked sleepy but happy, and they seemed to be completely at ease with one another.

I offered to drive her back into Oxford.

"No, that's OK. The guys will be here soon – I don't need to go back for anything right now."

Breakfast finished, she headed for the barn. Dan made to follow but I caught his arm.

"Everything OK?"

"Everything's wonderful! Sapphy's wonderful!..."

"That's great – Danny – you're a big boy now, but be careful – don't get hurt..."

He smiled, a little uncertainly.

"I'll try not to. I know what you are trying to tell me, and I know all the arguments, but I'm – she's –"

He sighed.

"Last night was very, very special, and I wished it could last forever. Part of me knows that it's unlikely, but I'm not going to run away just yet, even if my heart gets a bit dented in the process."

I hugged him tightly. I knew he had to go where his heart led him, but I also knew that the chances were that, in a week's time, Sapphy would have got bored and ditched him.

I let him go and he ran off towards the barn. Davey had obviously been watching from the window as he suddenly appeared beside me.

"All well?"

I nodded.

"Seems like it. She'll break his heart, but I think he now knows who he is better than he did yesterday. Our little lad's grown up!"

Danny stayed on with us until Sapphy and the band had finished recording and then, as they headed back to their base in London, announced he was going with them.

I took Sapphy to one side and asked her if that was a problem but, to her credit, she seemed as besotted as he was, promising to look after him and, if she had any concerns about him, to let us know immediately.

Chapter 47:

1998, Old Kennel Farm, Misty

Life moved on. Much to my surprise Dan and Sapphy remained an item, and he found himself on her band's payroll as a PA/facilitator/general dogs-body, tagging along happily as they circled the globe.

As we had found several decades earlier, what went down well in one country often bombed in another. They were, almost uniquely, a huge success in both the States and the UK, but had little or no success in mainland Europe or Australia. This however worked quite well for them, as they were able to spend much of their time at home, jet-hopping across the Atlantic when and if necessary, thus saving a lot of time and money which might otherwise have gone in endless touring and promotion.

Sally's live-in romance moved up a gear and she announced that she wanted to get married. Davey, taken by surprise, blew his top, but eventually simmered down when we pointed out that Sal was now twenty-five and more than old enough to know her own mind and that she had been living with Paul since leaving university four years before so, if she didn't know him well enough by now, it was unlikely that she ever would.

He was a nice enough lad; they'd met at Uni, albeit on different courses and, of the two, Sal was almost certainly the more intelligent, although he now had a good job at the Courtauld Institute – not all that well paid, but with good prospects for progressing up the career ladder either there or at some other institution. We didn't see a lot of him – he found our world a little too far out, although he sometimes came to stay if there was something on in Oxford that he wanted to attend.

Sal declared her wish to marry locally to us so that they could have the reception at home. This led to much head-scratching as to where to have the ceremony itself – there being little choice at that date other than a church or register office. Sal's inclination had been for one of the churches which I attended, despite not really having been raised as a Catholic, but Paul was not keen, his own family being Anglican, and eventually they settled on one of the stunning but tiny village churches within easy reach of the farm.

Even without their friends, the guest list would have been enormous, what with Tina's five siblings and their families, Davey's eight and theirs - and that was only Sal's side! After a lot of consultation and diplomacy it was decided that a line would have to be drawn, and that family would be limited to uncles and aunts only, except where certain cousins were also friends. The friends' list was likewise to be limited to very close friends only. By that means we managed to get the numbers down to around a hundred.

"Where are we going to put them all?!"

"I reckon we can probably use both gardens without too much to-ing and fro-ing."

"What happens if it rains?!"

"We can use the ground floor of the main house – if we move the dining room table back against the outside wall and move the sofa and chairs etc. in the library, plus the hall area, that should easily cope."

"They won't all be able to sit down. I thought Sal wanted a sit-down meal?"

"Well she'll just have to choose – if she wants to have it here then that's how it will have to be! The only other solution would be to get one of the fields mown and have a marquee, but then you'd need an army of waiters to ferry things around. The house and gardens will be a much better bet. We can lock the doors through to our part. If we don't book out the studio that week, we can use the kennel rooms as well as the four in the house and the guest room."

"If all the aunts and uncles come that still leaves us six rooms short, even without your mam! They won't all come! Will they?"

Davey suddenly looked alarmed.

"They might do, out of curiosity, if nothing else!" I said brutally. "I suppose we can use the games room and the rest area in the studio – that gives us another two rooms. Maybe we can borrow a couple of caravans if we're really stuck…"

"Or ask Ally if we can borrow a couple of stables…"

"Don't be fatuous! Apart from anything else, you're the youngest – some of the uncles and aunts are knocking on a bit!"

"Not that much. Tina was the eldest of her lot, so hers are younger than you. Mam can have the guest room – can't we shove someone in with her?"

"Like who? I was thinking that Sam and Jean would have that room…"

Davey groaned

"I suppose that makes more sense as it's the biggest room. Mam can have Dan's old room so she's next to Sal…"

The debate rumbled on. The biggest headache was what to do with my mam. If she came it could cause a massive problem with Jean but, on the other hand, she had become an extra grandparent to Sal and Dan, and it seemed cruel not to invite her. In the end Davey had a word with Mag who said very firmly that Mam had to be invited, could share with her, and that she would try to act as a bodyguard to make sure there was no problem with Jean.

The other minefield was Grace. Although she would never have admitted it, she was getting older and, while she could still cope admirably with a small dinner-party, it was obviously going to be an impossibility for her to cater the entire wedding, even with Sylvia and her extended family helping. When I said as much to Davey, he offered to talk to her, but I quickly told him to leave it to me, much as I dreaded the conversation.

To my surprise she agreed with me without any argument, but said that she would be happy to make the cake, as well as catering for our house guests, although she suggested that we got Sylvia's daughters in to help her with the breakfasts. I heaved a sigh of relief, although this now left me with the problem of how to engage an outside caterer for the wedding without offending Sylvia.

Luckily that problem also partially solved itself when we ended up having to book all the available rooms at the 'Swords for Paul's family, meaning that Sylvia would be fully occupied in looking after them.

The day before the wedding Davey and Dan both drove up to Manchester to fetch our respective mothers [Davey] and Sam and Jean [Dan]. We had hired a coach for the other family members, having decided that was preferable to having a dozen or more cars littering the drive. That in itself caused a further problem – it would be impossible to get a coach down the drive and under the railway bridge and even above it there was nowhere to turn it round. We managed to get temporary permission for a pull-off area at the top of the drive and Gerry kindly provided the pub minibus to use as a ferry for both guests and luggage from the main road to the house.

Chapter 48:

Late summer 1998, Old Kennel Farm. Misty.

I sat in the sun on my usual perch on the fountain wall, directing the various caterers, florists etc.

Dan arrived first with Sam and Jean. I was more than a little nervous that my emotions would get the better of me, but Jean took me by surprise by greeting me warmly.

My surprise must have shown because she said "Thank you for making Sam so happy! He told me what Davey had said – about you writing *You gave me life* for him. It's a beautiful song, and he's so proud of you!"

As she said this Davey drove up, and I wondered how far the mellowing would extend as Mag and Mam climbed out, but Jean hurried across to greet them. Sam turned to me.

"She's decided that forty-odd years is quite long enough to bear a grudge... she's determined to make this weekend special for Sal, and this is part of that."

I watched as Jean and Mam embraced, wondering if I was dreaming and whether I'd wake up in a minute.

"She really was knocked out when she first heard the song – we both were! I cried like a babby, and I'm not over given to that…I hope we'll see more of you from now on – without me having to sneak off behind her back!"

I hugged him, overwhelmed at how much better things suddenly seemed.

"OK, *son*, are you going to show me round the shack?"

I grinned. We did the tour, starting with the studio and then working round the house in the usual way and ending up with the guest suite.

"You've done well for yourself. Davey tried to describe it to me, but I thought he was puffing it up – if anything it's bigger than I expected!"

"To some extent it pays for itself. We get a good income from the studio and its accommodation, and any input we give to the artistes using it. Then the girl who runs the stables pays us for that bit, and we rent out most of the land to Eddie, one of our neighbours, who farms what used to be the main estate. Before *Angel,* things were getting a bit tight – we'd spent so much getting the place straight, although the price we paid included a lot of the building work."

"'We' paid? Or you paid? From what I saw, I don't think Tina left Davey any money when they divorced, and she seemed to have her hooks into everything he earned after that…"

I looked at the ground, reluctant to criticise her.

"Davey never criticised her either! It's OK, Micky – I know she was my daughter, but I saw how eaten up she was…"

"She had the kids to consider." I said quietly. "And she was my sister – I wish I'd known her better, and I wish I'd had time to talk to her as a sister…"

"One of these days we must talk properly. Davey's hinted that you didn't have a happy childhood – if I'd *known…"*

I sighed. "What would you have done? What could you have done? Old man Culshaw held all the cards…"

"I'd have found something, even if I'd had to defy Jeannie and bring you home! I thought you were in the best place – only child, plenty to eat, room to yourself…but I know that sometimes there are other things that are far more important... The other kids – my kids with Jeannie – had it tough, but they had each other…"

I nodded, a lump in my throat. There was so much more that he didn't know, and I wondered how I would tell him – IF I could ever tell him…

The rest of the day was a blur. It had never occurred to me just how much there was to do to set up an occasion. Sal, usually the model of organisation and calm, had, by her standards, totally gone to pieces. Davey, having completed his task by fetching Mag and Mam, was about as much use as the proverbial chocolate teapot. Even Grace began to look more and more flustered as the day wore on but, by around 4 o'clock, everything seemed to have more or less fallen into place.

We had decided the easiest way to deal with an evening meal was to get the coach to pick everyone up and take them into Oxford, where we'd booked the whole of Rosetta's restaurant for them, which meant ferrying them all back down the drive again, but at least this time we didn't have to deal with the luggage.

Davey and I bailed out and sneaked off to the 'Swords, Paul's contingent having been included in the Oxford expedition, so we were able to eat in peace with Sal and Dan. I think that Sam would have liked to have come with us but, if we had extended the invitation to anyone else, we would have ended up with everyone claiming special rights, and I felt that Sal should have the evening off before her big day. We had a lovely evening and I couldn't help thinking how life had changed in what seemed like a comparatively short space of time.

The ceremony was to take place at the comparatively early time of 11 o'clock. I'd tried to suggest that a later time would be better, to avoid the inevitable panic, but was overruled, Sal decreeing that the earlier, the better, so that there was less time for nerves to set in, and that it meant we would be back at the farm for lunch so that she would have more time with the guests.

I skipped breakfast and concentrated on getting Davey into his grey morning suit. He had tried to dig his heels in and wear a lounge suit, but had been heavily outvoted. Apart from the rather incongruous length of his hair he didn't look half bad. I had reluctantly bought a new, pale grey suit which was almost the same shade as the morning suit. Sal had selected a striped silk tie for me which alternated the colour of my eyes with a silver grey, worn with a very pale grey silk shirt.

I emerged into the hall to find Sal, still in her dressing gown, sitting on the bottom stair. Trying not to panic I asked gently "What's up – shouldn't you be getting dressed?"

She gave me a slightly wobbly smile.

"There's ages yet – I don't want to get there early…Micky..?"

"Mmm?"

I recognised the tone as the one she used when she either wanted to ask a special favour or to say something unwelcome.

"I know that Dad's walking me down the aisle and giving me away, but I want you to do it too…"

I yelped in alarm.

"No – don't be daft! Davey's your dad, not me!"

"You've been as much of a father as he has – more at times! *Please*, Micky! Dad knows I'm asking you – he told me to wait until this morning, so you didn't have time to panic…"

I closed my eyes, feeling sick – or faint – or…I took a deep breath, making my mind up, unable, as ever, to deny her anything…

"I would be honoured!" I said decisively. "If you're sure that Davey's happy with me stealing his thunder?"

"He's fine! He said you can make his speech too, if you want!"

"I'm sure he'd love that!"

The wretched speech had been driving me mad for more than the last few weeks. I'd had to listen to numerous re-hashes and had even offered to write it for him, but he was adamant that everyone would know I'd written it.

Sal hugged me gleefully.

"You are the most wonderful step-parent anyone could ever have! And you look absolutely gorgeous in that suit! I wish I was marrying you..!"

"I hope you don't!" I retorted. "I'd be no use to you whatsoever! And for God's sake don't let Paul hear you say that…"

She was halfway across the boot-room on her way back to her bedroom, but turned and gave me a radiant smile.

"He'll do!" She said brightly. "He'll make a great father, and we're good friends, which is the important thing…"

"You haven't said you love him…?" I prompted, a little anxiously.

She hesitated slightly.

"I *think* I do…I did when he proposed, anyway. Does love ever really last?"

I thought about it. Neither of us spoke for a while.

"I think it does." I said eventually, a little reluctantly, in case she genuinely had fallen out of love.

"I've loved Davey since we were kids, and he was the only one I ever really wanted, although I was in love with Alex, and I still have feelings for him, But when Davey and I got together – it was just so – so incredibly special – and it still is! I love him as much today as I ever have done, even when he does my head in!"

"But is it the same love? Is loving someone the same as being 'in love' – or can you stop being 'in love' but still love someone – and are there different types of love? We love our parents – we love our pets – we love our friends…"

"Maybe. Sal – are you sure you're doing the right thing? If you're not sure…?"

"I'm sure! We've lived together perfectly happily for over four years and we are good friends. He'll make a great dad…"

"You're not…?"

She gave me an enigmatic smile which didn't entirely confirm or deny my suspicions. I knew she hadn't confided in Davey – he'd never have been able to keep anything like that to himself. If I'd felt sick and faint a few minutes before, that was nothing to how I felt now… If I convinced her not to go through with the wedding, what then?

Visions of Mam's dilemma came to mind, but Paul seemed a million miles from Joe Culshaw and I could see that Sal was convinced that he was likely to be a good father. If they subsequently divorced? Was that worse, if I could have prevented her making a mistake in the first place? It wasn't a Catholic wedding but…

"I must go and get dressed!"

She'd gone before I could say anything more.

I turned and went into the boot-room, as I often did in moments of stress, to cuddle the dogs, forgetting that they had been removed to the stable yard for the day. One of the cats was sitting in the courtyard and I went out, intending to find solace there, but instead found Davey sitting on one of the benches. He looked up.

"We're going to have to leave shortly…"

"She's gone to get dressed – hopefully she won't be long now."

He gave me a wobbly smile.

"I didn't intend to eavesdrop," he said quietly, "but I heard what you were saying about loving me…"

"Oh lord! As if you aren't conceited enough…!"

He got up and came to me, putting his arms round me and hugging me tightly.

"I love you too! And you look gorgeous in that suit!"

I rested my head on his shoulder.

"Do you think she's doing the right thing?"

"I dunno…I'm probably not the right person to ask! Does it matter? We've been together all these years without getting wed, and I probably love you more now than ever…"

"But what if she meets someone else and really does fall in love with them?"

"Things have a way of sorting themselves out. Look at us! The kids seem to have survived somehow, despite everything. You're the one who had the really difficult times and, Yes, it's left its mark but mostly you've coped with it…"

"Only because I had you! And with a lot of help from Doc. Petersen…"

"What matters is that we are still here, together, and we still love each other. Sal's a big girl now – if this is what she feels is right for her, now, then we have to go along with it, even if we can both see that it's not perfect. Hopefully, if it all falls apart somewhere down the road, then we'll still be here to pick up the pieces."

The door from the music room corridor opened and Sal appeared, a vision in white silk and lace, surrounded by bridesmaids. She looked radiant and I sighed in relief that she seemed to have made her mind up, whatever my own misgivings.

We travelled to the church in the pub minibus, decked out with flowers and ribbons. As the '*Here Comes the Bride*' rang out we walked down the aisle, one on each side of Sal, followed by the flock of tiny bridesmaids. The congregation all turned to watch, and a buzz went round that there were two 'fathers of the bride', but somehow everyone looked perfectly happy and relaxed about it.

Sam was standing between Jean and Mam, one on each arm, which brought tears to my eyes. Dan was squashed into the pew next to them, Sapphy on his arm, looking totally gorgeous herself in her customary electric blue (with hair to match) but thankfully without the black lipstick!

The ceremony went without any hiccups, although I heard a giggle from somewhere when we reached the 'Who giveth this woman…?' and we both said "We do!" in unison. The music was beautiful and the happy couple walked back down the aisle to Beethoven's *Ode to Joy*.

The reception also passed off smoothly, helped along with an ocean of champagne. Davey managed to get through his speech as though he had been doing so all his life, despite, or perhaps because of, having imbibed at least a bottle of bubbly beforehand. I didn't recognise anything he said as having been part of any of the draft versions, and he admitted later that it had all been entirely spontaneous as he'd lost his notes and was too addled to remember anything of what he had prepared!

Once the speeches were out of the way we provided the entertainment; we had felt honour-bound to stretch a point and invite Paddy and Jan after all the time they had spent chaperoning the kids when they were younger, and Bird was already 'part of the family' so, as we were all going to be there, it seemed natural for us to provide the music.

The original plan had been to perform 'unplugged' and stick to our quieter material and whatever standards we felt we could do justice to but, after a number of pleas for specific things, the rules went out of the window and we rocked it up with a wide variety of stuff, some dating back to the late fifties, and we were treated to the sight of our elderly aunts and uncles, parents etc., jiving enthusiastically in their wedding finery.

By midnight we were well and truly knackered; Sal and Paul had already 'gone away' – spending their wedding night at a country house hotel close to Luton airport, before flying out the next morning for Venice. We played the *Last Waltz* – not one of my favourite songs but we played it through twice so that Sam could dance it with both Jean and Mam [!] – and then shoo-ed everyone off to bed or out of the door as appropriate.

It was gone two o'clock when we finally got to bed ourselves. Despite the quantity of bubbly we'd drunk I was well and truly sober again after all the singing. Davey went and fetched a bottle of Jack Daniels but I decided that mixing drinks was a recipe for disaster and sent him back to find a bottle of Dom Perignon – amazingly there were a few left over – and we drank it straight from the bottle before crashing into bed.

We woke late the following morning to hear a gentle knock at the door from the music room corridor. Davey looked at me, mystified, but I realised that the only people likely to be coming from that direction were Dan and/or Sapphy, who had drawn the short straw of having to sleep on the sofa in the music room. I crawled out of bed, pulling on a pair of jogging trousers as I went, and unbolted the door. Sapphy dived in, followed by a sleepy-looking Dan.

"Misty…" she began huskily, head on one side in what was obviously intended to be an endearing manner.

"Yee-ess?" I responded, a little nervously.

"Um – we were wondering if we could – maybe – borrow the house for our wedding…?"

"Nooo!!!"

Davey yelped in panic.

"No, you can't!! Dan – you're too young to get married!!"

"No, I'm not! You'd been married five years by the time you were my age!"

"My point entirely! What's the hurry? You've not been together that long…"

"Yes we have – nearly eighteen months now…"

"That's no time at all!"

I had been watching Sapphy's face and guessed there was something more.

"Is there something you want to tell us?" I asked gently.

She smiled a very gentle smile and peeped up at me through her eyelashes in that flirtatious way I'd got used to seeing. Davey intercepted the look and groaned.

"Oh my God! I'm too young to be a grandfather!!"

"Well, you'd better get used to the idea!" I retorted. "And you're not *that* young any more, either! Before you know where you are, you're likely to have at least a couple of grandchildren…"

"Or more!" Sapphy said mischievously. "I'm actually expecting twins…"

Davey clutched his head.

"Seriously, Sapphy…" I interrupted. "I hope you don't want as big a wedding as Sal and Paul had?"

She shook her head.

"It won't be! There won't be anyone from my side – apart from the guys of course…"

"What about your parents?"

"They won't come over, I can tell you that now! If one came the other wouldn't, anyhow."

"Where do you want to have the ceremony? The same church that Sal used?"

She pulled a face.

"I don't think so... I was raised a Catholic…"

"We've talked about this – we'd rather have a proper Catholic wedding or just a register office…" Dan finally found his voice.

"It may have to be a register office." I said as gently as I could. "The Catholic churches usually want at least six months' notice…"

Sapphy looked disappointed.

"That wouldn't work, unless we have the wedding and the baptism at the same time!"

"Isn't there anyone you can put in a word with?"

Davey was obviously getting used to the idea.

I thought for a couple of minutes.

"Maybe… But you may have to have the wedding in London…"

Sapphy brightened up.

"OK – but we could still have the reception here?"

I looked from her to Dan, worried that, so far, Sapphy had been making all the running, but one look at his face convinced me that he was still totally under her spell, and that he wanted nothing more than to spend the rest of his life with her and their babies…

"Of course!" I found myself saying.

As with the fateful day two summers ago when she had first cast a spell over me, I had the feeling that Dan wasn't the only one who had fallen for her, although in my case it was an odd mixture of fatherly feeling, a certain sympathy for her own unhappy background, respect for her as a performer and maybe other emotions that I couldn't quite identify.

I went through to the library and found my address book. I dialled a number which I had only recently added and, rather to my own surprise, found that it was answered almost immediately.

"Mulcahy."

"Father Sean? It's Micky Culshaw…"

"Micky! It's good to hear from you! What can I do for you?"

I decided that it was best to come straight out with it.

"Father, I am hoping that you can do me a favour…"

"Ahh…well, perhaps I can, but it may be a case of a favour for a favour…What is it you think I can help you with?"

I took a deep breath.

"Davey's son, Danny, is engaged to be married. His fiancée is a lovely American girl. She was raised as a Catholic and would like to get married in a Catholic church. Unfortunately, there is a little urgency…"

"Ahhh. I think I understand! Can she not get married in the USA? Her own local church...?"

"She's estranged from her parents – has been for a very long time – and is based here now. She's a musician, so she's not been settled anywhere for long enough to have a local parish..."

"And what of Danny? If I remember correctly his father is not a Catholic?"

"No...but his mother, my sister, was. She died last year. Because of the problems between Davey and her, the children weren't really brought up to be churchgoers at all, but I think Danny would be happy to take instruction and do things properly. He was baptised as a Catholic..."

"How much of a hurry is there?"

"Let's just say that when I told her that the church usually wanted six months' notice, she said something about having the wedding and baptism at the same time..."

"Ah! Well, as you know, I've not been back here all that long, so I'm not sure I have sufficient influence to lean on any of your local clergy..."

I must have sighed loudly, because he continued "...but if the couple are happy to come to Westminster, there's probably no reason why we can't have a quiet little ceremony here in the Cathedral. Will they be happy with that? It might be wise to only have the minimum number of guests here..."

I heaved a sigh of relief.

"I'm sure they will be more than happy! If we just have his grandparents, his sister and her husband and the two of us will that be OK?"

"I'm sure that we can manage that discreetly. Now, two things: one, you will need to bring them here so that I can meet them and talk to them, and in the meantime I will check for availability so that we don't clash with anything else, and two: I did mention a favour for a favour…"

"OK – what do you have in mind?"

"Well, Micky, it's come to my notice that, since we last met, you seem to have had something of a resurgence in your career?"

"Mmmm?"

"Would you consider putting on a concert to raise money for the homeless? We have a large number of rough sleepers who gather around the Cathedral piazza. We would never turn them away, but it does cause problems for people coming in to worship, especially in the early mornings and evenings. We would like to be able to offer a refuge for these people – perhaps somewhere they can get at least one meal a day…"

"I'll have to talk to the others but I'm sure we can do something for you."

I crossed my fingers as I said this.

"When can I bring Dan and Sapphy to meet you?"

"I could meet you this afternoon if that's not too short notice? I'm off to Rome tomorrow for a week or two, so if you're in a hurry…"

"Yes, OK, that's fine. What time?"

"Can you do 3.30? That should give us a clear hour before I have to be elsewhere."

"I'll make sure we're there. Where do we find you?"

"I'll meet you by the front door of the Cathedral – that's probably the easiest option."

I went back to find the others in the kitchen. Dan immediately offered to drive, knowing that I didn't like driving in London. Davey wanted to come with us, but I suggested that, this time, it should probably be just

Sapphy, Dan and me and, in any event, as Dan was supposed to be driving Sam and Jean back to Manchester, he was needed to act as a taxi for them as well as Mag and Mam.

We had a quick breakfast and I said a reluctant goodbye to the parents before we piled into Dan's 4x4 and headed up the motorway. At his suggestion we left the car at his flat and got a cab into Westminster, arriving a little ahead of 3.30, which gave us all the chance to have a quick look inside the Cathedral, none of us ever having been there before.

After the cathedrals and larger churches we had seen in Italy, the Cathedral came as something of a shock. It had little or no similarity to the great medieval cathedrals in the UK, with their huge blocks of Caen stone and elaborate tombs, nor to the Italian churches with their innumerable altars and chapels, huge oil paintings and ornamentation. The exterior was startling with its bands of red brick and, in some ways, bore a passing resemblance to some of the ancient mosques of Moorish Spain. The interior seemed deceptively plain at first sight, almost unfinished, but the more you looked, the more detail became apparent until you noticed the mosaic ceiling with its vibrant colour and gilding.

We had not been there long when Father Sean joined us. He greeted me warmly and I introduced him to the happy couple. Sapphy took it all in her stride but, knowing her as I did, I knew that she was a little over-awed, both by the surroundings and the fact that 'Father Sean' was now a Monsignor and a senior aide to the Cardinal Archbishop.

He took us through to his office and we sat and talked for a while, drinking afternoon tea. He questioned Sapphy closely as to her credentials, but it was obvious that she had indeed been raised and schooled as a Catholic in the States and that she had the remnants of faith, despite her unsettled upbringing and the various crises she had been through.

He turned to Dan.

"And you, Danny? Micky tells me that your mother was Catholic. I have met your father, and I know that he is not. You were baptised? Did you make your First Communion?"

"Yes, but we didn't go to Mass much after that. It was only a short time before Mum and Dad split up."

"Did you go to a Catholic school?"

"Yes, until I was thirteen, then I moved to the local Comp."

"How would you say you feel about the church – about God?"

Dan hesitated.

"I – I don't really know. I know that Micky believes and goes to Mass and I respect him for that – I know that it has helped him a lot, so I think there has to be something in that…"

"Sapphy has said that she would like to be married in church, and has indicated that she has faith and is happy to raise any children in the ways of the Church. How do you feel about that?"

"I want Sapphy to be happy. I think that marriage in church is perhaps stronger than a register office job."

"Catholic marriage is sacramental. That means that it is harder to undo than other forms."

"Yes, I know…I don't have a problem with that! I want my kids to have two parents who love each other.

I would love Sapphy whether we were married or not, but marriage is still important."

"Are you prepared to come along for a chat for a few evenings – a kind of refresher course to prepare you properly for marriage? And come to Mass? Where do you live?"

"Yes…I guess we're not going to be working much for a while. We're living in my flat at the moment, in the Barbican, so it's not too difficult to get here."

Father Sean nodded, apparently satisfied with this response.

We stayed on for the early evening Mass, Sapphy sandwiched happily between Dan and me, far more at ease with the ritual than Danny, who was patently struggling to follow, even with the aid of a missal and service sheet.

After the service was over, we dropped Sapphy at the flat and Danny drove me back to the farm. Davey wanted him to stay for supper, anxious to talk to him, but he was unwilling to leave Sapphy on her own in London and left early after loading their bags into his car.

It was good to have the house to ourselves after the intensity of the last few days. Grace looked exhausted and I insisted that she should go and rest, and that I would deal with our supper. I toyed with the idea of cooking but, as there was a fridge full of leftovers from the wedding buffet, I ended up filling several large plates and putting them on the table so that we could help ourselves.

Davey seemed rather down and admitted that, while he had enjoyed the wedding, he was not totally happy that Paul was the right choice for Sal, nor was he happy about Dan and Sapphy.

"Sal will be fine!" I said firmly. "OK, maybe Paul's not completely her speed but, as she says, they are good friends and know each other well enough by now. I don't think she'd leave him unless she found someone she fell head over heels for. She wants kids and I think her biological clock is ticking – she doesn't want to leave it too late. As for Dan, he's definitely head over heels for Sapphy, and I think she pretty much feels the same way. She's a lovely girl – he's a very lucky boy!"

"If I didn't know you better, I'd think you had fallen for her too!"

Davey looked at me, brows drawn together. I shrugged.

"Guilty!" I admitted. "I never thought I'd ever admit to that, but she certainly gives me feelings that I've never had for a lass before…"

He frowned.

"Oh God! You're not turning straight in your old age, are you?"

I grinned.

"Whose old age? You're nearly two years older than me remember! Don't talk soft! Whatever I feel for Sapphy, she's Danny's girl and, in any event, I'll never love anyone the way I love you."

He got up, came round the table, and pulled me to my feet, enveloping me in a bear-hug that left me breathless.

"I said this before, a long time ago, but I wish we could get married!"

His voice wobbled and he was trembling. I hugged him back.

"Davey, I'm not going to leave you! Nothing could tie me closer to you than I am now! Even if we could get married, what would be the point? We've been together all our lives and properly, as a couple, for fifteen years now! And whatever Father Sean said about the church being more tolerant towards gay relationships, I don't see them ever allowing gay marriage, and that would be the only thing that would matter to me... Please, get this through that thick head of yours, I love you, always have, always will!!"

I realised that he was crying and felt helpless. I was the one who usually cried enough for both of us, and only remembered him even coming close to tears on a couple of occasions.
"Are you OK? This isn't like you…"
He shook his head.
"Just tired I suppose…I've just given away one child and am about to lose the other – I couldn't handle losing you as well…"
"You're not going to lose me, you Muppet! What do I have to say to get through to you?"
I was tempted to add that if I did run off with Sapphy, he'd still have Dan, but thought better of it – in his present state of mind he'd probably brood on that idea and believe I was seriously thinking of doing so!

Things moved on rapidly over the next few weeks. Father Sean phoned me soon after his return from Rome, to say that he'd met with Dan a sufficient number of times to feel confident of his commitment both to Sapphy and to renewing his faith, and that we could now set a date for the marriage.

I had already contacted the various caterers, florists etc. to say that we would be requiring a (scaled down) re-run of our recent event, so I was now able to confirm a date with them. We were not going to invite all the uncles and aunts again, but there were still the grandparents, Sapphy's band and road crew, Sal and Paul and a good number of Dan and Sapphy's friends to accommodate.

I had hoped that Sapphy's 'guys' would provide the music for the reception as I felt that we might be rather too over the hill for the younger crowd, but Sapphy said very firmly that she would NOT be performing and that, without a suitable singer to front them, the band could not really do much. She added that, in any event, we had given such a great performance at Sal's wedding, she wanted the same, thank you very much!

The grandparents, who had not met Sapphy before, other than at Sal's wedding, had been almost as worried by the wedding announcement as Davey had been but, having now met her properly, declared themselves more than happy. The fact that the church wedding had been her choice obviously helped, Sam, in particular, seeing that as a sign of commitment which boded well. He was also very amused when he realised that she was up the duff, declaring that Dan was a chip off the old block!

Dan had originally asked me to be best man, but Sapphy had also claimed me in loco parentis and, in the end, Davey was best man while I gave Sapphy (or Sophia, as we now learned was her proper name) away. As she was already fairly obviously 'blooming', she didn't go for the full white dress and veil, but looked enchanting in a long, ivory silk, medieval-style gown with flowers in her hair, now restored to its natural black, as she had abandoned the blue dye during her pregnancy. We also wore suits rather than morning dress and, with no bridesmaids other than Sal as matron of honour, we were able to slip into the Cathedral virtually unnoticed and were back at the farm shortly after one o'clock.

The afternoon passed in a champagne-induced blur. The happy couple had decided to postpone their honeymoon until after the baby's arrival and were, instead, spending a few days at a country hotel in Cornwall, hoping to enjoy the tail-end of summer. For that reason they were staying overnight in our guest suite, leaving the grandparents to make do with the rooms in the bedroom range. The 'guys' had the kennel rooms and Paddy and Bird had to camp out in the studio rest area, although as Jan had remained in Manchester and Bird had left the present Mrs. at home, they actually were probably at least as comfortable as anyone else.

As before, we played a wide variety of stuff in an effort to keep everyone happy, and the 'guys' and Dan and Sapphy's friends all seemed to enjoy themselves. By popular demand Sapphy consented to join us on stage (in fact the mezzanine landing which, we had discovered last time round, provided a very suitable place to set up out of the way of the dancing, while allowing us to perform with a certain amount of freedom). She started by singing Silver's biggest hit and I tried to coax Jo to take over on guitar, but she shyly refused, still a little in awe of playing in front of Bird or myself. After this, and because we only really knew the material we had recorded for her, she switched to a handful of well known standards, before declaring herself to be tired and handing back to me.

Epilogue

Within a matter of weeks we were grandparents (strictly speaking, in my case, a great uncle or step-grandparent) when Saffy gave birth to twin girls, Michaela and Davina [!].

By then Sal's pregnancy had also been officially announced, and by Christmas the grandchildren total had risen to three when she produced yet another girl. She had been piqued that Saffy and Dan had gazumped her by using the name Michaela, but I gently suggested that I thought she should call the baby Christina after her mother. To start with she was not over-happy with that idea, and countered with the suggestion of Samantha, after her grandfather, but Davey and I both thought that the Sam name should be reserved for the first boy in the new generation and she reluctantly agreed.

After the second wedding Grace had, very reluctantly, decided that she should retire. Although I had actually made the suggestion a while before this, worried that if she did not, then she would never have the opportunity to have any time to herself until she was too old to appreciate it, when it came to the reality I felt almost the same sense of loss as I would have done if things had ended less happily.

We bought a tiny cottage for her near the 'Swords, ignoring her protests that she had enough tucked away to rent a small flat in Oxford, feeling that she would be far happier and safer near friends who could keep a regular eye on her, and that she could then use her savings to enjoy life.

For a few days after the decision had been taken, it looked as though we were going to find ourselves without our life support, but a solution suddenly presented itself from an unexpected source. Very sadly, and totally out of the blue, Gerry had collapsed and died some weeks beforehand. Sylvia did not feel able to carry on at the 'Swords without him – not only from a practical point of view, but also, having run the place together for the whole of their married life, from the constant reminder of her loss. The 'Swords was safe – one of their daughters and her husband, who had frequently helped out there in busy times or when Gerry and Sylvia had needed a break, took over and Sylvia, on hearing that Grace was to retire, offered her services, happy to live in as Grace had always done.

To say we were relieved would be a massive understatement! Sylvia had been almost as much a second mother to us as Grace had been. We knew she was an excellent cook and it also meant that we would still have access to her extended family when we needed more staff for any reason – the perfect solution all round.

Sam and I had bonded from that first meeting, and I quickly found myself able to talk to him about anything and everything, in a way that I would never have been able to do with anyone remotely like Joe Culshaw. I took a long time to decide to tell him about what had happened to me at school, but eventually I found it easier to tell him than to continue to skirt round the subject.

He had found it difficult to understand why, having acknowledged that I was gay while still in my early teens, I had only begun a relationship when I was in my mid-twenties. I had started by hedging around the subject, trying to throw him off the scent by pointing out that, in the early-1970s, things were still far from accepted, but he countered that argument by saying that he could not understand how someone who could perform in front of thousands of people on stage, would be that bothered by what people thought. Eventually I told him everything, including the beating that I had been given for 'lying'. By that point we were both in tears...

Sam had sat there for a long time, unable to say anything, just shaking his head in disbelief. Eventually he'd blurted out "My God, Micky! If I'd known, I'd have killed the bugger!"

I fully believed him, though I wasn't entirely sure whether he meant Father Flan or Joe Culshaw – most probably both! After that he rarely referred to what had happened, even indirectly, although I realised that he now understood some of the complications in my life.

He met Alex (and Nat) on several occasions, and I watched a little nervously as they walked off into the walled garden and talked for some time. Both had seemed a little uneasy to start with, but Alex's easy charm quickly won Sam over and he, in turn, impressed Alex with his own fearless simplicity.

Not too long after the 'Year of the Weddings', Nat had contacted me. He had sounded serious and I had a moment of panic, wondering if somehow there had been an additional twist of fate and I was likely to find myself facing yet another accusation of somehow being complicit in Andy's death, but, as soon as he realised the way my mind was working, he hurriedly assured me that it was nothing to do with that. He then gently told me that Alex was far from well and wanted me to visit him. I tried to get more information, but he just said that he'd rather leave Alex to talk to me.

Thoroughly alarmed now, and worried that, despite all my HIV tests having come back clear, Alex was going to tell me that he had AIDS and that I was also at risk, I rushed up to London to meet him at Nat's flat in the Temple.

Having never been there previously, I met Nat at a restaurant in Chancery Lane for lunch, and tried again to get more information from him. When he realised what I suspected, he again hastened to reassure me that I was on the wrong track, and apologised for worrying me, but I could see that, whatever the situation, he was deeply upset and that it was obviously something that was not going to improve.

After we'd eaten we walked down to Fleet Street, into the Strand and along to the Temple. I was amazed to find that, far from being some exotic enclave, the area comprised a complex of classic, timeless buildings including a church, with mature trees, parking areas, even restaurants, all insulated from the hustle and bustle of that part of London.

Nat's flat was in a building in a corner of one of the squares, and we walked up the staircase to the second floor. He unlocked the door and let me in.

"I'll speak to you soon." he said, a little cryptically.

"Aren't you coming in?" I asked, a little nervous that he was just leaving me there.

"No. Alex wants to talk to *you*, and in any event, I have an appeal hearing this afternoon."

He pecked me on the cheek and then he'd gone. Before I could wonder which way to go, one of the lobby doors had opened and Alex stood there. My feet felt as though they were glued to the floor and I stayed rooted to the spot. I surveyed him anxiously; he'd lost some weight, but other than that he looked more or less like an older version of the Alex that I'd known for nearly twenty years.

He smiled the smile I'd loved since that first morning.

"Don't look so scared!"

His voice was the same as ever, although I detected a slightly breathless quality that had not been there before.

"I promise not to die this afternoon!"

I felt the tears pricking at my eyes.

"Don't! Please don't talk about dying!"

"I'm sorry, Micky, but I must – talk about it, that is".

He took a step to me and put his hands on my shoulders, and again I remembered that first morning when he'd gently told me that I could change my mind if I wanted…

He kissed me, as he'd done before, and I wanted so much to respond as I'd done then, but I was afraid to, not knowing in what way he was ill. He felt me tremble and took me through into the sitting room. He poured a tumbler of gin and added a small amount of tonic to it, handing it to me before pouring a measure of Armagnac into a small, crystal cognac glass for himself, then came and sat beside me on the leather sofa.

I watched his every movement through a mist of tears, not wanting to believe that this could be the last time I spent with him. He smiled at me again.

"Now..." he said gently, "There are things I want to discuss with you. Nat has told you that I am unwell?"

I nodded miserably.

"But he has not told you how?"

I shook my head. He nodded, satisfied.

"That is good. I asked him to leave it to me."

"But it's not…not AIDS?"

"No, it's not that… It's nothing to do with my – our – lifestyle. I have cancer."

He let the word sink in.

"Don't ask me where – it's enough to say that by now it is pretty much everywhere. The doctors say that they could operate, I could have chemo, I could have pretty much any treatment you care to mention, but the result would be a great deal of mutilation, a great deal of disability, a lot of sickness and pain and, at the end of the day, I might live a few weeks longer…I prefer to let things take their course and use what time I have left to me to put my affairs in order and say goodbye to my friends with some dignity. I hope that when…the end comes…it will come quickly but, if it doesn't and I end up in a hospice or whatever, I do not want you to come to see me. I don't want you to see me like that – do you understand me?"

He bent his head to look into my eyes.

"I – I hear what you're saying…" I said quietly "But I…you saw me at my worst…why won't you let me be with you…?"

"You weren't able to forbid me. I have that luxury!"

I took a gulp of the gin – it was so strong that it took my breath away.

"Now, down to what I want to talk to you about. Micky, I am a very wealthy man – I don't think you realise quite how wealthy! I earned a lot of money early in my career at the Bar, and later through my political career and the various things that came from that. When my parents died, I inherited a lot of property in Sweden which I liquidated, as I had no wish to live there, and it seemed the easiest way to manage it. When I divorced Veronique it was a clean break, as she had little need of support from me, given that her new paramour was an aristocrat who also had more money than even she could spend, so I still own the house in Fulham that we shared. A friend died a few years ago and left me his very large house in St John's Wood, where Nat and I now usually live. Nat does not need my money – he is now wealthy in his own right from his career, as are you. It took me a long time to appreciate that you were independent, and I know that you have prospered further in recent years. I have no children to leave anything to, so I want to make sure that, when I am gone, my money does not just disappear into the tax system, but is used to do something good. That is how I want you to help me."

I bit my lip, trying to keep myself from the hysterical tears that were threatening to overwhelm me.

"I don't know the whole of your story. I know we talked, all those years ago, but there were things that you never told me. Anders Petersen was always very correct. and would only hint to me that there were things that happened to you which were very personal, and your father – Sam - has said similar things. Obviously, I know about what you suffered at the hands of Andy, and what happened to you in prison…but somehow I get the feeling that something had happened to you much earlier that is even worse?"

I nodded dumly, unable to speak.

"Micky, please…I realise this is difficult – maybe I should have asked you to bring Davey with you, or perhaps let Nat stay, but after all that there was between us, I hoped that you trusted me enough for us to talk freely…"

I nodded, reluctantly.

"Please, Micky – I want to set up some sort of trust or charity to help young people who have been through whatever it was that you went through – help them to build a good life, as you have done, possibly through music. You have the contacts, the resources, to help put that in place."

I nodded, realising the potential that Alex's idea had to help people.

"Micky, please…I need you to talk to me, to tell me what happened to *you*, so that I know how to set this trust up, who to specify should benefit from it…"

I nodded again, a shade less reluctantly.

"I – I was abused…by a priest – the headmaster of the school I went to. I was eight years old… I told my mother – she believed me - but my – my stepfather didn't. He beat me – beat me so badly I had to stay off school until I was well enough to go back…"

As always, talking about what had happened stirred up memories and emotions that I tried to avoid, and the tears that I had been trying to stop now broke. I doubled up, helpless to stop them. Alex quickly took the glass from me before wrapping his arms round me and hugging me tightly, holding me against him. I could hear again how bad his breathing was, compared with a healthy person.

"I'm so sorry! Micky – I'm so sorry! I – I thought it might be something like that, but I prayed that I was wrong! I didn't want to think that you had been through anything like that. Sam hinted that you'd been abused, but I thought – hoped – that he meant that your stepfather had hit you – not that you'd been - violated – when you were so young! I feel ashamed that it was me who…"

"For God's sake, Alex! I *wanted* you – I've never wanted anything so badly in all my life as I wanted you that morning! When you spoke to me, I couldn't believe that you were talking to *me*, and I was terrified that you wouldn't come back to the flat with me. When you told me that I didn't need to go through with it, I thought you were trying to back out…I was so desperate…that was the *best* day, the happiest day of my life!"

I could hardly speak for sobbing. Alex handed me the glass again and steadied my hand as I drank it down. He quickly refilled the glass, but I gently pushed his hand away, knowing that we needed to finish the conversation before I became too drunk.

"But you are happy with Davey?"

"Of *course* I am! He was all I ever wanted, but I never, in my wildest dreams, thought that it was a possibility at that time. As I've always said, he is the other part of me, but that doesn't change the fact that I loved you, right from the moment you first spoke to me, the – the way you made me feel when we first made love...Alex, I can't believe that this is happening, that you..."

"All things must pass" he said quietly. "We are both a lot older... at least this way I will never be a burden to you or to Nat. I worry about Nat – his feelings are far more engaged than mine, although I do care deeply for him. I hope that you will – keep an eye on him – he has no family as such, although we have a few close friends...YOU are the only one I have ever really *loved*, as opposed to wanted for sex... I hope that you believe me when I say that...I know that I upset you that afternoon, when I behaved so badly after bringing Davey home from court, but my emotions were...Davey was in such distress, torn between his children and you..."

I nodded, pulling myself together with an effort.

"We must...we must talk about your idea." I said reluctantly.

"Yes...So...something to help children who have been abused – in any way, I think. Not just sexual abuse, but physical abuse and possibly emotional or psychological abuse as well, but we must make sure that we prioritise the worst cases, otherwise the system could be manipulated. Provide scholarships or bursaries for those young enough to need to finish their compulsory education, and then work with them to find them employment in your world. If they have the ability, then as musicians. If not, then work of other kinds - maybe in recording studios, or as 'roadies' – is that the right word? – anything where you have the contacts to help them."

"We need to make sure they have somewhere safe to live…during school holidays and later, until they have the means to fend for themselves. I was lucky – I had the band and then the money to get myself away from home, but I could easily have ended up on the streets, selling my body…"

"Like I thought you were doing!"

Alex was smiling at me and I found my stomach lurching in that familiar way.

"I propose that Nat, and Angelo, and you, are the first trustees, and I will leave it to the three of you to put your heads together and work out how it will operate…"

"Don't smile at me like that! You'll start me off again!"

Alex got up and poured me another gin.

"Drink it!" He ordered "I don't propose to spend all my energy talking details with you, when you and the others are perfectly capable of dealing with such matters."

He sat down again, closer than before, using his free hand to turn my head towards him, kissing me softly, sensually, on the lips. I trembled, torn between desire and loyalty…

Desire won. Alex gently undressed me, using all his skill and experience to arouse me and take me to the highest possible state of rapture without using up his limited stamina. Afterwards I lay in his arms, hopelessly emotional, now torn between overwhelming guilt and the most incredible feeling of satiation and love.

Eventually I managed to force myself to get up and pull my clothes back on. Alex watched me, a tender smile lighting his face, although he now looked tired and, despite what we had been doing, pale.

"You look wonderful in a suit! You should wear it more often…"

I shook my head, his words reminding me of Davey's similar comments after Joe Culshaw's funeral, inflaming the massive sense of guilt I felt.

I tried to tell him my thoughts but found myself crying again; he tried to pull me back into his arms, but I evaded him this time.

"I'm sorry!" I sobbed "I have to go! We shouldn't have done that!"

"Why? It's not as though it is likely to happen again…You will go back to Davey – you don't even need to tell him…Nat knows how I feel about you – he gave me his blessing, although I'm not sure that he thought I'd find enough energy to…"

"Alex! I'm sorry, but somehow that makes it worse! I've betrayed Davey – you know how I felt about it last time you tried…I *loved* you, I *still* love you, but that's not the point…"

I was dressed now and hurtled out of the flat before he could say anything further, running headlong down the stairs and out into the square, desperately trying to clear my head enough to remember my way back to the Strand. Ducking through an archway I suddenly realised that I was there.

My intention had been to grab a taxi and go straight back to Paddington, but I suddenly heard a surprised voice call my name.

"Misty?".

It was Sal's husband, Paul – hardly a surprise as we were only yards from the Courtauld where he worked. I stopped abruptly, trying to pull myself together.

"Are you OK? You look…"

I shook my head, wondering what to say to him. We had never been close, despite my very close relationship to both of Davey's kids, but he knew most of my back story.

"Where are you heading for?"

"Paddington."

I managed to force the word out.

"You don't look as if you ought to be trying to travel by public transport. I can call Dan and ask him to take you home?"

I nodded, a little reluctantly, but Dan was a good choice, given the tricky conversations we had had in the past. Paul fished out his mobile and called Dan. There was a brief conversation before he rang off.

"He'll pick you up as soon as possible, but it could be an hour or so. Is there somewhere you'd prefer to wait? You can come into my office if you want, but it's not over private."

I suddenly realised where I wanted to be.

"I'll get a cab and Dan can pick me up at the Cathedral."

Paul nodded.

"OK, I'll call him back and tell him, once I've seen you safely into a cab. Have you got enough cash on you? Have you got your mobile so that he can call you when he gets there?"

I nodded. Paul spotted a cab with its light up and hailed it, surprising me with the way he had taken control of the situation, belying my usual opinion of him as a bit wet.

Despite the early rush-hour traffic, I arrived at the Piazza mercifully quickly. In the meantime, I had managed to call Father Sean and, in very few words, arranged to meet him.

He was waiting near the taxi drop-off and swept me quickly inside to his office.

"Micky? What's happened? Is Davey OK?"

I opened my mouth to try to explain but couldn't get the words out, beyond managing to say that Davey was fine.

"Tell me what's happened...are the children OK?"

"Yes...yes..."

Eventually he managed to coax it out of me – Alex's illness, my betrayal...

He smiled gently at me.

"Oh Micky! What are you going to tell Davey? ARE you going to tell him?"

I shrugged helplessly.

"Least said, soonest mended – that's what most people would say, but I'm not sure that's fair, between – between lovers in the true sense..."

"I don't know how to tell him! I don't know if I *can* tell him! I don't know anything anymore! Please...help me!"

Slowly Father Sean managed to get the whole story out of me, a few words at a time.

"Do you think that what he said about setting up this scheme to help abused children was true? Or was it just an excuse to get you there?"

"I don't think Alex would lie to me...any more than he would have forced me to have sex. Yes, he used the Trust as an excuse to get me there, but I'm pretty sure that he meant what he said. He's always been completely straight with me..."

"Then let's hope that he was this time and that some good will come out of it. Look at it that way, Micky. Yes, you're upset, but if you can help some of the kids who have been through some of the really bad things that happened to you…"

"But it's not what Alex did today – it's what *I've* done – I've been unfaithful to Davey – I've never done that before…"

"And I'm sure you won't do it again! There were exceptional circumstances today – firstly it was Alex, who you could argue had a prior claim, and then there is the very sad fact that it's not likely to happen again…"

I bit my lip, trying not to start crying again. I felt safe with Father Sean – he was totally non-judgemental and dealt with everything in such a gentle, prosaic way, that I was able to keep some semblance of calm, in spite of the emotions that kept washing through me like a flood, ebbing and flowing.

Once he realised that I had regained a reasonable level of control, he steered the conversation away from what had happened and heard my confession, after which, and after I had prayed my penance, we talked lightly of other things until my phone rang, announcing that Dan had arrived.

Father Sean escorted me out of the complex and saw me into the car. We swung out into Victoria Street and joined the queuing traffic.

"Are you OK? Paul was worried…and Dad's been on the phone, trying to find you…"

"He didn't ring me…my phone was on…"

There was an awkward silence.

"I think he tried to phone Alex…"

"We were at Nat's flat, in the Temple…"

Dan tried again.

"Paul said he thought you were upset…maybe more than upset…?"

I made a non-committal sound.

"Have you eaten? We could stop somewhere – it's going to take a while to get through this traffic…"

"Nat took me out to lunch – an Italian place in Chancery Lane."

I had started to feel cold – always a sign that I was going into a wobble. Dan knew me well enough to pick up on my mood.

"Micky – please tell me what's happened?"

"Alex has cancer. He's dying!"

The words tumbled out and I bit my lip so hard it hurt.

"Oh Micky! I'm so sorry! I know how much you…"

I whimpered, unable to say anything more.

"Is that why you were so upset? Why you went to see Father Sean?"

"N…No. There's more…"

Dan looked at me sharply, and then braked heavily as the car in front had stopped.

"You said cancer – it's not…?"

"No. Not that!" I said shortly.

We drove on in silence, taking an age to get clear of the M25. Dan had headed for the M4 rather than the M40 and, when we reached Maidenhead, he swung off the motorway and up towards Marlow, pulling off the road at Cookham and turning off the ignition.

"OK." He said quietly. "Talk!"

I shook my head.

"Please, Micky! You know you can talk to me – We've talked about all sorts of stuff in the past…"

I shook my head again, fighting back tears. He reached across and took my hand

"God! You're freezing!"

He reached into the back seat and pulled a rug over,wrapping it round me.

"Something happened, didn't it? Can't you talk to me? It's probably easier to talk to me than it would be to talk to Dad…"

I opened my mouth to try to say something, anything, but all that came was a strangled groan. Dan stroked my hair gently.

"Would it help if we went somewhere for a drink?"

"No! I had quite a lot at lunchtime and then…Alex kept pouring gin…I probably drank far too much…"

The words started pouring out. Dan waited patiently, not wanting to interrupt now in case I clammed up again.

"I – I – we had sex…I couldn't help – couldn't help myself…"

"Is that why you're so upset?" he asked gently, when he realised that I wasn't going to say anything further.

I nodded, trying not to sob out loud.

"Micky, you've always been open about how much you loved Alex – I'm sure Dad would understand, under the circumstances…He was out of his mind with worry when I spoke to him earlier. No one seemed to know where you were. Nat said that he'd left you with Alex, but he tried to ring Alex and got no reply. It was only when Paul rang me, that we knew you were OK – well, more or less OK, anyway."

I didn't reply. Whether or not Davey would understand, I felt an immense guilt over what had happened, now heightened by wondering why Alex had not answered the phone. There might be a simple explanation, but a creeping sense of dread made me wonder what might have happened after I had fled.

"Please…please take me home…"

I still dreaded what I was going to say to Davey, but I knew that, whatever had happened, I wanted to be at home and with him now.

We drove on, joining the M40 and heading for home. The traffic was still quite heavy but moving relatively fast and we reached the junction off the motorway reasonably quickly.

The last part of the journey, down the increasingly narrow, winding roads, seemed longer than ever but eventually we swung into the farm entrance, bumping down the older part of the lane, still unrepaired, before diving under the railway bridge and onto the drive.

The moment Dan pulled up in front of the house Davey hurtled down the steps and wrenched open the passenger door, dragging me out and into his arms.

"Thank God you're OK!" he sobbed. "I thought you'd done something stupid!!"

I clung to him.

"I did!!" I sobbed. "I'm so sorry! I'm so sorry!"

Dan helped get me inside and into the library. Davey turned to him, looking at him over my shoulder.

"Sylvia's got food ready for you – if you go through to the kitchen…"

"I'd better be getting back – Saff'll need my help with the kids…"

"Have something to eat first – you obviously had a rough drive here – I thought you'd be back ages ago…"

"We stopped for a while – but OK, I'll eat before I go. I'll come and say goodbye..."

He left us alone. Davey was still holding me tightly. We were both still trembling, and I realised how very upset he must have been.

"Oh Micky, don't EVER do that again!! I really thought that you'd done something stupid!"

"I did!" I repeated. "Just not what you thought I'd done..."

"I don't care what you've done, as long as you're OK!!"

I shivered.

"I don't know whether I am or not...I did something that I'm so ashamed of..."

He pulled me even closer into his arms and then kissed me so gently that it almost broke my heart. I could hardly breathe, but knew that I had to tell him *now*, otherwise the longer I left it, the more difficult it would be and the more damaging to our relationship.

I took a shuddering breath

"I – Alex and I – "

"I don't care! Micky – whatever happened, it doesn't matter! All that matters is that you're OK!"

"Why did you think I might not be?"

"Until Paul phoned Dan, no one knew where you were... Nat said he left you at his flat around 1.30. I rang him about 4.00 and he said you might still be there, but we both tried to phone the flat and Alex' mobile and got no reply..."

I could sense that there was something more. Davey hesitated before continuing.

"Nat went to the flat, thinking that you might still be there. Alex was...Alex told him that you had... got upset... and had run out...Alex had taken a...a massive overdose of morphine. He died shortly after Nat got there, although I think Nat probably wouldn't have called an ambulance anyway…"

My head was spinning. Alex had seemed so rational while I had been at the flat with him that what Davey had just said seemed impossible, and yet…and yet it made perfect sense. Alex had obviously planned this, although only he knew whether it was part of the plan to get me into bed with him as a last celebration.

I gently pulled away from Davey and sank onto the sofa, my legs shaking. I was finding it difficult to breathe.
"Is Nat OK?"
"I think so. He had called a friend who was going to stay with him. Obviously he will have to deal with the coroner and all that stuff, but their doctor knows the situation so there shouldn't be too much kerfuffle. Are you OK? Do you need me to call the doc for you?"
I shook my head, feeling guilty that I felt only a massive sense of relief, both from the fact that Alex was now beyond suffering, and that Davey seemed to be totally untroubled by what had happened that afternoon.

Postscript

Skilfully handled, Alex' death was reported as 'from cancer', with no inquest necessary.

We attended his funeral – a massive affair, despite his having been out of politics for many years. As he had indicated, his estate ran into many millions.

The Alex Hansen Foundation was established with Nat, Angelo, Father Sean (in a completely non-denominational capacity), myself and two other friends, an accountant and a politician, serving as the first trustees.

We agreed that we would select one candidate per year so that, at any one time, we are likely to be helping a maximum of twenty youngsters aged between six and twenty six, giving them a home in (to start with) the Fulham house and later, as the number grows to the maximum, in the St. John's Wood house as well. Scholarships are provided at several schools, in an attempt to match the child to the school most likely to give them the most beneficial experience.

During the school holidays Davey and I, with help from Saffy, Paddy, Bird and other friends, work with the youngsters, not only with their music, but simply to try to give them the skills they need to get by as adults, although the Foundation houses are also staffed with carefully chosen house parents to give them some sort of family life.

I find working with the youngsters to be rewarding, as I so often recognise the parallels between their experiences and my own, enabling me to talk to them with total honesty and authenticity. Being absorbed with the massive task of setting up the Foundation helped me recover from that last, traumatic day with

Alex, and I eventually came round to the opinion that those few hours' anguish were a small price to pay for the privilege of being able to help so many kids who had suffered similar childhood experiences. In my mind I forgave Alex his last fling and remembered only the love we had shared and his final, immense kindness.

No-one can know what the future holds; for as long as we can do so without making ourselves ridiculous, we will continue to write, record and perform. The family continues to ebb and flow, the new generation's increase filling the gaps left as the elderlies pass on. For now, I have two parents that I love, and I spend as much time with them as I can. Mag, being quite a lot older than Sam and Mam, is growing visibly more frail, and we have bought a modern house in a good location and moved both her and my mam into it so that they are company for each other and are close to everything they need, as well as to their surviving friends.